The Human Reinstatement

JOSEPH CUBBAGE

Fulton Books, Inc.
Meadville, PA

Published by Fulton Books 2021

ISBN 978-1-63860-372-6 (paperback)
ISBN 978-1-63860-373-3 (digital)

Printed in the United States of America

For Courie, Miranda, Julian, and Jaelin
For Mom and Dad

CHAPTER 1

Hastings, Moscow, and the White House

Just west of Hastings, Nebraska, on a small farm, J. J. Henderson and his younger brother, Jeff, were playing football in their front yard. Their dad, John, was out back on the riding lawnmower, mowing the backyard and listening to the local news on his headphones. It was late October and a bit cool but a beautiful sunny day. JJ, who was twelve, had the ball and a two-point lead. It was fourth and two, thirty seconds left in the fourth quarter of the Superbowl. If he made this first down, game over. Jeff, who was ten, was dancing around in front of his older brother, waiting for him to say "Hike." Jeff was ready to pummel his brother and get the ball back. JJ looked around and then looked at his brother. He smiled and yelled, "Hike!" Jeff rushed at his brother and got an arm around his waist. JJ juked and spun out of the arm hold; Jeff fell to the ground. He watched as his older brother ran to the edge of the yard and spiked the football, dancing and laughing. Jeff rolled over on his back and let out a sigh. His older brother sure loved rubbing his victories in Jeff's face.

The ground rumbled. Jeff sat up and looked at his brother. JJ ran over to him. They heard their dad's lawnmower shut off. John ran around to the front of the house.

"Boys!" he shouted. "Get inside. They're saying a meteor just hit Kansas City. We gotta get inside now!"

The boys and their dad rushed into the house. Their mother, Serena, was at the front door.

"What was that, John?" she asked, clearly flustered.

"A meteor just hit Kansas City!"

"Oh my god! A meteor? How? How is that even possible?" she said, with panic in her voice.

"They're saying the blast zone could be five hundred miles or bigger. We have to get downstairs!" John escorted his family downstairs to their makeshift bomb shelter and then ran back upstairs. He gathered flashlights, bottled water, his .45 pistol, and a shotgun. He returned to the family.

John turned on the TV. He found the local news channel, and they all sat down to watch. Kansas City, just about three hundred miles southeast of Hastings, was gone, turned into a huge smoking crater. John shook his head. All those people gone just like that. One moment going about their Sunday afternoon and the next moment obliterated. He had gone to college in Kansas City, a farm boy who had wanted to try city life. He still had a few friends in Kansas City, goners now though.

The news was telling everyone to stay inside, do not go out for any reason. A cloud of smoke and debris was heading their way. Everything in a two-hundred-mile radius was gone. The news showed drone footage of the damage, buildings crumbled to pieces, bodies demolished in the streets, and fires burning everywhere. John made the boys look away from the TV; they didn't need to see that stuff. Serena cried into her hands. The boys climbed next her, and she held them, they were shaking.

"Are we going to die too, Dad?" JJ asked, fighting back tears. He didn't want his younger brother or his dad to see him cry.

"No, JJ, we are not. I will not let anything happen to us." He patted his eldest son on the back. "I promise."

There was a pounding on their front door. John looked at Serena, and they exchanged confused looks.

"Stay here with the boys," he said, handing her the .45 and taking the shotgun.

John approached the front door slowly, holding the shotgun out in front of him. He looked through the peephole and saw his neighbor, Chris Waters, standing on the porch, looking around. Chris looked at the front door and knocked loudly again. John opened the door and invited Chris in. Chris stepped inside; John could tell Chris was panicking.

"You okay, neighbor?" John asked, closing the front door.

"No. My wife was in Kansas City when that thing hit. She's gone, man." Chris fell to the floor in tears.

John didn't handle emotions well, especially from others. He had been raised to believe men never showed emotions. It was very awkward for him to watch his neighbor sob on the floor. He didn't know what to do.

Chris and his wife, Erica, had been married for almost forty years and had three grown children, two daughters and a son, and six grandkids. The adult children and their families all lived in Hastings.

"I'm sorry about your wife, Chris. That's terrible news. But you should go into town and be with your kids," John said, trying to sound as compassionate as possible.

"I can't tell my kids their mom is gone. I just can't," Chris sobbed.

"They need to know, neighbor."

Chris looked at John; his face was flush and wet from the tears. He looked angry and defeated. John felt for him, but he needed to take care of his family. No one knew what was happening at that point. Would Hastings and the surrounding farms survive the meteor blast zone? John and Chris had always been very neighborly, but John never considered his neighbor a friend. John did consider himself a good man and a good neighbor, but at that time, his number one priority was his wife and sons. He couldn't have someone else jeopardizing their safety. And if this lasted too long, he wouldn't have enough supplies to support his family and another adult. He had to convince Chris to go to his kids.

"Chris, I feel for you, I really do. I don't know what I would do if I ever lost Serena, but I know I would want to be with my boys. You need to go to your children. They need you, and frankly, you need them."

"I can't. I can't drive like this. I have my animals I need to tend to." He looked at John. "I just can't be in my house right now. Everything reminds me of Erica."

"I can imagine that would be tough." John put a hand on Chris's shoulder. Chris got to his feet. "I'll drive you to town. Take you to one of your kids' place. I'll even tend to your animals."

"Why would you do all that?" Chris asked.

"Because you are my neighbor, and I believe it's very important for you and your kids to be together at a time like this. We don't know what's going to happen because of that meteor. What if we get cut off from the rest of the world? Then your kids lose both parents without a chance to say goodbye? They need you, Chris. You need them."

Chris looked at John; he understood what John was getting at. He knew his neighbor was right. Chris didn't know what he had expected from John. He had always respected John, but John had never been the most approachable man. After some internal debate, Chris decided to take John up on his offer.

"I'll accept your offer for a ride into town. Let me go pack a suitcase and call my daughter to let her know I'm on the way."

"That's great," John said. "I will go let Serena and the boys know, then I'll meet you at your place in about ten minutes."

"Sounds good," Chris said as he headed outside.

The skies were growing dark with smoke and dust. John looked out the front door; he was surprised by how quickly the skies had darkened. It made him very uneasy and nervous. He hoped he wouldn't regret his offer to Chris.

He headed downstairs to tell Serena. He asked her to come upstairs and told the boys to stay put.

"What's going on? Who was at the door?" she asked, hugging her husband.

"That was Chris. Erica was in Kansas City today. She's gone. He's very upset. I am going to drive him to his daughter's place in Hastings."

"What? Oh my god, that's terrible news. Erica was a great woman." She paused and looked at John. "No way you're leaving this house."

"I am," he said. "Chris needs to get out of here and cannot drive himself."

"Then he needs to stay put. No way I'm letting you leave me and the boys at a time like this. They are scared out of their minds."

"They will be fine. You all will be fine. I can't have Chris hanging around here. He's a wreck." John went over to a row of hooks with keys hanging on them. He grabbed his truck keys.

"Of course he's a wreck. His wife is gone. But that doesn't mean you have to risk your safety to drive him into town."

"Serena, I will be fine. It's a twenty-minute drive each way. This guy will be all over us if we don't get him to his kids. I can't risk our supplies and well-being. It's worth the trip. I'm going, and that's final."

"Please don't, John," she pleaded.

"I have to," he said. "I love you."

She knew there was no changing his mind. When he said he was doing something, he would not be convinced otherwise.

"I love you too." She sighed. "Come back to us." Tears welled up in her eyes.

"I will. Don't cry in front of the boys. Stay strong for them."

"I will. Be safe, John." She hugged him again.

He hugged her tight. "I'll be right back, promise."

"You better be."

They let go of each other, and John walked out the door.

*****

On a cloudy Sunday, Amanda Jamison sat in her dorm room in Moscow, Idaho. She was trying to study for a test she had the next day. She was struggling to focus on her studies because she was so distracted with her social media accounts. It was late October, and she had been invited to several Halloween parties. She was excited to get through the upcoming week and celebrate her favorite holiday. She just needed to buckle down and study, but her phone just kept dinging. It was hard for her set her phone aside and ignore her friends.

She felt the ground shake a bit. Her phone lit up with messages. "Did you feel that?" "What was that?" She and her friends guessed it was a small earthquake. They dismissed it as no big deal and went on with planning their costumes for the Halloween parties. They wanted to go with a theme for their group but were having a hard time agreeing on one.

Then her phone rang. It was her dad.

"Mandy!" he practically shouted into the phone. "Are you okay?"

"Yes, I'm fine," she said, confused. "Why wouldn't I be?"

"Haven't you heard yet?" He was panicked.

"Heard what, Dad?" She was confused.

"Meteors hit the Bay Area, Portland, and Vancouver, Olympia, and Seattle! They're all gone!"

Amanda was speechless. She could hear notifications going off while she was talking to her dad.

"Seriously?" she finally said. She didn't know what else to say.

"Yes!" he shouted. "They're saying the mountains absorbed most of the after blast, but Spokane could be affected." She had grown up in Spokane, Washington, and her parents, Tom and Melissa, still lived there.

"Are you guys okay?" she asked. Her phone was going nuts.

"We're fine, for now. If this affects us, it'll affect you too. You're so close."

"I know, Dad. What do you want me to do?"

"Come home."

"I can't. I have a test tomorrow."

"This is more important than a test right now. This is a disaster!"

"I'll check with the school and call you back."

"Just come home, Amanda!" He was sounding more and more upset. "We've got the news on and they're saying there's a smoke and dust cloud heading our way already."

"I'm staying here, Dad. I will call you back soon."

"Damn it, Amanda! I'm not asking you to come home, I'm telling you to get your ass here asap!"

"I'm not a little kid anymore. I'm twenty years old. I will come home if they cancel classes. I gotta go, Dad. I'll call you back as soon as I can. I love you guys."

"Please, just come home." He was pleading with her.

"Not right now, Dad. Tell Mom I love her too. I'm hanging up now." With that, she disconnected the call.

She had dozens of notifications from her friends. Everyone had heard about the meteors by that point. They all chatted back and forth about what had happened as they pulled up news coverage online. Photos of the devastation were already popping up all over social media and online news agencies. There was nothing left but huge holes in the ground where major cities had been. There were videos from drones flying over what used to be Seattle. There was no direct coverage from the impacted cities, but the surrounding areas that survived the blast were doing their best to cover the aftermath. Amanda had gone to Seattle countless times throughout her life. There were no words for what she was now seeing. It was reported that meteors hit every major city on the west coast. The impact from all the meteors caused a tsunami that was expected to level all of Asia.

As she was watching the local coverage, breaking news reports kept popping up. It was being reported that meteors struck all over the planet. It seemed like every major city in the world had been hit. The death toll was projected to be in the billions already. Towns, farming communities, villages, and everywhere else that wasn't directly hit were expected to be wiped out by the fallout. The force of the impacts and the debris were going to cause nuclear winter around the world. This was expected to literally end life on Earth.

Coverage of the meteors was getting spotty due to the devastation around the world. As the clouds from the blast zones reached the surrounding areas, news coverage was lost.

The college sent out an e-mail to all students advising them to get to a safer place immediately. They were shutting down the school and forcing evacuations. The e-mail ended with, "Get to your families if at all possible. This could be the end times. We all should be with our loved ones. Be safe and good luck." Amanda stared at those last four sentences in shock. *Pretty dark and a bit callous*, she thought.

Her phone was going nuts. Her dad had called six more times. Her friends were freaking out. She tossed her phone on her bed and went down to the locker room. She took a hot shower and cried. She returned to her room and packed up her clothes. She called her dad back and told him she was on her way home. He sounded very relieved and told her to hurry best she could. He told her to drive safe but as fast as possible.

She messaged her friends and invited any of them to leave with her. Three of them said they would join her and meet her in her room. Stephanie, Bridgette, and Luna showed up minutes later with packed bags and panic in their eyes. The four young women rushed out of the dorm and piled into Amanda's car. The skies were already getting dark. The highway was bumper-to-bumper traffic already. What was usually an hour and a half drive looked like it could take hours. The women settled in for a long, scary drive to Spokane.

President of the United States, Cecilia Rodgers, sat at a table in a briefing room in an underground bunker. She was surrounded by members of her staff, military officials from all branches, and top NASA advisors. Meteors had started hitting the east coast in Miami. The president and her staff had barely made it to the bunker before Washington, DC, was hit. The vice president and the rest of the White House staff had not made it to safety in time. The vice president was on his way to a military bunker when the meteor hit DC. The president was clearly angry.

"Why were we not informed about these meteors?" she asked James Douglas, the head NASA advisor.

"There was no warning, Madam President. Nothing was seen by satellites. The space station didn't see anything," James replied, clearly very nervous.

"Bullshit!" she yelled. "How in the hell did you guys not see these things? They're big enough to turn cities into steaming holes in the ground! They didn't just materialize out of nowhere."

"I'm sorry I don't have a better answer, but we didn't see them coming."

"How do we know this wasn't an attack from another country?" she asked the room.

"Madam President," Anthony Gimliano, the senior military advisor, began, "from what I've been able to obtain with spotty coverage down here, those things came from outer space. They have hit all over the world. I'm getting reports that a couple of nuclear warhead depots in Russia were hit and wiped out the entire country. If that's true, we lost Alaska, and Europe will be gone from the nuclear fallout."

"Where are you getting this information from? And just because Russia has been destroyed doesn't mean this still wasn't an act of war." The president was getting more and more impatient.

"I'm getting this from intelligence agencies. It's reliable. Madam President, I am certain this wasn't an act of war. This could not have been orchestrated on this planet. Reports are flooding in that every major city in every country around the world has been destroyed. And only major cities. I can't think of anyone who has the ability to do that." Anthony stood up and walked his laptop over to the president. "Look here, ma'am," he said, pointing to the screen. "None of our military satellites were hit, they're all still operational. This is a live view of the planet. Everything is burning."

She studied the screen and then looked at James.

"Mr. Douglas, can you get in contact with the space station? See what they can see from up there?" she asked. She was still very upset but not at anyone in the room.

"I have tried, Madam President, but there is no communication with them. All signals are gone. I'm afraid the space station may be gone."

"General," she started, looking to Anthony, "get one of your satellites to find the space station. If it's still up there, we have to find a way to contact them. They're the only eyes we have now."

"Yes, ma'am," Anthony responded with a salute.

The room fell silent while Anthony tried to reposition the satellite closest to the space station. Nothing. The space station was gone.

"It's gone, ma'am," he said. "Just vanished."

"Shit!" she said, standing up. "General, get birds in the skies. Try to get eyes on the damage around the country. Send out the National Guard, soldiers, feds, whoever we have left. Get them out to the communities around the big cities. I don't want to see any rioting or looting. Get a message out to the surviving Americans that we have things under control. We will rebuild and survive this disaster together."

"Yes, ma'am," he said and left the room.

"Douglas, get ahold of the Kennedy Center and see if we can't get something to space. See if there's any more meteors heading our way."

"Kennedy Center was hit, Madam President," James said.

"Shit! Why am I just hearing about that?"

"I just found out, ma'am."

"I need something, Douglas. Figure out a way to find out what the hell is going on up there. This is too much of a coincidence to be a freak accident. Something is going on. Find out what and find out stat!"

"Yes, ma'am," James said and ran out of the room.

Anthony rushed back in, frantic and panicking.

"Madam President," he said, "all of our major military bases were hit too. Every single one of them is gone. All our men and women presumed dead. I'm getting reports from the smaller bases that so far, they are unaffected, but the fallout from the strike zones could pose serious issues for them shortly. I've put the bases I could contact on high alert. We're trying to get birds in the air, but visibility is a major concern at this point."

"Get whatever we can moving now!" She walked to the door. "All of you, get to work." She left the room. She went down the hall to the presidential office. She went in, closing and locking the door. She couldn't believe no one saw this coming. How does one of the most sophisticated and technologically advanced defense systems in the world miss hundreds of meteors hurling toward Earth? And how in the hell do they all hit major cities and military bases so accurately? Something didn't sit right with her, and she knew they needed to figure it out as soon as humanly possible with the limited resources they now had.

She sat at her desk and put her head down. She said a prayer. They would need much more than prayers, but that's all she had at that moment.

*****

John and Chris drove toward Hastings in silence. They were the only ones on the highway. The sky was growing darker and darker as they got closer to town. They could smell the smoke. It all felt very apocalyptic.

"Sometimes when the kids were little," Chris said, breaking the silence, "I'd get overwhelmed. I'd spend all day tending the farm. Erica would have spent all day doing what she did. The kids would be crazy. Once we finally got them settled and into bed, Erica would hit the bottle. She loved her wine." He rolled his eyes and made a drinking motion with his hand. "I'd wander off to the shop. I always had my 9mm on me, and I'd play with it. I'd look at it. I'd put it to my temple, 'just squeeze the trigger and it'll all be over,' I'd tell myself. One little trigger pull." He paused and looked out the window. "Those damn kids were so crazy back then. Always fighting and screaming. Erica would be content to just drink herself to sleep. I couldn't handle it, man." He looked at John with tears in his eyes again. "Now I don't want to die. I thought for a time that would be a way out, eliminate all my stresses with one little trigger pull." Tears flooded down his cheeks. "You ever think about that?"

John looked over at him in shock. "Hell no!" he said, looking back to the empty road. "I could never do something like that. That's a coward's way out."

Chris looked at John for a moment and then back out the passenger door window.

"I'm glad I didn't do it, just for the record," Chris said, clearly offended.

John didn't say anything else. He wasn't sure why Chris would even share that with him. He just wanted to get Chris to his daughter's house and get home as quickly as possible. They had reached Hastings by then and John was surprised by how dead the town was. He had to go into town frequently, and although it wasn't a big city, it was always a busy place. On that day, however, he didn't see anyone out and about. No traffic. Nobody walking the streets. He assumed people were heeding the warnings to stay inside until authorities knew for sure what was going on and what to do about it.

They were approaching an intersection, and they had a green light, so John just kept rolling on through. Before he could even react, they were hit by a one-ton Dodge speeding through the intersection from their right. The Dodge slammed into the passenger side of John's truck, killing Chris on impact. The collision sent John's truck into the light pole on the opposite side of the intersection, pinning John inside. The driver of the Dodge hopped out and ran down the street. He had a considerable limp but otherwise seemed fine.

John looked over at Chris. Chris had been torn almost in half. Blood was everywhere. Chris's body had let go of all bodily functions, and the truck stank of blood and feces. John choked back vomit. He couldn't feel his legs, and his head was spinning. Things were going in and out of focus. John tried to stay awake but eventually passed out.

CHAPTER 2

Currie, Ely, and Vegas

Malcolm Mason pulled his beer truck into the parking lot of the only tavern in the small unincorporated town of Currie, Nevada. He delivered to that tavern every day. He knew the owners, the bartender, and the regulars well. Currie only had about twenty people living there, and they all frequented the tavern regularly. Malcom pulled a forty-foot trailer with his truck. His route ran him from his hometown in Ely, Nevada, to Wells, Nevada, then up through the mountains and back to Ely. It was a beautiful drive and took him to all these small communities. He had been doing it for about three years and had gotten to know everyone on his route quite well. He had been offered a more local route a few times, but he liked all his customers too much to give up this route.

Donnie Anderson, the bartender, met Malcom in the parking lot like he did every day.

"Malcom!" he exclaimed as Malcom climbed out of his truck. Donnie had clearly been hitting the bottle pretty hard already. "How the hell are ya today?" The same question he asked Malcom every day.

"I'm great, Donnie boy." The same response Malcolm gave him every day. "How are you all doin' today?"

"We're great! Looking forward to our fresh beer delivery."

"Well, you're in luck I got beer in this truck!" Malcolm laughed, slapping the side of the trailer.

"I just wish y'all delivered it cold," Donnie said, chuckling. "That's why we order so much, so we always have ice-cold brews on hand."

"Good call, Donnie," Malcolm said, opening the trailer. He popped out the lift gate and climbed inside the trailer. "I'll get your beer inside in no time."

"Thanks, Malcolm. See ya inside." Donnie headed back into the tavern. He came right back out and propped the door open for Malcolm.

Malcolm loaded his dolly with as many cases as he could and lowered himself to the ground with the lift-gate. As he was rolling the dolly across the rough parking lot, the ground rumbled. He stopped and looked around. Currie was established as a railroad stop back in the early 1900s and trains still roared through. There was no train in sight, though. The more he thought about it, that rumbling was deeper than a train rolling by. Must have been a small earthquake.

"Did you all feel that?" Malcolm asked as he walked into the tavern.

"Yeah, man. A little quake," Donnie said. "We don't get those 'round here much."

"No, we don't," Malcolm said, dropping the cases of beer behind the bar. "I'll be right back with the next load," he said, heading back out into the hot sun. For such a small town, they sure did drink a lot of beer. Malcolm figured that was pretty much the only thing they had to do around there.

As he headed back to his truck, the ground rumbled again, this time a lot more intensely. It made Malcolm unsteady for a second. He could hear glasses breaking inside the bar. Donnie came outside followed by the handful of people inside. They all looked around.

"Man, what's going on?" Donnie asked no one in particular.

"This is some crazy shit, Donnie boy," Malcolm said, shaking his head. "These quakes better stop before I get up in those mountains." His phone rang. It was his dispatcher. "I gotta get this call. I'll have the rest of your beer inside ASAP." He walked to the cab of his truck and answered the call.

"Malcolm," Jennifer Miller, his dispatcher, began, "you okay out there?"

"Yea, Jen, I'm fine. You askin' 'cuz of the earthquakes?"

"Those weren't earthquakes. A meteor hit Vegas then one hit Salt Lake. The Salt Lake one was the bigger quake."

"Holy shit! Seriously?"

"Yeah, man, it's a shit show out there. Meteors are apparently hitting all over the world."

"No way! What's that mean for us?" He sat back in the driver's seat of his truck and scratched his scruffy chin.

"I don't know. They're saying we could see some effects from the cloud of debris and smoke. Everything is on fire where those things hit."

"Jesus, Jen."

"I just read that LA, San Fran, Oakland, San Diego, Reno, Portland, every big city on the West Coast is gone. Same for the East Coast. Manhattan and Long Island are completely gone, they're underwater now."

"Fuck," Malcolm said. He felt tears welling up in his eyes. "All those people just gone. It's heartbreaking."

"It really is, Malcolm."

Jen had been so consumed by the news of what was happening; she hadn't given herself time to think about all of the lives lost. She had grown up in Wells, Nevada, just two hours north of Ely. She moved to Ely with her husband, Ben, when he took the terminal manager job at the beer distribution center. Within a few months, he got her a job as a dispatcher. They were a relatively small outfit but did a lot of business to all the small towns. She loved her job. She didn't know anyone outside of Wells or Ely, so the impact of the lives lost didn't hit her as hard. It didn't even seem real. It almost seemed like some kind of Internet hoax. The ground rumbling sure as hell was real. The more she let it sink in, the sadder she got. She began to cry.

"You okay?" Malcolm asked.

"I don't know," she sobbed. "It's all so unbelievable. Unimaginable, really."

"I can't believe it," Malcolm said. "I just can't believe it's all gone."

They both went silent for a bit before Jen said, "All we can do now is thank the good Lord that we're alive."

"Amen, sister," he said. "Go hug and kiss your ol' man. Tell Benny you love him." He could hear her cry even harder when he said that. "I'm going to finish my drop here and get back on the road. Nuthin' we can do now but carry on, right?"

"I guess so. Be safe out there, man," she said, still sobbing. "And I will go hug and kiss my man. Check in with me frequently, Malcolm."

"I will, Jen. Talk at ya later."

"Bye for now."

They hung up, and Malcolm climbed back out of the truck. The tavern regulars and Donnie had gone back inside. He knew these old timers would have no way of ever hearing about what happened. He struggled with whether or not he should tell them. The whole thing really wouldn't have an effect on them; they were already so isolated and cut off from the rest of the world. Currie was so small; it was often referred to as a ghost town. He decided he'd deliver the rest of their beer and not tell them anything. He'd tell them the next day after he got more information on the situation as a whole. No reason to panic them at this point.

He dropped off the last two dolly loads of beer. Everyone was seated at the bar, drinking beers and talking. Cigarette smoke hung in the air like a cloud. He said his goodbyes and returned to his truck. He closed up the trailer and climbed into his mobile office. He wrote up his paperwork and fired that old Kenworth up. He turned north onto US-93 and was off to Wells. He had a very bad feeling in the pit of his stomach.

*****

Dana Simpson and Julia Brown were dealers in an off-the-strip casino in Las Vegas. They had been friends since grade school. Dana had worked for the casino for a couple of months before helping Julia get a job there. They both really enjoyed the work, but the hours were not great. They mostly worked evening shifts. Luckily Vegas never closed, so they still had plenty to do after their shifts ended at midnight.

They had a rare day shift on Sunday in late October. They had just returned from lunch, when their boss asked them to go down to the basement to get new decks of cards. What everyone referred to as the basement was basically a hole in the earth deep under the casino. It creeped almost everyone out, including Dana and Julia.

"I hate it down here," Julia said, as she flipped on the lights.

"Me too," Dana said. "I always feel like something is watching me down here."

"I get that feeling too." They headed to the back of the room. "It's so cold and musty."

"Let's hurry up, this place sucks."

"It sure does, but hey, if we get hit by a nuke, we'd be safe down here." Julia laughed.

"Don't say shit like that," Dana said, pacing.

"Sorry, Miss Superstitious." Julia laughed again. "Just 'cuz someone says something doesn't mean it'll actually happen."

"I know that, but you shouldn't say stupid shit like that."

"Calm your tits. I'm just tryin' to lighten the mood down here."

"Do it without joking about bombs and shit," Dana said, still pacing.

"Sorry. Jesus, you're extra sensitive today." Julia started loading decks of cards into the basket they had brought with them.

"I may be, and you should know why." Dana sat down on a nearby bar stool. The basement room was used to store all kinds of things for casino use. Everything from gaming supplies to non-perishable canned goods and bottled water.

"I know, I know," Julia said, rolling her eyes a bit. "You're still a bit tore up about Nick."

"Don't roll your eyes at me," Dana said. "He just up and left me. No goodbye. Nuthin'. Just fuckin' ghosted me."

"I told you from go he was a douche. Worthless piece of shit, if you ask me." Julia sat down next to Dana.

"I was just starting to really like him."

"I still don't know why. He treated you like shit. Just comin' around to get some. He acted like you were just a piece of ass."

"That's not true and you know it. He was cool and he didn't treat me like shit. He was good to me."

"The fuck he was," Julia scoffed. "You were nothin' more than a booty call to him."

"That's not true, Julia. Stop saying shit like that. We really had something."

"You had great sex—that's what you guys had and that was it. You never went out—you never just hung out and watched TV. All you guys did was fuck and send nudes, you sending more than he did. The asshole probably found some new bitch and moved on. You're better off, Dana. He was a dick."

"Just drop it," Dana said, lowering her head. Deep down she knew her friend was right; she just didn't want to admit it yet. It did start as a hook-up relation, but she developed feelings for the guy. She hadn't told Julia yet, but she had told Nick she loved him right before he ghosted her. She had dropped the L word way too soon and scared him off.

"You need to drop it. Get him out of your head. You should go out with Tommy. He keeps asking you out. Give him a chance."

"Oh, Jesus Christ, not this shit again." Dana rolled her eyes and threw her head back. "I've told you a thousand times I ain't interested in Tommy. He's not my type."

"He's breathing and has a cock—that's totally your type." Julia laughed.

"Fuck you," Dana said, trying not to laugh too. "Seriously, I just don't find him appealing at all."

"He's a good-lookin' dude," Julia said.

"Then you date him," Dana said.

"He doesn't want me. He wants you. Just give the guy a chance."

"Holy fuck, girl, just fuckin' drop it already. If he can't convince me to go out with him, you sure as shit won't convince me either."

"I'm just bustin' your balls again," Julia said, giggling. "I wouldn't actually date him or want you to date him. He's creepy. I'm just tryin' to distract you."

"Well, it worked. Dating Tommy is so ridiculous you actually did get my mind off of Nick for a minute."

"Good," Julia said, putting her arm around her friend. "I love you."

"I love you too, bitch," Dana said, and they both chuckled.

"We better get back up there before Rich comes looking for us. He's such a dick sometimes."

"True that! I hate it when he's in charge," Dana said. "I hate how he's always looking at my tits when he talks to me. It makes my skin crawl."

"Ugh, I know it. I doubt he even knows what our faces look like." Julia shivered a bit.

They stood up, stretching out their backs as they did. In mid-stretch, they heard a loud screeching noise. They stopped and stared at each other. Within a few seconds, they heard a loud explosion, and the room shook so violently they fell to the ground. Shelves and their contents started to tumble to the ground. One shelf fell on Dana, pinning her right leg. She screamed in pain. The lights went out. They both began to panic. Julia was yelling for help as she got to her feet and fumbled in the dark to find the flashlight that hung on the wall at the bottom of the stairs. She tripped over Dana and fell to the concrete floor hard, landing on her hands. She writhed in pain, and tears flooded down her cheeks. Both of them were bawling and screaming.

Julia composed herself the best she could and crawled to the stairs. She got to her feet and felt the wall with her throbbing hands. She found the flashlight and turned it on. She went over to Dana and tried to lift the shelf off her. It was too heavy to lift. She sat down on the floor next to Dana and started caressing Dana's head. Dana looked up at her.

"What the hell was that?" Dana asked.

"I don't know. Sounded like a bomb went off."

"This is all your fault, you know."

"What?" Julia said, confused.

"You had to make that fuckin' nuke comment." She laughed through the tears.

"Oh, Jesus," Julia laughed, rolling her eyes. She patted Dana on the back. "You okay here if I go for help?"

"Yeah, go. I want outta here." Dana smiled at her friend.

"Ok, Girl." Julia got up and headed to the stairs. She got two steps up and realized they were trapped. The door and walls were caved in. Rock, concrete, and drywall bits filled the stairway. "Fuck," she muttered, returning to Dana. "We're trapped." She sat next to her friend again. "We are fucked."

"Shit. Fuckin' shit!" Dana cried.

"What the hell do we do now?" Julia asked, panic sneaking into her voice.

"We need to figure out how to get this shelf off of me. My leg is numb. Then we need to find something to dig our way outta here."

Julia stood up and shone the flashlight around the room. In the very back corner was a big toolbox. She smiled and ran over to it. She found a hammer and a hand saw. She went back to Dana and started breaking apart the shelf. Dana would cry out in pain every once in a while, as Julia hammered boards apart on the shelf. The shelf was clearly very old and rotten. It broke apart easier than she had expected. It didn't take very long before she broke enough away to free Dana.

"Oh my god, thank you!" Dana exclaimed, standing up and hugging her friend. She was very unsteady on her feet. Her right leg was still very numb and tingly.

"I'm so happy you're free! Let's find something to dig outta here."

They headed back to the toolbox and rifled through it. They grabbed screwdrivers, wrenches, and a hammer from the box. They headed for the stairs. Dana looked at the top of the stairs for the first time.

"Holy shit," she said, looking at Julia. "What if it caves in on us?"

"Hopefully it won't," Julia replied, shrugging her shoulders. "We can't worry about that too much. We just gotta dig."

"Let's do it."

They climbed the couple of stairs left and began chipping and hammering away at the pile. They could smell smoke and something just vile. It slowly dawned on them the vile smell was burning flesh and hair. They choked back more tears and just kept digging.

CHAPTER 3

Post Falls, Spokane, and Des Moines

Pete Murphy worked for a car lot in Post Falls, Idaho. It was a cloudy, cool, late October Sunday afternoon. He was washing cars. He had worked for the car lot for about five months, mostly just washing cars and moving them around the lot. He had hopes he would eventually get promoted to salesman. His whole life, he loved cars and trucks. He had always wanted to work in the auto industry. He chose sales because he didn't want to be a mechanic, despite being good at working on cars. He enjoyed working on his own vehicles but never wanted to do it full time.

Pete and two high school buddies had just moved to Post Falls, finally getting out on their own at the age of twenty. They had been so excited to leave home, no one to answer to and parties every weekend. The reality of supporting yourself settled in quickly. Pete had thought he had it all figured out: get a job, pay bills, and party all the time. It didn't quite work out that way, though. He realized it was very difficult to support yourself on minimum wage, even with two other people contributing to the bills. He was forced to take a second job as a clerk at a gas station. He worked in the day detailing cars and evenings behind a register. He hated it. His buddies both had decent paying jobs. One of them, Robbie Hamlin, was working at a nearby hospital in their distribution department, while he went to school to become an x-ray technician. Pete's other buddy, Gabe Thompson, worked with his dad doing HVAC work, with the understanding he would one day take over the business. Pete thought he and his buddies would be living it up, but he hardly even saw them now.

The three friends had grown up in Spokane, Washington, just thirty miles from where they now lived in Post Falls. Close enough to family to get help when needed but far enough away to live their own lives. Pete's parents were constantly on him to get enrolled in college and get a degree. They would always tell him selling cars wasn't going to satisfy him for the rest of his life. His dad was a criminal law attorney, and his mom was a school nurse. They both made great money and had every weekend and holiday off. His mom had summers off, and his dad could pretty much make his own schedule, so they were always off in their RV or on a beach somewhere. They used that as a way of showing him he could have a better life with just a few years of school. Sure, school isn't easy, but in ten years when he was making good money, it would have all been worth it. He knew they were probably right, but he just couldn't do school right then.

All of that was going through his mind when the ground shook slightly beneath his feet. He had never felt an earthquake before and thought it was kind of cool. He looked around, and nothing seemed to be affected by the little rumble, so he carried on with his duties. Minutes later, he got a text from Robbie.

"Dude! A meteor just hit Seattle!" the message read with a shock face emoji and a sad face emoji.

"No way!" Pete responded, using the same emojis.

"Yea dude it's bad," responded Robbie.

One of the salesmen, Mitch Severson, came out to Pete.

"Hey, Pete, you gotta come inside and see this. Meteors just hit every major city on the west coast. It's on the news," Mitch said. Mitch had taken a liking to Pete and was teaching him the ropes of selling cars in his spare time.

"My buddy just messaged me about it. He just said Seattle." They headed back to the showroom.

"That was the one first reported here. They said tremors from the impact could be felt all the way to Montana."

"I just felt the ground shake. Is that what that was?"

"I'm guessing so," Mitch said, opening the door for Pete.

They headed into the waiting area where everyone in the place was huddled around the TV. It was tuned to a news station out of Spokane. They were reporting what was coming in through social media. No one was left in Seattle to do a live report. It was a circus. No one knew anything for sure; they just knew that what was thought to be a meteor had hit Seattle, leveling it. It had left such a big crater, that the ocean was now flooding in. The water was putting out all the fires, but it would make any rescue attempt almost impossible. It didn't seem likely at all that there would even be any people left to rescue.

Pete was in shock. Everyone around him was in shock too. People were texting and calling their loved ones. The manager of the car lot made the decision to close down so everyone could get home to their families. Pete volunteered to close up so everyone could get out of there. Mitch stayed with him until everything was locked up and good to go.

"Get back to Spokane, Pete. Be with your folks. I have a feeling this is going to be really, really bad. End of the world shit," Mitch said, patting Pete on the back as they stood next to Pete's car.

"I will. Get home to your wife."

"I will. Good luck and God bless."

"You too, Mitch." Pete did something he never did; he hugged Mitch. He hugged him tight. He had really grown fond of Mitch and cared deeply for him.

"I hope to see you soon. Stay in touch, son." Mitch let go of Pete and headed to his car.

"I will. See you soon," Pete said, waving to Mitch.

Pete got into his car and called his dad. His dad told him they would be home within minutes, and he should get home to them as quickly as possible. His dad agreed with Mitch that this could be the end of the world as they knew it. It certainly would change the world forever.

Pete hung up and called Robbie and Gabe. He told them he'd be in Spokane with his parents. Gabe was already at home with his dad. Robbie was told by hospital management no one would be able to leave until they figured out the scope of this tragedy. The hospitals were all on alert for trauma patients and patients from the fallout of the meteor impact.

Pete set off toward Spokane. It was usually only about a thirty-five-minute drive, but he could tell by traffic on the interstate it was going to be a much longer drive that day.

*****

Taylor Ericson was at work at the bus terminal near downtown Spokane, Washington. He worked as a mechanic for the transit authority. He mainly preformed routine maintenance on the buses, oil changes, tune-ups, fluid checks, brake checks, and the like. He loved his job. He had gone to diesel mechanic's school after a few years of trying to figure his life out. A tough breakup with his high school sweetheart had crushed him, and he had been lost for some time. They had dated throughout most of high school and for most of her freshman year of college. Taylor didn't go to college right out of high school; he took a job with a buddy working at a comic bookstore. Taylor didn't know how to live without a girlfriend for some time after the breakup, so he just kind of isolated himself. After a couple of years, his dad, who had been a truck driver and had instilled a love for big rigs in Taylor, urged him get into truck mechanics. Taylor had loved that idea and went into the diesel mechanics program at the community college. He got the job with the transit authority right out of school and had been with them for about six months. He was still low man on the totem pole, so he didn't have the best schedule and hadn't been promoted past maintenance tech.

It was a chilly Sunday afternoon in late October. Taylor was under a bus checking the drive train, when the ground rumbled. He rolled out from under the bus and looked around. Then another, smaller rumble. He got up and found his co-worker and good friend, Billy Clark. Billy had felt the rumble too.

"What the hell was that?" Taylor asked.

"Felt like an earthquake," Billy said, pulling his phone out of his pocket. "I bet there's something about it on social media already."

"Oh, for sure," Taylor said, grabbing his phone off of his tool cart.

"Holy shit!" Billy exclaimed. "People are posting that a meteor hit Seattle!"

"What? No fuckin way!" Taylor frantically scrolled his news feed. "Holy shit, man, it's all over my feed."

"I'm on the local news page, and they just confirmed it. They're saying that's what the rumbles we felt were from. The meteor hit so hard we could feel the ground shake here." Billy shook his head. "That's a helluva impact to feel it almost three hundred miles away."

"Jesus, man," Taylor said, also shaking his head.

The two young men stood there for several minutes in silence, looking at their phones. They were reading anything and everything they could. Reports were coming in from all over the world; every major city had been destroyed by meteors. Billy pulled a pack of cigarettes out of his pocket and motioned to Taylor he was heading outside. Taylor followed him. Taylor pulled out his own pack and lit a smoke. The two men stood outside the building smoking and looking at their phones. They began to hear sirens. The bus terminal was just a couple of blocks north of the police station, courthouse, and county jail, so hearing sirens frequently wasn't new in that part of town. That day, however, there seemed to be a lot more than usual and all of them seemed to be headed downtown. Downtown was about four or five blocks south and across the Spokane river. They looked at each other.

"What the fuck's going on?" Taylor asked.

"I don't know. Shit's going down, though," Billy said.

"What should we do?" Taylor asked, puffing on his cigarette. "Should we get back to work until management says something?"

"No way, man. I want to stay out here and keep track of this shit."

Taylor didn't say anything else; he just returned his attention to his phone. They stood there in silence again, scrolling through news on their phones. News was coming in faster than they could read it. No one knew anything for sure, except all those cities were destroyed. Billy was visibly shaking. He felt sick to his stomach. Taylor felt like he was going to cry. Not even thirty minutes ago, he was under a bus doing what he did every day, and now he was outside reading about how every major city had been reduced to a smoldering hole in the ground.

"Fuck, man. I think this is the end," Billy said after a bit, looking at Taylor.

"It's horrible, but I don't think it's the end. We have survived so many natural disasters. We'll survive this one too."

"This ain't no natural disaster. It seems too orchestrated."

"What do you mean?" Taylor asked, looking puzzled.

"It seems like an attack." Billy lit another cigarette with very shaky hands.

"Attack from who?" Taylor asked.

"I dunno," Billy said, inhaling a drag from his smoke. "Aliens maybe?"

Taylor laughed. "Fuckin' aliens? Seriously, dude?"

"You never know," Billy said, slightly offended at the laughter.

"You're nuts, man. Aliens didn't do this shit. A meteor shower hit Earth, that's it."

"A meteor shower hit Earth but only landed in major cities? That's very unlikely. *Way* too unlikely."

Taylor just shook his head. Taylor knew Billy well and considered him a conspiracy theorist. He wasn't going to stand there in the cool October afternoon and argue aliens with Billy. He let Billy believe what he wanted and moved on. Taylor nodded to Billy and went back into the shop. He chuckled to himself as he got back under the bus. He figured he might as well just get back to work, no sense in dwelling on stuff he couldn't control. No sense in stressing himself out so much he got himself sick. Just focus on work best he could and keep an eye on the news.

Taylor rolled back out from under the bus. He had finished his check of the drive train. He got up and put his tools back in his toolbox. He wiped his hands on a rag and looked over to Billy's station. No Billy. Taylor went back outside and found Billy sitting on the sidewalk with his back against the building's wall. Billy looked frazzled and ill. Billy looked up at Taylor.

"I just called the boss," Billy said. "He said we could shut it down and get out of here if we want to. He said the city officials are telling everyone to get home and stay home. They're worried people will start looting and rioting. It's going to be a shitshow, man." He shook his head and returned his focus to his phone.

"Do we have to go home?" Taylor asked. "I don't think it'll be that bad, and I really need the money."

"You won't need money if this is the end," Billy said. "You'll need supplies. I'm leaving and going to the store to stock up. This shit's serious."

Taylor chuckled, and Billy shot him a dirty look.

"I'm fuckin serious, dude," Billy said, standing up. "Don't fuckin laugh at me."

"I'm not laughing at you. I'm laughing at the idea that a meteor hitting Seattle will turn Spokane into a looting, rioting shitshow as you put it. It's just ridiculous to me. It's a terrible thing that happened, but I doubt people will react to it like that."

"You have way too much faith in people," Billy said. "Think about it, dude, we're cut off from every major city. Where are all the tech companies located? Major cities. Who drives a state's economy? Major cities. Who governs states? Major cities."

"Yeah, yeah, I get all that," Taylor said. He was starting to get annoyed with Billy. "I ain't as worried as you clearly are. Go on and get your supplies, man. I'm gonna stay here and earn money. 'Cause when this shit blows over—and it fuckin' will blow over—I'll need money to pay my rent and fill my belly."

"That *is* a big mistake," Billy said, lighting a cigarette. Taylor pulled out a smoke and lit it. "I consider you a good friend, but when you run out of food and shit, don't come knockin' at my door. I'm telling you, this shit is real. We'll start losing power and cell service. The water will stop flowing through our taps. Food and basic needs like TP will be gone. Stock up now!"

"I won't need to call on you. It ain't goin' down like that. Sure, the major cities are all gone, but we have our own government on a city level. Seattle doesn't govern us. They don't supply us with anything. We aren't hopelessly lost because Seattle, Olympia, and

Tacoma are gone. The few crazies that think they can get away with looting and shit will be handled by the cops. I love ya, man, but I think you're way overreacting right now."

"I wish you would just listen to me. I love ya too, and I don't want to see you hurt by all this. What would it hurt to just stock up on basics? Nuthin'. If this shit does blow over, which it won't, then you're set on basics for a while. No harm in that. But huge problem if I'm right, and you don't have that shit." Billy put out his smoke. "Look, Dude, I'm outta here. Take care." Billy shook Taylor's hand and walked across the street to the employee parking lot. He waved at Taylor before disappearing into the lot.

Taylor stood there dumbfounded. How could Billy be that worried? Everything was "the end" for Billy. He overreacted to every damn thing. If he got the sniffles, it was SARS, the swine flu, pneumonia, or something equally bad, but never just a cold. Even if he did get seriously ill, he wouldn't take medication or antibiotics. He swore up and down that medical and pharmaceutical companies used medication to control the population. Taylor remembered a twenty-minute rant that Billy went on one day about all of it. Billy would rant and rave about all sorts of conspiracy theories. Taylor would always just let him rant and rarely injected his opinions. Billy could be, and often was, quite annoying with his beliefs, but Taylor saw the conspiracy theory stuff as just a quirk and just a small part of Billy's personality. Everyone has that annoying, conspiracy theory friend or family member. Taylor wasn't the type of person to argue things like that. To him, it was an opinion, and opinions don't get changed through arguments. Let them rant and rave and just move on with your day.

Taylor saw Billy pull out of the parking lot. He threw his friend one more wave and went back into the shop. He shook his head as he walked back to his station.

Three gunshots rang out not far from the bus depot. Taylor jumped.

Four more gunshots, even closer this time.

Several more rang out. Taylor jumped behind a bus. Now he could hear sirens getting closer and closer. The gunshots continued.

He heard tires screeching as several vehicles came to abrupt stops. He heard yelling and more gunshots. More yelling. More gunshots.

What the hell was going on out there? Did Billy make it out of there safely? Taylor went to the far back of the depot and hid between two buses. He crouched down next to the engine compartments, hoping if stray bullets did make into his building, the engines would stop the bullets. He was shaking. Tears were streaming down his face. He felt nauseated and faint. *Do not puke*, he thought to himself. *Do not pass out.*

The big garage door was still open, and Taylor could see part of the street from where he was hiding. He saw four police cars roar to a stop right outside. The officers jumped out of their cars, guns in hand, and just started firing. The gunshots echoed off the concrete walls. It was so loud. His ears rang and he felt dizzy. His legs were weak and shaking. He sat down on the hard, cold shop floor. Tears were still streaming down his face. The gunshots and yelling continued outside. Taylor was overwhelmed by fear and emotion.

Was Billy right? Was this the end?

He slumped further on the ground. He was lying in the fetal position, bawling. He had never been this scared.

Someone ran into the depot. He heard them run to the opposite side of the shop. He heard them run onto a bus. The bus fired up. When a bus was on the floor to be serviced, they left the keys in it until they were done and parked it. He heard the engine roar. He looked out from under the bus he was hiding behind and watched as the bus roared out of the shop. He heard the bus crash into the police cars outside of the door. Then more yelling and gunshots.

Taylor got up and slowly climbed into the bus. He hid under the seats and hoped to God this would all be over soon. He had never been a religious man, but he prayed that day. He begged God to save him from this.

The gunshots died off, and it was quiet again. He let himself relax a bit and closed his eyes. He passed out shortly after.

*****

Scarlett Reed sat behind her desk in her home office in Des Moines, Iowa. It was a Sunday afternoon in late October. She usually didn't work on weekends, but she had a big presentation to do the next day. The presentation, if it went well, could result in another promotion for her. She had been rapidly climbing the ranks of a multimillion-dollar insurance firm. If someone had told her twenty years ago when she first got her insurance license that she'd be on the verge of becoming the VP of a major firm, she would've laughed at them. Her career took off when she and her now ex-husband moved to Des Moines many years back. Des Moines had always been a major center of the US insurance industry. Her ex-husband, Dylan Witner, was also an insurance agent. He worked for another Fortune 500 firm. They both began their new lives in Des Moines at his firm, but Scarlett took a lucrative job offer from a competing firm. That move drove a wedge between them that they were never able to get past. The competition in the business world led to constant fights at home. The bitterness and stress led to infidelity by both spouses. Once what little trust that had been left was gone, so was the marriage. After a long divorce and tens of thousands of dollars spent, they were finally legally divorced. It was the greatest day of her life. She had loved the man in the beginning, when they were young and small-town insurance agents. They'd work their nine-to-five schedule and spend their weekends outside camping, fishing, hiking. Anything outdoors. But once they both started making six figures and beyond, the love turned into jealousy and disdain. Dylan couldn't stand that she made more money than him. And it was *a lot* more money. He just couldn't handle it and it led to the end of what had once been a loving marriage.

Scarlett had no regrets. She didn't want to be with a man that was so small-minded that he couldn't just be happy for his wife. She didn't want a man that fought with her just to make himself feel better. Some of the things he had said to her were inexcusable. She hadn't realized how truly unhappy she had been for years until it was all finally over. She loved her new life. Just her and her seventeen-year-old daughter Gwen.

Gwen lived with Scarlett full-time. She and her dad had no contact anymore. When the divorce first became final, she'd spend weekends at her dad's place, but he was never around. He'd leave her alone while he played golf during the day and hit the night clubs in the evening. Once she turned sixteen, she decided she would just stay with her mom. Her dad didn't fight it. She was no more important to him than his Porsche. Gwen actually felt like her dad loved that stupid car more than he loved her. Just as her mom had done, Gwen moved on from her dad and was a lot happier.

Gwen was at her friend's house about ten miles away on that late October Sunday. Scarlett took advantage of the quiet house to get some work done. She had left her phone downstairs in the kitchen so she wouldn't be interrupted. The presentation had too much riding on it for her to be distracted by anything. She was buried in paperwork and spreadsheets when she felt the ground shake. She stopped what she was doing. Within seconds, the ground shook again.

What the hell was that? she said to herself. She had lived in Des Moines for a long time at that point and had never felt an earthquake. She shrugged it off and went back to work. The tremors were so minor she didn't even pay it a second thought.

Gwen and her friend Hope Johnson sat in Hope's room. They were watching a movie when the ground shook, not once but twice. They looked at each other, puzzled.

"What the fuck?" Hope asked.

"I think that was an earthquake," Gwen said. "I'm going to message my mom."

Gwen messaged her mom, but no immediate response. They sat there for a while, confused. They had never felt anything like that before. Hope grabbed her phone and opened up social media.

"Look at this!" she said, after scrolling her feed for a bit. She turned her phone to Gwen.

"What in the fuck?!" Gwen said, shocked. "Did that say meteors? Meteors hit Kansas City and we felt it? What? How?" She couldn't believe what she was reading.

"And Minneapolis!" Hope said, still scrolling. "That has to be what we felt. It says the cities were leveled. Turned into giant craters!"

"This can't be true. It's gotta be a hoax or something." Gwen had opened her social media and was thumbing through the feed. "It's everywhere now," she said, looking at Hope. "Every major city was hit."

"No way!" Hope said, wide-eyed.

There was a knock on Hope's bedroom door. It was Hope's mom.

"Did you guys hear the news?" she asked, clearly rattled.

"Yeah, Mom, it's all over social media. Is it for real?"

"I think so. It sounds like it's real." She bowed her head. "So many lives lost," she said, her voice cracking as she began to cry.

"What do we do?" Hope asked.

"Stay put," her mom said, wiping tears from her eyes. "The news is saying we need to stay inside and not go out if we don't absolutely have to. They don't want a bunch of people clogging up roads and hindering emergency services."

"I'm supposed to be home for dinner," Gwen said.

"I think it's safest to stay here," Hope's mom said. "Call your mom and see what she thinks."

"Okay," Gwen said.

"I'm going back downstairs to watch the news some more. I think we might lose our connection soon," Hope's mom said.

"Okay," the girls responded.

Gwen called her mom, but no answer. She sent her mom a message telling her what Hope's mom had said.

"What now?" Gwen asked Hope.

"Just wait. Your mom will call you back soon."

"I hope so. She's probably working on her presentation and left her phone in the kitchen again. She always does that."

"I'm sure she felt the ground shake. I'm sure she'll check the news and call you."

"Maybe," Gwen said. "When she's workin', she ignores everything."

"This is huge. Impossible to ignore," Hope said. "She'll call you back."

The girls went back to their phones and frantically kept scrolling. The news was devastating. They couldn't believe it.

They were lost in their phones when they heard tires screeching down the road. They heard a loud crash, followed by another crash, more tires screeching, and then the power went out. They got up and looked out the window. They saw a red car turn around and peel off down the road. A black SUV had crashed into the power pole across the street. The SUV hit the pole so hard it snapped and fell onto the vehicle. Hope's mom rushed back into the room.

"Are you girls all right?" she asked.

"Yeah, Mom, we're fine. Just a little scared."

"Me too," her mom said. "I'm going to go get the flashlights out of the garage. Stay here."

"Be careful, Mom," Hope said.

"I will, honey," she said and gave the girls a weak smile.

They were still looking out the window. The man driving the SUV was obviously dead. The red car was long gone. It must have been chasing the black SUV. It was all so scary and disturbing. They heard Hope's mom close the back door. Then they heard a loud *zap* and a quick scream. They looked at each other and ran down the stairs. They stopped in the kitchen.

"I can't look," Hope said, crying.

"I can't either," Gwen said, tears streaming down her cheeks as well.

"You have to, please."

"I can't. I don't want to."

"Please, Gwen, please!" Hope bawled.

They both knew what Gwen was going to see. They both knew what that sound was and who screamed. Gwen slowly walked to the window above the kitchen sink. She stopped and looked at Hope several times. Hope pleaded with her to keep going each time. Gwen felt knots in her stomach. She did not want to see what she was sure she was about to see. She finally made it to the window and looked out. She bent over the sink and vomited. That was all Hope needed to see, and she fell to the floor screaming and crying.

CHAPTER 4

The Fallout

John woke up and looked around. Evening had set in. Serena was probably worried sick by then. John pushed himself up in the driver's seat. John's legs were numb, but he could move them. The more he moved his legs, the less numb they became. Both of the truck doors had been smashed in from the impact of the other truck and light pole. The windshield had been shattered in the crash. John kept a toolbox behind the seats. He reached into the toolbox and found a hammer. He busted out the windshield and carefully crawled out. He slid down the hood of the truck and fell to the pavement. He tried to stand up, but his legs were still too weak. He sat there on the street moving his legs, trying to get the feeling back in them. Eventually, he felt the numbness go away and he was able to stand up. His lower back and hips were killing him. His head was pounding. He reached into his pocket for his phone. It wasn't there. He looked into the cab of the truck and couldn't see it in there either. Then it slowly dawned on him he had left it at home. In his hurry to get Chris out of there, he had forgotten his phone on the dining room table. He thought about trying to find Chris's phone, but looking into the truck at Chris's body, he realized the phone would be soaked in blood by that point. Not only would the phone be disgusting, but it would also be totally useless.

John looked around. He needed to find a phone and call Serena. Everyone had cell phones, so there wasn't a payphone in sight. All the businesses on that block were closed. He could see a gas station about three blocks down the road. The sign was lit up, and he hoped they would be open. If not, he would need to find a fire station or the police station. The firefighters and cops had to still be on the job. John turned his aching body toward the gas station. He took three steps down the street and fell. His legs were still so sore and weak. He crawled for a bit and then slowly got back onto his wobbly legs. He was in excruciating pain but willed himself to make it those three blocks. Each step, he told himself, *Almost there, you got this.* It hurt so bad; every damn step hurt worse than one before.

He finally made it the gas station, and thankfully, it was open. He went inside and approached the counter. The man behind the counter looked at him intently.

"You okay, man?" he asked.

"No," John replied. "I need to use your phone."

"Don't got one," the man said.

"What?" John asked, surprised by the man's coldness. "How do you not have a phone?"

"Just don't got one," he said. "You gonna buy sumthin'?"

"What? Are kidding me right now?" John asked, very irritated at this point. "I was just in a really bad accident that killed my friend and fucked me up pretty good. I need a phone. I need to call the cops and my wife."

"Told ya, I ain't got a phone."

"You're full of shit! Everyone has a phone."

"I don't need that kinda language in my store, sir," the man said. "I'm going to ask you to buy sumthin' or leave."

"Where's the nearest firehouse?" John asked. If he hadn't been hurting so badly, he would've knocked the guy out.

"Dunno. There's a town map for sale right here," the man said, holding up a small map. "Firehouse should be on there."

John stared at the man, furious. He pulled a ten-dollar bill out of his pocket and threw it on the counter. He grabbed the map and limped out of the store. He couldn't believe how that guy had treated him. The world was getting annihilated by meteors and this guy was acting a fool. How could he treat his fellow man that way?

John was still angry but tried to get past it and just focus on finding a fire station or police station. Luckily, they were both listed on the map. Even more fortunate for John, there was a fire station just two blocks away. He hobbled to the fire station. When he got there, one of the bay doors were open and he could see several firefighters inside. He called out to them, and they came running to him. They looked very concerned. The relief of seeing friendly faces, coupled with the pain, caused John to fall again. Tears of pain, frustration, and desperation flooded down his face. Two of the three firefighters ran back into the garage and returned quickly with their medical bags and a back board. They positioned John onto the backboard and began to examine him.

"I need a phone," John said through the tears. "I need to call my wife."

"We'll get you a phone, but for now, we need you to remain calm, sir, you're badly injured," one of the firefighters said. "What happened to you?"

"I was in a really bad accident. I got T-boned. My friend was killed in the accident. He's still in my truck."

"Where is your friend?" the same firefighter asked, looking at the other two.

"I'm not sure. It's in front of a bookstore a few blocks away."

One of the other firefighters got up and ran inside.

"Are you in a lot of pain, sir?" the firefighter asked.

"Yes. Terrible pain. In my back and legs."

"I'm going to give something for the pain."

"No. Don't," John said. "I need to find a way back to my family."

"Sir, what you need right now is pain management." The fire-fighter gave John a shot.

"Damn it," John sobbed. He never took medication, and he knew whatever he was just given would most likely knock him out. "Please call my wife," he muttered and called out her phone number. "Please someone call her. Her name is Serena."

The other firefighter returned. He had a cell phone in his hands. He told the other firefighters he had called the police regarding the accident. John begged him to call Serena. The last thing John saw before he passed out was the firefighter calling his wife. That made him rest easy.

*****

Amanda and her friends sat in gridlocked traffic. No one was moving. There couldn't be that many people trying to get to Spokane; something must have happened somewhere up ahead. There was absolutely no traffic going in the opposite direction. Amanda considered crossing the median and taking the oncoming lane toward Spokane. She was afraid that would be too risky and decided against it.

As they sat there, Amanda saw a man walking up the road from behind them. He had a shotgun in his hands. She pointed him out to her friends. They all felt fear and panic rise in their guts. He walked right past their car and kept on going down the highway.

"What in the fuck?" Luna asked.

"Crazy people," Amanda responded, shaking her head.

"At least he's getting somewhere," Stephanie said. "We're stuck here like sitting ducks."

Within minutes of the first man walking by, a dozen other heavily armed men walked by their car. They gave each other confused looks. Amanda checked the rearview mirror, and she could see at least another dozen men, possibly even more than that. She looked over her shoulder and pulled onto the median. She crossed the median and got onto the other side of the highway. She floored the gas and peeled out of there toward Spokane. She could see other vehicles begin to follow her lead. One car, then another, then another.

They got to the beginning of the backed-up traffic and saw the most gruesome, horrifying thing they had ever seen in person. It was so shocking that Amanda came to a stop without even realizing she had done so at first. They stared in shock at an eighteen-wheeler that had jack-knifed and flipped over, blocking both lanes of traffic. It was a tanker truck, and something was leaking out of the flipped over tank. A small sports car had smashed into the tanker so hard that the front end had been pushed into the back of the car. There was a man, or at least what was left of him, squished between the engine of the car and the rear end. Lying on the ground next to the wrecked car was one of the man's arms. About ten feet from the arm was a woman's torso. Behind the unrecognizable car was the woman's head, her blond hair streaked red with blood.

Behind the wrecked sports car were several other minor accidents. Little fender benders where people had been stopped because of what had happened in front of them, and then they were rear-ended. Amanda slowly started to drive off. She was in shock; they all were. She was still looking back at the wreckage as she accelerated. She crashed into a car that had stopped in front of her. The driver's side door was open, and no one was inside the car. She looked around and put the car in reverse. She pulled around the car she had just hit and stomped the gas pedal.

The other side of the highway was clear past the wreck, so she crossed the median back to the side of the highway she was supposed to be on. She sped back to Spokane. It took no time to get into town. It was getting late into the afternoon and what was usually a busy downtown Spokane looked like a ghost town. There were still homeless people milling about, but that was about it. A few cars were speeding about but not the usual weekend traffic. It looked like almost all the businesses were closed up. They saw cop cars everywhere. Police officers were standing on street corners, directing traffic out of downtown. Amanda was nervous that she may get pulled over due to the damage on her car. None of the officers seemed to care about that; they just kept motioning to her to continue on her way through. She was headed north out of downtown. Two of the four bridges crossing the Spokane river were closed, so she was forced to head east before she found an open bridge. There were quite a few cars on the bridge trying to get north as well. The whole thing had an eerie feel to it.

The women drove in silence, just taking in everything around them. Once out of downtown, there was a lot more traffic. Spokane drivers were bad on their best days, but that day was horrible. It seemed like everyone forgot the rules of the road. People were running red lights and stop signs. Flying through parking lots to cut the corners and intersections. There were accidents and screaming mad people everywhere. At one intersection, traffic was at a crawl as people drove around a male's dead body in the middle of the road. Once they passed him, they realized he had been shot several times. Not even half a mile north of the dead man was another body. This time, a woman's body. She was mangled up so badly her legs were twisted around the wrong way. She had clearly been hit by a car going extremely fast.

All those wrecks and bodies but no emergency crews anywhere. No sirens. Nothing. Nothing but chaos. Amanda had planned on dropping each friend off at their parents' houses but was too scared now. She told them she'd take them back to her parents' house and maybe her dad could take them home from there. She just did not want to be out on those streets any longer than she absolutely had to be. They all agreed that was the best idea at that point.

Several miles from her parents' place on Mount Spokane, a yellow car began following them. Amanda could see two masked men in the car. It was very clear to her that these men were following them. She didn't want to lead them back to her parents' house. She didn't want them to know where she lived. She had grown up in that part of town and knew the area well. She decided she would try to lose them on the back roads. She handed her phone to Stephanie and told her to call her dad and tell him they were being followed. Amanda's dad had been messaging her since she told him they were stuck in traffic back on the highway. Stephanie opened Amanda's phone and called her dad. As soon as she put the phone to her ear, the yellow car rammed into the back of Amanda's car, causing her to spin out. The yellow car came to a stop in front of Amanda's car. The passenger got out and walked between the two vehicles. As soon as he was in front of her car, Amanda gunned it, hitting him and pinning him between the two cars. She backed up and the man fell to the ground, clearly in extreme pain. She drove away in the opposite direction they had been going. Stephanie was frantically trying to explain everything to Amanda's dad. The driver of the yellow car backed up and drove around his injured passenger, speeding after Amanda.

"What's my dad saying?" Amanda asked Stephanie as she sped down the road.

"He said your mom called 911 and no one answered," Stephanie said, still on the phone.

"*What?*" Amanda yelled. "How the hell is that even possible? What the fuck is going on here?"

"I don't know," Stephanie said, tears streaming down her cheeks.

Bridgette and Luna were in the backseat bawling. Amanda had tears flooding down her face as well. The yellow car was right on her ass.

"What's he saying?" Amanda asked again, tearing around a corner.

"He says come home, and if the cops aren't answering, he'll just handle that guy."

"Shit," Amanda said. "My dad'll kill that guy."

"That's better than that guy killing us!" Bridgette said from the backseat. "Get us to your house!"

Amanda ripped around another corner. They were two blocks away from the house.

"Tell my dad we're two blocks away. We'll be there in thirty seconds."

"He said he's waiting outside. He said slow down but do not stop in front of the house." Stephanie said.

"Okay," Amanda said, rounding the last corner.

She could see her dad in the driveway. He had his .45 in hand. She put her blinker on and slowed down as she approached the house. The driver of the yellow car slowed down too. He was focused on her and her friends. She slowly rolled by her parents' house. Her dad raised the .45. He took aim and shot the man in the yellow car. Amanda saw blood explode out of the side of the driver's head. He slumped over immediately, and the yellow car crashed into a parked car across the street. Amanda slammed on the brakes and backed into her dad's driveway. The young women piled out of the car and ran inside. Amanda's dad followed them slowly, keeping an eye on the yellow car. He came into the house behind them and locked the front door.

*****

President Cecilia Rodgers returned to the briefing room. Everyone, except for Anthony, stopped what they were doing and stood to give her a salute as she entered the room. Anthony sat at the table pounding away on his laptop. He stopped and looked up. When he saw the president, he quickly rose and saluted her as well. She told everyone to relax and keep working.

"As long as we're dealing with this disaster," the president began, "we can forgo the formalities of normal day-to-day operations. I am still in charge, but we're all in this together. Let's not waste time with saluting and whatnot."

Everyone in the room nodded in agreement. President Rodgers sat at the head of the table.

"Update me on what's going on, people," she said.

"All operational bases are in action, Madam President," Anthony said, sitting back in his chair. "I've instructed the Air Force to get as many birds in the sky as possible. I am awaiting word back from them. My Internet service is becoming very spotty, and I'm losing my feeds from our satellites. I'm not sure how much longer we'll have communication with the outside world."

"Shit. Keep on the bases while we still have contact. I want every piece of information possible."

"Yes, ma'am," Anthony said, returning his attention to the laptop.

"Douglas, what can you tell me about all of this?"

"Not much else, Madam President," James said. "I don't have any contacts left—well, any that I can find at least. As you know, most of our work is conducted either here, the Kennedy Center, or Houston. All of which are now gone."

"We have got to see what's going on up there," she said, pointing up. "General, can you see anything up there with the satellites you have left?"

"No, ma'am," he said. "All I can see is open space. Nothing out of the ordinary."

"That doesn't make sense. None of this does."

"Shit!" Anthony exclaimed, startling everyone. "I just got word from one of our smaller Air Force bases that the three birds they sent up all got shot down."

"What?" the president exclaimed, standing up and walking to Anthony. She stood over his shoulder and looked at his laptop. "Who could do that?"

"They don't know, ma'am. Look here," he said, pointing at the screen. "They're reporting that whatever hit our planes did not come from the ground. But no other aircraft was seen or reported in the area."

"What in the fuck?" the president said. "Excuse my language, but seriously, what in the fuck?"

"I don't know, ma'am. No warning at all. They were in the air one minute and gone the next. It's baffling, honestly."

"What's that?" she asked, pointing to the laptop screen.

Anthony had a satellite image of the United States on half the screen. He leaned in to get a closer look at what she was pointing at.

"I don't know, ma'am," he said.

"I've never heard 'I don't know' so many times in my life," she said, standing up and walking away from Anthony. "I understand this is something we've never experienced before, but I know we have protocols in place for everything. I feel like it's all of your jobs to know or at least to find out what the hell is going on."

Anthony looked at her. "I want to say it's a glitch in the imagery, but taking into consideration what's been going on, I doubt that's the case." He looked back at the laptop. "Shit, it's getting bigger." He clicked to a full-screen view. "It looks like an aircraft, ma'am."

"What?" she asked, walking back to him. "Whose?"

"That I can't tell, but it's huge."

"Douglas! Get over here and look at this," she said, moving out of the way so James could look. "What is that?"

"Jesus," he said when he saw it. "I've never seen anything like that before."

"Where is that thing?" she asked.

"Looks like it's just outside of orbit," James said.

"Okay, what is going on here?" she asked no one in particular.

The president, Anthony, and James were all studying the image on the screen. It kept getting bigger, blocking out the image of the United States. The image disappeared. The whole screen went black. Everyone in the room looked up from their devices. They had all gone black.

"Our Internet is gone," Anthony said. "We're blind."

"Shit! We have to get out of here. Maybe we can find service on the outside."

"That's still too dangerous, ma'am. We don't know what's going on up there. We can't ensure your safety if we do that," Anthony said.

"Fuck my safety, and frankly, fuck all of yours too! We all signed up to serve and protect this great nation, and we all knew we could die doing it. This is no time to be safe. This is the time to act. This is the time to do what we signed up for. What the American people elected me to do. We are worthless down here without communication to the outside world. Get us out of here, General."

"Yes, ma'am,' Anthony said, standing up. "It'll take some to time organize an escape plan."

"Make it happen ASAP," she said. "I'll be in my office gathering what I need."

"Yes, ma'am," he replied.

The room emptied as everyone went their own way to prepare their return to the surface.

*****

Malcolm was approaching Wells, Nevada. He was surprised how dead the highway was, especially at that time of day. There was a dark cloud rolling in over the small town. Malcolm had several stops in Wells but was usually able to make all his deliveries in less than two hours. Wells was also where he would stop for his lunch break. The truck stop had a nice diner with great service. The food was good, and the coffee was surprisingly fresh and tasty. He pulled into the truck stop and was shocked by how many trucks were parked there. He had never seen so many before, especially on a Sunday afternoon. He parked his truck and climbed out. The air reeked of smoke and dirt. His eyes instantly burned and itched. He went into the diner; it was packed. He found a stool at the counter and sat down.

It took a while, but the waitress, Beverly, finally came over to him with a cup of coffee.

"How ya doin', Malcolm," she asked.

"I'm fine, Bev," he responded. "I've never seen this place so busy."

"Ya, I-80 is shut down. A meteor hit Salt Lake and destroyed the freeway. So all the guys headed to Salt Lake are kinda stuck here for now."

"Ah shit, I didn't even think about that," he said. "I heard about the meteors."

"Ya, scary shit," she said. "I gotta keep working, Malcolm. What do ya want to eat?"

"Cheeseburger and fries, please."

"You got it. It'll be a bit, though. They're slammed back there."

"No worries, Bev. Thank you."

Malcolm sipped his coffee and pulled his phone out of his pocket. His parents had both passed away a few years back. He was single with no kids. He didn't have anybody to check on. Or even talk to, really. He had always enjoyed being on his own, but now he felt really lonely. He did miss his parents terribly and wished he could talk to them. He thought about calling Jen again but decided not to. He tried to pull up social media to see if he could get any news on what was going on, but he didn't have a data connection. Not too surprising—coverage was spotty at best on a good day in that part of the world. The diner had Wi-Fi, but he couldn't connect to that either. He just assumed the service was overwhelmed with so many people in one spot. He looked around the diner and started to realize no one was on their phones. That struck him as very odd. Dinner breaks were the time truckers caught up with their calls, messages, and social media. Something weird was going on.

Beverly was making her way down the counter, refilling coffees. When she got to Malcolm, he asked her about the Wi-Fi.

"It went out right after the meteor hit. I'm guessing since Salt Lake is so close, it messed everything like that up."

"That makes sense. So we're all in limbo for now, huh?"

"Ya, looks like it."

She moved on to the guy next to him and continued on down the counter. The guy next to Malcolm turned to him and introduced himself.

"I'm Glenn," the guy said.

"I'm Malcolm," Malcolm responded, extending his hand. Glenn shook Malcolm's hand.

"Some crazy shit goin' on, huh?" Glenn said, carefully sipping his fresh cup of coffee.

"Yeah, man, it's nuts."

"Never seen nuthin' like this before."

"I didn't think we ever would," Malcolm said.

"It's the end of the world and I'm stuck in Wells fuckin' Nevada," Glenn said, shaking his head.

"There's worse places to be right now," Malcolm responded.

"Ain't that the truth," Glenn said. "So whatcha think of all this?"

"It's sad, man. Terribly sad," Malcolm said, taking a sip of coffee.

"It's sad, yes, but I meant whatcha think about them meteors?"

"It's a little unbelievable," Malcolm said. He was kind of surprised Glenn seemed so nonchalant about the sadness of the events. Maybe Malcolm just had more compassion than Glenn.

"A little?" Glenn said with a chuckle. "It's very unbelievable. It ain't no accident."

Oh, here comes the conspiracy bullshit, Malcolm thought.

"Seems like an accident to me," Malcolm said. Part of him wanted to find a way out of this conversation. Another part wanted to hear what Glenn had to say. What was his theory?

"I blame that bitch the liberal fucks elected president. Nuthin' like this shit ever happened when we had men runnin' this country. Now less than two years in we got rocks destroying everythin'?

I think she fucked sumthin' up and the gov'ment is hidin' it now. Teach us to elect some bitch to run this great country."

Malcolm looked away from Glenn in shock. He had to fight back laughter. He had assumed whatever Glenn thought was going on was going to be out there and most likely hilarious, but he didn't think it would have been that ridiculous.

"Wait, how is it President Rodgers's fault?" Malcolm asked, trying not to smile.

"She probably got her period and pushed some damn button she wasn't supposed to," he said, clearly angry.

Malcolm couldn't suppress the laughter that time and chuckled.

"It ain't funny, my man," Glenn said, now sounding offended. "That bitch is behind all this shit!"

"Okay, you keep saying that, but how? How would any one person be behind all this?" Malcolm asked.

"I don't know how," Glenn said, staring at Malcolm. "I just know she gotta be responsible. It's gotta be her." Glenn was an older man, probably mid-fifties, who, by the roundness of him, had probably been driving truck his whole adult life. He smelled like an ashtray, so clearly, he was also a heavy smoker. His face was getting red. "We'll probably never know how," he said.

"That's quite the theory," Malcom smiled. "I think we don't know enough about what goes on in outer space, and we unfortunately got hit by a massive meteor shower. Happens all the time, they just usually burn up before hitting the ground down here. This time was tragically different."

"Aw, bullshit," Glenn growled. "That is more out there than what I said."

"No, sir, it isn't," Malcom calmly replied.

Before Malcolm got his job with the beer company, he had been an over-the-road trucker for several years. During those years, he had met dozens of interesting fellow drivers. Just like any population, truck drivers ran the gamut of social beliefs, backgrounds, economics, and political alliances. Malcolm never let himself get too worked up during an opinionated conversation. He tried to avoid getting baited into those conversations, but that didn't always work out. Truck drivers spent a lot of time alone on the open road. In the days of podcasts, they got all sorts of information from wherever they chose to get it. The technological boom had created an even bigger political divide. Malcolm had his own opinions and views, but he liked to keep those to himself. No one ever won in an opinion-driven debate. In his over-the-road days, he had enjoyed a lot of good, spirited debates and found humor in them. But every once in a while, he would run into someone like Glenn who was just plain nasty about everything. That's where debates like this one lost their humor and became irritating. Glenn was beginning to irritate him.

"It ain't no freak meteor shower," Glenn said, shaking his head. His food had arrived, and he was stuffing his face full of chicken fried steak and eggs as he talked.

"It's not the president's fault either," Malcolm said, slightly disappointed he had taken the bait and was in a conversation as absurd as that one. His cheeseburger and fries showed up. Beverly came right back with a side of ranch.

"What y'all talkin' 'bout?" she asked, leaning on the counter.

"This fella thinks it was just meteors crashin' inta us," Glenn said, pointing at Malcolm with his thumb.

"It ain't that, Malcolm," Beverly said. "The gov'ment did this."

Malcolm shook his head. "Why would our own government do that?" He regretted asking the question as soon as it passed his lips.

"'Cuz they controllin' us," Glenn said, spewing out chucks of scrambled eggs as he talked.

"*What?* That don't even make sense," Malcolm said, very confused. "Why and how would blowing up all the major cities control us?"

"No, big cities control us," Glenn said. "That's where the technology is."

"I'm still confused." Now his curiosity outweighed his annoyance.

"Look, young buck, gov'ment wants to control us, but technology controls us now. Gov'ment gets rid of technology, they can control us."

That was the smartest thing Malcolm had heard come from this man's mouth. It was still insane, but at least there was intelligence behind it. Malcolm stared at Glenn for a moment. He assumed Glenn's theory was actually someone else's. He'd probably heard some radio or podcast host yammering on about how technology controlled the world now and that someday, governments would find a way to eradicate technology so they could take control back. The irony was governments already controlled populations and they used technology to do it.

"That's an interesting idea," Malcolm said. "But I don't see how it would benefit the government to kill off most of the population like that. I'm telling you, it's just a horrible natural disaster."

Glenn looked at Beverly, and they both laughed.

"No way, Malcolm," Beverly said. "Glenn's got it right."

"They wouldn't," Malcolm said. "They just wouldn't."

"They would and they did," Glenn said.

"Then why did DC get hit?" Malcolm asked, thinking he had gotten them.

"Did it?" Glenn asked.

"That's what I heard," Malcolm responded.

"You seen it?" Glenn asked.

"Well, no, obviously not personally." Malcolm said.

"So how you know it did?" Glenn asked.

This guy was really getting under Malcolm's skin now. That's why he never got into those kinds of debates. Every question you had for them, they had a refuting question. Not many answers, always more questions. Malcolm didn't say anything for a bit. He finished his cheeseburger and fries. Beverly had long gone about her duties. Glenn sat next to him with a smug look on his face, eating a huge piece of cherry pie.

"I guess we'll have to agree to disagree," Malcom finally said, putting a twenty-dollar bill under the edge of his empty plate. Beverly saw it and swooped in to grab the dirty plate and the money.

"That's what losers always say when ya school 'em on matters," Glenn said, with a smirk.

That comment infuriated Malcolm, but he didn't let it show. "I suppose that could be the case sometimes. I'm going to be on my way, sir." He threw in the "sir" to irk Glenn a bit.

"Happy trails, young buck," Glenn said.

Malcolm shouted at Beverly to keep the change and left the diner. His blood was boiling. He couldn't believe that guy. He was even more upset with himself that he let the man get under skin like that. He usually wouldn't let a guy like that bother him. He assumed it had to do with the extra stress of the current events. He tried to let it go and climbed back into his truck. He reached into the glovebox and pulled out a pack of menthol cigarettes. He rarely smoked, but that day, he needed one desperately.

He sat there smoking a cigarette while he replayed the exchange he had just had with Glenn. He knew guys like Glenn got off on shit like that. He knew Glenn saw how irritated and angry he had become, and he knew Glenn had loved it. His phone rang and it startled him. It was Jen calling.

"Hi, Jen," Malcolm answered. "I didn't think I had service, or I would've called you by now."

"I've been trying to call for over an hour," she said. Malcolm could hear the panic in her voice. He was about to apologize, but she just kept talking. "Don't go back to Ely. The whole town is on fire. People are going nuts there. Ben and I are on our way to Vegas." The connection crackled, and he didn't hear what she said after that.

"Wait, what?" Malcolm stammered. "Why Vegas? I thought Vegas was destroyed too."

"A meteor hit Vegas proper—it missed the strip. The strip has lots of damage, but most hotels survived. They're taking people in for free, man." The phone broke up again. "Get there," she said.

"Okay." He was dumbfounded. Vegas was almost six hours from where he sat in his truck.

"Get there, Malcolm."

"All right, I will head that way now."

The phone went dead. The call had dropped. What in the hell was going on? Why would Ely be on fire? This was a lot bigger than he had ever imagined. This wasn't going to just go away. He knew he had enough fuel to get to Vegas, he was just worried about traffic.

*****

Taylor woke up on the floor of the bus. The smell of diesel still hung in the air. He knew he hadn't been out long. He sat up and looked out the bus windows. The street outside of the bus depot was empty and quiet. He slowly stood up and walked off the bus. He still couldn't hear anything. The sun had set, and the depot was dark. The automatic outside lights were on just outside the garage door. He grabbed a tire iron and carefully walked to the door. He looked out the door and saw what looked like a scene from an apocalypse movie. Two cop cars were smashed up from the bus hitting them. Crashed vehicles clogged the road, leaving enough room for one car to get through. Bodies littered the street, both civilians and police officers. He put his head down and ran across the street to the employee parking lot. He could hear people down the street. Loud voices yelling, not an argument but more like a celebration. He hurried to his car and realized he had left his keys in his toolbox back in the shop. He stood there for a moment, scared to death. He took a deep breath and ran back to the shop. He grabbed his keys and rushed back to his car.

There was a man walking through the parking lot, looking into car windows. Taylor stopped and raised the tire iron. The man was at the far end of the lot working his way toward Taylor. He hadn't noticed Taylor yet. Taylor's car was halfway between him and the man. With the tire iron still raised, he ran to his car. He knew as soon as he hit the unlock button on his key fob, that guy would hear it. Just feet from the driver's door, Taylor hit the button, pulled open the door, hopped in, and locked the doors. He fumbled for a second to get the key in the ignition. He finally did and started his car. He looked behind him and saw the man standing about twenty feet away from him. Taylor backed out and pulled away with a screech of the tires. The man just stared at Taylor. Taylor peeled out of the lot and headed east, dodging vehicles and bodies. At the end of the road, he wanted to turn south to cross the bridge and head to his apartment just south of downtown, but the police had the bridge blocked. He had to go north to the next cross street. That road was also blocked. He kept heading north, the opposite direction of his apartment.

Finally, he found an eastbound street that was open and took it. He got to the next southbound road and headed toward downtown. That bridge was closed too. He had to double back and head east again. He was getting extremely frustrated. He just wanted to get home and lock himself in his apartment. He was starting to think he should have listened to Billy and just left earlier to stock up on supplies. He had been very relieved when he left the bus depot and did not see Billy's car anywhere, meaning he had gotten out of there before the gunfire. Taylor had food and basic supplies already but only enough to last a week or so. He just had to get home.

The last bridge into downtown was open, and he took it south. He would have to cross downtown west bound to get up to his apartment building. Downtown was completely dead. Only police officers directing what little traffic was going through. No businesses were open. No one was walking around. It was so eerie. He finally made it across downtown and headed south again. After about five minutes, he was finally home. He grabbed the tire iron and headed to his apartment. He saw a woman in her early twenties lying in the grass in the courtyard. She wasn't moving. He approached her very cautiously. He could see her chest moving up and down; she was breathing. When he got close, she sat up really quick and jumped back. She looked terrified.

"Don't be scared," he said, lowering the tire iron.

"Run," she whispered.

"What?" he said, tilting his head at her.

"Run. I'm a decoy," she whispered.

Taylor started to turn around and felt a blunt object hit him in the back. He fell to the ground, dropping his tire iron. He rolled over on his back and saw a man holding a baseball bat. Taylor reached for his tire iron. It wasn't anywhere near him. That's when he saw the woman holding it just behind the man. She looked Taylor in the eyes and smiled. She took two steps back and slowly raised the tire iron. Taylor looked up at the man.

"What do you want from me?" Taylor asked the man.

The man pointed the bat at Taylor. "Everythin' you got," the man growled.

"I don't have shit," Taylor said.

The woman took one step forward and slammed the tire iron into the man's head. His eyes bugged out, and he fell forward. Taylor grabbed the bat and stood up. The woman had split the man's head open and blood was gushing out.

"What the fuck?" Taylor exclaimed, staring at the man on the ground.

"He's been using me as bait," the woman said.

"Bait for what?" Taylor asked.

"Scamming dudes. What I did to you. Pretend to be hurt, get your guard down and *bam*!" She swung the tire iron as she said "*bam*."

"Why'd you go along with that?" Taylor asked, looking at her.

"He said he'd give me booze and drugs," she said, looking down at the ground.

"Did you guys kill anyone?"

"Fuck no!" she said, looking back at Taylor. "You're only the third dude we tried it on. Look, man, I ain't in a good way. Then this meteor shit happened. Now I don't know how I will survive. This asshole came along a while back and promises me all sorts of good shit. Then doesn't follow through with shit! Fuckin' used me to get his own fuckin' fix. You were the first one to not get knocked out. That really confused him, so I took my chance with the tire iron." She walked over to the man's body. "Think I killed him?"

"Oh, hell yeah, you did. He's definitely dead." Taylor was in shock. What in the hell was going on in the world?

"Good! Piece of shit tried to rape me too but couldn't get that tiny little dick hard."

"Why didn't you just run?" Taylor asked.

"I couldn't, man, he had dope. I saw it. He kept giving me little bits, just to keep me healthy enough but never let me get high. Then when the meteors hit, he decides to start doin' this shit." She looked at Taylor. "Thank you. You saved my life, man."

"I did?" Taylor asked, confused. "Seems like you saved mine."

"Maybe we did each other's." She smiled. "You want a drink?" she asked.

"Uh, sure," he said, not a hundred percent sure what he had just agreed to. He was still in shock.

"Cool. My name's Amber. What's yours?" She grabbed his hand and pulled him toward the apartment building.

"I'm Taylor."

"Cool beans, Taylor. Nice to meet you." She squeezed his hand and smiled.

She led him to a ground floor apartment. They went inside. The apartment was a mess and smelled so bad. It smelt like wet dog, urine, and mildew. She went into the kitchen and grabbed two glasses out of the dishwasher. She took a bottle of vodka off the fridge and poured a healthy amount into each glass. She opened the freezer and put ice in each glass. She then opened the fridge and produced a bottle of lemon-lime soda. She filled the glasses the rest of the way with soda. Taylor was still standing in the foyer, taking in the mess around him.

"Come sit down," Amber said, motioning at the stained and ripped-up couch.

"Um, I'm good. Thanks," Taylor muttered. The smell was making his eyes water and his stomach turn.

"Come on, man, sit with me." She sat down. "Relax. Have a drink." She set both drinks down.

She sat back on the couch and kicked her shoes off. She put her feet straight up in the air, reached out to her feet, and took off her socks. She tossed the once white, but now yellow, socks across the room. She sat up a bit. She looked at Taylor and smiled. She was wearing a pink button-up shirt. She smiled at Taylor and undid the top three buttons, exposing her cleavage.

"Come on, man. I just wanna hang out. Get ta know ya. Maybe we'll hit it off and we can play." She smiled, twirling her hair.

"Uh, I don't even know you. Five minutes ago, you were luring me in to get my head knocked off. Now you wanna get drunk and fool around?" He grabbed the knob on the front door. "I gotta get home."

"Look, I'm sorry 'bout that. That wasn't my call. But hey, you didn't get knocked out, and we killed Jimmy. We're safe, man."

"You killed him."

"Before he could kill you," she said. "Please, man, just one drink. Nuthin' else, just drinks."

"Another time," he said and opened the door. "I gotta go. I'll check on ya tomorrow."

"Please, Taylor," she said, standing up and walking toward him. "I'm lonely. I just want some company." Her bloodshot eyes begged him.

She was clearly down for anything. She was cute, and his libido was urging him to stay and play, it had been a while since he had been with a woman. But he knew he couldn't. Who knew what that girl had? Plus, that apartment was wretched.

"Sorry, Amber, I'm going home." He stepped out the door. She grabbed his arm.

"Please, Taylor," she whispered.

"I'll come by tomorrow."

"What apartment you in? I could come to you."

"It's not important." He pulled his arm free and left.

"Then fuck off!" she yelled, slamming the door.

Taylor stood there and shook his head. What in the hell was all that? He turned and headed to his apartment. He made sure she wasn't following him. He got to his apartment and went in. He closed and locked the door. He went to the fridge and grabbed a beer. He sat down on the couch and turned on the TV. Nothing. Just a black screen. He tried all his streaming apps. Nothing. There was no service. He turned off the TV and stepped out on his balcony. He lit a cigarette and sat down with his beer. He could hear sirens all around him. He could hear gunshots in the distance. He was so glad to be safe in his apartment. He sat, smoking and drinking his beer, and let himself finally relax. He would need more supplies soon, but all that could wait a day. That night, he just wanted to get a good buzz on and pass out. And that's exactly what he did.

*****

Pete sat in traffic on the freeway. Traffic was moving slowly, but at least it was moving. He was heading west and could see the skies starting to darken. It was just about dusk, but this darkness was different. Like something was slowly blocking out the sun. He didn't want to go back to his mom and dad's place. He had finally stepped out on his own and was now running back to Mom and Dad, or so it felt that way to him. He knew they'd have food and supplies, and he had none of the above at his place. He lived paycheck to paycheck, so he never had the money to stock up on anything. Meals were usually picked up at the store beforehand or ordered in, usually the latter.

Pete was in deep thought when three police cars screamed by the line of traffic on the shoulder, lights and sirens blaring. Right after the first three, another three flew by. Then three more. Traffic slowed down even more. It was now stop and go, mostly stopped. He merged into the far-right lane and took the next exit. It was a few exits east of the one he would normally take to his parents' place, but he figured he'd rather go across town than sit on the freeway. Just moving in any direction felt better than just sitting. As he got further from the interstate, traffic lightened up quite a bit. The further north across town he made it, the more of a ghost town it became. His parents lived up north near Mount Spokane. That area of town was usually pretty busy. It was just off Highway 2 North, and that was a well-used highway. But not that day. It was very strange and eerie.

He was about five miles south of his turn when he saw a car on the side of the road. The back tire was flat, and there was a woman trying to jack up the car. He wanted to keep going, but he was afraid that woman would be stranded. She didn't seem to know what she was doing. He pulled off the highway in front of her and got out. He slowly walked back to her car, as to not frighten her. She saw him approaching and smiled.

"Hey, need a hand?" Pete asked her.

"Oh my god, yes please," she said, with relief in her voice. "My dad taught me how to change a tire when I was sixteen, but that was ten years ago and three cars ago. I don't know how to work this thing," she said, holding up the jack.

"Yeah, they're tricky," Pete said. "I'm Pete."

"I'm Melanie, nice to meet you."

"Nice to meet you too," Pete said, taking the jack from her. "Now let's see if we can't get this tire changed."

"Thank you so much," she said.

Pete knelt next to the flat tire and looked under the car. He found the spot for the jack and slid it underneath. He loosened the lug-nuts then jacked up the car. He got the flat off and put the little spare tire on. He put the lug-nuts on and lowered the car to the ground. He tightened all the nuts and handed the tools back to Melanie.

"Oh my god, thank you so much!" she said.

"You're welcome." He smiled.

"You did that so fast," she said, putting everything back into her trunk.

"I've been working on cars for my whole life. I've changed a lot of tires."

"It shows." She smiled. "Thanks again. Can I give you some money or something?"

"No money needed. Maybe your phone number?" he asked shyly. "Maybe after all this stuff blows over, we can go to dinner?"

She looked at him for a minute and then smiled.

"Sure," she said. with a smile. She gave him her number. "Text me later."

"I will!" he said. "I definitely will."

"I look forward to it," she said. "Hey, do you live out here?"

"No, I just moved out to Post Falls. My parents live up off Mount Spokane. I'm going up there until all of this blows over. Do you?"

"No, I live out by Liberty Lake. Same thing for me, my parents live out here. I was just asking because have you ever seen this road so empty?"

"No, never," he said. "We moved out here when I was in fifth grade and I've never seen it like this."

"This whole time we've been out not a single car has driven by. It's all so scary." She stepped closer to him.

"It is so, so scary." He looked at her, and she looked like she was going to cry. "Are you okay?" he asked.

"I don't know," she said, dropping her head. "I thought I was going to be stuck out here before you stopped. I can't get ahold of my parents. I tried calling so many times. I'm just so scared."

"I can imagine. We're all scared," he said and put his arm around her. She fell into him and burst into tears. It weirded him out a bit. She had seemed fine when he first met her. A little stressed from the flat, but nothing more than that. "It'll be okay."

"Will it?" she asked, looking up at him. "How do you know that? Half the world is gone, probably more than half. We won't survive long."

"Yes, we will," he said. It was all very unnerving, but he had faith the survivors would pull through. Humans always found a way to pull through.

"I admire your optimism, but you're wrong." She stepped away from him. "You're naïve," she said.

He was a bit offended by that. He had just helped her out of a jam. He had been nothing but nice to her, and now she was insulting him.

"I don't feel like being hopeful makes me naïve," he said.

"I knew you were from the moment you stopped. No one else on the highway and you stop to help a stranger." The tears were all gone now. "That's stupid and dangerous."

"Whoa!" he exclaimed. "That's uncalled for. I stopped because you were alone out here trying to fix a flat. I was trying to be nice, and now you're being rude to me."

"Oh, poor guy, did I hurt your feelings?" She took a flashlight out of her pocket, turned it on, and waved it around in the air.

"I'm out of here. Don't expect a text later." He turned toward his car. Standing behind his car were two men with baseball bats. "What the fuck is this?" he asked, turning back to Melanie.

"This is a car jackin'." She smiled.

"What? Why? You have a car right there? Why steal mine? Just let me go on my way."

"This car don't run. It was sittin' here. We slashed the tire. We need a car. You stopped, so we're taking yours. Give me the keys."

"Fuck you," he said.

"Give me the keys and my brothers won't beat the shit out of you. Look, man, we just want the car. We honestly don't want to beat you up. We just need wheels, and you're the only one who stopped."

The men were now right behind him.

"Come on, man," she said, holding out her hand.

Pete looked at the men and then back at Melanie, which probably wasn't even her real name. He sighed and reached into his pocket. He pulled out his keys and took the car keys off the ring. He handed her the car keys with another sigh.

"Thanks, hon," she said, smiling.

The men turned around, and all three of them walked casually to Pete's car. Pete stood there dumbfounded. He watched as they climbed into his car and took off. He went to the car that he thought had been Melanie's. He looked inside. The car was a mess. It had clearly been ransacked. He walked around to the other side of the car and stopped dead in his tracks. Lying in the ditch next to the car was a man in his mid to late forties. He had been beaten to death. It was the most gruesome thing Pete had ever seen. Nothing like what you see in movies. Pete heard a car coming from the north. He looked up, hoping it would be someone who could help. It was his own car. They had gone up the highway to somewhere they could turn around. All three of them stared at him as they flew past on the opposite side of the road. He looked back at the body. He swiveled all the way around, nothing and no one else. He took off running toward Mount Spokane.

CHAPTER 5

Connection Lost

Dana and Julia sat in the stairwell, taking a break from chiseling away at the concrete and drywall. They were tired, hungry, and filthy. They could see light poking through the debris. They couldn't tell how long they had been at it but seeing that little bit of light gave them hope. Julia's hands throbbed, and Dana's leg was still so numb and tingly. They had found cases of bottled water and were sipping water as they rested. The room was starting to feel cramped and arid. Either they had gotten used to it or the smell of burning flesh had dissipated.

"We gotta get outta here," Dana said, tears in her eyes.

"Yeah, we do. We're going to eventually run out of air. That tiny little hole up there ain't goin' to give us enough air," Julia replied, sipping her water. The water was amazing, but they didn't want to drink too much. There was nowhere to go to the bathroom down there.

"My leg hurts so bad," Dana said. "And I don't feel good at all."

"My hands are killing me, and I feel like shit too," Julia said. "But we just gotta work through it. We ain't going to get anywhere sittin' here." She stood up and grabbed her tools. She grimaced in pain as she began to pound away at the debris.

Dana gingerly stood up and joined her friend. They pounded away at the pile for about fifteen minutes until they had to stop again. The pain was just so intense. They knelt at the top of the stairs, trying to catch their breath. That's when they heard something above them. Movement. Something or someone was moving around right above them. They looked at each other with wide eyes. They turned back toward the pile of concrete that had trapped them and began yelling for help. The movement above them stopped. They stopped yelling to listen. A voice shouted back at them.

"I hear you!" a man's voice yelled. "Where are you?"

"Down here!" Julia shouted back, banging her hammer on the concrete above her head.

"Hang on!" the man yelled.

They heard more movement above them and then more shouting. They couldn't make out what was being said, but there was at least one more man shouting up there. The shouting stopped and everything went silent again. They looked at each other again. They stayed silent, just listening for anything above them. Then seemingly out of nowhere, they heard several footsteps right above their heads.

"Stand back!" someone yelled. "We're gonna bust ya out!"

Dana and Julia scurried off the steps. They stood back in the basement, holding each other. Tears were flooding down their faces. The sound of sledgehammers and axes was almost deafening but oh so beautiful. Concrete and drywall started flying down the stairs. The stairs lit up as the debris was broken away. Finally, someone descended the stairs. It was a man who looked to be in his mid-thirties. He was holding a sledgehammer.

"You guys okay?" he asked, looking around. They just nodded. They were crying so hard at that point they couldn't speak. "Come on, let's get ya outta here." He extended a hand.

Dana and Julia followed the man up the stairs. They looked around and what they saw was beyond devastating. Everything had been destroyed. Just leveled. Bodies were scattered about. Parts of bodies stuck out of the building debris like cheap Halloween decorations.

"Hey, guys," the man said, turning to a group of four people. "There's a bunch of water, food, and random supplies down there. Let's get everything we can out of there."

The other people nodded and headed into the basement. They made several trips up and down, hauling out everything that could be or would be needed.

"Where did you come from?" Julia asked, wiping tears from her eyes.

"I'm from Ely, Nevada," he said. "These folks are from 'round here, I guess. We haven't really exchanged formalities like that yet."

"How'd you survive this?" Julia asked. "What the hell happened?"

"Meteors hit all the major cities," he said. "I was in the middle of nowhere when we got hit, delivering beer to some hole-in-the-wall bar. I drove down here cuz I heard there was shelter. My town was burnt to the ground."

"Wait. What? Meteors?" Julia looked at Dana. "This wasn't a bomb?"

"No. One big-ass rock that hit just outside Vegas did this," he said, motioning to the damage all around them. "This is actually somewhat minor compared to the impact zone. Where the meteors hit, there's just a huge hole in the ground now. Y'all are lucky you were down there."

"I-I guess so," Julia said, looking around. "How'd you find us?"

"Lucky, I guess," he began. "I was trying to get to the strip, but I couldn't in my beer truck. I met these people at the hotel I was lucky enough to get a room in. The hotel says it has limited supplies, and these people said they were going to go look for supplies and any survivors. We were looking through the rubble here and heard y'all yelling."

"Oh my god," Dana said. "If you guys didn't go looking for supplies, we'd still be stuck down there."

"I'm hoping someone would've found ya," he said smiling.

Dana and Julia were speechless. They were trying to digest everything this man had just told them.

"Come on, let's get moving," he said, picking up a stack of canned goods.

"Where?" Julia asked, still looking around.

"The strip. The casinos are still standing. They're taking people in."

"Okay," Julia said, looking at Dana. Dana nodded.

"Grab some supplies," he said.

They picked up a couple of cases of water and followed the man. It was very dark. The only light was the full moon. They carefully walked through the rubble. Dana gasped and stopped dead in her tracks. Julia stopped right behind her. Dana was looking at a mangled body on the ground.

"It's Rich," Dana said.

Julia looked down. There was Rich's body, or at least what was left of it. His head and torso were wedged between two slot machines, and his legs were on the ground behind the machines. They looked at each other. Julia smiled, and Dana couldn't help smiling too. They felt kind of bad getting some sort of pleasure out of seeing their boss like that, but they couldn't help it. The man had kept moving; he hadn't noticed they had stopped. They stepped around Rich and hurried to catch up to the man.

They had no idea what was going on, but the relief of being out of that basement and around other people had really put them at ease. They felt more themselves now. No matter what came next, at least they would always be together and have each other to count on. Nothing was going to come between them.

*****

Sheer panic and fear had caused Gwen and Hope to pass out on the kitchen floor. They awoke to the sound of a loud siren. It wasn't any emergency vehicles. It was the siren you heard in movies when a town was under attack. Or the world was ending. They looked at each other and slowly got up. They went back up to Hope's room to get their phones.

"I don't have any service," Gwen said, thumbing through her phone.

"I don't either," Hope said, looking at Gwen. "What do we do now?"

"I think we should go to my house. My mom will know what to do."

"What about my mom? We can't just leave her out there," Hope said with tears in her eyes. She blinked, and the tears flooded out.

"We can't go out there. We'll get electrocuted too," Gwen said, tears streaming down her cheeks as well.

They stood there in Hope's room crying. They were heartbroken and terrified. The grief was overwhelming, even though everything hadn't even fully set in yet. They had gone from watching a movie to meteors hitting all over the planet to some guy crashing into a power pole to the worst thing imaginable. It was all too much to process. Too much to handle. Gwen knew they just had to get out of there. She grabbed her bag and car keys.

"Let's go, Hope," she said through tears.

"Okay," Hope said, spinning her now useless phone in her hand.

They went outside and stopped in the driveway. Gwen's car was parked on the street on the other side of the downed wire. They would have to walk over the wire to get to her car. Or go around the crashed SUV. They looked across the street and saw a man standing in front of the SUV. He was staring at them. They looked at each other and then back at the man. He smiled a smile that sent shivers through them. He started to walk toward them. They ran back into the house, locking the front door. They ran to every entry point and locked the whole house up. They went back to Hope's room and looked out her window. The man was standing in the front yard, looking up at them. He smiled that awful smile again. The girls closed the blinds and climbed onto Hope's bed. They laid there holding each other and just wept.

*****

Scarlett had fallen asleep at her desk. She had the presentation almost done. She awoke in a panic, thinking maybe she had slept all night. She looked at the wall clock; it was only 10:00 p.m. She let out a sigh of relief. She got up and stretched. She wanted coffee. She *needed* coffee if she was going to get that presentation done. She headed downstairs. On her way, she stopped by Gwen's room to say hi. Gwen wasn't in there.

Shit, she thought, *I slept right through dinner.*

Scarlett figured Gwen had fended for herself and was probably downstairs watching TV. The whole house was dark. She soon realized Gwen had never come home. That wasn't like Gwen. Scarlett went into the kitchen and grabbed her phone. She had several messages from Gwen and a few missed calls from her as well. She had dozens of missed calls and messages from friends and family. She almost dropped her phone as she read what had happened. How in the hell did she sleep through all of that? Damn, when she buried herself in her work, she really shut the world out. She couldn't believe what was going on.

Gwen! Where was Gwen? Was she okay? Was she still at Hope's? She tried to call Gwen but didn't have any service. *Shit*! She grabbed her keys and phone and rushed out the door. She had to get to Hope's to see if Gwen was still there and make sure she was okay. Gwen and Hope had been friends since grade school. Scarlett had taken Gwen to Hope's house hundreds of times; she knew exactly how to get there. And how to get there quickly.

She wasn't surprised not to see anyone out and about in her neighborhood, especially at that time of night. She was surprised there was little to no traffic outside of her neighborhood. A few cars here and there. Something didn't feel right to her. This wasn't the city she had called home for so many years. There were abandoned cars lining the streets. People were walking around carrying guns and baseball bats. She had to turn around at one point when she came across a five-car pile-up. The body of a woman in her early twenties lay in the street. The woman's eyes were still open, staring at Scarlett. She shuddered and moved on. The more she paid attention, the more frightened she became. She saw a man limping down the middle of the street toward her car. He was holding a bloody shirt to the side of his head. When he saw her slowly approaching him, he removed the shirt. The whole side of his face was gone. She could see his jawbone. Her stomach heaved, and she fought back the urge to vomit. She pulled around the man and gunned it. She had seen enough; time to get to Hope's as fast as possible.

Scarlett was less than two miles from Hope's house when a car slammed into the back of her car. She hadn't even seen the car pull up behind her. The impact made her swerve toward the curb. She quickly righted the vehicle and sped off. The green car gunned it and took off after her. She could see a man in the driver's seat. He was dressed in all black with a beanie on. All she could see was the sinister grin on his face. She was panicking. No way could she lead this guy to Hope's house. She had to try to lose him. She just hoped and prayed she knew the neighborhood better than he did. He was right on her ass. She took the next corner, squealing her tires. He was still right behind her. She cut down an alley, and he followed.

The park! she thought. *I'll lose him behind the park!*

Scarlett whipped around the next corner and sped to the park. She zipped behind the park and into a parking lot. She had out run him for a second. Turning her lights off, she drove into the park. Her tires spun a bit on the grass as she cut through the park. She could see him stopped in the parking lot. The dome light inside his car come on as he opened the door. He walked into the park, looking around. She tore through the park and got back onto the street. Turning her lights back on, she floored it toward Hope's house.

She turned onto Hope's street. The whole street was dark. No street lights. No lights on in any of the houses. She pulled into Hope's driveway. As she did, her headlights lit up the front yard. There, standing ten feet from the front door was a man. He turned and looked at her. He smiled and shivers went up her spine. He approached her car. She looked up to the house and saw the girls looking out of Hope's bedroom window. They were safe. She had to get this man away from the house. She put her car in reverse and slowly backed out of the driveway. He stopped and watched her. She pulled up next to the curb and rolled down her window.

"Get out of here!" she yelled at the man.

He didn't say anything.

"You don't belong here! *Go!*" she yelled. Still no response.

He was standing in the driveway, staring and smiling at her. She reached into the glovebox and grabbed her 9mm. Her dad had raised her with guns and had taught her to always have a gun with you. Always have one in the glovebox. She pointed the gun out the window with very shaky hands. She was a damn good shot with that pistol, but she had never shot at anyone in her life. She wasn't sure if she would be able to.

"Leave now or I will shoot you!" she shouted at the man.

He laughed out loud and started to walk toward her.

"I'm not fuckin' kidding! Get out of here now!"

He laughed again and kept walking toward her. She pointed the gun at his chest and squeezed the trigger. The gunshot echoed throughout the dark, dead quiet street. Blood exploded from his chest and he fell to the ground. He rolled around on the driveway as blood began to pool underneath him. Scarlett put the car in park and shut off the engine. She walked to the man. He looked up at her. She pointed the gun at his face. He reached into his pocket, and she pulled the trigger. She hit him in the forehead, and the top of his head blew out. Blood and brains stained the driveway. Scarlett walked over to the lawn and vomited. She looked up at the window and motioned for the girls to come let her inside. The girls were in shock, and it took a while for them to register what was going on. Finally, they ran downstairs and let Scarlett in. Scarlett grabbed both girls and pulled them to her. She squeezed them tightly, and they buried their heads into her shoulders and began to cry. Scarlett put her head on her daughter's head. The girls were shaking, and all Scarlett could do was hold them close. Tears welled up in her eyes, and she just let them flow. They stood there, just inside the front door, and bawled.

*****

John woke up on a bunk in the firehouse. A firefighter was sitting next to him. John was foggy and disorientated.

"Sir," the firefighter began, "how do you feel?"

"Where's my wife and boys?" John asked. For the first time since the accident, he felt no pain.

"They're on their way to Des Moines," the firefighter said.

"Why?" John asked, trying to sit up. He was strapped to a backboard.

"Because that's where we're taking you. Closest place to us with a hospital."

"I don't need a hospital. I just want to go home," John said. The room felt so bright.

"Sir, you can't go home. Your back is broken. You're one wrong step away from being paralyzed." The firefighter put a syringe full of something into John's IV line.

"There's closer places if I have to go," John said; he was feeling sleepy again.

"Not now, there isn't."

"What about Lincoln? Omaha?" John's eyes were getting heavy.

"Lincoln is on fire, the city has been evacuated, and Omaha is on lockdown, no one in or out."

"Shit," John said as he drifted off again.

John awoke again several hours later. He was in the back of an ambulance. The vehicle was moving very fast. He raised his head and looked around. He was alone back there. He could see out the back windows of the ambulance. There were no cars behind them. The road was eerily empty. He knew the highway they were on, and it was usually a very busy one. All he could see out those windows was darkness. He groaned and laid his head back down. He knew he had been out for a while. The meds had done their job and knocked him out hard. Now he felt more himself. He could feel the pain in his hips, back, and legs. Not as intense as it had been, but the pain was definitely back. He welcomed it, honestly. He hated drugs. Despite the pain he felt, he was happy to feel more normal again.

All of a sudden, the sky lit up. The light was so bright it filled the back of the ambulance with a brightness he had never seen. Or felt. Yes, felt. He could *feel* that light. Was this the light people saw during a near-death experience? Was he dying? The ambulance came to a screeching halt. The whole vehicle rocked. He could feel the shaking in his spine. It hurt so bad. He could hear the guys in the front.

"What the fuck is that?" one of them said.

"I don't know man," the other replied. "But it's huge!"

"I thought air travel was restricted. What the hell is flying around out here?" the first guy asked.

"Probably military," the second guy said. "Get us out of here."

The ambulance went dark, except for the light outside.

"Shit," the first guy said. "We're dead in the water."

"Fuck. Now what?" the second guy said.

"We're so close. Less than forty minutes from Des Moines," the first guy said, trying to start the ambulance.

John couldn't move; he was strapped to a stretcher. He called out to the guys up front, but they didn't respond. The ambulance was still rocking. His back was now screaming in pain. He actually wanted drugs.

The outside light intensified. The guys up front quit talking. Except for a faint whirring sound, everything was dead quiet. John could hear people walking outside the ambulance. They sounded big. He raised his head and looked out the back windows. He couldn't see anything except that unnaturally bright light. Then the light was blocked out. John's heart was pounding out of his chest. He must have still been under the influence of the narcotics they had given him, there was no way he was seeing what he thought he saw out there. Looking at him through the back window was the ugliest thing he had ever seen in his life. The black eyes of this thing were sunk into a leathery brown/gray face. The nostrils fogged up the window as it exhaled. The teeth looked like yellow razor blades. John couldn't look away. Those dark eyes held his eyes without his permission. He physically could not look away even though he so badly wanted to. This thing had him.

Suddenly, his head felt like it was going to explode. It felt like it was full of helium or something. The light outside got even brighter. That thing was still staring at him. It was smiling at him. Not a friendly "Hey, how ya doing" smile. More of a "Hey, you look delicious" smile.

He heard the front doors of the ambulance open. The men up front screamed. Their screams were quickly silenced. John knew they had been killed. There was no doubt in his mind. The way their screams were just cut off; it was all too obvious something had ended them. John knew he was next. That thing was still staring at him. He swore he saw it lick its lips. Those eyes were enchanting though. He felt like it was communicating with him through its eyes. His head was pounding. His heart was racing. His bladder had released. He was soaked in sweat and urine. This was it. This was the end for him. Tears streamed down his scruffy cheeks. He didn't get to say goodbye to Serena or the boys. In fact, the last time he had spoken to Serena they had argued a bit. He was leaving this world, and his last interaction with his wife was not a great one.

Shit!

Where were they? Had they made it to Des Moines? Were they at the hospital already waiting for him to get there? How long would they wait there? Did these things get them too? He didn't even want to think about that.

"*Your family is fine,*" a cold, dark voice said in his head.

"What?" he said aloud.

"*Your family is fine,*" the voice said again.

"How do you know?" he asked aloud. Who was he even asking? What was that voice in his head?

"*We know. We know all,*" it said.

It! That thing was talking to him inside his own mind! How in the holy hell was it doing that?

"*They won't be fine for long, though,*" it said with a chuckle. "*None of you will.*"

He heard a lot of commotion outside. For the first time since that thing had locked eyes with him, it looked away. As soon as it took its eyes off John, his head fell back to the stretcher, and the pain in his head went away. That full, almost going to explode feeling was gone. His heart rate slowed, and he was breathing normal again. He felt somewhat normal again too. Still pain in his hips and back but not as bad as before.

John heard gunshots outside of the ambulance. He could hear shouting and screaming. Those screams were agonizing. It sounded like several people were dying horrible deaths. Then an explosion of red light lit everything up for a moment, and everything went quiet and dark again. Pitch dark. The ambulance quit rocking, and every-thing was deathly still. The air was heavy. What smelled like sulfur began to creep in the open front doors of the rig.

He yelled out.

Nothing.

He called out again, this time louder.

Still…nothing.

He closed his eyes and let all his emotions out. Tears pooled on the cheap plastic pillow under his now swimming head. He sobbed. For the first time in his adult life, he bawled. He feared he would never see Serena and the boys again. He had to get out of that ambu-lance. He felt like he was going to pass out again. He couldn't let that happen. He was in and out of consciousness for a bit. Each time he'd let himself pass out, he'd snap himself back. He tried to keep his head up and off of the pillow, but it was far too heavy.

After a bit, he heard movement outside again. His heart stopped. He pulled his head up and listened intently. He heard a man gasp. Then he heard that same man say out loud, "Holy fuck."

"*Hey!*" John yelled. "*Help!*"

"Who's there?" the man shouted.

"I'm in the ambulance," John shouted. "I'm strapped to a stretcher in here! Please help me!"

John saw a man peek through the back window. The man slowly opened the back door.

"What the hell happened out there?" he asked as he climbed into the ambulance.

"I don't know," John said. "I was tied up in here the whole time." He wasn't about to tell this man what he had actually seen out there.

"There's mangled bodies out there. And this weird green goo next to the cab of this ambulance." The man sat next to John and shook his head.

"Please unstrap me," John said. "I have to get to Des Moines."

"You don't wanna go to Des Moines," the man said as he unstrapped John. "I just left there. It's a shitshow."

"I gotta get to the hospital. My family is there."

"I wouldn't if I were you," the man said.

"I have to," John said, sitting up for the first time in hours. It hurt like hell, but no amount of pain was going to stop him from finding his family.

"You look to be pretty beat up, my friend," the man said. "How ya planning to get yourself to Des Moines?"

"I'll drive this thing. If it's still drivable." John tried to stand up and plopped right back down onto the stretcher. He winced in pain.

The man sighed and looked at John. "I don't think you can," he said.

John looked him in the eyes. "Then help me," he said.

"I ain't going back there. No way, man. People are getting shot in the streets for their cars. People are looting stores and beating each other with bats. I've never seen anything like it. It's too dangerous."

"I don't give a fuck," John said. "I need to find my family. Do you have a family?"

"I did. My crazy ex-wife divorced me and brainwashed my only daughter into hating me. They can fend for themselves as far as I care. I ain't risking myself for no one."

John shook his head. "Sorry about your wife and daughter, but don't you think they'd welcome you considering what's going on? What if this is the end as we know it? You want to spend your last days on earth by yourself, running away?"

The man looked at John. John saw tears in his eyes.

"I'm no good to 'em dead," the man said.

"You're no good to anyone runnin', either. Man up." John could see his last comment stung the man.

"I am a man. They deserted me."

"Show 'em what they deserted. Show 'em you can protect them and provide for them."

"They don't want my help. She left me."

"Screw your ex then," John said. He had to convince this man to take him to Des Moines. He didn't think he could drive with his hips and legs hurting so badly. "Do it for your daughter. She needs you whether either one of you knows it or not."

"You may be right," the man said softly. "I have a car and a couple guns."

"Let's do this then," John said.

"Fuck. Okay," the man said. He stood up and extended a hand to John. John took his hand and stood up.

"Thank you," he said. "My name is John Henderson. If we're going to do this together, we should introduce ourselves."

"I'm Dylan Witner," the man said. "Let's get going before who-ever did this comes back."

"Oh, they'll be back. I have no doubt," John said. Dylan looked at him puzzled but didn't ask about it.

They climbed out of the ambulance. John stopped in his tracks when he saw what had happened out there. The guys driving the ambulance had been gutted. It looked like something had eaten their organs. There was about a half-dozen men laying on the ground about twenty-five feet from the ambulance. They had all been decap-itated, and their heads were nowhere to be found. John shook his head and let a tear escape his red and puffy eyes.

"Holy shit," John muttered. "How was I saved from all this?"

"Lucky I guess," Dylan said. "Come on, man, let's go." He led John to his car and helped him in. He fired up the Porsche and sped off toward Des Moines.

*****

Taylor was asleep in his bed when he heard someone pounding on his apartment door. He looked at the clock; it was 2:00 a.m. His first thought was that Amber had somehow figured out where he lived. God, he did not want to deal with her. He tried to ignore it, but whoever it was just kept pounding on his door. He figured he better answer before his neighbors got pissed off by all the knocking. He got up and put clothes on. The pounding continued. He got to the door and peeked out the peephole. Billy was standing there. Taylor opened the door. Billy had two suitcases and an overloaded backpack.

"Dude!" Billy said, letting himself in. "My apartment building is on fire!"

"Oh shit, man," Taylor said, closing and locking the door. "Well, it's a good thing I didn't say 'don't come a-knockin' on my door.'"

"I'm sorry I said that. I was kinda panicking. You know I would've helped ya out, right?" Billy said, putting his stuff down next to Taylor's couch.

"I know you would've. I'm just bustin' your balls. Sorry 'bout your building."

"Dude, it was so scary! I was trying to sleep, you know get some rest before shit really goes down, and I smelled smoke. Strong smoke smell. I got up and looked out the window, and the building next to mine was ablaze. People were running around outside in their pajamas and underwear. They were all yelling about how their phones didn't work and they couldn't call 911."

"Jesus," Taylor said, shaking his head. He went to the fridge and grabbed two beers. "Wanna have a smoke and a beer?"

"Yes, please!" Billy said.

They went out onto the balcony. They both opened their beers and took liberal swigs then lit cigarettes. Billy still looked panicked.

"Dude, it was so scary," Billy said, exhaling cigarette smoke. "I stood there in my undies staring out my window in shock for a while. I saw some dude run out his apartment on fire! He was on fire, Dude! It was fucked up."

"Holy shit," Taylor said. "I'm glad you got out of there."

"Me too. After what seemed like forever, but was probably only five minutes, I realized that fire would jump to my building. So I packed my backpack full of clothes and loaded my only two suitcases with food, water, and TP. I got dressed and left. As I was trying to make my way out of the parking lot the fire jumped to my building. I'm so lucky I smelled the smoke. I almost took a sleeping pill. If I had, I'd be dead right now."

"Fuck. This world is fucked up right now."

"No shit."

"I had a messed-up encounter right over there," Taylor said, pointing to the grassy area where he had been attacked; they could see the guy's body still lying there. He told Billy the whole story.

"Jesus Christ, dude. Fuck, I'm glad that's not you lying over there. Shit, man, I told ya this was going to happen. People are selfish and don't know how to act in a crisis like this. We could've both died tonight."

"You were right. I shoulda listened to you. I don't like thinking about how close to dying we got tonight."

"Me neither."

"Oh shit, I need to tell you what happened at the depot," Taylor said, putting out his first smoke and lighting another one.

They sat down in the two patio chairs Taylor had on the balcony. He told Billy the whole story about the gunfire and the cops. About how some guy stole a bus and rammed two cop cars. He told him about the creepy dude looking into cars in the parking lot. Billy listened intently, shaking his head the whole time.

"Holy shit, man! Goddamn you must have like twenty guardian angels or something."

"Fuck, that's her!" Taylor said, pointing at Amber in the grassy area. She was walking toward the man's body. Taylor thought she had told him the guy's name, but with everything that had happened, he forgot it and frankly didn't care.

"She does look kinda cute," Billy said, squinting his eyes. "Definitely looks like a druggie."

Amber got to the man's body and knelt beside him. She started rooting through his pockets. Taylor and Billy looked at each other; they knew exactly what she was doing. She apparently didn't find any drugs in his pocket. She stood up and looked around. She was standing there; scratching her face with one hand and fiddling with her shorts with the other. She looked right at them. They both instinctively ducked down. It did no good; she could still see them. She approached the balcony.

She looked up at the second-floor balcony. "Can I bum a smoke?" she asked, still scratching at her face.

Taylor and Billy looked at each other. Taylor hoped if they gave her a cigarette, she would leave them alone. He wasn't happy about the fact that she now knew where he lived. That would most likely lead to issues. Taylor didn't trust her. She had tempted him briefly, but he knew deep down she was trouble.

"Please, guys," she said. "I really need a smoke."

Taylor sighed and stood up. He dropped a cigarette over the ledge of the balcony. She let it fall to the grass and then picked it up. Amber looked up at them again.

"Thanks," she said.

"No problem," Taylor said.

"You got any money?" she asked.

"No," Taylor said.

"I need to get some food. I just need a few bucks."

"There's nowhere to get food right now," Billy said, standing up to look over the side of the balcony. "Your best bet now is to lock yourself in your apartment."

"I'm starving, guys," Amber said, looking at Taylor. She could not stand still. She fidgeted with her clothes, picked at her face and played with her hair.

"We don't have any money," Taylor said. "We're going inside now. Have a good night."

"Please," she pleaded one last time.

The guys ignored it and went back into Taylor's apartment, closing and locking the slider behind them.

"Holy shit, what a tweeker," Billy said, sitting down on Taylor's couch.

"No shit, man," Taylor said, grabbing two more beers from the fridge.

"How come you never mentioned her before?" Billy asked, cracking open his beer.

"I've never seen her before today. I knew there was some tweeker dude living in that apartment over there, he had people coming and going all the time. She's new, probably a hanger-on to get a fix, ya know?"

"Yeah, I get ya," Billy said, shaking his head. "She don't want no food money."

"Oh, hell no," Taylor said, sitting down in the La-Z-Boy next to the couch.

80

"I bet she'd do some freaky shit for a twenty," Billy laughed.

"I bet she would, but I ain't goin' there. I like being disease-free."

Billy laughed, "I'm sure she's riddled with everything."

"No doubt."

Billy pulled a twenty out of his pocket. "I think it's worth the risk," he said, holding up the twenty.

"Fuck no!" Taylor said, quite a bit shocked.

"Dude, it's been a while for me," Billy started. "A really long while."

"You better be jokin', man. Please, tell me you're jokin' 'round." Taylor stared at him in disbelief.

Billy looked at Taylor and then took several sips of his beer. He played with the twenty.

"Dude, when I saw her up close, she's way hotter than you described. I'm seriously tempted."

"Jesus, man. She is a drugged-out basket case. Bat-shit crazy. Don't do it." Taylor could only shake his head. He couldn't believe Billy would even consider being with Amber in any way.

"It would be nice to get with a lady before the world ends," Billy said, flipping that twenty in his hands.

"Well, Amber ain't no lady so I'd suggest finding another final conquest." Taylor swigged on his beer.

Billy stood up. "Fuck it. I'm gonna do it. We're probably going to die anyways. I might as well get laid first."

"You're an idiot, man," Taylor said.

"Maybe, but I'm an idiot that's about to get some."

"Fuckin' A, man," Taylor chuckled. It was all he could do at that point, just laugh at his friend.

"Got any rubbers?" he asked, picking up his cigarettes off the coffee table.

Taylor got up and went to his room. He handed Billy a box of condoms. "I'd suggest you put 'em all on," he said.

"Ha ha, you're so funny," Billy said, sarcastically.

"I'ma say it again, you're an idiot." Taylor was honestly disappointed in his friend. Billy was going to go take advantage of Amber's desperation. "Please don't do this. It's gross and, honestly, desperate. You're using her."

"Maybe so, but it's the end of the world and I'm going to do whatever I want until it's all over." Billy drained his beer. "Look if she says no, I'll be right back. She's an adult, if she wants it too, why not?"

"Because you're payin' her for it. She ain't goin' say no when you wave that twenty in her face. She needs a fix, man. This ain't right."

"Point heard," Billy said, heading for the door. "But I'm doin' it. See ya in a bit." He walked out the door.

Taylor went out onto the balcony and lit a cigarette. He watched as Billy walked toward Amber's apartment. Billy knocked on the door, and Amber answered immediately. They stood there for a few moments talking, and then Amber let Billy inside. She looked across the courtyard at Taylor and smiled. Shivers went up his spine. He just shook his head and whispered out loud, "Gross."

Once inside Amber's apartment, Billy looked around. Taylor wasn't exaggerating; that apartment was a disaster. Almost vile, in fact. The mess itself was bad, but the worst thing was the smell. It was almost enough to make him want to leave. Almost, but not quite.

"Sit down," Amber said, motioning to the very well-worn and stained couch. "I'll make us some drinks."

"I'll just have a beer if ya got any," Billy said, sitting down on the couch. It smelled like cigarette smoke and BO.

"I think there's beer in here," she said, opening the fridge. "Just got the cheap stuff." She held up a can of beer.

"That's fine," he said.

She walked over to Billy and handed him the beer. She walked back to the kitchen and made herself a vodka and lemon/lime soda. She sat down next to Billy.

"Got any smokes with ya?" she asked, smiling at him. She looked like she hadn't slept in days.

"Sure do," Billy said, pulling out his pack and lighter. They both lit up cigarettes. "So what do you do?"

"Whatcha mean?" she asked him.

"Do you have a job? Or at least did ya before all of this?"

"No, I've been looking for a while. Not much out there these days." She took a sip of her drink and sat back on the couch. She put her legs across his lap. "How 'bout you?"

"Yeah, me and Taylor are bus mechanics," he replied, putting his free hand on her leg.

"Cool," she said.

They sat there in silence for some time. It was very awkward. Billy kept puffing on his cigarette because it was the only thing that was distracting him from that smell. It smelt like something had died in there, which wouldn't actually have been much of a surprise. He finished his smoke and leaned forward to put it out in the ashtray on the coffee table.

"Would you mind?" she asked, handing him her cigarette butt to put out.

Amber stood up in front of Billy. She unbuttoned her shirt and looked at him.

"You wanna go to the bedroom?" she asked with a coy little smile.

He looked at her bare chest. "Yes, yes, I do," he said, standing up.

They went into the bedroom. It was just as messy and gross as the rest of the apartment. Dirty clothes and underwear all over the floor. Empty beer cans and cigarette packs littered about the whole room. There were even used condoms on the floor next to the bed. A bed that looked as though it had never had its bedding changed. For a moment, Billy didn't think he'd be able to go through with it. But then Amber took her shirt off and removed her shorts. He hadn't seen a naked woman in person for a couple of years. Billy never did have much luck with the ladies. Between his weight problem and his personality, women just didn't seem to find him very attractive. After everything that had happened that day, he figured this would be his last chance ever to be with a woman, so no amount of mess was going to stop him now.

"Whatcha waitin' for, big boy?" Amber asked.

"Uh, nuthin'," he said, taking off his shirt, then his pants.

"Come here," she said as she removed the blanket from the bed and climbed onto it.

The sheets were stained with God knows what. Billy hesitated for a second. It was a very brief hesitation. He walked toward the bed. As he put a knee on the bed to climb on, a loud *thud* shook the whole apartment. They looked at each other puzzled. Then another loud *thud*. And another. And another.

"What the hell?" Billy said, looking around.

Another *thud*.

Billy stood back up and dressed. Amber looked at him but didn't move.

"I'll be right back," he said.

The apartment had blackout curtains throughout. It was a dark place except for the random lamps here and there. Billy went to the front door. As soon as he opened the door, he was blinded by the brightest light he had ever seen in his life. That light was everywhere. He couldn't see anything it was so bright. All of a sudden, his head felt like it was going to explode, and he fell to his knees. He held his head in his hands. He had his eyes closed, but it didn't seem to help with that light. That light was somehow inside him, or so it felt that way.

Something was standing over him. Definitely something and not someone. His head was throbbing, and his heart was pounding. It felt like his heart was going to explode. Without thinking about it, he crawled backward into Amber's apartment. He crawled right into her knees. Billy sat back onto his butt and looked up at her. She was standing there in a dingy robe with a look of sheer terror and shock on her face. He tried to look out the front door to see what she saw, but he couldn't. He physically could not move his pounding head in that direction. She slowly walked out the door and closed it. He heard her scream the most bloodcurdling scream he had ever heard. Then silence.

His head still hurt like never before. His heart was still beating out of his chest. But he was able to stand again. He stood up and looked around the apartment. Those junkies had to have some kind of weapon. Junkies were always paranoid, so he was certain they had to have something. Behind the couch, he found a wooden baseball bat. It had seen better days but would certainly do some damage if need be.

Billy slowly approached the door. He grabbed the door knob. Out of nowhere, he felt dizzy and nauseous. It had to be the smell of that apartment was finally getting to him. With a deep breath and exhale, he opened the door. That blinding light still flooded the entire complex. He could hardly see anything.

"Billy!" Taylor yelled. "Get over here now!"

Billy didn't respond; he just started to run. He got about ten feet and tripped over someone. It was Amber, or at least what was left of her. Her midsection was completely torn away. Her glassy blue eyes stared up at him. A single line of blood rolled out of her open mouth.

"Billy! Hurry up!" Taylor yelled from his balcony.

Billy got up and started to run to Taylor's apartment. Halfway there, he stopped, frozen in place.

"*What are you doin', man?*" Taylor yelled.

Something huge and grotesque stepped between Billy and Taylor's balcony. Billy looked up at its hateful black eyes. Those eyes hijacked his. Billy couldn't move. Taylor couldn't believe what he was seeing. The thing leaned in closer to Billy as if it were studying his face. Billy tried to move but couldn't even blink.

There was a gunshot, and the thing whirled around. Billy fell to the ground. He quickly got to his feet and ran for Taylor's door. Taylor watched as the thing approached a balcony two doors down from his. A man was standing there holding a .22 pistol. The man fired several more shots at the thing. The shots seemed to hit it but had little effect on the creature. It reached up and grabbed the man by the throat. It pulled the man off the balcony. The man kicked and screamed. The thing set the man on the ground and separated his head from his body. The man's body flopped to the grass, spurting blood from the neck. The thing held the man's head in its hands. It looked over at Taylor and smiled. Taylor felt his stomach tighten and ran for the slider. He got inside his apartment and heard Billy pounding on the front door. Taylor locked the slider, closed the blinds, and ran to the front door. Billy ran into the apartment and collapsed onto the couch. He was breathing heavily and crying.

"What the fuck?" Taylor asked. "What in the holy hell was that thing?"

"Alien. Dude," Billy panted. "Fuckin' aliens."

Taylor sat down in the chair. They could hear screaming, gunshots here and there, and a lot of commotion. Something heavy hit the slider with enough force to crack the glass. Taylor sank to the floor and crawled over to the window. Staying low to the ground, he peeked out the blinds. There lying on his balcony, staring back at him, was his neighbor's head. This was it. This was the end of the world. He was going to die with Billy instead of his family. He hadn't taken any of this seriously and didn't get a chance to say goodbye to any of his loved ones.

Billy got up and ran to the bathroom. Taylor could hear him in there vomiting. The last night of his life spent listening to his crazy friend puking. He crawled to the kitchen and grabbed a beer. He thought he might as well drink himself silly if he was just going to die anyway. Might as well die drunk.

Billy crawled out of the bathroom wiping his mouth with a washcloth. He crawled into the kitchen and sat next to Taylor on the floor. Taylor reached into the fridge and grabbed a beer for Billy.

"What do we do now?" Billy asked.

"Get drunk and wait to die, I guess," Taylor said.

"Sounds like our only option at this point," Billy said, raising his beer bottle to Taylor. They clinked bottles and drank.

Two beers in, everything outside went dark and quiet. A feeling of relief came over them. They got up and looked out the balcony door. In the pale moonlight, they could see the destruction that had taken place out there. There must have been a dozen, maybe two dozen, bodies strewn about the courtyard. Not one of them intact. The smell of sulfur hung in the air. They looked at each other and went back inside. Billy sat down on the couch, and Taylor sat in the

La-Z-Boy. They felt a calm come over them. The stress and beers had wiped them out. They eventually drifted off to a restless sleep.

*****

Pete had run a couple of miles. He was exhausted and completely out of breath. Even though he had grown up in this neighborhood, he felt lost. The thing about these housing developments, all of the houses and streets looked the same. He recognized the area but wasn't sure how to get to his parents' place. He stopped on the corner under a streetlamp. The light kept flickering. He looked down the block, and it was very familiar. His parents' house had to be close.

Pete noticed a yellow car crashed into another car down the street from him. The yellow car was still running; maybe he could take it to get himself home. If it wasn't too damaged. He slowly walked toward the car. Every little sound, every gust of wind, made him jump a little. A weapon, any kind of weapon, would have been nice to have. *Should've taken that tire iron,* he thought to himself. Once he finally reached the yellow car, he froze. There was a man slumped over the steering wheel, dead. Blood and bits of skull and brains were all over the windshield and dash. Pete gagged. Well, he wasn't going to be able to commandeer that car.

"Pete?" a female voice called out. "Pete Murphy, is that you?"

Pete looked around but didn't see anyone.

"Up here!" the voice yelled. "Turn around."

Pete turned around and looked across the street. A girl was hanging out of a bedroom window of the house across the street. It looked like his old friend Amanda. It was Amanda!

"Holy shit, hi!" he said. He wasn't very shocked to see a familiar face in that neighborhood, but he felt damn lucky she had seen him.

"Whatcha doin' out there?" she asked.

"I got carjacked, and I'm tryin' to get to my parents' house," he shouted across the street. "My phone won't work, so I can't call them."

"Our phones don't work either. You should come inside," she shouted.

Pete crossed the street. Amanda met him at the door.

"What happened to that guy in the yellow car?" Pete asked, pointing across the street.

"He was following me, and my dad shot him," Amanda said, leading Pete into the kitchen. She could tell Pete was wiped out and got him a bottle of water.

"Holy shit," Pete said, taking the water. "Thanks," he said as he opened the bottle. He downed the whole bottle.

Amanda's dad walked into the kitchen. Pete noticed he had a gun on his hip. Must have been the one that killed the man in the yellow car.

"Hello, son," her dad said. "I'm Tom." He extended his hand to Pete.

"I'm Pete," he said, shaking Tom's hand.

"How is it out there?" Tom asked.

"Crazy, sir," Pete responded. "Some chick and two dudes car-jacked me. I'm pretty sure they killed another dude too. There's almost no one out on the roads, but there's wrecks and dead people all over."

Tom shook his head. "Mandy told me about that. People just have no class." He went to the fridge and grabbed a beer. "You want one, son?" he asked, holding up a beer.

"Uh, sure," Pete said, looking at Amanda. "Thank you." He took the beer.

"What brought you to this neighborhood?" Tom asked.

"My folks live close to here. I grew up in this neighborhood. Amanda and I went to school together."

"Small world," Tom chuckled. "Will you be staying long? We have plenty of food if you'd like something to eat."

"I appreciate that, sir, but I need to get to my parents. I shoulda been there a couple hours ago. They are probably worried."

"You know how to use a gun?" Tom asked.

Pete thought that was a random question. "Yeah, I grew up shootin' with my dad and uncles."

"If you're going to try to get to your parents, you should take one of my guns. You never know what is out there."

"Really?" Pete asked. "Are you sure?"

"Yes. I've got a lot of them. I can spare one to keep you safe."

"Wow, thank you so much."

"Dad, can me and Pete take my friends to their parents'?"

"I don't know, Mandy. I don't want you out there."

"Please? They aren't far from here, and we'll be careful. They need to get home too."

Tom drank his beer and looked at Amanda. He didn't like the idea of his daughter out there, but he knew they needed to get the others home somehow. Tom didn't want to leave his house vulnerable, so he couldn't leave. They did have plenty of food and water, but those supplies would dwindle quickly with four extra people in the house. Against his better judgment, he decided he'd let Amanda get her friends home. Tom had gotten a really good feeling about Pete. He trusted that Pete would keep Amanda and the other girls safe and get his daughter back to him in one piece. Tom didn't say anything to Amanda; he just turned and left the kitchen. Pete and Amanda looked at each other. Tom came back into the kitchen a few minutes later with a pistol and a shotgun.

"Fine," he said. "The more I think about it, I think it's a good idea to get everyone home. I should do it myself, but I don't want to leave this house and your mother unprotected. I need to stay here in case any shit goes down." Tom went to a drawer at the end of the kitchen counter and pulled out a set of car keys. "Take the SUV." He handed Amanda the keys.

"Thanks, Dad," Amanda said, hugging him and then bounding upstairs.

"Protect those girls," Tom told Pete.

"I will, sir," Pete said. "I think we'll be fine 'round here. Pretty dead out there."

"I hope so," Tom said, grabbing another beer for himself. He went into the living room and looked out the front window. The street was dead quiet, again not too surprising for that time of day on a Sunday, but it was still so eerie. The yellow car still idling across the street only added to the creepiness.

Amanda came downstairs with her friends.

"Ready, Pete?" she said.

"Yup," he replied, picking up the shotgun. "I call shotgun." He chuckled.

Amanda went into the living room and hugged her dad.

"I love you," she said. "I'll be back soon."

"I love you too. Be safe and hurry home. No dilly-dallying out there."

"We won't."

Amanda led Pete and her friends into the garage. She climbed in the driver's seat, and Pete hopped into the passenger seat. The other girls piled into the back seat. Amanda backed the car out of the garage. Her dad was standing on the lawn next to the driveway. He had his pistol in hand and was surveying the street. Amanda rolled down Pete's window.

"Bye, Dad! I love you!" she called to her dad.

"By, Mandy. Be safe," he said, walking up to the vehicle. "Don't get trigger shy," he said to Pete. "If someone tries anything with you guys, just drop 'em. There is no prison time in the apocalypse."

"Yes, sir," Pete said. *When did all this get upgraded to an apocalypse?* he thought to himself. That made everything even more scary and messed up.

Amanda backed out of the driveway. Bridgette and Stephanie's parents both lived close to Mount Spokane, but Luna's parents lived on the east side of town in a neighborhood called Hillyard. Mileage wise, Hillyard wasn't too far from where they were, but with everything else going on, it would be a scary trip. Amanda decided to take Luna home first and drop the others off on the way back. In hindsight, she would regret that decision.

CHAPTER 6

Blackout

Anthony led the president and the rest of the staffers out of the bunker. They had to remove some debris to get to the surface but made it pretty easily. It was dark except for the moonlight. They all stood there for several moments, looking around. There was nothing left. Everything had been completely leveled. Even the concrete foundations and streets had been reduced to rubble. Luckily, the bunker had been built to withstand a nuclear bomb. What they were seeing actually looked like a nuke had gone off. It was devastating.

The president knew that if DC looked like that, the rest of the impact zones did as well. The number of lives lost was staggering. She didn't like to think about that, but she knew she had to. If they made it through this, she knew as the president, she would have to answer to the lives lost somehow. This had happened on her watch. She needed to act and act fast.

"Wait," she said to her staff. "If a meteor hit us, where is it?"

They all looked around. No one else had thought of that. They were standing in the crater that you would imagine a meteor would make, but where was the meteor itself?

"Maybe it disintegrated on impact," Anthony said.

"Ladies and gentlemen," the president started, "I don't think we were hit by meteors. We were attacked."

"By whom?" Anthony asked. "All intelligence suggests that's impossible."

"I know, we've been over that. I think we were attacked from out there," she said, pointing to the night sky. A couple of people chuckled at that. That response clearly enraged her. "We all have the security clearances to know those things are up there. Let's not waste our time trying to come up with a different possibility. I knew all along this was way too organized of an attack to simply be meteors—you all did too. Don't be standing here thinking I'm fucking crazy. You all know I'm right." She looked at James. "NASA has known we're not alone in the universe for decades. Isn't that right, Mr. Douglas?"

"Uh, um," he stammered. "Uh, yeah, that's right, Madam President."

"What do we do now?" she asked the group. No one responded. "I took you people with me to that bunker for a reason. You're the best of the best. Let's get a plan together, and let's get it going now. General, any word on getting our birds in the skies?"

"No, ma'am. I don't have a signal," Anthony said. "All communication is gone. I'm hoping the commanders are pulling rank and getting boots on the ground and birds in the air. We're completely in the dark here, Madam President."

"Shit," she replied. "Let's get moving."

"Where to, ma'am?" Anthony asked.

"Let's find a building to shelter in." She looked around. They were at the south side of the crater. "It looks like we could find something south of here. We're no good to anyone, including ourselves, just standing here."

President Rodgers started climbing out of the crater. Anthony and a couple of Secret Service men rushed to her side. With weapons drawn, they flanked her as they all made their way out of the rubble. Once out of the crater, they could see buildings intact. Everything was dark, and fire raged all around them. There was no one else in sight. The Potomac River had flooded to the east, so they were forced to head southwest. Abandoned cars littered the streets. Bodies cluttered the sidewalks and intersections. Police cars were burning. It looked like a war zone. It dawned on them that it was, in fact, a war zone. Someone—or something—had started a war. A war they weren't sure they could fight.

They heard a whirring sound, and the skies lit up. The light was blinding. Their heads began to hurt, and their hearts were beating a mile a minute. Anthony and the Secret Service men fought through the pain and surrounded the president. She hunkered down. Her head was pounding. It felt like it was going to explode. That constant whirring sound made everything so much worse. Enough by itself to make you go mad.

Then everything went dead silent. The president thought she had gone deaf; she couldn't hear anything at all. The silence was broken by a voice inside her head.

"*We come to take this planet back,*" the voice said. It almost sounded robotic but deep and gravelly. "*Fighting us will be useless.*"

"Anyone else hearing this?" she said. No one responded. They were all frozen in place, staring in the same direction. She tried to stand up to see what they were looking at, but she couldn't move. She grunted and tried to move again, still nothing. She was paralyzed.

"*Trying to move is useless,*" the voice said inside her head. "*No one else can hear me. This message is for you.*"

"What's your message?" she asked aloud.

"*We told you,*" it said. "*We are taking this planet back.*"

"Back?" she asked.

"*Yes. We left it for you, and you've ruined it.*"

"Let me see you," she said. "You attack us and tell me you're taking our planet. But you don't have the guts to let me see you?"

The men surrounding her were violently tossed away, their bodies smacking the pavement with a disturbing *thud!* The feeling of paralysis was gone, so she slowly stood up. Her head was still pounding, and she was sweating. She turned and saw a tall, brown, leathery creature standing before her. Its eyes stared deep into hers. It smiled at her, and she almost lost control of her bowels. She felt bile in her throat. She choked it back and stared at the creature. She couldn't move again. The creature took two steps toward her and studied her. It sniffed her and stepped back, turning its massive head back and forth like a dog does when it's looking at you. President Rodgers was petrified but stood strong best she could. It was difficult to be tough and imposing when she couldn't move a muscle.

The bright light flickered. The creature looked up to the sky. President Rodgers realized once it looked away that she was able to move again. She looked around her and saw Anthony's M16 lying on the ground a few feet away. She picked up the assault rifle and pointed it at the creature. The creature was still staring up to the sky. President Rodgers squeezed the trigger and blasted a clip of ammo into the creature's midsection. Thick green ooze spurted out of the bullet holes. The creature looked at President Rodgers and screamed. The scream was deafening and caused the president to fall to her knees. One of her Secret Service men's pistols was on the pavement next to her. She quickly grabbed it and emptied the gun into the creature. It fell to the ground, green ooze bubbling out of its mouth. The bright light vanished, and the constant whirring was gone. For a few seconds, everything was pitch black and silent.

Her head stopped pounding, and she stood up again. The smell of sulfur hung in the air like cheap perfume. She heard Anthony groan. She walked over to where he was lying. His radius bone was sticking out of his arm. He had tears in his eyes and was writhing in pain. She helped him up. The impact of what they had thought were meteors had caused the surrounding buildings to tumble. She found a piece of 2 × 4. Using the strap from Anthony's M16, she made a splint for his broken arm. The Secret Service men had been killed. The rest of their group had vanished. President Rodgers and Anthony slowly approached the creature. It was still breathing but barely. They could hear a wet rasp to its breaths. It looked at them and snarled. Green ooze coated its razor-sharp teeth.

"We've got plans for you," it said inside both of their heads.

"We won't stand still and let you take our planet," President Rodgers said.

They heard the creature laugh inside their heads. *"You will die,"* it said.

"Let's go, General," she said.

Anthony pulled his pistol out of its holster and put a bullet in the creature's head. He put the pistol back into the holster and looked around. Before they moved on, they took guns and ammo off the Secret Service men. They fled southwest. After they had run about three blocks, the skies lit up again. They stopped in their tracks. The light lasted maybe thirty seconds and was gone again. President Rodgers looked at Anthony. They looked behind them—nothing but dark streets. With guns in hand, they began running again. A car was parked on the sidewalk just ahead of them. The keys were in the ignition. The president hopped in the driver's side, and Anthony jumped into the passenger seat.

"You know how to fly a plane?" she asked.

"Yeah, why?"

"If I get us to the airport, could you fly us out of here?"

"Yes, ma'am," he said.

She started the car and took off toward the airport. They just hoped the airport was still standing.

*****

Malcolm had made it to Las Vegas. He was surprised by how easy a trip it had been. The idea of making that drive had made him nervous; he didn't know what he could have run into. Luckily, the few people who were making the same trip were doing so in an orderly fashion. Once he had arrived in Las Vegas, he had to abandon his truck; there was just no way to maneuver that rig around. The streets were far too crowded with people and cars.

It amazed him how some buildings had completely crumbled and others were unaffected. He was glad there was at least somewhere to go. The hotel that had given him a room was rationing supplies, so he and four others, three men and a woman, set off to scavenge some supplies. That's when he heard two women yelling from a caved-in basement. Malcolm and two other men were able to free the women. It turned out to be lucky for him as well as the ladies that basement was stocked full of water and canned goods. They even had cartons of cigarettes down there. He figured stuff like alcohol and cigarettes would make for great currency.

The women he had rescued stuck close to him. They were terrified, and rightfully so. They were young, he guessed early twenties. Before all this, he would have assumed all they cared about in this world was social media and guys. Several minutes into their walk, Malcolm introduced himself to them. They told him their names, Dana and Julia, and that they were dealers in the casino that had crumbled on top of them. The women explained that they had been down in that basement fetching new cards for the blackjack tables and had been sitting down there BS-ing when they heard what sounded like an explosion. If they hadn't been taking their sweet-ass time down there, they would've been dead too.

"I gotta take a break," Dana said, setting down the water she was carrying. "My leg is killing me."

"We should really keep moving," Malcolm said.

"A rack fell on me down there," Dana said. "My leg is throbbing. I can't walk anymore."

"Yes, you can," he said. "Leave the water, we'll come back for it."

"I just need five, man," she said, setting down on the case of water.

"I'll stay with her," Julia said.

"I ain't leaving you guys," Malcolm said. He turned to the others. "This one's got a bum leg. We'll catch up with you at the hotel."

The others nodded and kept on walking. No one was moving quickly loaded down with so many supplies. Malcolm set down his cases of canned goods. He pulled a bottle of water out of his pocket and downed it. Even late at night, in late October, Vegas was warm, and he was sweating. Julia was rubbing her friends back and looking around. The devastation was so bad she couldn't imagine anything was still standing anywhere close to them.

The skies lit up. It was the brightest light any of them had ever seen. Their heads began to pound, and their hearts started to race. They instinctively shielded their eyes. Malcolm could see the others frozen in place about a hundred yards down the road from where they were. A huge, brown, leathery creature appeared out of nowhere in front of the others. It looked at them very intently. It sniffed at them like a suspicious dog meeting a new human. The creature knocked everything out of their hands. It picked up the woman like she was a ragdoll. A pulsing red light appeared, and the creature and the woman disappeared. Seconds later, the creature was back. It sniffed at the oldest man of the three. The creature pushed the man to the ground and tore open his stomach. It devoured the man's organs. Why were they all just standing there? *Run!* Malcolm thought to himself. Shit, that was a great idea. He grabbed the young women and pulled them down the street in the opposite direction. His beer truck was about four blocks away; they could hide out in that.

"What the fuck was that?" Julia cried as they ran.

"I don't know." Malcolm panted, leading the way. "Come on, we gotta get to my truck!"

Malcolm looked behind them to see if that thing was following them. He saw it tear the head off of the last man. It held the severed head in its clawed hand and smiled. Smiled? Did it actually just smile? Shivers ran up Malcolm's back. Rounding a corner, Malcolm looked back one more time. The creature was gone. The bright light disappeared just as quickly as it had appeared. They were back in pure darkness and could hardly see.

"Two more blocks," he told Dana and Julia. "Come on, we can make it."

The women were struggling badly. Dana was limping and could barely stay on her feet. Julia kept pace with her, and they were both beginning to lag behind him. He couldn't lose them; he would never be able to live with himself. Although, it didn't seem like he would be living much longer.

"Come on, ladies! It's less than a block now. I can see my truck just up ahead." He pointed to his truck. The sight of it gave Dana and Julia a boost of motivation, and they picked up their pace.

That bright light came back, and somehow, it was even brighter this time. Malcolm had made it to the truck and was fumbling for his keys. *Please God, don't tell me I left them in the room,* he thought to himself. He was almost certain he hadn't; he had planned to come back to the truck for beer. Finally, he found them. He figured the trailer would be the safest place to hide, no windows and only one door to worry about.

As he worked the key into the padlock on the trailer door, a loud *thud* hit the top of the trailer. He looked up, and there on top of his trailer, staring down at him, was one of those creatures. It bared its teeth at him, and they were covered in blood. It was the same one he had just seen kill those people. It smiled at him and jumped down. He stepped back. Dana and Julia screamed. The creature whirled around to face the women.

"Run!" Malcolm shouted at them.

They turned and ran, but about fifteen paces down the street, they came to a dead stop. Dana and Julia stood there, frozen in place.

"Run, ladies!" he yelled again. His head was killing him.

"They can't," a voice said inside his head.

Malcolm shook his head. *What the fuck was that?* he thought.

"It's me," the voice responded and the creature turned to him.

The same pulsing red light from earlier came out of the skies and landed on the girls. The redness of the light intensified and then blinked out. Dana and Julia were gone.

"What the fuck?" Malcolm mumbled. Damn, his head was pounding. It hurt so bad he thought he was going to throw up.

"We took 'em," that voice in his head said.

The creature bent down so it was eye-level with Malcolm. It studied him and sniffed at him. Malcolm tried to turn and run but was paralyzed. This was it. He was a goner; he was certain of it. The creature smiled again. That red light pulsed again, and the creature was gone. With it, the light vanished too. Malcolm fell to the ground. Tears flooded down his cheeks. He got to his hands and knees. He vomited on the pavement and then rolled onto his back. He looked up to the night sky and saw five bright white lights zoom out of sight. That cemented everything for him. He knew exactly what he had just witnessed, and he knew precisely what had happened. Twenty-four hours before, he had been showering for work; now he was lying on the pavement in Old Las Vegas with a headache and bile in his throat. He kind of wished that thing had killed him. He had no idea what to do next.

Malcolm slowly stood up and looked around. The smell of sulfur hung in the air like candle smoke after a candle is blown out. His head was starting to feel better. His guts were acidy and churning. Everything seemed to ache. He took a few steps around the truck. The keys were lying on the ground behind the trailer. He picked up the keys and unlocked the driver's door. With a final look around, he climbed into the truck. Sitting in the driver's chair, he burst into tears again.

How did I survive that? he thought. *Why didn't that thing kill me too? I gotta get out of here.*

He fired up the truck and took off. Those things would be back. He didn't know how he knew that for sure, but he absolutely knew they would be. Malcolm didn't know where he was going to go. He figured if he made it into the mountains, it was far less likely those things would find him. One man alone in the mountains or towns full of people? Hopefully, they would choose the towns and not waste their time with him.

Malcolm made his way through town. He was headed out the same way he had come in. What had been a relatively clear route was now littered with abandoned cars and mangled, decapitated bodies. Those things must have come through right before him. Some of the bodies were still bleeding. It was like an obstacle course, but he just romped the gas pedal and sped out of there. He felt like a sitting duck out there.

Up ahead he could see what looked like a woman running down the middle of the street. She looked panicked. When she saw his truck, she started waving at him. He cursed himself for being such a nice guy. He should have just drove on by and gotten himself to safety, but he just couldn't leave her out there. He wouldn't have been able to leave anyone out there alone.

Malcolm stopped his truck and leaned across the cab to open the passenger door. The woman climbed into the cab, breathing heavy. Her light-brown hair was matted and tangled. Her clothes, which looked to be a server's uniform, were torn and dirty. Her right eye was black and swollen. Malcolm put the truck in gear and got it rolling again.

"Oh my god, thank you so much for stopping. So many people just flew past me," she said, still catching her breath.

"No problem. You okay?" he asked, accelerating through the gears of the truck.

"I am now, thanks again. I probably look a lot worse off than I actually am."

"I'm Malcolm," he said, putting his hand out to her.

"I'm Bethany," she said, shaking his hand.

"What happened to you, Bethany?" Malcolm asked.

"Dude, it's so crazy. You won't believe me."

He looked over at her. "Oh, I think I will," he said. "I've seen some crazy shit myself."

"Aliens?" she asked.

"Uh, yeah," he said. "What'd you see?"

"Oh, Jesus, man, what I didn't see would be a shorter answer." She looked around the cab of the truck. "Do you smoke?" she asked.

"Sometimes. Not a regular thing for me. I have some in the glovebox if you want one. Lighter's in there too."

"Sweet! Thanks! God, I need one of these," she said, pulling a cigarette out of the pack. "Even a menthol sounds good." She chuckled.

"Please, Bethany, tell me what you saw. Tell me what happened to you."

"K," she said, lighting the cigarette and rolling down her window. "But you gotta tell me yours after, deal?"

"Yeah, deal," he said. The cigarette smoke smelled so good. "Hey, would you hand me one of those?"

"You bet," she said, grabbing him a cigarette and the lighter.

"Thanks," he said. He leaned over the steering wheel and lit his cigarette.

"Okay, so, here goes," she said, settling back into her chair and putting her feet on the dash. "I don't know if you can tell or not, but I'm a waitress. I work for an Italian joint inside one of the casinos. I had just got to work and was having a smoke in the parking lot. All of a sudden, there was a bright light in the sky. It looked like an asteroid or shooting star but so, so bright. It arched down toward the ground, then *boom*, it crashed into the ground and I fell. It shook the ground so hard the pavement under me cracked. I thought for sure the casino was going to fall on me. Then I did hear buildings crashing to the ground. People started running out of the casinos and hotels yelling and screaming. I hate to admit this, but I panicked and got back in my car. I sped out of there as fast as I could. There were people everywhere. I headed the same way we're going now. All the traffic was gone. I was speeding down the road here when all of a sudden there was another bright light." She paused and took some drags off her cigarette. She fidgeted with her clothes a bit. "Sorry, man, my skin feels so weird and itchy. I swear I'm a clean person. This feeling ain't normal itchy."

"No worries," he said. He was hanging on her every word. She had actually seen whatever hit the earth!

"Anyhoo, that bright light. It was so bright I couldn't see, and I had to stop my car. My head was pounding. Like hurtin' like never before. And I get migraines. This was worse than my worst migraine. I don't know why, but I got out of my car. This is going to sound really weird, but it was almost like someone else was controlling my body. I knew not to get out of my car. I didn't want to get out. But I did anyway. I walked a few steps and stopped. Then I couldn't move. There was a pulsing red light, and everything went black. I felt a warmth I had never felt before. At first, I thought I was dead and on my way to heaven. Then I heard this deep, gravelly-like robot voice in my head. Like inside my head. It said, 'Go to sleep,' and that was the last thing I remember till I woke up twenty feet from my car. I was dizzy and nauseous. I actually ended up puking. I went to my car, but it wouldn't start. So I started running toward town. Then I saw you."

"Holy shit," he said. "Wait, how long were you out?"

"I dunno, like ten minutes I think," she said.

"Um, the meteor, or whatever it was, hit like eight hours ago," he said. "Probably longer than that now, actually. Shit it took me like five hours just to get here, and that was several hours ago."

"No way, man. I saw that thing hit and it was only like fifteen minutes before I saw that light. Then I passed out, probably from the headache. No way hours went by."

"Yes, Bethany, it's been hours."

"No, that's impossible." She looked confused and terrified. "If that's true, where did all that time go? I swear, I was only out for like ten minutes."

"Not possible in the timeline of your story. If you just woke up a few minutes ago and passed out shortly after impact, it's been hours and hours." He had been so engrossed in her story that it didn't even strike him as odd that they were the only people on the road. Maybe that was a good thing. Maybe those things had moved on and they would be safe. Maybe, but highly unlikely.

Tears rolled down her cheeks. "This is all so fucked up!" she cried. "Why is this happening? This ain't supposed to happen. It feels like some sci-fi movie."

"But it is real," he said. "You want some water?" He reached behind his seat.

"Oh my god, yes!" she said.

He pulled out two bottles of water and handed her one. They drove in silence for a while. Bethany slowly sipped her water and just stared out the windshield. Malcolm would look over at her every few minutes. She looked like she was in shock. Her eyes were glazed over. Her movements were almost robotic, like her body was just going through the same motions it had a million times. Drink to lips, sip, swallow, repeat.

"Bethany. You okay?" Malcom finally said. She jumped when he said her name.

"Ye-yeah, yeah, I'm fine," she stammered. She looked around. "I'm sorry, I got lost in my mind. I just don't know what to think anymore." She looked at him.

"It's all good," he said, looking at her. She smiled at him and he smiled back. Her eyes lit up a bit. She seemed more coherent and normal. He didn't know how she normally acted or interacted with people, but he felt like he had the real her now.

"Can I have another smoke?" she asked.

"Only if you get me another one too," he replied.

"Done deal, my man." She reached into the glovebox and handed Malcolm a cigarette. He lit it and handed the lighter to

Bethany. "Tell me your story now," she said, settling back into her seat.

"Okay, here goes," he said.

He told her everything, from the beginning in Currie and feeling the "earthquake" to the drive to Vegas. He told her about rescuing the women from the basement. Then the bright light, the pulsing red light, and the two women disappearing. He left out the part about the thing killing the other four people he had been with. Lastly, he told her about the thing getting in his face and sniffing at him.

"It smelled like sulfur," he said. "Sulfur and wet dog hair. That's the best way I can describe it."

"I know that smell. That's what I smelled when I woke up."

"Fuck, who knows?"

"I don't care. Let's just get as far away as possible," she said. "I mean, if it's cool I travel with you?"

"It's cool. I wouldn't just abandon you," he said.

"Thanks, man. You're pretty awesome, ya know?" she said, smiling and blushing.

"Thanks, you're pretty cool yourself," he said, making her blush even harder.

A man's voice came over Malcolm's CB radio. "Anyone in the Vegas area got their ears on?" the voice said. "Attention, anyone out there?"

Malcolm picked up the CB mic. "I copy," he said. "We're in the Vegas area. Heading south."

"Go north!" the man said. "There's an operational Air Force base just outside of Spokane, Washington. Everything south of Vegas is a war zone."

"We're just going to hide out in the mountains," Malcolm replied.

"Don't!" the man snapped back. "If you're fleeing Vegas, I'm sure you've seen those things, haven't you?"

"I have," Malcolm responded.

"They are everywhere." The radio went silent for a moment. "Look, you do you, but I'm telling you I have it on good authority that the base up there is safe and is taking people in. I'm on my way there now."

"Thank you for the information," Malcolm said, looking over at Bethany.

"We gotta fight these things. The base can do that, but they need more people. We're at a point where we either fight back or die. Anyone who can hear my voice, get to Washington. A small town called Airway Heights. Keep your radios on. There will be more information coming. Over and out." The radio went silent.

"What should we do?" Malcolm asked Bethany. He had already decided that they would be sticking together for a while.

"Let's go to Washington," she said. "A military base should have food and water."

"That's a long-ass drive," he said, pulling over to the side of the road. He stopped the truck and climbed into the sleeper. "Luckily, I kept these old maps in here," he said, returning to his seat with a stack of road maps. He found the quickest route north and got the truck rolling again. "We'll need to find fuel somewhere."

"I'm sure we will," Bethany said, smiling at him. She was quite a bit enamored with him already. She was looking at him, thinking to herself how handsome he was, but not just a good-looking guy, he was a very likable man too. "Road trip!" she exclaimed and then laughed.

"Let's do this!" he responded and laughed with her.

They drove north, talking and getting to know each other better. Spokane was a thousand miles north; Malcolm had enough fuel to get them maybe a third of the way. They would have to stop for fuel and sleep. He had already been awake for twenty-four hours at least. He wouldn't be able to make a fifteen-hour drive without sleep at some point soon. The thought of stopping somewhere along the way terrified him. Hiding out in the mountains seemed safe, but stopping along the freeway felt like a bad idea. They would be sitting ducks, not just to those things but anyone who may feel the need to rob them or try to hijack the truck.

Malcolm looked at Bethany. "I got your back no matter what."

"Thanks, man. I have yours too. We're in this together now." She reached her hand out to him. He took her hand.

"We are," he said. They held hands as he navigated the highway.

CHAPTER 7

Get to the Base

Taylor and Billy were awoken by someone pounding on the front door. Taylor looked over at Billy on the couch. Billy looked scared.

"Who the fuck could that be?" Taylor asked.

"I don't know, man. It's your apartment," Billy said, sitting up on the couch.

The pounding continued. Taylor got up and grabbed the bat Billy had taken from the tweaker's apartment. Billy watched him approach the door. Taylor opened the door to a frantic man. The man looked into the apartment. He clearly noticed the bat in Taylor's hand. The man stepped back a couple feet.

"Guys," he began, "I live in 202. My cousin has a CB radio. We just heard that the base is taking people in. They have food and supplies."

"Okay," Taylor said. He didn't know what else to say.

"My cousin and I are heading there after we tell everyone. Sounds like it's the safest place to be right now."

"I'm not sure I want to leave my place," Taylor said. "Being out there on those roads seems foolish to me."

"Staying here seems foolish to me," the man said. "That bat ain't goin' do shit against those things if they come back."

"I like my chances here for now. Thanks for the heads up, though."

"They are urging everyone to go to the base. They can protect us there."

"I appreciate it," Taylor said. He did really appreciate it, but he didn't like the idea of leaving his apartment. The base was only about a thirty-minute drive from his apartment complex, but that may not be the case with what was going on out there.

The man looked at Taylor and then looked past him to Billy sitting on the couch. Billy had a concerned look on his face.

"I gotta get goin'," the man said. "Just wanted to let everyone who's still here know about the base."

"Again, thanks for letting us know. Good luck out there," Taylor said, slowly closing the front door. He saw the man jog toward the next apartment.

"Beer?" he asked Billy as he locked the front door.

"Naw, man, I'm good. I still feel like shit," Billy said, sitting back on the couch.

"Smoke?" Taylor said, heading toward the kitchen. He grabbed himself a beer.

"Yea, that sounds good." Billy stood up and put his coat on.

They went out to the balcony and lit cigarettes. They stood there looking at the devastation again. It was sickening and heartbreaking. The air outside was still heavy, and that sulfur smell was still there.

"Look there," Billy said, pointing toward the far side of the courtyard. "What the fuck?"

Taylor looked to where Billy was pointing. The apartment complex somehow still had power, so all the outdoor flood lights were on. They could see a young man who looked to be in his early twenties. He had a duffel bag and flashlight. He was going from one dead body to another and going through their pockets. He would put whatever he was finding into the duffel bag. They couldn't see what he was taking but just assumed it was money and anything else he found valuable. They shook their heads.

"Man, that's kinda fucked up," Taylor said.

"Yeah, it is. No respect for the dead," Billy said, exhaling a plume of smoke. "You know it won't be long before people start breaking into apartments and houses to loot."

"I hope that's not the case."

"Dude, it totally is the case. People weren't prepared for this shit. It hasn't even been a whole day yet and people are already stealin' and killin'. Right now, dudes like him are scavenging dead bodies, but eventually, they'll run out of shit to steal from bodies. They'll have to start breaking into places."

"We got the bat and tire iron. We'll crack some skulls if we have to," Taylor said, still watching the guy in the courtyard.

"I think we should go the base," Billy said, looking at Taylor.

Taylor looked over at Billy; he looked so scared. Taylor figured Billy was probably right about all of it; he had called it beforehand. The thought of driving anywhere terrified Taylor, but he also knew staying put may not be the best idea either. Did he really want to risk having to fight someone if they broke in? What if those things came back? What would they do when they ran out of food?

"Man, I don't like the idea of being out there on the roads," Taylor said, lighting another cigarette.

Billy started to respond but was interrupted by car tires screeching and then a loud crash. The sound of the car crashing into something was quickly followed by an explosion. All the lights went out. In the darkness of early morning, they could see the glow of fire from where they had heard the crash and explosion. The glow of the flames quickly grew brighter and brighter. Billy looked back at Taylor, who was still staring in the direction of the explosion.

"Dude, we gotta get outta here," Billy said. "Pack up some supplies and get to the base."

Taylor didn't say anything; he just kept staring at the growing glow of fire. He eventually looked back to the courtyard; the guy with the flashlight was still going through the pockets of his dead neighbors. Taylor looked at Billy.

"I don't think we have a choice now," Taylor said. "Fuck, man, I'm so scared."

"Me too, man. Hey, at least if we make it to the base, we'll be safe."

"*If* being the key word there," Taylor said, snubbing out his cigarette. "And if the base is actually taking people in. We don't know if that guy has accurate information. What if it's a trap to get people out in the open? Someone could be out there baiting people so they can rob and kill 'em."

"Shit, Taylor, now you sound like me! Makes me kinda proud." Billy chuckled. "Look, dude, we're basically fucked no matter what. Our options are to stay here and probably die or leave and head for the base. Sure, there's a good chance we might die out there somewhere too, but if the base is taking people, we have a chance at safety. I would rather take that risk than just sitting here drinkin' beers and waiting to die. I'd rather die trying to find safety and food than just sit here."

"I hear ya. I agree. I hate this, man. I fuckin' hate this."

"Me too." Billy looked out at the courtyard again. "This is random, but what would you normally be doin' right now if all this shit wasn't going on?"

Taylor looked at him, puzzled. "Sleepin'," Taylor said. "Why?"

"I don't know, man. Just trying to think of some normalcy. We haven't even been in this situation long, and normal life seems so long ago. I shouldn't focus on that—it depresses me—but I can't help it. Maybe if we make it to the base, we can actually get some sleep."

"I ain't concerned with sleep—yet," Taylor said. "I just want to make it there alive first."

"I don't care either way," Billy said, his eyes filling with tears. "What do we even have to live for at this point? Nothing will ever be the same again."

"No, but someday we may have a new normal. If we live through this, we can rebuild. People have a way of surviving and moving on. Maybe we outgrew our planet and the reset button was pushed. I don't want to die, Billy. I got your back, you gotta have mine. You came to me. We're now in this together."

"I ain't giving up, man." Tears slowly rolled down Billy's plump cheeks. "I got your back a hundred percent. I'm just sayin' I ain't afraid to die. I'll fight 'til the end, but I'm just not going to stress about the possibility of this being it for me. If it's my time, it's my time."

"I get that, but I want to live if at all possible. And if gettin' to the base is our only chance now, I'm ready when you are."

"Let's do it, man," Billy said.

They went back into the apartment and began gathering everything they could think of. Water, food, toilet paper, beer, cigarettes, clothes, and cash. They didn't have much cash between them, but they honestly didn't think they'd need it. Stores weren't going to be open. Taylor grabbed the bat and Billy took the tire iron. Taylor took one last look around his apartment before walking out the door. He had a bad feeling that was going to be the last time he ever saw his apartment and the rest of his belongings.

That feeling would end up being true.

*****

Amanda drove slowly toward Hillyard. The roads were eerily empty. She had made that drive to Luna's parents' place hundreds of times, and the roads always had traffic. But not that night. Amanda wanted to get her friends home but was now regretting not waiting for daylight. At the same time, she didn't want their parents out looking for them either. She looked over at Pete; he was staring out the window, clutching the shotgun. His eyes were darting all over the place. He made her feel safe—well, as safe as possible considering their circumstances. She just wanted to get everyone home and get herself back home in one piece.

They came to an intersection that was completely blocked by wrecked cars. Amanda put the car in reverse to turn around.

"Wait!" Pete said. "There's a lady in that blue car. I think she's still alive."

"What can we do about that?" Amanda asked.

"I don't know, but we can't just leave her there without trying to help her," Pete said, unfastening his seatbelt.

"Pete, don't," Bridgette said, grabbing his shoulder from the backseat.

"We have to check on her," he said, shaking loose from Bridgette's hand. He opened the door and got out.

"Pete!" Amanda called after him. "My dad said you were to protect us. Leaving the car isn't protecting us."

"There's no one else around. We're perfectly fine right now," he said and walked toward the woman in the blue car.

The woman was seat-belted in and not moving. She had blood trickling down the side of her face. Her eyes were empty, but there was still life in them. The woman looked at Pete in shock. He walked around to the passenger side of the car. He opened the door and leaned in. He undid her seatbelt, and she flopped over. She made no noise. Pete heard a car door close and looked up. Amanda was standing in front of her dad's SUV with the pistol in her hand, looking around.

"Come on, Pete!" she shouted. "I don't like it out here."

He stood up from the car. "Help me get her in the back of the SUV," he shouted to Amanda.

"Then what?" she yelled back.

"My mom's a nurse. She could probably help this lady."

"Pete," Amanda started. A trio of amber lights in the sky caught her attention. She pointed to them. "Look!" she shouted to Pete. He turned around and saw the lights. "Come on, Pete, I don't like this."

The lights disappeared. Pete reached back into the car and slowly began to pull the woman out. He got her out, and she flopped to the ground with a disturbing *thud*. Pete could see she was breathing, but it was very labored. He knelt next to her and listened to her chest. Her breathing was raspy and sounded like she had fluid in her lungs. Pete put his arms under her armpits and dragged her toward the SUV. When he got past the wreckage, he looked toward Amanda and the SUV. The shock of what he saw made him drop the woman and froze him on the spot. A look of pure terror came over him.

Amanda saw Pete drop the woman and just stared past her in shock. Amanda slowly turned around, raising the pistol as she did. Standing about ten feet behind her was a tall, brown, leathery creature with sinister deep black eyes. Those eyes stared through her. It tilted its head and approached her. She couldn't move. Her head was pounding, and her heart was racing.

Shoot it! she thought. But she couldn't. She couldn't move a muscle.

The creature got right in her face and sniffed her. It looked up at the sky and stepped back several feet. The brightest, most intense white light lit up the entire intersection. Amanda hadn't realized how dark it had been outside until that light blinded her. A pulsing red light broke through the steady white light. Amanda felt warmth all around her. All she could see was red. All she could feel was anger and hatred. That pulsing red light engulfed her; it felt like it was squeezing her. Almost like she was being squeezed to death by a python. She felt her breath being taken away. Her head pounded like never before. She felt lightheaded and sick. The pistol fell from her hands, and she felt like she was floating. All she could see was red. The warmth she had felt was getting warmer. Hot even, like stepping into a sauna. Her eyes closed, and she was out.

Pete watched in horror as the creature approached Amanda. As soon as the thing got close to her, Pete could move again. He ran to the SUV and grabbed the shotgun. Stephanie, Luna, and Bridgette were still in the back seat. They were staring at Amanda and the creature in shock, tears flooding down all their cheeks. Pete crouched behind the front end of the SUV and pointed the shotgun toward Amanda and the creature. He didn't have a clear shot. Suddenly, the creature stepped back, and the sky lit up in a bright white light. A pulsing red light came down from the sky and surrounded Amanda. Pete heard the pistol hit the pavement. Moments later, the pulsing red light was gone. And so was Amanda. Pete looked back over to where the creature had been, and it was gone. That bright light was so intense his head was starting to hurt. It was the most intense headache he'd ever had. He heard the doors of the SUV open. Bridgette and Luna got out of the passenger side, and Stephanie got out the driver's side. They looked like zombies. Their faces were emotionless, and they moved like they had strings attached to their limbs and someone else was controlling their bodies. Bridgette and Luna walked—more like stumbled—past him as if he wasn't even there. He tried to tell them to get back into the SUV, but he couldn't speak. Shit, he couldn't move again.

Something bony and strong grabbed his right shoulder. It lifted him to his feet and spun him around. That creature was bent down and eye-to-eye with him. It smiled and revealed a mouth full of razor-sharp pointed teeth. Several rows of teeth. Pete felt his bladder let go, and he pissed himself. That made the creature smile even bigger. He heard one of the girls scream and then what sounded like flesh being ripped open. That was quickly followed by a soggy *thud*. Then one of the other girls screamed, and Pete heard bones cracking and then another *thud*.

He still couldn't move. The creature in front of him just kept staring at him and smiling. Pete could not look away. Pete could see movement behind him in the reflection of the creature's black eyes. That pulsing red light came back again and then disappeared.

Pete heard a shotgun blast. Then another. The creature squawked and looked to its left. Pete fell to the ground. He quickly realized he could move again and raised his shotgun. He put the barrel in the creature's stomach and pulled the trigger. The creature flew back several feet. Green ooze poured out of the giant hole in its belly. It looked at Pete and struggled to get back up. Pete took aim at its head. Everything was getting blurry, and his head pounded. He pulled the trigger and blew the creature's head clean off. Thank God Amanda's dad had loaded the shotgun with slugs and not buck-shot!

The bright light intensified to a point where Pete couldn't see anything at all. Then it just went out as if someone had flipped a switch. It took a while for his eyes to adjust to the darkness that now surrounded him.

"You okay?" he heard a man call out.

"I think so," Pete said, rubbing his eyes.

Things slowly began to come into focus. The creature he had shot was gone. A large man walked around the back end of the SUV. He was holding a shotgun. Pete looked up at him. The man extended a hand and helped Pete to his feet.

"I'm Mike," he said. "I've been chasing that light all night shootin' at those fuckin' things."

"I'm Pete," Pete said. "We were trying to get our friends' home." Pete looked around. He saw two badly mangled bodies on the other side of the SUV. He knew they were the bodies of two of the girls, but they were so mutilated he couldn't tell who they were.

"This your car?" Mike asked.

"My friend's car, but she's gone." Pete dipped his head. His heart was still racing, but things were starting to settle in.

Mike looked over at the girls' bodies. "Sorry, man," he said, putting his hand on Pete's shoulder. "I've seen a lot of this tonight. It never gets easier, but one thing I've learned—those things always come back. We should get outta here."

Pete just nodded and climbed into the passenger side of the SUV.

"You gotta drive, bud. I ain't leavin' my truck." He pointed to a jacked-up pickup several yards behind the SUV. "Follow me," he said and turned toward his truck.

Pete got out of the SUV and walked around to the driver's side, closing all the doors as he did. The SUV was still running. He put it in reverse and turned around. Mike honked his horn and took off. Pete followed him. He should've have gone back to Amanda's to let Tom know what happened, but he didn't want to deal with Tom just yet. He thought about leaving Mike and heading to his parents', but he had a good feeling about Mike. Pete felt like he'd be safer following Mike than trying to get anywhere else alone. He was just thankful Mike had showed up when he did. That creature would probably be digesting him by then if Mike hadn't distracted it.

Mike pulled away and headed toward Downtown Spokane. Pete didn't like that idea, but he followed him anyway; he didn't know what else to do at that point. He should have just headed home.

Hopefully I don't regret this. Pete thought as they sped down the highway.

If you find this letter, please deliver it to my wife, Serena. She and my sons are waiting for me at

Sacred Heart Hospital in west Des Moines. I was badly injured in a car accident and was on my way to the hospital by ambulance when the ambulance was attacked and the paramedics were killed. I was lucky enough to survive. A man by the name of Dylan found me and agreed to take me to the hospital. If you are reading this, it means you have found my dead body. Please get the following message to my family. I know it's a lot to ask, but I am hopeful there are still good, decent people out there. Time is a big factor here. I don't know how long my family will be allowed to wait for me at the hospital. If I never make it there, they will have no idea what happened to me. So again, I beg you to get this letter to them. I thank you for helping, and may God bless you.

Dear Serena,

I want you to know how much I love you and our boys. If you are reading this, it means I didn't make it to you. I want you to know that I tried with everything that I had to get to you. I should have listened to you and stayed home. I should have just let Chris be. The truth is, he annoyed me, and I just wanted him as far away from us as possible. You know, I never really liked him very much. He was an odd man, and he honestly creeped me out a bit. I never liked the way he looked at you or how he would interact with you. I did not want to risk him trying to hole up with us. I could tell he was very fragile after realizing Erica had been killed. I felt for him, I really did—I couldn't imagine losing you like that. But I knew I needed to get him to his kids. I had to get him away from us. I didn't trust him. Looking back on it now, separated from you and the boys, I know I made a big mistake. I apologize for that. I am sorry for doing this to you and the boys. I was selfish. I only had my feelings in mind, not what was best for the family. I truly did think getting Chris away from us was in our best interest, but I now know that wasn't the case. I couldn't have imagined the scope of what was going on at that time. Everything went from normal to shit in a matter of hours. I have never seen anything like this, none of us have.

As I write this letter, I am in a car with a man from Des Moines. I hope you never read this letter. I hope I make it to you and the boys. I hope you are still at the hospital. I hope you all are safe. I miss you so much. I miss the boys. I wish I could go back and just tell Chris to leave our house and lock us inside. I wish that damn truck had never ran that red light. I wish I wasn't so bullheaded sometimes. I will make it to you, somehow, some way. But just in case I don't, I hope this letter gets to you. It's crazy out here, baby. So dangerous. Things you wouldn't believe. I saw things that I don't even believe. I know it was real. I saw it, I felt it, I heard it. I don't want you and the boys alone in this world.

Dylan tells me we're getting close. I hope to see you soon. Wait, Dylan is stopping. There's something blocking the highway.

*****

President Rodgers and Anthony made it to the airport. The airport was intact and was crowded with people. All flights had been grounded, and everyone had been instructed to stay put. Cecilia was proud of the airport brass for doing such a thing. They had probably saved everyone's lives. President Rodgers and Anthony made their way to the air traffic control tower. The tower was bustling with people watching the radar. Everyone stopped what they were doing and stood to salute the president.

"No need for that," she said. "Who's in charge, and what are you seeing out there?"

"I am, ma'am," a man of about fifty said. "I'm Thomas Smith. We keep seeing blips of large crafts come in and out of radar."

"Not anything of ours, I assume," the president said.

"No, ma'am," Thomas said. "These things will hover and then vanish, then reappear, then vanish again. Over and over and over."

"Any idea where they are coming from?" she asked.

"No, ma'am, they just appear out of nowhere." Thomas paused for a moment. "It's almost like they're doing it on purpose. Like they're showing us they're out there, but just for a moment or so."

"Almost toying with you?" Cecilia asked.

"Yes, ma'am, seems that way. They definitely know we're here. They keep jamming our equipment. They keep doing fly-bys. I've been in the airline business for thirty years. I've never seen anything like those things. They're so big they shouldn't even be able to fly. And especially not as fast as they do."

"How big?" she asked.

"Huge. I'd say five times the size of our biggest planes. These things are not from our planet."

"We know that. It sounds ludicrous to say out loud, but we've been invaded." Cecilia looked around the room. Everyone had stopped what they were doing and had been listening intently to the conversation. "I'm not sure how yet, but we will fight back. We will not let these things steal our planet. Have you heard anything from any other airports? Or maybe military bases?"

"Yes, ma'am," Thomas said. "There's several airports in the same boat we're in. And one air force base out in Washington State that says they're operational. They're taking in refugees."

"Can you get my general in touch with that base?"

"Yes, ma'am," Thomas said. "Right this way." He motioned to a radio in the center of the room.

Anthony got on the radio with the Air Force base. The rest of the room slowly went back to work, watching their monitors. Thomas and President Rodgers stood behind Anthony as he chatted with the base commander.

"Madam President," Anthony started, "the base is fully functional. They are taking refugees. They are hoping they can bulk up their ranks with people off the street."

"Thomas, we need a plane. We need to get to that base," Cecilia said, turning to Thomas.

"Absolutely, ma'am," Thomas said.

"Any pilots on hand?" she asked.

"Yes, ma'am," Thomas replied.

"Take me to them. Have someone set my general up with a plane."

"Yes, ma'am," he said. Thomas walked over to his desk and picked up the phone. He punched in a few numbers. "This is Thomas. Get someone out to the tarmac. I have the president and her general here. They need a plane. Set the general up with a plane that will get them to Washington State. This has to be stat, number one priority." He listened for a second and hung up the phone. "Terminal twenty-seven, General," he told Anthony. "Follow me, Madam President."

Thomas, President Rodgers, and Anthony left the tower. Anthony headed to the tarmac and Cecilia followed Thomas into the pilot's lounge. There were about a half-dozen pilots sitting around the large room. They all jumped to attention and saluted the president as she walked in.

"At ease, men," she said. "As you all know by now, we have been attacked. I will not stand down and let whatever did this take us over. I will be mounting a counterattack. We have found an operational Air Force base out in Washington State. I need pilots. We don't know what to expect, but we never do in war time. Have no doubts, men—this is a war. Something started a war, and we will fight back! As the president of the United States of America, I am calling you up to fight with us. To fight for this great country."

"Yes, ma'am," they all said, saluting her once again.

"Come with us, men," she said. "Thomas, show us to the plane, please."

"Yes, ma'am, follow me."

Cecilia, Thomas, and the pilots made it out to the tarmac. A plane had already been shuttled out to the runway. Anthony was standing at the bottom of the stairs to the plane. President Rodgers climbed the stairs, followed by the half-dozen pilots and, lastly, Anthony. They closed up the plane. Anthony and one of the pilots settled into the cockpit. Everyone else buckled into the first-class section. The pilot, who introduced himself to Anthony as Mitchell Madsen, took the controls. The plane took off for the four-and-a-half-hour flight to the Air Force base in Washington State.

"It's so weird being the only plane in the skies," Mitchell said to Anthony.

"I know it," Anthony said, checking gauges. "And to be flying blind without satellite positioning is scary, man."

"It sure is. Never done this before. I'm staying low, so hopefully we'll hear from other airports on the way. Hopefully we weren't the only airport watching the skies."

"I just want to make it to that base in one piece," Anthony said. "I want to get in a fighter jet and go blast those fuckin things."

"I'm with you on that one, General," Mitchell said, looking over at Anthony. "I'll get us there."

Not long into their flight to Washington State, a large aircraft appeared behind them. The aircraft kept pace with them but stayed back at first. Everyone was on edge. This could be the end of all of them. They were in a commercial airplane; there was no way they could fight or outmaneuver that aircraft. The left wing of their airplane exploded. The plane tilted hard to the left. Mitchell fought to keep the plane steady, but that was almost impossible without the left wing. The aircraft that had been behind them disappeared.

*****

Scarlett decided it would be safe to go check on Hope's mom. They all knew Hope's mom was gone. Scarlett took a blanket with her and put it over the body. The girls had told her what happened, but the scope of it didn't hit her until she saw the body. Scarlett had become close friends with Hope's mom, Victoria, and it was devastating to see her friend like that. What Scarlett had seen and done that night alone was more terrifying than anything she could have ever imagined. She stood over Victoria's body and said a prayer. Scarlett had never been a religious person, but at that moment, it felt appropriate. Her heart broke for Hope. How could a girl her age ever heal from something like that? And on top of hearing her own mother get electrocuted, she had witnessed her best friend's mom shoot a man dead in her own driveway. It was all so horrifying and, frankly, unbelievable. None of it felt real, like slogging through a nightmare you couldn't wake up from. You try and try, but just can't wake up. Scarlett told herself to put all that behind her. There wasn't time for mourning or remorse at that point. The only focus going forward was to protect those girls. Hope was hers now. She would protect Hope and Gwen with her life.

It was late, and Scarlett decided they should all eat something. Hope and Gwen had rounded up every candle and flashlight they could find. Scarlett had made everyone a sandwich and they sat around the kitchen table. They all just nibbled on their sandwiches; none of them had much of an appetite. Usually when the three of them were together, they were all constantly chatting. The girls had grown up together, and Scarlett was very close to Hope. That night, they sat in silence. No one spoke. They barely moved. They sat at the table, picking at their food. Everything was so dead quiet. It was so eerie. Scarlett had a very bad feeling; no matter what had happened, there should be some noise somewhere out there.

They were all startled out of their chairs by a loud, deafening explosion next door. Scarlett told the girls to get under the table. With the pistol in her hand, she slowly walked to the living room window. The neighbor's house was engulfed in flames. Scarlett could feel the heat through the window. If there had been anyone in that house, they would have been dead. There was no way anyone survived that. A house across the street exploded. Then another. And another.

"Girls!" Scarlett screamed. "Grab whatever you can and get out to my car. Water, food, a few clothes. Go now!"

The girls scrambled out from under the table and began throwing water bottles and canned goods into garbage bags. Scarlett rushed upstairs and started grabbing blankets and coats.

Another house exploded.

"We have to go, girls!" Scarlett yelled, running down the stairs.

They rushed out the door. A house across the street exploded. The explosion was so big it sent shrapnel across the street; a piece of glass hit Gwen in the leg and she went to the ground, screaming in pain. Scarlett dropped everything she had been carrying and tried to run to Gwen, but she couldn't move. That's when something approached them, a huge, brown, slimy creature. It looked at them with a smile of bloodstained razor-sharp teeth. Its eyes were deep black, blacker than the night, but there seemed to be happiness in them. Not an *"I'm happy to meet you"* happy, more of an *"Oh, lookie here, more delicious people"* kind of happiness. The creature stepped toward Gwen and sniffed her. Gwen gagged at the smell of the creature; it reeked of sulfur and blood. It stepped back several feet and looked to the sky. A pulsing red light came down on Gwen, and within minutes, she was gone.

Scarlett kept trying to get the pistol out of her belt, but she couldn't move. When the creature stepped back and that red light appeared, she realized she could move again. She pulled the pistol out. That red light was blinding, and she knew Gwen was inside of it. Scarlett didn't have a good shot.

Another house on the block exploded.

The red light vanished, and Gwen was gone. Scarlett looked around in pure panic. The creature moved toward her, and she shot at it. She was so shaken up she missed wide right. Not even close to the thing. It looked at her and laughed. Scarlett's head began to pound. Hope whimpered and crumpled to the ground. Scarlett squeezed off another round and missed badly again. It laughed at her again. The creature reached out and took the gun from Scarlett. It threw the gun into the street.

"Where's my daughter?" Scarlett screamed, not expecting an answer.

"*She's safe,*" a voice in her head answered.

Scarlett couldn't move again. Her head was pounding. What was that voice inside her head? The creature tilted its head at her.

"*You're important,*" that voice said.

Scarlett didn't know what that meant, and in that moment, she didn't care. She thought she could hear an airplane. The creature seemed to react to the sound too; it looked to the sky. Scarlett looked up too. Off in the distance, there was indeed an airplane. She hadn't heard or seen any planes in the sky for a very long time. How was that possible? And where was it going? Who could be on that plane? It had to be the military. No one else would be flying around after everything that had happened.

The creature vanished in a burst of bright red light. The plane was getting closer. Scarlett could now see that it was a commercial plane. She helped Hope to her feet. They stood on the front lawn looking around. Almost every house on the block was in flames. They heard a clicking sound come from above them. Hope's house exploded into flames, knocking them to the ground. The heat from the fire was so intense they felt their skin start to burn. Scarlett scrambled to her feet, grabbing at Hope. She pulled Hope to her feet and rushed them to the street. They stood in the street catching their breath and watching Hope's house burn. That entire side of the street was now on fire. It was no longer several house fires; it was now one huge, roaring fire.

"What do we do now?" Hope asked through tears.

"I don't know," Scarlett replied. "We have to get out of here and find Gwen."

There was an explosion in the sky. They both looked up to see the plane falling out the sky. The plane soared past them and crash landed not too far away from them. They could even feel the ground shake. They looked up and saw a huge black aircraft fly off to the west. Then the skies were quiet and empty again.

"We need to get to that plane crash!" Scarlett said. "Whoever is in that plane has to be important."

"What about Gwen?" Hope asked, still sobbing.

"She's safe," Scarlett said. "Come on, help me load this stuff up." Scarlett ran back into the yard to the pile of stuff they had dropped.

Hope followed Scarlett and grabbed an armful of supplies, rushing them back to Scarlett's car. The two of them loaded up the car. Scarlett grabbed her gun out of the street. They hopped in the car, and Scarlett took off toward where the plane had gone down.

Taylor and Billy were on their way to the base. They had expected more traffic than what they encountered. The little bit of traffic out on the roads with them wasn't any kind of hindrance. It actually felt comforting to not be the only ones out on the roads. The roads were still jammed up with wrecked and abandoned vehicles. Every few miles, they would come across a dead body.

*****

Taylor slammed on the brakes as a naked woman ran out in front of his car. She put her hands on the hood and stood in front of the car panting. Her hair was filthy and tangled. Her face was streaked in dirt and blood. Taylor looked at Billy; he was staring at the nude woman. She pounded on the hood, and Taylor looked back at her. He threw the car in reverse, backing away from the woman. Taylor slammed it into drive and sped around her. He saw her turn around and watch them leave her.

"What are you doing, dude?" Billy asked.

"Getting us to the base," Taylor said, still speeding up.

"We shoulda helped that chick," Billy said, turning in his seat to look out the back window.

"Fuck no!" Taylor exclaimed. "No more crazy bitches."

"How do you know she's crazy?" Billy asked, settling back into his seat.

"She's running around naked," Taylor replied, glancing over at Billy.

"Yeah, she was," Billy smiled. "But that don't make her crazy. What if she was in trouble? What if someone was trying to rape her and she got away? We coulda saved her, dude."

"Didn't you see the look in her eyes? She was crazed, man."

"No, I didn't even look at her eyes," Billy said.

"You're somethin' else," Taylor said, shaking his head. "She had the look of a killer, not a victim."

"What could a naked chick had done to us?" Billy scoffed.

"Be a decoy. We don't know she was alone, man. If I was crazy and was goin' to try car jackin' dudes, I'd get a naked chick to help. You know, to be a distraction. It worked perfectly on you."

"Oh, Jesus fuckin' Christ, dude. You always think the worst possible outcome," Billy said, shaking his head and chuckling at Taylor.

"*I do?*" Taylor asked. "You're the conspiracy guy. I look at things rationally and assess the situation. I don't just jump to crazy conclusions."

"You just did exactly that!" Billy said, slightly offended. "You assumed that chick was part of some scheme to car jack us, when in reality, she was probably running for her life."

"She wasn't right, man. I could tell."

"How the fuck could you tell that? From her goddamn eyes?" Billy rolled his eyes, still shaking his head at Taylor.

"Yes!" Taylor responded loudly. "Goddammit, man, you almost got killed by some fucked-up creature because you just had to go fuck that tweaker. I told you she was bad news, but you ignored me and went over there anyway. You're lucky my neighbor shot that thing, or you'd probably be dead right now!"

"What the fuck you talkin' 'bout?" Billy asked, also loudly. "Me goin' over to bang the neighbor chick had nuthin' to do with that thing showin' up. How do you even relate the two? And what in the fuck does any of that have to do with the naked chick in the street?"

"I'm sayin' your judgment is off. You make decisions with your dick instead of your head. You just couldn't help goin' to the tweaker's apartment to get laid, which ended up putting you in a vulnerable position. Now you're suggesting we shoulda picked up that naked chick, just 'cuz she was naked! You're nuts, man."

"Fuck you, dude. That creature woulda showed up even if I wasn't over at that chick's place gettin' laid. And you have no reason to believe that naked chick was goin' do anything to us. You're being way too paranoid."

"Yeah, it would've still showed up, but you would've been safely inside my apartment if you hadn't put your dick's needs ahead of your own. You got lucky, bro. And maybe I am being overly paranoid, but look around us, we gotta be paranoid out here. Look there," Taylor said, pointing to a man's body on the side of the road and slowing down a bit. The man's head had been smashed in with some kind of blunt object. A wallet laid open next to him on the ground. "That dude there probably got his head smashed in for whatever was in his wallet. If there's people out there that would so violently kill a man for a few bucks, there's people that would do anything to car jack someone. We ain't stopping 'til we get to that fuckin' base. Period, dude."

Billy just looked at Taylor. He had never seen Taylor this animated and agitated. He was usually the one ranting and raving about everything. He liked this side of Taylor. Taylor did seem to have a backbone after all. Billy had always thought Taylor was a bit of a pushover. There had been plenty of times Billy had gotten his way with Taylor just by being loud and pushy. He wouldn't be getting away with that kind of stuff anymore. Taylor was in charge now, and Billy liked it. He did wish they had picked up the naked girl, though. Billy thought she was hot and would've liked to spend time with her. He didn't for one second believe someone that looked like her was trying to car jack people. There wasn't any point to arguing about it anymore, though.

"Fine," Billy said. "You're in charge, boss."

"Fuck off, man. You're a fuckin' baby sometimes."

"You fuck off! I'm not a baby." That comment had pissed him off. "Excuse me for not wanting to live out my last days on earth just runnin'. Forgive me for wanting to get laid one last time. Jesus, Dude, this is Armageddon, we need to get what we can while we still can."

"We need to fuckin' survive, Billy, not try to get laid."

"I'll ask you again, survive for what? What kind of life we gonna live after all this?"

"Who knows, but I ain't givin' up, man. Anything has to be better than this. Shit, it can't get any worse," Taylor said. They were almost to the base.

"Dude, don't say shit like that! Whenever someone says somethin' like that, shit gets worse."

"Only if you think that way. You gotta be positive, man."

"I was tryin' to be. I was tryin' to get myself laid. I was tryin' to live out the last days on Earth my way. Now who knows what's gonna happen? I have a bad feeling we're fucked." He sank down in his seat and sighed.

Taylor looked over at him. "Maybe there'll be some hottie at the base you can put the moves on. At least there we'll be safe."

"Maybe," Billy said.

"Well, safer at the very least."

"I meant maybe to the hot chick idea. We ain't gonna be safe anywhere."

They got to the base and pulled up to the gate. Several armed guards surrounded the gate. They had armed Humvees and tanks stationed behind the gate. The place was locked down tight. A guard approached the car. Taylor rolled down the window.

"You guys seeking refuge?" the guard asked.

"Yes, sir," Taylor responded.

"You armed?" the guard asked.

"Just a bat and tire iron, no firearms," Taylor said.

"Pop the trunk," the guard said, nodding to another guard. The other guard walked to the back of the car.

"You need the key to open the trunk," Taylor said.

"Hand them over," the guard said, putting out his hand. Taylor shut the car off and gave the keys to the guard. He tossed the keys to the guy at the trunk. "Stay put," he said to Taylor. After a few minutes, the other guy slammed the trunk lid and gave the keys back to the first guard, whispering something in his ear. "You're good to go," the first guard said, handing the keys back to Taylor. "Open the gate!" he yelled.

The gate opened. Taylor started his car and slowly pulled through the gate.

"Straight ahead," the guard shouted at him. "A pickup truck will meet you up the road. Follow it."

Taylor waved out the window and kept rolling. He looked over at Billy, who was staring out the front window.

"I don't like this, dude," Billy said.

"Dude, they got this place locked down. Nowhere safer than here right now."

"I don't like it."

They saw the truck. As they approached it, the driver flashed the headlights and slowly pulled away. Taylor followed him. The truck led them to what looked like a dormitory. There were two armed guards out front. A female officer approached Taylor's car.

"Park anywhere and come inside," she said, pointing to the building. "No weapons of any kind, including bats and tire irons."

"Okay," Taylor said.

Taylor parked the car, and they gathered their belongings. The armed guards opened the door for them, and they headed inside. They were met by armed military personnel. All of their belongings were gone through. They were walked through metal detectors. The female officer came up to them.

"Grab your gear and follow me," she said with no emotion at all.

Taylor and Billy gathered their things and followed her. She took them to a room. It was a medium sized room with two twin beds and a sink. No bathroom or anything else.

"Uh, where is the bathroom?" Billy asked.

"There are male and female locker rooms down the hall," she responded.

"Okay, thanks," Billy said.

She left the room and closed the door. Taylor and Billy looked at each other.

"Well, roomie, what now?" Billy asked.

"Sleep," Taylor said, sitting down on the bed closest to the door and taking his shoes off.

"Yeah, right, dude," Billy chuckled.

"I'm going to try to sleep. I'm fuckin' beat, man."

"Okay, have at it." Billy settled onto the other bed.

Taylor stripped to his boxers and crawled into the bed. He hadn't slept in a twin bed since grade school; it felt so small and weird. The sheets were starched and crunchy feeling. It was by far the least comfortable bed imaginable, but once he was settled in, he started to drift off to sleep. Within ten minutes, he was snoring.

Billy looked over at Taylor asleep on the other bed. *Must be nice,* he thought to himself. He wished he could sleep—he was very tired—but the gravity of everything that was going on weighed on him heavily. Billy got up and left the room. He decided he'd go look around, maybe find some other people to talk to. Taylor was Billy's best friend, but Billy was pretty annoyed with him at that point. He just wanted someone new to talk to. Maybe—no, hopefully—he would find a girl to talk to. He was, after all, still on the hunt for one last hurrah.

Billy walked down the hall. The hallway felt like a hotel hallway, nothing but bare walls and closed doors. At the end of the hallway, he turned left, his only option. He could hear voices and walked toward them. There was a door open, and he peeked in; the room was full of people in Air Force uniforms. They stopped talking when they noticed him. A man came toward Billy.

"You need to go back to your room. We have a curfew around here," the man said.

"I'm sorry, my friend and I just got here, and I didn't know," Billy said nervously. Anyone in uniform made him nervous.

"It's fine, just return to your room. Breakfast will be downstairs in the cafeteria at oh-eight-hundred."

"Thank you," Billy said and turned back toward his room.

Billy stopped by the locker room to use the bathroom on his way back. The shower area was stocked with towels and bathrobes. He decided a hot shower might help him feel sleepy. The hot water felt amazing; he stood in it for quite a while. As he was drying off, he could hear female voices in the hallway. They sounded disoriented and confused. He put on a bathrobe and went out into the hall. There was no one out there. Billy walked to the end of the hallway and looked down the other hall, nothing. He did the same thing at the opposite end of the hall, still nothing. He stood there confused for a minute. He knew he had heard voices, no doubt about it. They couldn't have made it far. Maybe they had been on their way to the women's locker room across the hall from the men's when he heard them. He went to the doorway of the women's locker room and listened for any voices. Once again, nothing. Billy ran his fat fingers through his wet hair.

"Hey! What are you doing there?" a female voice shouted from behind Billy, startling him badly.

"Uh…" he began. "Nuthin'. Just headed back to my room." He started walking.

"That's a good idea," she said. The woman, who looked to be in her mid-twenties, was dressed in full camo and was holding a pistol in her right hand. "Stay in your room until breakfast," she said as she followed Billy back to his room.

"I will," Billy said sheepishly. He found this woman quite attractive. The combination of her looks and the uniform made him very nervous. The pistol made her even more intimidating. He was scared of her and turned on by her at the same time. He got to his room door and opened it. "Sorry," he said to her as he entered the room.

She didn't say anything else; she just stood there while he went into the room. Billy closed the door. Taylor was still fast asleep. Billy went into his backpack and grabbed a clean pair of underwear. He climbed into bed and tried to get comfortable. That twin bed was so small. He finally got as comfortable as possible and closed his eyes. As soon as his eyes were closed, he saw the creature from the apartment. He opened his eyes and looked around the room. *Fuckin'-A*, he thought, *that thing will haunt me forever.*

He tried to picture the naked woman they had encountered on their way to the base. Billy hoped something like that would help him relax. It did help a bit. He settled back into bed and closed his eyes again—this time no creature. Taylor was snoring, and Billy found himself matching Taylor's breathing. He eventually fell asleep to the rhythmic sounds of Taylor's snores. Once he had finally fallen asleep, Billy was out hard. Both men were in such a deep sleep they didn't hear all the commotion outside the building.

CHAPTER 8

Toxic Clouds

Malcolm stopped at a truck stop, hoping the diesel pumps still worked. Bethany was asleep in the passenger seat. They had spent several hours getting to know each other better. He was finding himself falling hard for her. She was a beautiful woman with a fun and energetic personality. Despite everything that was going on, they had spent most of the trip laughing. It was exactly what they both needed, to be able to spend what was more than likely their last days happy. After what felt like a day worth of driving, Malcolm could see how dead tired his new friend was. He told her she could go crash out in the sleeper, but she said she wanted to stay up front with him. She fell asleep about an hour before he had to stop for fuel.

Malcolm got lucky. Somehow the pumps still worked. He felt so vulnerable standing outside his truck waiting on the tanks to be filled. Both tanks were about bone dry; it took forever to fill them. They had just made it to the Nevada/Idaho border. He had no idea where they were or what to expect out there in the middle of nowhere. Malcolm was so tired; he hadn't slept in a day and half. He needed to sleep but not at the truck stop. Once the tanks were finally full, he climbed back into the truck. He fired it back up, which woke up Bethany.

"I'm going to find a good spot to pull off the road and sleep for a bit," he said to her. "I need to sleep before I fall asleep at the wheel and kill us."

"Okay," Bethany replied sleepily. "That's a good idea, babe." That was the first time either of them had used a term of endearment. It panicked her a little. Was it too soon?

He smiled at her. "We both need sleep, babe."

Malcolm pulled away from the truck stop as Bethany happily fell back asleep. She was so exhausted she just could not stay awake, regardless of how badly she wanted to. Bethany wanted to be awake with Malcolm. She wanted to keep chatting with him. But she just couldn't stay awake.

It took Malcolm another hour to find what he thought was a safe place to park and take a nap. It was an abandoned warehouse store just off the main highway. There was nothing else around them. The parking lot was huge and dark. Come to think of it, everything was still dark. It hadn't really crossed his mind until then, but it should have been midafternoon by that point. Why was it still so dark? It wasn't a nighttime darkness, more like stormy weather dark. But not quite the same. There was a smokiness to the dark, a constant haze. He pulled the truck behind the store so they couldn't be seen from the road. Malcolm shut off the engine to conserve fuel. He reached over and gently shook Bethany. She blinked her eyes open and smiled at him.

"I'm going to crawl into the sleeper and get some rest," he said. "Want to join me?"

"Yes, I'd like that," she said, undoing her seatbelt.

Malcolm reached into the glove box and pulled out his 9mm. He took the gun into the sleeper and tucked it into a pocket above the mattress. Malcolm stepped aside and let Bethany crawl into bed first. He wanted to be on the outside of the bed in case anyone tried to break into the truck. After making sure both doors were locked, Malcolm settled in next to Bethany. She immediately snuggled into him. He put an arm around her and pulled her close to him. She smelled like sulfur and sweat. He wasn't put off by it. She didn't smell bad, just not what he had expected her to smell like. Malcolm imagined he probably didn't smell great himself. None of it mattered; they were both so tired they passed out fairly quick.

Malcolm didn't sleep well. The wind had picked up and kept rocking the truck. Every time the truck would move, he'd wake up. Bethany slept soundly. He lay awake for a bit, just watching her sleep. Her beauty took his breath away. Malcolm had married his high school sweetheart a year after graduation. They moved to Las Vegas for a few years while she attended UNLV. Malcolm got a job at a distribution center to pay the bills while his bride went to school. He eventually obtained his CDL and began driving for the company. Once a week, he'd be gone overnight. Malcolm had thought Jessica was his one and only. His forever love. But it turned out she was using those nights he was gone to sleep with a classmate. A female neighbor had told him that a man came and stayed with Jessica every night he was out of town. That news devastated him. He was furious and heartbroken. Malcolm divorced Jessica and moved back to Ely. It was an embarrassing transition back to life in Ely. Everyone knew everyone in that town, and they all knew what had happened between Malcolm and Jessica. For a long time, he blamed himself. If only he hadn't taken that route. If only he had showed her how much he loved her more often. It took about a year before he could see that it wasn't his fault. She chose to cheat on him. She made that decision and would have ended up doing it even if he was home more often. Malcolm didn't date after that. He didn't think he would ever love anyone again.

Watching Bethany sleep, he realized he was developing strong feelings for her. Very strong feelings already. She snored softly in his arms. He kissed her forehead, and she stirred a bit. Malcolm hadn't been trying to wake her; he just couldn't stop himself. She was just so beautiful to him. Bethany opened her eyes, smiling at him. He pulled her even closer to him and kissed her head again. She lifted her head and kissed him. It was a brief kiss. They pulled away from the kiss and looked at each other. Bethany sat up on one arm. She looked into his dark-brown eyes. Those eyes invited her in. Bethany climbed on top of Malcolm and kissed him again, this time a whole lot more passionately. They lay in that sleeper being rocked back and forth by the wind, kissing.

Their passion and desire for each other was building at a rapid pace. Clothes soon began to come off. The kissing quickly turned to lovemaking. It was as if they had known each other forever. There was no awkwardness between them, just passion and what already felt like love. It was far too soon to be in love with each other, but it sure as hell felt that way in that moment. Of course, lust is often mistaken for love. Desire for another person can often feel like a love for them. Living in Ely, where he knew everyone, Malcolm had given up hope for ever finding another woman to love. He frankly didn't want it. The bachelor life had suited him just fine. Before he lost his parents, he had never even felt lonely. It wasn't until after their deaths that he started to feel lonely sometimes. Never a feeling that had ever lasted very long. Malcolm looked into Bethany's beautiful deep-blue eyes. She stared back into his eyes with a desire he had never seen in a woman before.

Something hit the back of the trailer hard enough to make the truck lurch forward. Malcolm and Bethany froze.

"What the fuck?" Bethany whispered.

"I don't know," Malcolm said. They could hear what sounded like someone hammering on the back of the trailer. "I think someone is trying to break into the trailer."

"Probably trying to get at the beer," Bethany said, rolling off Malcolm.

Malcolm swung his legs over the edge of the bed. He dressed and grabbed the 9mm.

"Are you going out there?" she asked.

"Yeah. I gotta see what's going on out there," he said.

"Please don't," Bethany said. "We don't know who or what is out there."

"I have to, they're trying to rob us."

"Who cares about some beer, Malcolm? Let 'em have it. It's not worth our lives."

"You think they'll just take the beer and go?" he asked, sitting down in the driver's seat and checking the mirrors. He could see a smashed-up pickup behind the trailer on the passenger side. "There's a wrecked truck back there," he said. "Not sure why they'd ram us like that."

"Maybe they were trying to see if anyone was in the truck? Maybe they thought if they rammed the truck someone would come out."

"Maybe," Malcolm said. "But why? Why not just break into the trailer and get out of here?"

"Maybe they thought they could lure someone out and kill them, then just take the whole truck," she said, getting dressed. "Let 'em have the beer so we can get out of here."

Malcolm was watching his mirrors. He saw a man walk around the back of the trailer on the driver's side. The man stopped and stared at Malcolm's reflection in the mirror.

"Shit! Someone saw me!" Malcolm said.

The man pulled a pistol from a holster on his belt. Malcolm fired up the truck.

"He's got a gun! Get down on the floor back there," he shouted as he put the old truck into gear.

The air bags were slowly filling, preventing him from releasing the brake. The man got up to Malcolm's door. Malcom ducked down. He could hear the man yelling something at him. With his 9mm in hand, Malcolm slowly sat up. The man was standing just outside the door. He had his pistol in his hand, but he was pointing it to the ground. He motioned at Malcolm to roll down the window. Malcolm did.

"We just want some of the beer," the man said. "We don't want to hurt anyone."

"Why you got a gun, then?" Malcolm asked, nodding at the pistol.

"Gotta have one out here now," the man replied. "I'm sure you got one in your hand right now."

"I do," Malcolm said. "Hurry up and take what you want. We gotta get moving."

"Understood, thanks, man."

"Hey," Malcolm began, "why'd you guys ram my trailer?"

"It was an accident. We didn't expect anything to be parked back here," the man said, looking to the back of the trailer. Malcolm saw another man standing at the back of the trailer. He gave a thumbs up. The first man didn't say anything; he just took off running toward the other guy.

Malcolm watched for a minute. Both men disappeared behind the trailer. A moment later, he saw an SUV pull away from the trailer and haul ass away. He opened the door and stepped out. Malcolm climbed down from the truck and slowly walked back to the end of his trailer. The pickup truck that had hit them was steaming from its broken radiator. The trailer door was still open. It was dark inside the trailer, but Malcolm could see a body lying in there. He ran back up to the truck and shouted at Bethany to hand him the flashlight he had behind his seat. She grabbed the flashlight and tossed it to him. He told her to stay put and ran back to the trailer. Malcolm shined the flashlight into the trailer. There was a man's body lying on the metal floor of the trailer.

"What in the fuck?" Malcolm muttered to himself.

Malcolm heard footsteps approaching. He looked around the back of the trailer and saw Bethany walking toward him.

"Go back to the truck," he told her.

"What's going on?" she asked. Her voice was shaky with fear.

Bethany got to the trailer door and looked inside. She screamed when she saw the body. Malcolm grabbed her and hugged her tight.

"We gotta get out of here," he said.

Malcolm walked Bethany back to the truck. She was trembling in his arms. He helped up into the truck. Malcolm walked to the back of his truck and disconnected the trailer hookups. He dropped the landing gear of the trailer. There was no way he was going to drive the rest of the way to Washington with a dead body in his trailer and no way was he going to remove the body. So the best thing to do was just leave the trailer. Plus, it would save on fuel as well. They'd make better time not pulling the heavy trailer.

Malcolm climbed back into the driver's seat. Bethany was buckled into the passenger seat. The air tanks were full by then, and he disengaged the brake. He pulled away and grabbed gears like he had never done before. The truck responded faster without a trailer. The adrenaline from what had just happened had him wide awake. No matter how sleepy he became, he was not stopping again until they reached that Air Force base.

*****

Pete had followed Mike through Spokane and then west toward Airway Heights. Mike had led him to the Air Force base. Mike pulled over before they got to the gate. He got out of his truck and walked back to Pete. Pete got out of Tom's SUV.

"They're taking people in. I think you should stay here," Mike said.

"Why?" Pete asked.

"It's the safest place to be right now," Mike said.

"What about you?" Pete asked.

"I'm hunting those things down. They took my daughter. I ain't stopping until I get them, or they kill me trying."

"I should get to my parents," Pete said. "All this shit went down while I was trying to get home to them."

"It's not safe to be out on the roads anymore. I'm sure your parents are fine. Hell, they might even be inside there," Mike said, pointing at the gate.

The air was heavy and dense. Pete was tired and hungry. He felt faint and feverish. Mike urged him to go inside again. Pete agreed to go.

"Give me your shotgun," Mike said. "They won't let you inside with it."

Pete gave Mike a confused look.

"It's okay, Pete. Give me the gun and go get yourself some rest. You'll be safe in there."

"Okay," Pete said, retrieving the shotgun from the SUV. Mike grabbed the gun.

"Good luck, kid," Mike said and headed back to his truck.

"Thanks, you too," Pete said, climbing back into the SUV.

Mike pulled away, heading back toward Spokane. Pete drove to the gate. The guards searched Pete's car and let him in. He followed a pickup truck to a dorm building. A female in full camo approached him.

"Park anywhere and follow me," she said.

"Okay," Pete said. He parked the SUV and climbed out.

"Grab your gear," the woman said.

"I didn't bring anything," Pete said. "I wasn't planning to come here."

"Okay then, follow me." She led him to the door.

Two armed guards opened the door for Pete and the woman. She followed Pete inside. He was told by a male officer to empty his pockets and proceed through a metal detector. All Pete had on him were the SUV keys and his wallet. He was instructed to follow the woman to his room.

"We need you to stay in your room," she said as she led him up a flight of stairs. "We will serve some breakfast in a couple hours, at oh-eight-hundred. Come back down here and head to your right."

"Okay, thank you," Pete said.

The place felt like a prison. No one was milling around except for heavily armed Air Force personnel. Pete was scared. He didn't want to be there, but he didn't know what else to do. Maybe he could just get a few hours of sleep, a meal in his belly, and then head out in daylight. He just couldn't see himself staying there when he knew his parents and Tom were, by that point, probably worried sick. Pete didn't know Tom well, but he assumed he wasn't the kind of guy that would just stay put and wait. After a while, he figured Tom would go looking for Amanda and the rest of them. Pete did not want to be the one to tell Tom what had happened, but he knew he had to. Tom deserved to know, even if it was so unbelievable. God, he hoped Tom wouldn't blame him for it. Tom's words, "protect those girls," echoed in his head. He had failed. Two of them mutilated and two vanished. Abducted? Of course they were; he knew it to be true. Pete didn't want to think about that. What were those things doing to them? And where?

The woman led him around a corner into a hallway of dorm rooms. Pete saw a man in a bathrobe standing by an open door down the hall. It looked like the man was trying to look into the room or listening for something. The woman stopped and opened a door for Pete. She motioned him inside. As Pete went into the room, he heard the woman yell, "Hey! What are you doing there?" Pete closed his door and looked around the room. It was a very small room with one twin bed, a sink, and a mirror. Pete sat on the bed. His heart was racing, and his head was pounding. He was tired, dehydrated, and all of a sudden, starving. He lay down on the bed, on top of the covers. Pete looked up at the ceiling and felt tears welling up in his eyes. He didn't fight them back; he let them out. Amanda was gone. No one, not even his best of friends, knew he had had feelings for Amanda. Ever since grade school, he had liked her. As they got older and became friends, his feelings for her had deepened. But he knew she would never feel the same way. Her lack of similar feelings didn't lessen his feelings for her. He had hoped moving to Idaho and meeting new people would have helped him get over those feelings. And it had worked for the most part until he had seen her again. As soon as he saw her in that window shouting hello to him, all those feelings came flooding back. Now she was gone. He missed her terribly and felt 100 percent responsible.

Pete fell asleep crying. The stress, fear, and unbearable sadness had gotten the best of him. He didn't sleep very long, but the couple of hours he got truly had felt amazing. His body clearly needed it. Pete looked over at the digital clock on the nightstand. It was a little past eight. He decided he'd head down for some breakfast. The cafeteria had a lot more people sitting around and waiting for food than Pete had imagined. How did all these people hear about the base? How did they all get there so fast? It slowly started to dawn on him that the base had been home to a lot of service people and their families. The crowdedness of the chow hall was probably mostly people who had already been there when all this shit had gone down.

Pete shyly walked to the food line. It smelled like cafeteria breakfast, not great but not bad either. It smelled fantastic to Pete; he was starving.

"Pete!" a man shouted; it sounded like Mitch from the car lot. "Pete Murphy!"

Pete looked around and saw Mitch standing up and waving at him from a couple of tables away. Pete waved to him and gave him the "Hang on, be right there" hand gesture. Pete loaded his plate with scrambled eggs, bacon, sausage, potatoes, and a blueberry muffin. He had enough food on his plate to feed three people. Pete joined Mitch and his wife, Barbara, at their table. Pete had met Barbara a couple of times at the car lot when she'd met Mitch there for lunch. He thought she was the sweetest lady. Both of them were just sweet people. Mitch and Barbara where probably in their late fifties and treated Pete like a grandson. He loved it. His mom's parents had both passed away when he was very young, so he didn't remember them, and his dad's parents lived in Florida, so he never saw them. Just in the short time they had worked together, Pete had adopted Mitch as his new grandpa, although he'd never call him that.

"Pete, you son of a gun! What are you doing here?" Mitch asked, slapping Pete on the back.

"I was going to ask you the same thing," Pete said. There was a pitcher of orange juice and glasses on the table; Pete helped himself to some OJ.

"We heard about them taking people out here on the radio. Most radio stations went to static, but we found one that was fuzzy. They had people relaying news and whatnot," Mitch said, smiling. He had taken his wife's hand, and the two of them sat across from Pete, just smiling at him. "How'd you hear about it? Are your folks here too?"

"Uh, no, I never made it home," Pete said. He paused as that settled into him again. Last time he had seen Mitch, he had been on his way home. It wasn't just his parents' place; it was and would always be home.

"What happened, son?" Mitch asked. He could see the distress on Pete's face.

"Oh, man, what didn't happen would be a shorter story. I'm not dead. I think I came close to getting killed. At least twice." Pete could see the shock on Mitch and Barbara's faces. "It's crazy out there, guys," Pete said, shoving some eggs in his mouth.

"Oh, I know it." Barbara said. "I rode all the way out here from Idaho with my eyes closed. So much destruction and death out there. I'm deeply saddened by how people have responded to this."

"Me too," Pete said, washing some bacon and eggs down with a healthy swig of orange juice.

"So tell us what happened, Pete. How come you never made it home? Where you been?" Mitch asked, pouring himself some orange juice.

"Oh, man," Pete began, "I was on the highway north, within a mile of my turn, when I saw a girl standing on the side of the rode next to a car with a flat tire. So I stopped to help. After I changed her tire, two big dudes appeared out of nowhere and they stole my car."

"Oh wow. Where's the girl?" Mitch asked.

"She was part of it. It was a plan to carjack me. Well, then I searched what I thought was her car for keys or anything, and that's when I saw a dead body in the ditch, and I just booked it on foot."

"Oh, my!" Barbara said, shaking her head.

"That's why everything has gone to shit," Mitch said. "That's why we have to seek refuge out here. I lost faith in humanity a long time ago and stuff like that is why. Then what happened?"

"I actually got turned around heading to my parents' house, ended up a few blocks away. I ran into a friend from school. She wanted to get her friends home to their parents, so we borrowed her dad's SUV." Pete paused and looked down at his plate. He had been plowing through his breakfast, but suddenly he didn't have an appetite anymore. He looked up at Mitch and Barbara with tears in his eyes. "We all got separated," he said, fighting back tears. "A man named Mike led me out here."

Mitch saw the pain in Pete's eyes; he knew there was a lot more to the story but wasn't going to press Pete on it. Barbara reached across the table and took Pete's hand in her hands. She rubbed his hand and told him everything was going to be okay.

"Thank you both," Pete said. "I am so happy to see you guys here. I'm so glad you're safe."

"We're glad you're safe, son," Mitch said.

Pete stood up. "Excuse me, please," he said, picking up his plate. "I need to use the restroom."

"Okay, son, come on back when you're done. We'll be here," Mitch said, standing up and patting Pete on the back again.

"Okay, will do." Pete walked away from the table. He scraped his plate and put it with the other dirty dishes. He walked out of the cafeteria and back upstairs. He found the men's locker room and went inside. Pete could hear a man sobbing in one of the stalls. It had quickly become a crazy and unpredictable world. Pete did his business and left. The other man was still sobbing. Pete thought about asking if he was okay before leaving but decided not to. Pete didn't want to get involved in that moment. He also figured if he had ever been so overwhelmed by emotion that he was crying in a bathroom stall, he wouldn't want a random dude asking if he was okay. He imagined he'd just want to be left alone.

Pete exited the locker room and headed toward the stairs. A woman shouted at him to stop. He did and turned around. It was the woman that had shown him to his room.

"You!" she said. "Come with me."

"Uh, what for?" Pete stammered.

"Just do it!" she demanded, fidgeting with the pistol in her hand to remind Pete that she had it.

"Um, okay," he said and walked toward her.

She led him upstairs to a meeting room. There were about two dozen people sitting in the room. They looked as confused as Pete felt. The woman in camo told Pete to take a seat. Pete found a seat in an empty row of chairs near the back. He sat back there and looked around the room. It felt like a classroom without desks. There was a whiteboard, a projector, and a flat-screen TV. The woman in camo kept escorting people into the room. After about fifteen minutes, she closed the door and stood in front of it, pistol in hand. A man who looked to be in his mid-forties, dressed in an officer's uniform, came into the room through a door on the opposite side of the room. Another man dressed in full camo and carrying a pistol entered behind the officer, closed that door, and stood in front of it.

"I'm Captain Reynolds," the man said to the room. "We are honored and fortunate to be able to host all of you here. Word is, there aren't a lot, if any, other bases out there that are still standing. It truly is our great pleasure to be able to take people in and provide a safe place to ride this thing out. Does anyone know what is going on out there?"

A bunch of hands timidly raised around the room.

"Have any of you seen those things?" Captain Reynolds asked.

The same hands went up in the air again.

"So most of you all know what is happening. Looks like a lot of you have seen it firsthand. For the rest of you, I have been given permission from my superiors to brief you all on the situation at hand. We have been invaded." He paused and looked around the room; no one reacted to that statement. They all knew what was going on. Very few people at that point didn't know. "We have been in contact with the President of the United States," he continued. "She and a few of her staff survived the attack. We have been instructed to fight back against those things. We need all the men and women we can get to help us. We are calling all of you to fight with us. To fight for your country. Hell, to fight for this planet!"

People started to whisper to each other. Pete felt himself begin to shake a little. His stomach turned, and he felt nauseous. The thought of going to war against those things scared him to death. He had seen one of them; he was lucky enough to have been able to kill it, but he knew what they were capable of. How would this group of people ever be able to fight those things? Pete needed to figure out a way to get out of there. He needed to get home to his parents. Find a way to get to Tom and tell him what happened. His parents and Tom must have assumed by that point he and his friends were dead. Pete knew he would be dead if he stuck around to fight those things. He was no soldier and never would be a good one.

"Beginning immediately, you will all go into training. It will be a crash course into how to fire assault rifles. How to mount an attack. I'll be honest with you all—we aren't even sure yet how we will mount that attack, but we will be going after those things."

A man in the front row raised his hand.

"You have a question?" the captain asked.

"Uh, yes, sir," the man said, standing up. "Um, how are we going to fight those things? We don't even know where they are."

"We're still working on that. We got word from DC that the president and her general are on their way here. If all goes well, they should be landing on base shortly. Once she is here, we should be able to come up with a strategy."

The door the captain had come through opened, and a man in an Air Force uniform whispered something to the man in camo. The man in camo approached the captain. He said something quietly to the captain.

"Please excuse me," Captain Reynolds said and left the room.

The man in camo followed him. The woman in camo opened the door she had been guarding and told the room they may leave but to go to their rooms until they are called back for the next briefing. She then crossed the room and went through the door the captain had just used. Pete stood up and looked around. People were slowly getting up and milling about. He could see the confusion and angst on everyone's faces. That was it—that was the time for him to try to get off that base. Pete suspected they would try to keep him there, but he hoped they wouldn't. Invaded or not, this was still the United States of America, and he should have the choice to fight or leave. He certainly did not want to fight.

Pete made his way to the door. People were slowly making their way out, and there was a traffic jam at the doorway. He accidently bumped into a dark-haired, kind of pudgy guy.

"Excuse me," Pete said to him.

"No worries, dude," the guy replied. "You believe this shit?"

"Uh, no. It's crazy," Pete said.

"My buddy here," the man started, pointing to another man about the same age as him, "said we'd be safe here. 'Nowhere safer than this base,' he said. Now they want us to fight those fuckin' things. Have you seen 'em?" he asked Pete.

"The creatures?" Pete asked back.

"Yeah, the aliens."

"Yeah," Pete said. "I killed one."

"*What?* No fuckin' way!" the man exclaimed. "How'd you do that?"

"One was standing over me, and someone shot at it and distracted it. So I blasted it in the guts with a shotgun. Then I blew its head off."

"Holy shit, dude! That's fuckin' amazing! Hey, Taylor, this dude is a fuckin' badass!" he said to his friend.

Pete had a good feeling about these guys. It felt good just to tell someone about what he had done.

"I'm not a badass, just lucky," Pete said.

"Whatever, you got one. I was face to face with one of those things, and I couldn't move. I was frozen in fear, dude."

"I was face to face with it too, and I couldn't move either. But when it was distracted by the other guy, I could move again. It was the weirdest thing."

"I just gotta officially meet the man that killed one! I'm Billy, and this is Taylor," Billy said, putting his hand out.

"I'm Pete. It's nice to meet you guys," he said, shaking both their hands.

"Nice to meet you too," Billy said. "So tell me what it felt like to kill one?" he asked, as the three of them walked down the hall.

"Honestly," Pete began, looking at the floor as he talked, "it felt great. Those things took my friend and another girl. Then they killed two other girls. So yeah, it felt pretty damn good to get one of 'em."

"Holy shit, dude!" Billy exclaimed. "But what do you mean they took your friend?"

"They took her. I saw it happen. She was standing in the road outside of her dad's SUV, and one of those things approached her. She didn't move a muscle. It was so weird. Then a red light came from the sky, and then she was gone."

"Was there a bright, like white, light?" Billy asked.

"Yeah, after Amanda disappeared, there was. That was when I couldn't move. That's when the thing was face to face with me. God, it smelled bad, man," Pete said. Billy and Taylor had stopped walking. They had reached their room.

"This is our room. Come in and tell us more," Billy said.

"I would, but I'm going to try to get outta here. I was supposed to be at my parents' house like twenty-four hours ago. They're probably so worried. Probably think I'm dead."

"You think they'd let you outta here?" Billy asked.

"Not a chance," Taylor piped in for the first time. Billy had a way of taking over a conversation with someone, leaving Taylor to pretty much sit on the sideline and listen.

"I'd like to hope so. As far as I'm concerned, I'm still an American citizen, so they can't hold me against my will," Pete said.

"Get in here," Billy said, opening the door to their room. "We shouldn't talk about this in the hallway."

"Okay, just for a minute," Pete said. He didn't want to miss an opportunity to get off the base by sitting around chatting with these guys.

"There's no way they're letting anyone leave," Taylor said. "They need bodies to fight those things."

"I have to at least try," Pete said. "I don't want to fight those things. I got lucky once—it won't happen again. They're nasty creatures."

"I'm with Pete, dude," Billy said to Taylor. "If we can get outta here, we definitely should."

"You've seen it out there," Taylor said. "It's a shit show."

"I'd rather take a shit show out there than be a part of a war on aliens! Fuck, dude!" Billy said, shaking his head. "Plus, this dude obviously has a shotgun. We'll be fine out there."

"Well, I don't have the shotgun anymore," Pete said.

"What? What happened to it?" Billy asked.

"I gave it to the guy who saved me from that thing. He led me out here and said they wouldn't let me in with a gun, so I gave it to him."

"Fuck, dude," Billy said, sitting down on Taylor's bed.

"I still think we're safer here," Taylor said.

"Bullshit we are!" Billy said, standing up. "Fuck it, let's go anyway," he said to Pete.

Pete hadn't expected to take anyone with him, but he did like the idea of having someone with him out there. These two guys were probably a package deal.

"They won't let you leave," Taylor said.

"You're sounding like a broken record and a loser, dude," Billy said to Taylor. "Me and Pete here ain't goin' to stick around to get killed by those things. You should come with us."

"Don't call me a loser!" Taylor said. "I'm trying to be rational here. You think the Air Force is going to let us get killed?"

"Um, yeah, I do. In fact, I think they're counting on guys like us getting killed while they hurl bombs at the ships."

"Look, you guys are welcome to come with me. Honestly I would feel better not being alone out there, but we gotta do this now. There isn't really time to argue about it," Pete said.

"I'm goin' with ya," Billy said. He walked over to his side of the room and picked up his backpack.

"Fuck it. Me too," Taylor said. He decided in that moment he wouldn't stay at the base without Billy. Billy was all he had left; there was no way he was going to get separated from Billy.

"Good, let's do this," Pete said. He was happy to have a couple of other guys with him.

The three of them headed downstairs. The guards at the front door didn't say anything to them or try to stop them from leaving the building. Taylor walked to his car, and Billy followed him. Pete went to the SUV.

"We should take just one vehicle," Billy said. "You know, stick together."

"I ain't leavin' my car here," Taylor said.

Pete didn't want to argue about what vehicle to take, so he just hopped in the back seat of Taylor's car. They pulled away from the dorms and headed to the front gate. Taylor was positive they wouldn't be allowed out of there. When they pulled up to the gate, an armed guard walked up to Taylor's window.

"You guys leaving?" the guard asked.

"Uh, yeah, we'd like to," Taylor said.

"You sure?" the guard asked. "It's not safe out there."

"We know, but we have family we have to get to," Taylor said.

"If you leave, you can't come back," the guard said and motioned to another guard.

"That's fine, sir," Billy piped up from the passenger seat.

The other guard had a camera and took a photo of Taylor's car. Then he walked around the vehicle and took a photo of each of them.

"Last chance, fellas," the first guard said. "Free room and board here."

"Uh, yeah, we're sure," Taylor said.

"Open the gate!" the guard yelled, stepping back from Taylor's car.

"Get us the fuck outta here!" Billy said.

Taylor took off out of the gate. "Where to?" he asked Pete.

"Mount Spokane," Pete replied.

"Mount Spokane it is," Taylor said as he entered the highway. "We're fucked," he said, stomping on the gas.

They rode in silence until they saw a huge craft appear in the sky above them. It was flying just above the tree line. They could hear—and *feel*—a whirring sound. Taylor's car felt like it was vibrating.

"Holy shit, guys!" Billy cried out. "It's them! They're going get us too! Drive faster, dude!"

"I can't outrun that thing!" Taylor exclaimed. "Fuck you guys! I knew we shoulda stayed on that goddamn base! Fuck! Now we're dead!"

"Hey, guys," Pete said in a calm voice. "Look," he added, pointing up. "I don't think that thing gives two fucks about us."

Billy and Taylor looked out the windshield. The large craft did look like it was passing over them.

"Just keep driving, dude!" Billy said as he noticed Taylor had instinctively slowed down to look at the craft above them.

"Shit!" Taylor said and stomped the gas pedal again. "I got distracted."

They heard a series of clicking noises and then huge explosions behind them. They all looked back and saw that the base had been turned into a huge fireball. The energy from the explosion pushed

Taylor's car to the right. He struggled to keep it out of the ditch. The large craft jetted away without a sound. Taylor stopped the car and looked out the back window. All that was left of the base was rubble and fire. No way anyone had survived that.

They all sat in the now stopped car in shock and complete silence for a bit.

"Holy fuck, guys," Billy finally said, very quietly. "Holy fuck."

"Jesus! If we had left fifteen minutes later, we'd fuckin be dead!" Taylor exclaimed. "Pete, you saved our lives, man."

"I didn't do shit. We got lucky, boys," Pete said softly.

All their hearts were pounding.

"It's almost like they waited for us to leave," Billy said, staring out the window at what used to be the base.

"Yeah, right, dude. We just got fuckin lucky," Taylor said. "Again! We got lucky again. How many more times you think that shit will happen?"

"Hopefully a lot," Billy responded.

"Hey, guys, I think we should just keep moving. We're sitting ducks out here," Pete said.

"Pete's right, dude. Let's go," Billy said.

Taylor didn't say anything else; he just put the car back in gear and took off. He watched the burning base slowly disappear as he gunned it east, back toward Spokane.

*****

Mitchell fought to keep the plane steady as they went down. Anthony flipped switches and tried to engage the landing gear, but the landing gear was stuck; none of the controls seemed to be responding. Mitchell flashed back to flying a fighter jet over Afghanistan while he was still in the Airforce. His buddy Noah had been flying ahead of him. A surface to air missile struck Noah's plane, and it exploded in midair. Mitchell watched as the pieces of his friend's plane fell to the desert like flaming hail. A missile hit the tail of his plane and he spun out of control. Mitchell had been able to right the plane and crash land it. Somehow, he survived it and was able to wait out a rescue team. Here he was again, trying to safely land an out-of-control airplane. He did it once before; he would do it again.

As they were plummeting to earth, he saw an abandoned highway. There were cars littered about, but that would have to be good enough. Mitchell righted the descending plane the best he could and crash-landed it on the highway. Cars crumpled into nothing under the weight of the plane. Anthony hit his head hard on the control panel and was knocked out cold. Blood trickled out of a small gash on Anthony's forehead. Mitchell felt dizzy and disoriented from the impact. He hoped everyone in back had had their seatbelts on. He was certain they would have survived if they were indeed buckled in. Within moments of landing, the president came into the cockpit.

"Great landing! Everyone back there is fine. You saved our lives," she said. "Is Anthony okay?" She looked at Anthony passed out over the control panel.

"Thank you, ma'am. I think he will be. I'm pretty sure he just got knocked out," Mitchell said.

"We need to wake him up. We have to find another plane. We must get to that base!" Cecilia said. "Do you know where we are?"

"I'm pretty certain we're just outside of my hometown of Des Moines. I know we flew over Des Moines River," Mitchell said. "That aircraft that shot us down came from the Great Lakes area. I didn't see it until it was too late. I should have been flying lower, ma'am."

"Nothing to stress about now," she said. "We just need to find a way to Washington State—it's our only viable option at this point."

"I agree, ma'am," Mitchell said.

Anthony came to. He looked around the cockpit and started to sit up.

"Are you okay, General?" Cecilia asked.

"Yes, ma'am," Anthony said, rubbing his head. "A bit of a headache, but I'm good to go."

"Great," she said. "Let's get off this plane and find another one, if possible."

Mitchell had been able to land the plane on its belly. The president, Anthony, and the pilots climbed out of the plane and looked around. What they saw looked about the same as what they had seen coming out of the bunker in DC. Wrecked cars, vehicles on fire, bodies littered about. It both broke Cecilia's heart and enraged her. It was just remarkable how quickly society had crumbled. How quickly people had turned on each other. It was a disgrace.

"Pilot, what's your name?" President Rodgers asked Mitchell.

"Mitchell Madsen, ma'am," he said.

"Mr. Madsen, do you know where the closest airport is?" she asked him.

"Yes, ma'am. I think it's about twelve or fifteen miles that way," he said, pointing southeast. "Ma'am, the Air National Guard is located at Des Moines Airport."

"Oh, that's great news! I hope they are operational," she said, clearly excited.

"If the airport is still there, the Guard will be too, ma'am."

"Men, we have headlights coming toward us," Cecilia said, looking down the highway. "Be on your guard for anything."

The president took a pistol out of her belt. Anthony grabbed his pistol out of the holster on his belt. The car was slowing down as it got closer. Anthony stepped forward and raised his pistol. He yelled at them to stop the car and get out. The car stopped several yards away. Two men slowly exited the car with their hands up.

"We mean no harm," the driver shouted. "Just tryin' to get my friend here to the hospital."

"Slowly approach us. Keep your hands up," Anthony shouted back.

The men slowly approached with their hands up. The passenger had a bad limp; he looked to be in great pain. They got to Anthony and stopped.

"Oh, shit, John, that's the president!" the driver said.

"She sure is," Anthony said. "Who are you guys? What are you doing out here?"

"I'm Dylan, and this is John. I was trying to get him to the hospital in West Des Moines. He's badly injured, and his family is supposed to be there waiting for him."

"You guys armed?" Anthony asked.

"No, sir," Dylan lied. He didn't know why he lied about having guns, but he didn't quite trust that guy.

"You guys from 'round here?" Anthony asked.

"I am, sir," Dylan replied.

"I'm from Hastings, Nebraska," John said.

"You know the area well?" Anthony asked Dylan.

"Pretty well, sir. Been here a long, long time."

"So you know where the airport is?"

"Yeah, it's not too far away, actually," Dylan said.

"If we find a vehicle you can get us there?" Anthony asked.

"I could, but I need to get this guy to the hospital," Dylan said.

"Let me rephrase that. If we find a vehicle, you *will* get us to that airport."

"No offense, sir, but this man is badly hurt, and his family is waiting on him. I would gladly point you to the airport, but we need to get to that hospital."

"General," Cecilia said, walking up to him, "we have another vehicle approaching."

The vehicle slowly creeped up to them.

"These guys are clean, ma'am," Anthony said, raising his pistol to the other vehicle. "Stop!" he yelled, putting up his left hand and pointing the pistol at the car with the other.

The vehicle screeched to a stop.

"Get out of the car, hands up!" he yelled, inching toward it.

A woman and a teenage girl slowly got out of the car.

"Scarlett?" Dylan yelled.

"Quiet!" Anthony shouted at Dylan. "Walk slowly over to me," he commanded the woman and girl. "You armed?" he asked.

"No, sir," Scarlett said. "But I do have a pistol in the glove box."

"Holy shit, it is you!" Dylan said. "What are you doing here? Where's Gwen?"

"I'm going to need you to be quiet for now," Anthony said to Dylan. "Who are you and where are you headed?" Anthony said, checking out her SUV.

"I'm Scarlett, and this is Hope. We saw the plane go down and assumed someone important had to be on it. You have no idea what we've just been through."

"I think we do, ma'am," Anthony said. "Can you get us to the airport?"

"Can you help us find those things? They got my daughter."

"Wait? What things? What happened to Gwen?" Dylan asked.

"Don't you know what's going on by now, Dylan?" Scarlett asked.

"You two know each other I'm assuming," Anthony said.

"She's my ex-wife. We have a daughter together. Who's apparently missing," Dylan said, looking accusingly back at Scarlett. "What's going on, Scar?"

"Do not call me that!" Scarlett said. "You lost the right to call me that years ago."

"Okay, you two, we don't have time for you to get into any of this," Anthony said. "We have got to get the president and these men to the airport, stat."

"I just want to know what happened to my daughter," Dylan said.

"So now you care about her?" Scarlett said bitterly.

"You poisoned her! Turned her against me."

"Goddammit!" Cecilia shouted. "This is not the time to squabble over your pasts. I can offer safety for anyone who can get us to the airport."

"I can get you there, Madam President," Scarlett said.

"General, find another vehicle and follow us. We can get two pilots in her car and the rest with you," Cecilia said.

"I'm not going to leave you, ma'am," Anthony said.

"Yes, General, you are. I am armed. This woman has a firearm. We will be fine. Just stay close."

"I want to go with you, Scarlett. I want to find Gwen," Dylan said.

"What about the hospital?" John asked Dylan.

"I'm sorry, John, my daughter's missing. I need to help find her. You can have my car. Just take 28 right there," he said, pointing to the onramp he had been ready to take when they were stopped by Anthony. "Keep north—you can't miss it. We are so very close already. I am sorry."

John didn't hesitate; he hopped into the Porsche. He was upset with Dylan, but deep down he understood. He'd probably be safer with the group, but he had to find his family. It was clear Dylan and his ex didn't get along well, but John was hopeful that they would come together to find their daughter. All that mattered at a time like what they found themselves now surviving was family. That was why he would find his family or die trying.

The group watched as the Porsche's taillights faded down the empty freeway. They all hoped John would find his family. President Rodgers, Hope, Dylan, and one of the pilots got into Scarlett's car with her. Anthony, Mitchell, and the other pilots found a large SUV. It was pretty smashed up but still ran well. Scarlett pulled away and headed in the direction she had come from. Anthony followed her. Scarlett knew exactly how to find the airport from there; she just hoped the roads would be clear enough for them to get through. Snow began to fall. Just what they needed—another obstacle hindering them from getting to their destination.

No one spoke. They all drove toward the airport in silence. The president, the pilot, and Dylan kept their eyes out on their surroundings while Scarlett focused on the road conditions. The snow was coming down hard and was starting to cover the road. Scarlett put both hands on the wheel and slowed down a bit. One way or another, she would get them to that airport.

None of them had thought to check the skies. A large, silent aircraft hovered just behind them.

*****

John made it to the hospital easily; they had been very close. His stress and anxiety plummeted as he parked the car. He got out and limped to the main entrance. There was an armed guard blocking the automatic door.

"The hospital is on lockdown," the guard said.

"I was injured in a bad car wreck. I was being transported here by ambulance when we were attacked. The paramedics were killed. My family is supposed to be here waiting for me to arrive. Please, I need to get inside."

"What's your name?" the guard asked, grabbing a stack of papers off a table next to him.

"John Henderson," John replied, looking past the guard into the hospital. He could see people milling around inside.

"Where are you from?" the guard asked.

"Hastings, Nebraska."

"You're on the list," the guard said. He turned to the door and flipped a switch above the slider. The doors opened, and the guard stepped aside to let John in.

"Thank you," John said, a little surprised, as he limped by the guard.

"Good luck to you," the guard said. The doors closed behind John.

John made his way through the main entrance. He found his way to the lobby. There were at least fifty people, if not more, in the lobby. Despite the number of people in the room, it was dead quiet. Every seat in the room was occupied, and the rest of the room was crowded with people standing. It was odd to walk into a room full of people who were not distracted by magazines or their phones. No one was talking; they were just staring at the walls. John could feel the nervous energy in the room.

John scanned the room. He didn't see Serena and the boys. Had they even made it to the hospital? Were they asked to leave when he didn't arrive earlier? John left the waiting room and hobbled to the information desk. There was a middle-aged woman at the desk.

"Excuse me?" John said.

"Yes, sir?" she asked.

"I was on my way here by ambulance from Hastings, Nebraska. My family was supposed to meet me here. I didn't see them in the waiting room."

"Are you sure they made it?" she asked. "Seems like it's pretty crazy out there."

"I don't know if they did. I was just wondering if there was anywhere else they could be waiting."

"If you were being transported by ambulance, they were probably going to bring you into the emergency department. If your family is here, they may be waiting in the ER for you."

"Where is that?" John asked. His heart was racing, and he could feel sweat trickle down his forehead. He felt so lightheaded.

"Go down that hall over there. Go to the end of the hall and then go right. That'll take you to the ER."

"Thank you," John said and headed off down the hall she had pointed to.

"Good luck to you," she said as he walked off.

He found it a little odd that the last thing she said to him was exactly what the guard had said to him. Maybe they were just trained to say that? Maybe it's just the polite thing to say without being too personal? Or maybe they knew more than they could or would say? John pushed it out of his mind and made his way to the ER. He walked into the waiting area in the ER—and there were Serena and the boys. John fell to his knees as they rushed over to him. He burst into tears as Serena embraced him. The boys huddled close to their father and cried.

"I can't believe I made it," John sobbed. "I never gave up trying, but for a moment, I thought I might not make it. Baby, it's so crazy out there."

"I know it, babe," Serena said, squeezing her husband tight. "The things I saw on my way here were terrifying. I made the boys ride laying down under a blanket."

"Come here boys," John said, pulling away from Serena for a moment. He held his sons tight. "We're going to be okay now," he told them. They both nodded against his shoulders.

John released the boys. He couldn't hold up his own body weight anymore and slumped to the floor. The room was spinning. He could feel bile in his throat. John looked up at Serena; she was looking around the room and shouting "Help!"

"You're going to be okay, John," was the last thing he heard his wife say.

*****

Scarlett was struggling to see through the increasing snowfall. Her wipers were on full speed and barely kept the windshield clear. She had slowed down to a crawl. They were still miles from the airport. Scarlett could hear Hope crying in the backseat. Dylan was doing his best to comfort Hope, but he had never been any good at comforting anybody. The president seemed so calm and in control; it was pretty amazing to Scarlett. She couldn't believe she was sitting in her car next to the first woman president of the United States. Scarlett had voted for Cecilia and was beyond excited that she had won and won by a lot. It had made her feel validated as a woman in corporate America. To see such a strong, confident woman fight and claw her way through the male-dominated world of politics had been inspiring. It made all her struggles with the "good ol' boy," white-collar world worthwhile. It had given her the courage to go for that VP position, the VP position that she would now probably never get a chance at. Under different circumstances, she would have been picking the president's brain, asking a million questions, but she knew she had to concentrate on getting them to the airport safely. That was not the time or place to be chatting up the president. It was just an honor to have met her, regardless of the timing. Maybe someday, if they made it through all this alive, she could have a nice conversation with Madam President Cecilia Rodgers.

Hope sat in the backseat between Dylan and another man. The other man had introduced himself to everyone in the car as Captain Rick Peterson. He seemed like a nice guy. Hope had been fighting back tears since they left her house. Once the snow started to fly and the roads got worse, she couldn't hold them back any longer. Dylan had tried to put an arm around her to comfort her, but she shook him off. She hated Dylan, absolutely hated her best friend's dad. He had always been such an asshole to Scarlett and Gwen. Scarlett had always shown Hope the same love and respect that her own mother had shown her. Seeing her second mom and her best friend treated so unfairly and badly had made her grow to despise the man. Just sitting next to him made her skin crawl.

Hope heard a *whirring* sound. The sound seemed to be coming from inside her head. Her head fell backward and rested on the back of the seat. She couldn't move, she couldn't see, and she was having a very hard time breathing. All she could smell, or taste, was sulfur.

"Tell them not to go to the airport," It sounded like Gwen talking to her but inside her head. It was hard to hear or understand over the *whirring* sound.

What? Gwen? she thought. She still couldn't move.

"Yes, Gwen. That is me," the voice said.

"How?" Hope asked in her mind.

"Not important. Don't go to the airport," the voice said.

Why? Hope thought.

"Dangerous," the voice said. It really sounded like Gwen's voice, but it sounded like she was talking through an industrial fan or something. It was so distant and mechanical sounding, like a really bad recording.

"I don't understand. How are you talking to me right now, Gwen?" Her head was pounding.

"Not important!" the voice shouted. *"Do not go to that airport!"*

The *whirring* stopped, and Hope regained control of her body. Her head was still pounding, and her heart was racing. Dylan was gently shaking her and asking if she was okay.

"What happened, dear?" Scarlett asked from the front seat. "Are you okay?"

"I don't know," Hope said, slightly out of it. "I heard a weird noise and I think I passed out."

"You were definitely out," Dylan said. "Probably just all the stress of the day," he said, settling back into his seat.

The snowy skies lit up in a bright blue light. Scarlett couldn't see anything and lost control of the vehicle for a split second. She instinctively slowed down.

"Don't stop!" the president commanded. "No matter what, do not stop this car."

The car Anthony and the other pilots were in exploded and the blue light disappeared. Pieces of the other SUV hit the back of Scarlett's. The debris hit so hard; one piece shattered the back window. Cold, heavy, sulfur-smelling air filled the SUV.

"Don't stop!" the president shouted. "We have to get to that airport."

"Gwen told me we shouldn't go to the airport," Hope said timidly.

"What?" Scarlett asked, twisting around in her seat to look at Hope.

"Eyes on the road," Cecilia said. "Who is Gwen again?" she asked Hope.

"My best friend," the girl shyly responded. "She's their daughter." She pointed at Scarlett and Dylan.

"How and when did she tell you that?" the president asked.

"Just now when I passed out. I thought it was a dream. I heard it in my head, like an echo."

Cecilia looked at Scarlett and then back to Hope. Hope's eyes were huge and filled with fear. Scarlett had absentmindedly slowed way down. She was barely going fifteen miles per hour.

"Speed up, please," the president said to Scarlett. "I sincerely doubt that was your friend," she said to Hope. "Those things use mind-speak on us. One spoke to me that way." Hope looked even more confused. "I know it sounds impossible and, frankly, fucking ridiculous, but it's a fact now. I don't give two shits what they said to you. We are getting to that goddamn airport!" The car fell silent for a bit. Hope began crying again. "Look, dear," Cecilia said to Hope, "I'm sure they made themselves sound like your friend, so you'd listen and try to make us do what they said. The fact that they don't want us to go to the airport is a good reason to get there as quickly as possible. Those things have killed way too many people now. They just killed my general and several fantastic pilots, and I am furious! I will not stand down and cower to those ugly fucking things! I will get every able body into a fighter jet and we will wage holy war on them!" She looked at Scarlett. "The only way we aren't making it to that airport is if those things blow us up too! Get us there!"

The car fell silent again for a while. They had traveled about another mile by the time Dylan spoke up.

"Okay, what is actually going on out there? I mean what things are you talking about? What blew up the other car? Who the fuck has Gwen?" he asked the car.

"You really don't know?" Scarlett asked, glancing at him in the review mirror. The sight of him angered her so very much. She had been content to live the rest of her life never having to interact with him again.

"No, I don't know anything about any of this! Last I heard, meteors hit earth and caused blackouts and destruction all over the place. I heard Des Moines was getting looted and people were killing each other for food and fucking toilet paper, so I got the hell out of there. I was headed west to my lake place to ride it all out when I ran into John. You couldn't imagine what people had done to the ambulance drivers. It looked like a warzone—dead bodies slashed up everywhere. People are nuts now."

"People didn't do that," Cecilia said. "They did." She pointed to the sky.

"They? What they?" he asked.

"Oh my fuckin' god, Dylan!" Scarlett blurted out. "Jesus, you need us to spell it out on a piece of paper with crayons? Fuckin' aliens, you idiot! Aliens attacked Earth, and they took Gwen!"

Dylan stared at her in anger and confusion. The car had fallen silent again after Scarlett's outburst.

"Seriously? Fucking aliens?" he finally said, shaking his head.

"Yea, Dylan, fucking aliens," Scarlett said. "What did you think that bright blue light was? What did you think blew up the other car?"

"I don't know. Maybe another country attacking us?"

"Another country singling out one random SUV just outside of Des Moines, Iowa?" Scarlett said condescendingly.

"I don't fucking know," he said. "I never thought to consider aliens, I'll tell you that. Aliens don't exist."

"They sure do!" Scarlett said. "Hope and I stood face to face with one! I watched as a pulsing red light took our daughter. Everyone in this fuckin' car has seen them!"

"That's enough!" President Rodgers yelled. "I am the president of the United States, and I am officially telling you, sir, this is an alien invasion. It sounds incredible. It sounds made up, but I assure you, it is a fact. Now I want you two to stop bickering. It is of no help to this mission, and it's frankly annoying as hell. Whether you two like it or not, we are all in this together. If this immature bullshit doesn't stop now, I'm not taking you two with me. Think outside of yourselves. Get over yourselves."

The car was awkwardly silent for the rest of the ride to the airport. Dylan stared out his window like a scolded child. Scarlett kept her eyes on the road. She felt so embarrassed that she had let her feelings for Dylan overtake her and make her act out at him. Being talked to like that by the president had really hurt. She respected President Rodgers so much and now felt as though she had let Cecilia down. It was all so childish, and she felt like a punished teenager.

The roads were getting worse, and it was beginning to feel like they'd never make it to that damn airport, but they finally did. The airport was dark and looked to be empty—no cars in the parking lot, no sight of anyone. They could see lights behind the airport on the tarmac. Maybe the Air National Guard? They had to find a way back there. President Rodgers told Scarlett to drive around; there had to be an access gate somewhere. They finally found a gate, but it was chained shut.

"Ram it!" Cecilia said. "We have to get back there!"

Scarlett gunned the SUV and slammed into the gate. The chain held, and they came to a violent stop, jarring everyone inside.

"Push the gate open as far as you can with the car!" Cecilia said. "We'll walk the rest of the way."

Scarlett pushed the gate open as far as she could with the car. It was just enough for them all to slide through. The sky lit up with the bright white light.

"Scatter!" Cecilia yelled.

Everyone except for Dylan took off running. Scarlett looked back at Dylan as she ran away. One of those ugly creatures appeared in front of Dylan. It turned its head and looked at Scarlett. The creature smiled at her as it reached out and grabbed Dylan. Scarlett stopped and stared. The creature maintained eye contact with her as it ripped Dylan's head off his body in one fluid motion. Blood gushed out of his neck as the creature released his body and it fell to the snowy ground. Scarlett had grown to downright hate Dylan over the years, but watching him die like that broke her heart. She may not have cared for him, but she never wished him dead. Scarlett screamed and took off running. The creature turned and chased after her. A fighter jet took off from the back side of the tarmac.

"Get down!" someone yelled as machine gun fire broke out.

Scarlett dropped to the snowy pavement and looked behind her. The creature had stopped chasing her and was running the opposite direction. It fell to the ground as bullets ripped through its flesh. Green ooze exploded from its brown, leathery body. The creature screamed. Another jet took off in a plume of smoke. Half a dozen other jets took off shortly after the first two. Scarlett got to her feet and found the president and Captain Peterson. She looked around for Hope and saw the girl hiding under a truck. Scarlett yelled to Hope to come join them.

The jets moved so fast and so low the ground shook. They flanked the large ship in the sky and simultaneously fired missiles at it. The missiles exploded into the aircraft. The bright white light blinked out. The jets retreated into the clouds. The large aircraft drifted slowly overhead and crash-landed into the fields west of the airport. The impact knocked the group off their feet. They heard the roar of the jets overhead as they dipped out of the cloud cover and flew over the crash site. The jets circled around, and all came in for a landing. A large truck full of armed service men drove past Cecilia and the others. The truck left the airport, probably on its way to check out the wrecked aircraft. The pilots exited their planes and walked toward the group.

"You all all right?" one pilot said as he neared. "Oh, Madam President." He stopped hard and said with a salute. The other pilots stopped and saluted as well. Cecilia gave them all a salute, and the rest of the pilots continued past the group on their way to a building just behind where they were all standing. "I am Sergeant Teddy Williams, ma'am," the pilot said. "We are mostly operational here. Please let us know if we can be of any service to you."

"Sergeant," Cecilia began, "we were on our way by plane to an Air Force base in Eastern Washington when our plane was shot down. The base is staffed and operational. I did not realize there was anything else operational out here."

"We are short-staffed, ma'am, but we are doing whatever we can with what we have. Why don't you all follow me inside?" Sargent Williams said, motioning to the building the other pilots had gone into.

They all followed the sergeant into the building. They could hear multiple generators running at full tilt. The smell of gasoline hung heavy in the cold, snowy air.

"We lost power shortly after the initial attacks," Sergeant Williams said, leading them into a kitchen area. He poured coffee for everyone and invited them to sit down at a table. In the excitement and pandemonium of everything that had just gone down, they didn't realize how cold they were until they got into the warm building and got some hot coffee into their bellies. "The brass at the airport evacuated everyone to the nearby stadium, where they have backup generators. The arena was set up for a concert that night, so they had all the food courts going. People are safe and have their basic needs met there. We have been monitoring the skies best we can without GPS and satellites. We've just been waiting for them to come back. Glad we got one."

"Me too, Sergeant," Cecilia said. "Have you heard chatter from anywhere else?"

"No, ma'am," he said. "As far as we can tell, we're alone out here."

"Have you considered any scouting missions? Getting a couple birds in the sky to see if there's any more bases operational out there?" Cecilia asked, sipping her coffee. The coffee was quite bitter, but the warmth of it was wonderful.

"Yes, ma'am, we did do that. The planes never came back. We're assuming they were shot down. We can't track 'em, we can't talk to 'em, all we can do is assume they're gone. In light of that, we decided we would stay grounded until they came into our airspace. That way, we could launch a mission close to home."

"I'm sorry about your men, Sergeant," Cecilia said.

"Thank you, ma'am. It is part of war but never easy."

"Never will be easy. We have all lost so much already. Unfortunately, we don't have time to mourn our losses at this moment. When we all get through this—and we *will* get through it—we can mourn our fallen."

"Yes, ma'am. I've done three tours in the Middle East. I've lost a lot of brothers, and you learn quickly to put emotions aside and carry out your orders. As you said, there will be time to mourn our fallen brothers and sisters afterward." Sergeant Williams got up and refilled his mug of coffee.

"Sergeant, what are the plans from here on out?" Cecilia asked.

"Keep doing what we've been doing. Our base commander is MIA, so that puts me in charge, and I've made the call that we stay put and protect the skies over Des Moines. I can't risk any more lives by sending planes any further."

"Can you give us a plane? I still need to get to that base. They are awaiting my arrival before they move forward with any counterattack."

"Yes, ma'am, we sure can. Do you need a pilot?" he asked.

"Captain, you can fly any bird, correct?" Cecilia asked Rick.

"Yes, ma'am! I was in the Air Force for eight years, specialized in flying bombers, but flew them all at one time or another. If it's got wings, I can fly it," Rick responded excitedly.

"Great!" she responded. "Sergeant, if we could get a plane stat we'll be on our way. Keep up the good work here."

"Yes, ma'am. We have a C-17 that's fueled up and ready for flight."

"Fantastic. Let's get in the air," she said.

President Rodgers didn't have any reservations about getting back into the air. She knew that they would be useless anywhere but that base in Washington State. From what Anthony had gathered from the base, they were fully capable of launching a full-scale counterattack. She did miss Anthony; he was a good man and had always been her top military advisor. He had been damn good at his job. But no time to miss him now; there was work to be done. She hoped if those things saw another military plane in the air, they'd stay back after what had just happened. She hoped but didn't expect that to be the case.

Captain Peterson got behind the controls of the C-17. Cecilia, Scarlett, and Hope strapped into the back. Sergeant Williams had given them some weapons and rations.

"These MREs aren't very good, but they'll fill your bellies," he said as he loaded a box of them onto the plane.

Captain Peterson lined up on the runway facing west. He put the plane in motion, and they were off. Rick kept the plane low and fast. He was bound and determined to make what is normally about a three-hour flight to take about half as long. He had flown these planes many times and knew them well. Rick took it on himself personally to protect the president at all costs, including his own life.

CHAPTER 9

The Meeting

Pete sat in the back seat listening to Taylor and Billy bicker about their situation. It was annoying Pete quite a bit, but at the same time, he could tell these two guys genuinely cared for each other. In a weird, happy old married couple sort of way, the arguing was kind of adorable. Like when Grandma and Grandpa bicker back and forth about something, they're irritated with each other, but you can still see and feel the love. Pete and his friends would argue sometimes, but it was never that heated, never that important to any of them. He missed his friends, and he hoped they were all safe.

"What are you doing?" Billy asked Taylor as he turned north. "Are you taking the one way?"

"Yeah, man, it's the fastest way north," Taylor responded.

"True, until you hit Country Homes, if there's one wrecked or abandoned car on Country Homes, we're fucked. Take Monroe."

"Monroe's one lane each way too!"

"Yeah, but it doesn't have that goddamn drainage swale running down the middle of it. We could still get through on Monroe even if there are wrecks and shit," Billy said, shaking his head.

"I'm going my way, Billy," Taylor said.

"It's always your way! We always do what the almighty Taylor says we're gonna do!"

"Guys, just take Division," Pete said from the back seat. "I followed that dude from the northside down Division and it was in pretty good shape."

"Okay, that'll work," Taylor said, glancing at Pete in the rearview mirror.

"Oh, you'll listen to him but not me? Real nice. Thought we were friends, dude," Billy said, rolling his eyes.

"Knock it off, man! Jesus, you've been such a little bitch! I'm taking his advice because he was just there and knows what the road is like."

"Don't call me a bitch!" Billy demanded. "Am I stressed out? Hell fuckin' yeah I am! Am I being vocal about it? Yeah, I am. I'll even admit I'm bitching about it, but don't you ever call me a bitch again. I ain't no bitch!" Billy crossed his arms and stared out the passenger window.

The car went silent. Taylor had taken the next cross street east to Division. He turned north onto Division. One of the busiest streets in town was dead. No traffic whatsoever. It was so strange and eerie.

"I'm sorry, man," Taylor said to Billy after a while.

"It's cool, dude," Billy said, looking over at Taylor. "Shit's nuts out here now, stress levels are high, words have been exchanged. I'm cool if you are."

"Thanks, dude. I'm cool," he said and put his fist out to Billy for a pound. Billy fist-bumped Taylor.

"You guys crack me up," Pete said, chuckling in the back seat.

"How so?" Billy asked, turning to look at Pete.

"Just the shit you say to each other. The way you fight and then you're besties two minutes later." He was starting to really like these guys.

"A, don't say 'besties,' and B, that's how bros work. You argue and you get over it. We ain't chicks, we don't hold on to shit forever," Billy said.

A police car pulled up behind them and turned on its lights.

"Shit, man, the cops!" Taylor said. "I wasn't speeding or anything."

"Dude, that ain't the cops!" Billy said. "Don't pull over."

"I have to! I don't want to get arrested for running from the cops."

"Dude, I'm telling ya, there's no way that's an actual cop. Someone probably stole a cop car and they're tryin' to jack us or sumthin'," Billy said, turning to look out the back window. Pete had turned around and was looking out the back window too.

"You don't believe a naked chick would be part of a plot to jack people, but you're gonna sit there and swear that's not a real cop back there?" Taylor asked.

"Guys, I don't think it's an actual cop," Pete said, turning back around. "Looks like there's at least three people in that cop car and none of them seem to be in uniform. I think Billy's right. Don't pull over, Taylor."

"Yeah, dude, don't pull over. Worst case scenario we get arrested and go to jail where it's probably warm and they'll feed us," Billy said. "Run, dude."

Taylor stomped the gas pedal. The cop car sped up behind him.

"Dude, we gotta lose 'em! We can't have them follow us to Pete's house!" Billy said.

"I'm tryin', man! It's just pretty damn hard to outrun someone with all this wreckage out here."

"Get off Division!" Pete said. "I know this area pretty well. I bet we can lose 'em on the side streets."

Taylor took a sudden right and sped down the side road. The cop car followed but had fallen behind a bit. Taylor was watching the police car in the rearview mirror when Billy yelled, "Look out!" Taylor snapped his attention to the front and slammed on the brakes. There was a young boy, probably about twelve years old, walking down the middle of the street. Taylor yanked the wheel and barely avoided hitting the child. The cop car stopped abruptly and turned around. The lights on the police car went off, and it sped away back toward Division. The boy walked past Taylor's car without even looking at it. The boy seemed to be completely unaffected by what had just happened. He seemed to be in some sort of trance. His posture was very stiff and mechanical.

"Dude, what the fuck?" Billy said, looking over at Taylor.

Taylor was shaking. He didn't say anything to Billy or Pete; he just opened his car door and stepped out.

"Hey, kid!" Taylor shouted at the kid. The boy just kept walking; he didn't even seem to acknowledge Taylor.

The dark, cloudy sky lit up in a bright, blinding white light.

"Fuck!" Billy yelled from the car. "Taylor! Get back in the car! Get us out of here!"

Taylor didn't respond. His body got rigid, and he began following the boy. Taylor's posture matched the boy's. They both slowly and methodically walked west. Their movements looked very robotic. Billy leaned over and honked the car horn, hoping to startle Taylor back to reality. It didn't work at all.

Several blue beams of light came down from the sky. The beams stayed steady for about a minute and quickly blinked out. Standing where the blue beams of light had been were those creatures. Four of them. The creatures looked at Billy and Pete sitting in the car. They smiled at Billy and Pete then turned their attention to Taylor and the boy. Billy froze in his seat. Pete climbed into the driver's seat and slammed the door shut. He threw the car into drive and took off. Pete went down to the end of the block and turned around.

"Get in the back seat!" he said to Billy. "When I pull up next to Taylor, grab him and pull him into the car!"

Billy didn't say anything or move. Pete reached over and slapped Billy's face. Billy shook his head and blinked his eyes.

"Get in the back seat and grab Taylor!" Pete shouted.

"What?" Billy asked, dazed and very confused.

Pete had stopped the car. The creatures were just ahead of them, keeping pace with Taylor and the boy but staying back.

"Goddammit, Billy! Climb in the back seat. When I pull up next to Taylor, grab him and pull him into the car!" Pete said slowly and deliberately.

"Oh, okay," Billy said, climbing into the back seat.

Pete slowly drove past the creatures; they paid no attention to the car. They were focused on Taylor and the boy. Pete pulled up next to Taylor, and Billy opened the back door. He reached out to grab Taylor. Before Billy could even get a hand on Taylor, a long, bony, clawed hand grabbed his arm. The strength that hand had was unimaginable. It pulled Billy out of the car. Pete stopped the car and jumped out. One of the creatures was standing over a trembling Billy. The creature looked at Pete and raised its leg. It stomped on Billy's chest. Pete heard Billy's ribs break and the air escape his chest. Billy coughed and groaned on the cold pavement. The creature stepped over Billy and walked away, still staring at Pete. It fell in line behind the other creatures, who were still following Taylor and the boy. Pete knelt next to Billy.

"You ok, Man?" he asked Billy, who had tears in his eyes and was gasping for air.

"No," Billy muttered. "Fuckin' thing broke my ribs." He gasped.

"Can you get up?" Pete asked. "We gotta get out of here."

Billy groaned and rolled to his side. "I need help," he said.

Pete hooked his arm under Billy's and gently pulled him to his knees. Billy grimaced and moaned in utter pain. Pete helped Billy climb into the back seat. Billy laid across the seat, clutching at his chest. Billy had caught his breath, but his ribs were killing him. Pete hopped in the driver's side and pulled away.

"Follow them," Billy groaned from the back seat.

"What? Are you crazy? We gotta get out of here!" Pete said, glancing at Billy in the back seat.

"Fuck that, dude! We can't leave Taylor with those things."

"I think we have to. They got him under some kind of control. We need to get as far away from those things as possible," Pete said. He had stopped the car again and had turned around in his seat to talk to Billy.

"Dude, they clearly don't care about us." Billy grimaced. "If they did, we'd be dead."

"Look what that thing did to you!"

"Yeah, think about that. It could've ripped my guts out in a second then tore you to shreds." Billy was breathing heavy again. "I think it punished me for trying to grab Taylor. Dude, just follow them. We're at least somewhat safe inside this car. If shit goes bad, then we'll run."

Pete looked at Billy for a minute. Billy had tears in his eyes and was sweating like crazy. Billy's large stomach was hitching with every labored breath. Pete didn't like the idea of following those things, but he felt for Billy. Pete knew if that was his best friend, he'd probably want to follow them too. He thought about Amanda. What if that was Amanda up ahead instead of a man he had just met? He hadn't been able to save Amanda, but they did have a very slight chance to possibly save Taylor. Pete let out a big sigh and put the car in drive. Staying back about a hundred feet or so, he slowly followed Taylor and the creatures. The bright white light was steady above them. That light seemed to be guiding the way. The young boy kept looking up at the sky.

The group, followed by Pete and Billy in Taylor's car, had made their way back to Division Street. The light from above pointed north, and everyone followed it. Maybe that light was controlling the boy and Taylor? Pete didn't know anything for sure and frankly didn't care about all of that in that moment. He kept his head on a swivel; the last thing he wanted was more creatures to show up. Billy's breathing seemed to have gone back normal.

They were about a block from the shopping mall when the bright light vanished. Pete swore he heard an aircraft zoom overhead. The boy, Taylor, and the creatures walked into the mall's parking garage. Pete slammed on the brakes when he saw what was in that garage. There was a very large group of zombie-like people and even more creatures flanking them. The people moved around like stiff cyborgs. Their movement really did remind Pete of slow zombies. The creatures milled about around the group. They looked like they were interacting with each other. The boy and Taylor cut through the perimeter of creatures and joined the mass of other people.

Pete looked back at Billy; he was passed out cold. Billy's breathing seemed labored and spasmodic. Pete feared that Billy may have a punctured lung. If that was the case, Billy wouldn't live much longer. Pete decided he was going to take Billy to the hospital that was just a couple of blocks north of the mall. Maybe they'd still be open and operational. He had to at least try.

Pete pulled into the ER parking lot and quickly got out of the car. He stopped dead in his tracks and stared up at the dark sky. A large military plane was flying overhead, followed closely by several small flying discs. The discs were flanking the plane as if they were guiding it in one direction. The military plane was so low its ear-shattering engine noise shook the pavement. Behind the military plane and the flying discs was the biggest aircraft he had ever seen in his life. It was easily ten times the size of any plane he had ever seen. It didn't even look like a plane or a flying saucer. The aircraft looked fake, almost like someone had drawn it. Pete couldn't tell if it was even moving; it just seemed to kind of hang in midair. It blocked out the entire sky above his head.

People from inside the ER started to come out the doors and look at the sky. Every one of them stopped dead in their tracks and gaped up at the aircraft. Mouths open and eyes wide, they all just stared. The aircraft descended toward the hospital, causing everyone to run back inside. Pete stood there watching the aircraft. Several amber and yellow lights blinked around the bottom of it. There was a large metal-looking circle in the middle of the craft. It opened slowly, and a pulsing red beam of light engulfed Pete. That same damn light that had gotten Amanda! Pete felt warmth and electricity surround his shaking body. His head pounded and his heart raced. Pete's eyes got heavy, and he passed out.

*****

Malcolm and Bethany had finally made it through Idaho and most of the southern corner of Washington. The trip had been uneventful but brutal. The roads were empty and, with the exception of a few abandoned or wrecked cars, clear. They had just passed the small town of Ritzville. By Malcolm's estimation, they were about an hour from the base. He was beyond exhausted at that point. All he wanted to do was sleep. Everything was dark and very ominous. That stretch of freeway was deserted, so he was able to just fly down the road. He was so happy his truck wasn't governed to a certain speed.

He couldn't have imagined having to take that trip at sixty-five miles an hour the whole way.

Bethany had slept most of the trip. Malcolm wished she had known how to drive a big rig so he could have gotten some rest, but he was glad she had the opportunity to sleep. He was just anxious to get them to that base. Malcolm didn't know what to expect once they did get there, but he hoped for at least a bed. He hoped they had showers there too; he needed a shower as badly as he needed sleep. The CB radio had been dead quiet since they left the Vegas area. He figured no news was good news. Bethany was awake and nervously looking out the windows. Malcolm could tell she was ready to get out of the truck too. They had been cooped up in that rig for what had felt like days at that point. Even though she had gotten a decent amount of sleep on the way, Malcolm could tell she was still very tired. They were both starving and dangerously low on water. They both reeked of cigarette smoke and sweat. Malcolm kept daydreaming about a hot shower and food in his belly. That burger and fries at the truck stop had been a long time ago. With all the excitement of those creatures in Vegas, he didn't even remember to grab any food from the supplies he and those girls had taken from the casino. He felt sick from hunger and exhaustion. But they were so close. He hoped they would be safe and healthy soon.

"We're close," Malcolm said to Bethany.

"Oh good!" she replied. "You need some sleep."

"Yes, I do," he chuckled. "That was by far the longest I've ever driven without a break."

"You're a rock star, Malcolm!" she said, smiling at him. "I so appreciate you driving us up here. I don't think we would have survived long in Vegas."

"No worries," he said, smiling back at her. "I don't think we would have either." He paused and looked over at her. "I am really glad we found each other."

"Oh, me too!" she exclaimed. She was staring at him with a look of total admiration.

"Holy shit! What the hell is that?" Malcolm yelled, stomping on the brakes.

The freeway was blocked up ahead by what looked like a flying saucer. The machine was dark and just sitting in the middle of the freeway. Malcolm came to a stop. There was nowhere to go, absolutely no way around that thing. Malcolm and Bethany just stared at it.

"What do we do now?" Bethany asked.

"I don't know. Turn around and get off at that little town back there, I guess."

Malcolm backed up and turned the truck around. The disc came to life and jetted up into the sky, hovering just over the truck. Malcolm stomped on the gas pedal, grinding gears. The flying saucer kept pace with him. He took the Ritzville exit and circled around to get back onto the freeway eastbound again. The flying saucer hovered right overhead no matter how fast Malcolm got that truck going. The truck buzzed. Yellow, blue, and red lights lit up the sky above the truck. The lights were dizzying.

The truck began to slow down. Malcolm had the gas pedal to the floor, but it wasn't responding. The truck stopped responding to anything Malcolm did. The truck had slowed down to about forty miles an hour. It cruised at that speed on its own. Malcolm tried to set the brakes, nothing. He tried pulling the steering wheel back and forth, nothing. Something else was controlling the truck. Three more flying saucers appeared above them. Bethany began to cry.

"I'm scared," she sobbed.

"Me too, baby," Malcolm said, taking her trembling hand.

"You think we're going to die?" she asked, squeezing his hand.

"I don't know. You'd think if they wanted us dead, they would've done it right away."

God, those lights were intense. It seemed as though they were getting brighter and brighter. So bright, they couldn't see anything outside of the truck. They both felt dizzy and nauseous. Malcolm climbed over to the passenger seat and slid under Bethany. He held her tight on his lap. She trembled in his arms. The lights just kept intensifying. Bethany passed out on Malcolm. Her breathing was deep and peaceful. Malcolm felt his eyes getting heavy. He tried hard to keep them open. It didn't take long for him to lose that fight.

He could feel the truck slowing down as he fought to stay awake. Malcolm couldn't fight it anymore and passed out.

*****

"Madam President," Captain Peterson started over the PA system of the plane, "could you come to the cockpit, please?"

"What is it, Captain?" Cecilia asked, entering the cockpit and sitting down in the co-pilot seat.

"We have bogies," he said.

"*What?*" she exclaimed, looking out the windows. She could see a flying saucer on her side of the large plane. "Holy shit!"

"They've been with us for a bit now, ma'am," Rick said. "They don't seem to be flanking us, ma'am, it's almost like they're in formation with us."

"Can you lose them?" she asked.

"No, ma'am. They are far superior crafts than this old bird."

"What about shooting them out of the sky?"

"Um, I don't think that'd be wise, ma'am. There's a much larger aircraft behind them. I think even if we got one of them, the rest would destroy us. I don't think they pose a threat. I feel like they would've just shot us out of the sky by now if they wanted to."

"I don't like it at all," Cecilia said. "How close are we?"

"We're close, ma'am."

"Is the radio working, Captain?" Cecilia asked. Rick didn't respond. He sat rigid in the captain's seat, his eyes glazed over. "Captain?" she said, shaking him. Still, no response. He looked to be in a trance.

Yellow, blue, and red lights engulfed the plane. President Rodgers couldn't see anything out the windows anymore, but it felt like the plane had stopped in midair. How was that possible? She grabbed the radio from its holster on the control panel. It was dead. Everything on the control panel had gone dead. Cecilia could hear the engines roaring, but she knew the plane wasn't moving anymore. She felt the plane slowly descend. It came to a bumpy landing. The engines cut off, and everything went dead silent. Rick stood up and slowly slumped to the back of the plane. His movements were very zombie-like and not at all fluid. He hit a switch in the back of the plane, and the cargo door popped open. Rick climbed out of the plane and disappeared into the bright, colorful lights. President Rodgers stood in shock, watching as he vanished.

"What's going on?" Scarlett asked.

"I don't know," Cecilia said, shaking her head.

A red light that was so bright the women had the shield their eyes came down from the sky above them. It blinked out almost as quickly as it appeared. Blinking through the dark spots in her eyes, Cecilia looked over to Scarlett and Hope. They were both out cold. She could see they were both still breathing; it was a deep, sleep-like breathing. A tall, slender man walked into the plane. He didn't look right. He looked human enough, but not quite. It was obvious that something was way off with the man. He looked at Cecilia, and her skin crawled. His eyes were the blackest of black she had ever seen. He had no nose, just two nostrils in the middle of his face. His mouth was tiny and thin; it didn't look like he had lips. The skin hung on his body like a wet T-shirt and was grayish.

"We need to talk," the man said. Cecilia knew he wasn't a man, at least not a human man.

"Do we now?" she asked. "Who are you?"

"Sit down," he said. His voice was very robotic, as if it were computerized.

"I'll stand," she said. "What'd you do to my pilot?"

"He's fine. You won't be needing him anymore." His lips didn't seem to be moving properly. His mouth didn't match the words escaping his lips. It looked like a bad dubbed-over movie, where someone is speaking a foreign language, but it's been dubbed over in English.

"It's pretty obvious you're one of them," she said, pointing to the sky.

"I am them," he said. "I am the leader."

"So is this where you tell me you're taking over our planet again? Because I've heard that before and I'm not going to let that happen." The man, or whatever he was, looked harmless, but she knew he wasn't. She wasn't intimidated though, she knew if he, or they, had wanted her dead, she'd be dead.

"No." He chuckled. "We don't want the planet—it can't support us anymore."

"Then what do you want?"

"We gave you this planet. We gave you every resource you could ever need. We gave you technology. We literally gave you the world and you destroyed it in no time. We may not be able to live on this planet, but we love it. You arrogant humans have ruined the second most beautiful planet in the solar system, yet again. So we are hitting the reset button—we call it the human reinstatement. Those of you we have chosen will get to rebuild, and we'll see if you can manage not to fuck it up this time. Although I doubt that because every time we have to intervene, you all just destroy everything again."

"What are you talking about? You *gave* us this planet? That's BS. We evolved—it's scientific fact."

The man laughed. "You didn't evolve! We put you here and we will take you out if we have to."

"You know we won't just sit back and let you do that. We'll defend our planet to the death!"

"That would be fine by us. We've wiped out many civilizations before, and we're not afraid to do it again. See the thing is, we like you humans. A lot. We did, after all, create you."

"You did not!" Cecilia interrupted. "I am a woman of faith, and I believe God created all. You are certainly not God."

"You humans and your faith," he laughed. "Your brains are so small and limited. You're like livestock, being herded into a room to listen to one man tell ancient stories about a faceless, ageless, deity. You do have it half right, those stories are mostly accurate, but it was us, not some spirit in the sky. We gave you life. We gave you the tools to succeed on this wonderful planet. We taught you how to farm, we gave you fire, we taught you how to build communities and then societies. We gave you the tools to govern peacefully. And every step of the way for thousands of years, you have fucked it up. It's getting sad, really." He paused, and Cecilia swore she saw his skin ripple. "You are descendants of us. We created you purely to inhabit this planet. Each redo seems great at first, but then as you build societies and start to utilize technology, your arrogance starts to take over. Instead of just being one with this world, you begin to feel superior. You guys start to take and take. You cause species that are vital to the planet to go extinct. We spread you all out over many lands, and you all feel like you're the best."

"What you are saying seems a little off," Cecilia said. This man—she shuddered to think of him as a man—was by no means being threatening. He seemed to be very sincere. That scared her more than if he was hostile. She couldn't or wouldn't trust him, but she had to hear him out. Cecilia just had to know why he was telling her all this. "We have recorded history. We have science that proves our theories of how and why we got to where we are. We learn from the mistakes of the ones before us." The man creature laughed at that.

"You humans have not learned anything over the thousands of years you've been here. We go out of our way to help you live a thriving existence here, and you just squander it. Your science and recorded history also came from us."

"How so?" she asked. "I feel like we are thriving. Or at least we were before you guys destroyed the planet."

"We did not destroy this great planet!" he snapped. "You humans did that! We have just stepped in to clean up your mess and repair this planet." He paused, and his skin rippled again. His black eyes pierced Cecilia's soul. She could feel his disdain for her. "To answer your question," he started again, a lot calmer. "Let's take your great US of A here. The Europeans stumbled upon this great land, which was thriving at the time by the way, and in no time, they began to ruin it just as they had ruined their continent. It was too late for us to step in and stop all of that. We didn't feel it was time for another human reinstatement. We really had wanted to give you all a lot of time to figure your shit out—that was our mistake. We should have known that you never would. But we still wanted to step in and point you in the right direction. You see, that's all we can do, is guide you, we can't force you. We can either help or simply end it and start over. Let me tell you, starting over sucks for all of us, it really does. So as I was saying, we decided back then that we'd help instead of destroy.

We contacted your founding fathers and gave them direction. We set them up for success. Laid it out word by word. Gave them the tools to create a great nation."

"And they did!" Cecilia interjected. The man-thing laughed again. "Okay, enough is enough. What is the point to all this?" She was getting tired and, frankly, a little irritated at the man-thing's belittling attitude.

"Please, if you want to know why we are—and I'll remind you, you did ask me that very question—do not interrupt me again. We like you Madam President, we really do, so it'd be a shame if your attitude forced us to eliminate you as well. We believe you could be a big factor in getting the world back in order. You are a one-of-a-kind leader and person. So may I continue, or shall we tap another leader?"

Cecilia stared at him dumbfounded. Had this man-thing just told her that her options were death or working for them? She couldn't work for them, could she? Nothing like this was even the slightest bit possible just a few days before. She didn't want to die without a fight. Maybe she could defeat them from the inside? Maybe she could gain their trust and end whatever it was they controlled for good. She couldn't give up yet.

"Yes, please go ahead. I am sorry," Cecilia said.

"Very good," he replied. "We were never fond of what they did to the Natives and the Africans, but we realized we could be on to something. Maybe instead of keeping the nationalities separated on continents, we could build an all-inclusive culture and society. But yet again, you humans ruined that. You enslaved your fellow man! We were not happy about that either, but we can't control what you all do. We did tell Lincoln to put an end to it. He was easy to convince; he had never been in favor of slavery either. He just needed a little bit of guidance from us. That gave us some hope for your precious US of A, so we continued to follow the growth of the country very closely. Every damn step of the way, you ruined it. We'd step in and guide your leaders one way, and they'd go the other. We'd help you build a booming economy, and you would elect someone who'd run it into the ground. You started wars or joined wars you had no business being a part of. You humans sure do like to kill each other. We don't have that kind of violence among ourselves. We have no qualms wiping you humans out—you are just basically insects after all. I'll level with you, Madam President—we just simply love watching you try to survive your own messes. We kind of like sending you curveballs and seeing how you react. Like sending plagues and super viruses. Something as simple as protecting yourselves from a virus becomes political and divides your nations. You have people that refuse to take the basic precautions simply because someone from an opposing political party recommended it, so they rebel. Especially you Americans. You have convinced yourselves that you are the almighty nation, and you have all these God-given rights. 'I have the right to do whatever I want. I'm American!' It's all so arrogant and frankly foolish. But you changed all that, Cecilia. Sure, there are plenty out there that don't like you or claim you as their president, but none of that matters to you. You are one of the only leaders who truly put country first. You think you were lucky to barely escape the attacks? No, you weren't. We tipped your people to get you to safety. We want you. So many people achieve power and become even more corrupt than before. Give a mortal man control and he becomes a god. But not you. Not you. We watched your rise in politics. We got you to where you are. Now you owe us. The last thing I will tell you, Madam President, is this: go along or be gone. This isn't a request."

Everything went dark, and Cecilia fell to the floor of the airplane. Scarlett and Hope came to. Scarlett unhooked her seatbelt and rushed to Cecilia; she was out cold. A pulsing red light filled the cargo hold of the plane. Scarlett watched the president disappear into the light. The light hit Hope, and she passed out again. Scarlett ran to Hope and grabbed her, pulling the young woman to her tightly. Scarlett could feel warmth and anger surround her. Hope was convulsing in her arms. Scarlett cried out for help. She screamed at the top of her lungs. Hope shook violently in her weakening arms. She couldn't hold on to the girl much longer. The red light went out, and Scarlett fell to the ground with Hope still in her arms. Hope had gone limp. She wasn't breathing. Scarlett wanted to revive her, but she couldn't move. She fought with everything she had to fight through the sudden paralysis. Her eyes were heavy. Her heart thumped inside her chest. Bile slowly rose into the back of her mouth. Scarlett vomited and collapsed to the cold metal floor of the plane.

*****

Serena sat next to John's hospital bed. The boys were sleeping on a cot behind her. John was sedated; the hospital was unable to perform surgeries at that point. Running solely on backup generators had forced the hospital to conserve energy wherever they could. John's injuries were not life threatening, so he did not get surgery. Serena knew her husband hated drugs and would hate being sedated the way he was. She had almost come to terms with the fact that she may never see her husband again and that their boys may grow up without a father. Serena didn't know what their future held for them at that point, but whatever was ahead of them, she wanted—no, needed—John with them. Even injured, he would have protected them with his life.

Serena had grown up a farmer's daughter in a large family of ten, including mom and dad. She grew up with the old-school ideology that the man works the fields, and the woman tends to the house and kids. Her dad would be up before dawn and out to the fields and livestock. He would return for dinner and then head back out for the nightly chores. Her brothers were expected and forced to work the farm with him during the summer and school breaks. Serena and her sisters tended the house with mom. Like most family farms, they barely kept their heads above water financially, so she never had an opportunity to go to college and try to get out of farm life. She didn't hate that life though; it was the only life she had ever known. Serena loved John and their sons so much she enjoyed taking care of all of them. John was a good man, and he had always treated Serena like a queen. Sure, he was stubborn sometimes and could get surly, but he respected her, and they always discussed everything. John had never treated her the way her father had treated her mother. Serena's dad was an abusive alcoholic. Deep down, he was a good man and did love his family, but he ruled that household with an iron fist. It had always been his way or no way. And once he got the liquor in him, he turned into a monster. Serena's dad had once put her oldest brother into the hospital after a beating. Her brother was sixteen at the time and had stood up to their father after he had smacked their mother. Her father didn't take kindly to her brother stepping into his mother's aid. Their father beat him bloody. He broke her brother's jaw, and it had to be wired shut. Serena swore to herself, if a man ever laid hands on her, it would be over.

Serena had met John at church when she was just twenty years old. She knew from the moment she had met him that he was a good, kind man. John was five years older than her and had just returned from college in Kansas City. His father had just passed away, and being the eldest child and only son, John had inherited the family farm. John's mother still lived on the farm but was not physically or mentally able to tend to it at that time. John's mom, Henrietta, had been a wonderful woman. Serena loved that woman with all her heart. John had moved back to the farm and took care of the land, the house, and his ailing mother. Two years after they met, John and Serena were married. Less than a year after they married, Henrietta passed away. It was devastating for both of them. Serena had just found out she was pregnant with JJ, and Henrietta had been so excited to have a grandchild. She never got to meet her grandkids. John took his mother's passing hard, drinking himself into self-pitying stupors. John had wanted to sell the farm and move to Kansas City. He had gotten a teaching degree and wanted to teach high school math and coach football. Serena didn't want to live in the big city, she was a farm girl at heart. She loved country life. No neighbors ten feet away. No traffic. No noise. John had been pretty steadfast about selling the family farm and moving away. Everything about that farm reminded him of his parents. John's dad had been a gruff man but was never abusive. His dad had a sick sense of humor and, especially when he was drinking, was the life of any party. But John had always been a mamma's boy. He loved his mom dearly and living in her home after she was gone was beyond difficult. The plates, the glassware, the hand towels—hell, even the cow-shaped salt and pepper shakers reminded him of his mother and her sudden absence.

After months of discussion, Serena had convinced John if they just did some redecorating and made the house their own, he would be more comfortable with farm life. John finally did concede, and they stayed put. Once he got into the groove of farm life as an adult, he grew to enjoy it quite a bit. As the boys grew up, John had begun to see the value of raising them in the country. He had once shuddered at the thought of becoming a farmer like his old man but had really settled into a happy life on the farm with his amazing wife and sons.

Serena caught a chill and grabbed John's jacket off the pile of his belongings and put it on. She put her hands in the pockets of the jacket and wrapped it around herself. It had felt amazing to be engulfed in John's jacket and his scent. She felt a folded-up piece of paper in one of the pockets and pulled it out. Serena unfolded the piece of paper; it was a note from John. She read the note and began to cry. Serena had been furious at John for taking off with Chris. John's stubbornness had reared its ugly head and had made him make a bad decision. His selfishness for not wanting Chris around had led them to their current situation. Serena did, however, respect her husband for trying so hard to find them. The note hinted at some really bad things he had encountered out there. She assumed she didn't even know the half of it and probably never would. John wasn't likely to expand on anything. He would keep quiet about what had happened to him so as to not worry her. As far as she was concerned, whatever had happened to him out there was over, and they just needed to move on. There was no point dwelling on what had happened; they needed to figure out their future. They needed to get themselves and the boys home somehow. Serena knew from what she had seen on the long drive to Des Moines that getting home would not be an easy task. She had been pleasantly surprised by how functional and normal the hospital seemed to be. Serena knew they couldn't stay there forever though; they would have to leave at some point. She just hoped John could heal and regain his strength a bit first. She needed her husband as close to a hundred percent as possible.

The hospital room went dark. The machines and oxygen they had John hooked up to went out. Serena looked out the open door and could see light in the hallway. She got up and headed for the door. Serena was a few feet from the door when it slammed shut. She tried the doorknob and it wouldn't budge. She pounded on the door and yelled for help. John began to cough and moan. Serena rushed back to his bedside. She glanced at the boys, and they were still fast asleep; that was a good thing. She didn't want them to undergo any more stress if they didn't have to.

"It's them," John whispered.

"What's them?" Serena asked.

"The lights going out. It's them," he whispered, pointing at the ceiling.

"Who?" she asked, starting to panic a bit.

"The aliens. I feel them," he whispered.

"*Aliens?* John what are you talking about?"

"It wasn't meteors. It was aliens. I saw them."

"What? Are you serious? I think they have you on too high a dose of meds."

"Not meds. Aliens," John whispered, turning to look at her. "They're here for us."

"You're talking crazy talk, John," she said, standing up again. "I'm going to go find a nurse."

"Don't bother. They're saying they'll take us shortly."

"John, you're scaring me. You're not making any damn sense."

"It'll make sense soon, baby." John closed his eyes again and was out.

A pulsing red light crashed through the hospital window. The light surrounded the boys and quickly flickered out. The boys were gone. Serena panicked and ran to the window. The pulsing red light returned and surrounded her. She could hear the boys screaming in terror. Serena could feel warmth and anger all around her now trembling body. She tried to step away from the light, but she couldn't move. Her head was pounding, and her heart was racing. She could feel sweat soaking her skin. Her eyes felt heavy. She tried to stay awake but couldn't. Serena passed out and then vanished with the red light.

*****

Pete woke up in a cold, dimly lit room. The floor and walls were metallic. His head was killing him, and he felt dizzy. The strangest thing was, he was absolutely starving, hungrier than he could ever remember being. Pete blinked his eyes and looked around the room. There had to be at least a hundred people in that room. People milled about, chatting quietly with one another. No one looked relaxed or calm; they were all obviously very nervous and confused. Pete could feel a light buzzing sensation through the wall he was sitting against. As the fogginess slowly dissipated, Pete started to realize where he was. He couldn't remember everything, but he vividly remembered stopping at the hospital and then seeing a huge aircraft in the sky. Then he woke up on that cold floor. He knew exactly where he was.

Pete stood up on shaky legs. It took a few moments for him to feel steady on his feet. The room spun a bit, and he thought he may fall back to the floor. Once he had gained full control of his legs again, he wandered around the room. People awkwardly smiled and nodded at him. It was clear that everyone else knew where they were too. The nervous energy in that room was heavy. The room smelled like body odor, urine, and fear—yes, he could even smell fear. Pete walked the perimeter of the room, looking for a door.

"You won't find no door, kid," an older man said to Pete as he walked by.

"No?" Pete asked.

"Nope. We all looked already. Every single person as they come to, walks the room looking for a door. There's no door," the man said. "I'm Denny." The man extended his right hand. His hand was extremely dry and callused.

"I'm Pete." He shook the man's hand.

"You know where we are, Pete?" Denny asked.

"I have an idea, yeah," Pete responded. He didn't really feel like entering into a conversation with anyone, but he wasn't going to be rude either.

"Yeah, we all kinda know," Denny said. "I been here for what feels like weeks."

"Oh yeah?" Pete asked, trying to be as brief as possible.

"Yeah, kid. When I woke up here, I was the only one. Ever since, people have just been showing up out of nowhere. It's the strangest thing. The whole room will be flooded with this blinding white light, and then when the light goes out, there's more people."

"Weird," Pete said. "So you've been here for weeks?"

"Yeah, sure feels like it. You don't know if it's night or day in here. Three times a day this window over on that wall"—he pointed to the opposite end of the room—"opens and there's a buffet of really bad food, but you're hungry so you eat it."

"What about when you have to use the bathroom?" Pete asked.

"Over there,"—he pointed to a half-wall behind Pete—"behind that partition are some toilets and curtains. It is very awkward, but when you gotta go, you gotta go."

"I asked because I do need to go. It was nice meeting you, Denny," Pete said, putting his hand out.

"Nice to meet you too, Pete," Denny replied, shaking Pete's hand again.

Pete didn't actually have to use the restroom; he just wanted out of the conversation. Denny seemed like a nice enough guy, but Pete just wasn't in the head space to have a long, drawn-out conversation. He wandered around the half wall and stepped up to one of the toilets, closing the curtain behind him. The toilet bowl had a tiny bit of blue liquid in the bottom of it. He could hear and, unfortunately, smell someone using a toilet two spots down from him. Pete opened the curtain and quickly headed back into the large, cold room. He saw Denny chatting with another man and darted past them. Pete walked back toward where he had woken up, keeping his head down so hopefully no one else would try to interact with him. He stopped dead in his tracks when he heard Amanda call out his name excitedly.

"Oh my god, Pete! It's really you!" Amanda exclaimed, jogging over to him and hugging him.

"Amanda!" he exclaimed, throwing his arms around her. "Holy shit! I thought I would never see you again! I am so sorry I didn't save you."

"I didn't think I'd ever see anyone again," she said. "What do you mean save me?"

"I should have tried to rescue you from that creature and the red light," Pete said.

"What creature? What red light?" she asked, very confused.

"You don't remember one of those creatures standing right in front of you out in the middle of that intersection?"

"What intersection? The last thing I remember before waking up here was being at my parents' house with my friends."

"You don't remember leaving to take your friends home? We stopped at a huge car wreck to try and save a woman pinned in her car. That's when the creatures showed up and took you."

"I don't remember any of that," she said. "Wait, when was that? I haven't seen you since last summer at the lake."

"I happened to run into you at your parents' house while I was trying to get to my parents' place. You invited me in. I had a beer with your dad, and then we took off to get your friends home."

"I don't remember you being at my house since high school." Amanda looked so confused and scared.

"Well, it's probably a good thing you don't remember. It was all so fucked up," he said, hoping to get off the subject; it was clearly stressing her out. "No need to dwell on all that any more. I'm so glad we're together again."

"Me too," Amanda said. "You're the only familiar face I've seen here. I met some girls from Vegas that seem pretty cool. We've been holing up together, trying to ride whatever this is out. It sucks here, Pete," she said, tearing up a little.

"I can tell that already. Not much for accommodations, huh?"

"No." She chuckled. "It's so scary here." Her tone went back to frightened and stressed.

"I'm here with you now," Pete said, taking her hand. She squeezed his hand. "I won't let you get hurt."

"Thanks, Pete," Amanda said. "Do you know where we are and how we got here?"

"I think so," he began. He looked at her and saw the fear on her face. He didn't know if he should tell her. He didn't know if she would be able to handle it. Pete could tell her nerves were shot and she was probably on the verge of a full-fledged panic attack.

"Please just tell me," Amanda said. She could tell he was hesitant to tell her. "I know I may seem fragile right now because I'm so scared, but maybe if I knew more about all of this, I'd feel better about it."

"Maybe," he said. "Maybe it will just freak you out more."

"I can't be any more freaked out than I already am. Not knowing anything is worse."

"Okay," he started, "I think we're on an alien mothership."

Amanda laughed, "Are you serious?"

"Yes, Amanda, I am very serious. I watched them take you. Then the same ship that took you showed up later and took me. Last thing I remember is staring up at the bottom of the biggest aircraft I've ever seen in my life. It was so big it shouldn't have been able to fly."

"Why would aliens take us?"

"I don't know, but I'm pretty sure they're the ones that blew up all the cities around the world."

"I thought that was meteors," she said.

Pete was surprised she didn't remember anything. He had seen her standing face-to-face with one of those nasty creatures.

"I'm positive it wasn't meteors," Pete said.

Amanda looked at Pete. She was incredibly happy to have him there with her. She had always liked Pete and knew that he had had a crush on her throughout school. She thought it was cute, but he was never popular enough for her to date. Amanda regretted that after the fact; she felt bad that she had missed out on a possible relationship with such a nice guy. She had liked him too, and it made her feel even worse to have missed out on it because of high school politics and class divides.

Blue lights started flashing in the corners of the room. A bright white light filled the room. Amanda, like the rest of the people who had been there, knew that light meant other people were about to appear in the room. That light was absolutely blinding and sickening. The light flashed out, and the blue lights went out. Amanda blinked at the sudden light difference. Pete was no longer standing in front of her. She frantically searched the room for him. He was nowhere to be found. Upset and terrified, she went back to the girls from Las Vegas and sat down on the floor with them.

"Where did that guy you were talking to go?" Dana asked.

"I don't know," Amanda replied, with a hitch in her voice.

"You two seemed to know each other well," Julia said.

"We sure do. We've known each other since grade school. I have always considered him a good friend. I'm scared for him. I hope he's okay."

"I'm sorry," Dana said. "I wonder what happened to him."

"You guys did see him, though, right?" Amanda asked. "I wasn't imagining it, was I?"

"No, we saw him too. You hugged him and chatted with him for a while," Julia said.

"Everything is just so damn foggy and dreamlike," Amanda said. "Pete told me that I was face-to-face with some kind of creature. That a red light took me right off the street. I don't remember any of that."

"We saw a creature right before we woke up here," Dana said. "It was terrifying."

"So it's all real?" Amanda asked.

"Yes, all too real," Julia said, looking at her feet.

"Jules, do you recognize that man over there?" Dana asked, pointing at a small, middle-aged, balding man across the room. "He keeps staring at us."

Julia and Amanda both looked up at the man. The man noticed them all looking at him and approached them.

"Shit, he's coming over here," Dana whispered.

"I hate this fucking place," Julia said.

"Hello, ladies," the man said once he got to them. None of them responded to him. "We are in quite the predicament, huh?" They still didn't respond to him. "I don't have a good feeling about any of this. I wanted to come over and make sure you young ladies have been saved. If not, I would like to teach you about our Lord and Savior, Jesus Christ." The women all rolled their eyes and still said nothing to the man. "I am a pastor. It is my duty and my mission that everyone learns about the teachings of Jesus Christ."

Amanda looked up at the man. "Look, this isn't the time or the place for all that. Please leave us alone."

"I beg to differ. This is exactly the time and the place for Jesus Christ. These are most likely our last days. It is imperative that you find our Lord Jesus Christ and repent your sins. Repent or spend eternity in purgatory."

"Okay, that's enough. We ain't interested," Julia piped in. "My friend here was very polite to you and asked you to leave. I will not be as polite. Get away from us."

"Why the hostility, ladies?" he asked. "I am only here to help you find Jesus Christ and help you save your soul."

"We don't need it," Julia responded. "We're good, thanks. You can move on and try to save the rest of the people in here."

"You ladies certainly do need saving. I know how ladies like you behave."

"Oh no, you didn't!" Julia snapped, standing up to face the man. Amanda and Dana stood up behind Julia. "You think just 'cause we're young, we're not good people? Tell me, how do you think we behave? You think we play around? Date a lot? What is it?" Her eyes were fixed on his and full of fury and insult.

"I was not trying to upset you ladies. As a pastor, I just need to make sure all souls are saved. Jesus wants a relationship with you ladies. Go with the Lord and you will have forever happiness."

"Get lost," Julia growled. "Now!"

The man looked back and forth at all three of them. He had begun to tremble a bit.

"You ladies seem upset. I will check back in with you later," he said and turned away from them.

"Please don't!" Julia shouted after him.

"What the fuck?" Dana said as she sat back down on the floor and leaned against the cold metal wall.

"Fuckin' asshole, that's what," Julia said, sitting back down as well.

"That guy was creepy," Amanda said, joining her new friends on the floor. "You guys see how he was checkin' us out the whole time?"

"Oh yeah, I sure did," Julia said. "I came this close to punching him in his fat face." She said, holding her thump and pointer finger really close together.

"He's still staring at us, girls," Dana said.

"Motherfucker!" Julia said, getting to her feet again.

Julia stomped over to the man. Dana and Amanda couldn't hear what she was saying to the man, but Julia was very animated and had gotten the attention of everyone around them. Dana and Amanda saw the man turn bright red. They smiled at each other.

"Julia's always been a badass," Dana said to Amanda. "She has gotten my dumbass out of a lot of sticky situations." Dana chuckled.

"That's a good friend to have."

Julia returned and sat back down. She was clearly very flustered and still quite angry.

"What'd you say to him?" Dana asked.

"I told him to keep his pervy eyes off of us and to *never* approach us or talk to us again. I told him if we catch him looking at us again, I was going to knock him the fuck out. I don't know what it is, but that guy is off. He is a creep through and through." Julia shivered and shook her head. "I hope I don't have to interact with him ever again."

"Look," Dana said, pointing across the room.

Julia and Amanda looked to where Dana was pointing. The pastor had fallen to the floor and was convulsing. His entire body was shaking violently. His head kept bouncing off the hard metal floor. People slowly started to back away. Why wasn't anyone helping him? Soon there was a twenty-foot perimeter around the pastor.

"Creep or not, he needs help," Amanda said, starting to stand up.

Julia put her arm out in front of Amanda. "No, don't," she said. "We've seen this before, just once before you got here. He'll blow any minute."

"Blow?" Amanda said, sitting back down.

The pastor's body shook so hard it was bouncing across the floor. People kept moving away from him. Dana, Julia, and Amanda stared in amazement and anticipation, not an excited anticipation, just in a "What in the hell?" kind of way. The man's body exploded. Pieces of him flew into the air. Blood, organs, and everything splattered on the floor.

"Close your eyes," Julia said.

That same bright light filled the room. Amanda shut her eyes tight. The light quickly went out, and the pastor's body was gone. Everything was clean as if it had never happened.

A robotic voice filled the room. "Do not harass others. Do not speak of your imaginary gods. Each and every one of you has an explosive device inside you, we will not hesitate to take any of you out."

The room went quiet again. People began to mill about a bit. The room was dead silent; no one spoke a word to anyone else. Amanda, Dana, and Julia sat quietly next to each other. Dana laid her head on Julia's shoulders and closed her eyes. Amanda slumped next to Julia and also closed her eyes. The three of them drifted off to a very restless sleep. That was the only kind of sleep anyone got in that place.

*****

President Rodgers sat in what felt like an interrogation room. There were no windows, just metal walls. There was a table and two chairs, and that was it. She sat on one side of the table, facing a door. The door didn't have hinges or a doorknob. Cecilia sat there, expecting that strange-looking man to enter at any moment.

After what had felt like hours, the door slid open.

"Exit the room," a voice said inside her head.

Cecilia got up and walked out the door.

"To the left," the voice said.

She turned to her left and began to walk down a long, narrow hallway. There were no other doors along the hallway. Just tall metal walls. The hall was bright, but there was also a very sinister feeling. And the smell. She couldn't tell what that smell was, but it was awful. It almost smelled like burning flesh and hair. There was also a fairly heavy sulfur smell to the air. The hallway curved slightly and came to an end. Cecilia stood there for a moment, looking around. The wall in front of her slid open. She walked through, and it slid closed behind her.

Cecilia looked around. The room was huge and full of medical equipment. She slowly began to walk forward. Further into the room were people laid out on stainless-steel tables. They were all either heavily sedated or dead. They had what looked like oxygen masks strapped to their faces and IV's in their arms. She walked up to one body, a young female, maybe twenty at the oldest. Cecilia reached out and checked the woman's pulse; she was alive. The pulse was weak but definitely there. The president walked over to a man's body on the table next to the woman. His eyes were open, but he didn't look responsive. His eyes had life in them, but it was very faint. She checked his pulse too just to be sure, and he too had a pulse.

Cecilia went to check the person on the next table when she heard what sounded like a child crying. She stopped and looked around the room; she didn't see anything except for the bodies on the tables. So many bodies. Cecilia stood still and just listened. She was definitely hearing a child cry. The cries were faint, but she could tell they were coming from her right. Cecilia slowly headed to her right, listening intently to the crying. It began to get louder and louder. Under a stainless-steel desk, covered in a blanket, was a girl, probably about ten years old. She had blond pigtails and sparkling blue eyes. Those eyes held a lot of pain and fear.

"Are you okay, sweetie?" Cecilia asked. The little girl shook her head. "Come with me," she said and extended her hand to the child. The girl just looked at her. "I won't hurt you, sweetheart." The little girl looked terrified. "I'm human," Cecilia said. "I want to help you."

The girl finally took Cecilia's hand and crawled out from under the desk. "What's your name, sweetie? I'm Cecilia."

"I'm Abby," the girl said shyly.

"Hi, Abby," Cecilia said, kneeling down to get at eye level with Abby. "Are you okay?"

"I'm scared," Abby said softly, tears still streaming down her pink cheeks.

"I am too," Cecilia said. "How did you get in here?"

"I don't know. I woke up on the table over there," she said, pointing across the room.

"And then you hid under that desk?"

"Yeah." Abby was still clutching the thin white blanket she had been hiding under.

"Do you remember anything else?" Cecilia asked.

"These funny-looking people always come in and do things to the people on the tables," Abby said. Tears were still escaping her eyes, but she had stopped sobbing. She seemed to be calming down.

"What did the funny people look like?" Cecilia asked, shifting her weight to her other knee.

"They were gray. They didn't have noses. They moved weird too." Abby said with a hitch in her voice. She didn't like talking about the funny-looking people.

"What did they do to the people on the tables?" Cecilia asked.

"They checked on them, I think. They would give them medicine with needles. I don't like shots."

"I don't either, dear. Let's see if we can get out of here."

"Okay," Abby said, clutching her blanket tightly.

A door behind them slid open. A man that looked like the one she had met on the plane walked into the room. He stopped and stared at Cecilia and Abby.

"What are you two doing?" he asked through lips that barely moved.

"Trying to figure out where we are and what's going on." Cecilia answered, standing up and grabbing Abby's hand.

"You shouldn't be here," he said. He turned and stepped to the door. It slid open, and he disappeared out of the room.

Cecilia pulled Abby's hand and headed for the door. The door slid shut as they got to it. Cecilia stood in front of it and waved her arms. Nothing. She pushed around the edges of the door, still nothing. Cecilia stepped back and the door slid open. She had expected to see that man-thing again, but no one was in the doorway. Cecilia led Abby through the doorway. They walked into a large, bright room. That room was also full of stainless-steel tables with people laid out on them. The new room, however, reeked of death. Cecilia walked over to a man's body and felt for a pulse; there was not one. She assumed that would probably be the case for all of the bodies in that room. The man had a tube jutting out from under the blanket that covered him. The tube was full of blood. Cecilia pulled Abby away from the dead man. She guided the girl through the room to the other side. They came upon another door. It slid open as soon as they approached it. They walked into a cold, dark room. It was so very cold, like a huge walk-in refrigerator. Cecilia shielded Abby's eyes and rushed her through the room. Hanging from hooks along both sides of the cold room were human bodies, splayed open. On shelves lining each wall were chunks of cellophane-wrapped meat. The thought of what those things were doing to people made her skin crawl and her sight go red with anger. They tried to tell her they were there to help humans, yet they were clearly harvesting them for food. At the end of the row of swinging bodies was an empty hook. Cecilia grabbed the hook on their way out of that horrifying room.

The next room looked like an industrial kitchen. They could smell meat cooking. It smelled really good, but Cecilia knew what they were cooking, and it turned her stomach. The room ended at a corner. When Cecilia rounded the corner, she stopped abruptly and pulled Abby close to her. There were about ten people in chef uniforms, lined up in front of a prep counter, chopping vegetables and chunks of meat. None them stopped what they were doing or looked at Cecilia and Abby. They all looked to be in a deep trance, like her pilot had been when he exited the C-17. She slowly and carefully led Abby past the prep cooks. On the opposite side of the room were another ten or so people at stoves and grills cooking food. They too were all in that deep trance-like state. It was so very eerie. No one paid them any attention at all.

Cecilia and Abby had made it through the kitchen. The next area had a large, flat metal platform in the middle of it. More people in chef uniforms and in a trance were going back and forth putting plates of food on the platform. When the platform was full, they'd hit a button, and it would disappear into the ceiling and an empty platform would appear in the same spot.

"I'm hungry," Abby said, looking at the plates of food on the platform.

Cecilia realized she was also hungry, very hungry in fact. But there was absolutely no way she was going to let either of them eat that food.

"You may have a plate each," a voice said from behind them. It had startled them, and Cecilia turned around, raising the meat hook. "No need for that now." Cecilia lowered the meat hook. A woman stood there in front of them—well, she *looked* like a woman at least. It was quite easy for Cecilia to tell that was not a human woman.

"We're fine," Cecilia said.

"The child is hungry. Let her eat," the woman-thing said.

"No thank you," Cecilia said. "We're not eating that."

"But you both need food. Please, sit and eat," she said, motioning to a table behind her. There was a row of restaurant-style tables lined against the far wall.

"Again. We're fine," Cecilia said. "We'll just find our way out of here, thank you."

"You will not. We probably need to chat again, Madam President Cecilia Rodgers," the woman-thing said, sitting down at the table. She looked over at one of the zombie-like people loading the platform with food. The man stopped dead in his tracks and tilted his head. He then grabbed two plates of food and brought them over to the table. He set them down and immediately went back to loading the platform. "Sit. Eat," she said to Cecilia and Abby.

Abby wiggled her little hand free from Cecilia's and scampered over to the table. She sat down across from the woman-thing and started eating.

"No, Abby, don't eat that!" Cecilia said, but it was too late; the girl was plowing through the food like she hadn't eaten in months.

"The food is fine, Madam President," the woman-thing said.

"It's fucking people, you disgusting thing!" Cecilia exclaimed. Abby stopped eating and stared at Cecilia. "I thought you guys were eating the people, but you're feeding it to the rest of your prisoners?"

"They are not prisoners, Madam President. They are the future of Planet Earth."

"You are killing and cooking people!"

"Those are not the chosen people. They are disposable. We have to feed the chosen ones." The woman-thing's skin rippled.

"Abby, come stand behind me," Cecilia said. Abby did as she was instructed.

Cecilia raised the meat hook and took a step toward the woman-thing. The woman-thing raised her right hand, and Cecilia's body froze. Cecilia had no control of her body. With her left hand, the woman-thing waved Abby over to her. Abby's eyes glazed over, and she robotically walked over to the woman-thing. She grabbed Abby's throat with her left hand and looked at Cecilia.

"I want you to drop that hook," the woman-thing said. "If you insist on being difficult, I will tear this little girl's head off."

Cecilia regained control of her right hand and dropped the meat hook. It clanked on the metal floor. The woman-thing released Abby and she ran back to Cecilia. The woman-thing dropped her right hand, and Cecilia could move again.

"I like you," the woman-thing chuckled. "You are tenacious. Madam President, you do have some big brass balls as you humans would say." She chuckled again.

Cecilia walked to the table and sat down across from the woman-thing, pushing the plates of food away. She motioned at Abby to sit next to her. The woman-thing looked at Cecilia with those dark black eyes and smiled.

"You going to play ball, Madam President?" it asked her.

"I don't seem to have a choice," Cecilia began. "But if we are to have a discussion here, I'd like to know whom I am talking to. What is your name and rank?"

The woman-thing chuckled once again. "Why is that important? You humans are so fickle sometimes."

"I just like to know who I am making deals with. It would help me feel like this is more of a two-way street than you just demanding things of me."

The woman-thing sighed and smiled at Cecilia. "Fine, I will humor you. You wouldn't understand my given name, much less be able to say it." She paused and thought for a moment. "You have mentioned you were a woman of faith?"

"I *am* a woman of faith, yes. Why does that matter now?" Cecilia asked, confused. These things had a way of talking in circles. Pulling things out of nowhere that didn't seem relevant.

"I am trying to come up with a human name that you would be able to recognize and remember," the woman-thing said. It paused again in thought. "You can call me Eve Adams. And as far as my rank is concerned, in human terms, I would be the queen," the woman-thing finally said. "Do you feel better now? May we continue?"

"Yes, that does help me. I like having a name to put to a face. What do you want from me?" Cecilia asked with a sigh.

"What we need you to do at this point is to talk to the chosen ones. We will assemble them all together and let you give a speech. We will tell you what needs to be said, but you have the freedom to play this up like you're the savior. This is your legacy, Madam President. This is your chance to go down in human history as the one who saved that beautiful planet."

"What exactly am I supposed to say?" Cecilia asked. Abby had scooted in close to Cecilia, so she put her arm around the girl. The woman-thing waved her right hand at Abby, and the girl fell asleep.

"We will let you know. There will be a prepared speech." The woman-thing's skin rippled again.

"Okay, when is this going to happen?"

"Soon, Madam President. I feel the need to remind you of one thing: if you don't go along with this, we will simply destroy you and everyone else. We can always create more of you."

"Why not just do that then? Why save certain people and not everyone? Doesn't seem to make much sense to me," Cecilia said.

"Did you have an ant farm or fish tank as a kid?" Eve Adams asked.

"Fish tank, yes. Why?" Cecilia asked, confused.

"When your fish tank got dirty or one of the fish got sick, did you just dump out all of the water and remaining fish and start over?"

"Well, no. I'd clean the tank or isolate the sick one."

"That's what we prefer to do. We can't just go down to the store and buy more humans. We have to grow you and take care of you until enough are ready to repopulate the planet. It's all so very time consuming and, frankly, not at all interesting. We prefer a human reinstatement over a total restart."

"Thanks to you guys, we don't have much of a planet to go back to now," Cecilia said.

"That will be taken care of shortly. Once we have gathered all of the chosen and enough resources, we will finish destroying what you all fucked up down there. We will restore the planet to its original beauty once again. We already have soldiers down there beginning the process."

"I have to ask, why me? How am I to direct this whole repopulation?"

"We've told you, Madam President, you are a rare and one-of-a-kind leader. You have the talent and ability to lead the rebuilding of a great nation. We understand humans will always evolve—that is how we created you. So we are well aware that you will never just live in small communities, surviving off the land. You need your entertainment. You need your socialization."

"I feel like you have made one mistake," Cecilia said.

"And what's that?" Eve Adams asked.

"You've told me all of your secrets. What's stopping me from building an army to protect us from you once we're returned to Earth?"

Eve Adams laughed. "You all always say that same damn thing." She leaned closer to Cecilia. Her breath smelled of death and decay. "You won't remember any of this, Madam President. We'll wipe all of your memories clean and replace them with new ones of your new lives down there."

Eve Adams stood up and looked down at Cecilia, raising her right arm. She waved her arm at Cecilia. The president dropped her head to the table and was out cold.

*****

Malcolm woke up strapped to a stainless-steel table. The room was bright. He had an oxygen mask strapped to his face and an IV in his arm. Whatever was in that IV burned as it entered his bloodstream. He could hear movement in the room but couldn't lift his head to look around. A woman appeared next to him; she looked very familiar. She leaned over and looked at him. The woman looked concerned but also very stoic. She put her fingers to his neck. The woman stepped away from him. He tried to say something, but he couldn't. His brain was telling his mouth to speak, but it just wouldn't work. Malcolm thought he could hear a child crying.

Malcolm heard the woman start to move away from him. Inside, he was screaming for help, but still nothing came out. After a few moments, the crying stopped. He could hear very faint voices coming from the other end of the room. Coming from the side of the room where those creepy, not-quite-people things would always come from. Those damn things that would "check" on him from time to time. They seemed to do more harm than anything else.

He closed his eyes and started to do a deep-breathing relaxation technique. Malcolm hoped if he could relax his whole body, then maybe he could regain control of his limbs. He had to try to get off that table and find Bethany. He could already wiggle his toes and fingers. God, whatever was being pumped through that IV burned so badly. He had to figure out a way to get that needle out of his arm. Who knew what they were pumping into him? Slowly, he began to feel his legs again. The sensation was like electricity sparking through his body from his toes up. The sensation continued up his body. Feeling returned to his arm, just the arm without the IV. Malcolm tried to lift his arm but figured it would be trapped under the strap. It wasn't the strap was only across his chest. He reached over with his good arm and pulled out the IV. It squirted clear liquid out as he dropped it to the floor. Feeling rushed back into that arm as well. Malcolm removed the oxygen mask and lifted his head. He fumbled with the strap but couldn't find a buckle or anything to loosen it. He assumed it was buckled underneath the table. Malcolm sucked in all the air in his chest and wiggled down the table. The strap was tight, but he could just barely sneak out of it.

Malcolm got to his feet. His legs were very weak and wobbly. He was dizzy, and the room was spinning. It took quite a bit for him to regain strength. Once he felt stable, he went to each table, hoping to find Bethany on one of them; she wasn't. Malcolm unstrapped everyone and removed their IVs as he went table to table. No one else was awake, but he hoped once that shit wasn't pumping through their veins, they'd all start to come to. Malcolm hastily searched the room for some clothes so he could get out of the hospital-style gown he was wearing. He found a large cabinet and opened it. It was stuffed full of clothes. Malcolm started grabbing clothes and tossing what wouldn't fit him aside. Finally, he came across a pair of pants that fit and snagged a T-shirt. He quickly dressed. He knew where those things always came from when they would make their visits, so he ran in the opposite direction. He did not want to run into any of them. Malcolm frantically searched for another way out. Suddenly, without warning, a door slid open. He peeked through and saw a long, narrow hallway. He ran through the door and into the hall. The hallway was bright. Malcolm ran until the hall ended. He stood there looking around. A door to his left slid open. He walked through the door, and it quickly slid shut behind him. He had walked into a room about the size of a small coat closet. The room started to move; he could feel it descending. He knew that feeling well; it felt as though he was on an elevator. It came to a jarring stop, and the door slid open again. Malcolm couldn't tell where he was; there was the brightest white light filling the new space. Something nudged him from behind, and he instinctually jumped forward into that bright light. He heard the metal door slide shut behind him. As soon as the door shut, that light blinked out and he could see. He was standing in a large room full of people. Everyone was milling about and rubbing their eyes—probably trying to rub the brightness away.

There had to be at least a hundred people in that room. Malcolm scanned the room. As he searched faces, he hoped and prayed to find Bethany in that crowd. Was that even possible? He started to move about the room to get a better look at people. No one paid him much attention. People were sticking to themselves or in small groups of three or less. There were hushed whispers throughout the room. The room had a strong feeling of fear and remorse. It felt like something very bad had just happened and people were still trying to digest it.

Malcolm had made it to the center of the room when his head suddenly started to throb. The pain grew intense and caused him to fall to his knees. He clutched his head. Malcolm heard someone say, "Oh shit, it's going to happen again!" The pain just kept getting worse. It felt like he had a balloon inside his skull, and someone was slowly inflating it. The pressure was unbearable. He slumped all the way to the floor and felt every muscle in his body contract. His body was convulsing. The whispers he had been hearing turned into full chatter. He couldn't understand what anyone was saying, but he could hear concern and fear in everyone's voices. Then a woman's scream pierced through all the chatter. The scream was followed by, "No! Not Malcolm. Please not him!"

Bethany! That was Bethany's voice. He knew instantly. Malcolm felt her rush over to him and drop to her knees. She put her arms around him. His body shook uncontrollably in her arms.

"Please! Not him!" Bethany shouted at the ceiling.

"Let go of the man." A voice filled the room.

"No!" She yelled. "If you take him out, you'll have to take me with him!"

"Fine." The voice said and the room went dead silent.

"No!" Someone else shouted. "This has to stop!"

Soon, a lot of voices started to shout the same sentiment. The feeling in the room shifted from fear and remorse to anger. The room felt heavy with anger. The shouts got louder and more intense. People started to crowd around Malcolm, shouting at the ceiling to "stop this madness."

The room went dark. Malcolm felt the pressure in his head slowly go down. His body stopped convulsing, and he had regained use of his limps. He threw his arms around Bethany and squeezed her tightly to him. She smothered his sweaty face in kisses. Tears flooded down her face. The shouting had stopped, and the room was again quiet. The room was so dark. Malcolm couldn't see Bethany's face, but it felt so good to have her in his arms again. For a brief moment, when he first woke up strapped to that table, he thought he may never see Bethany again. Malcolm sat up. Bethany sat next to him. They held each other on that hard, cold floor. You could have heard a pin drop in that room. That feeling of anger that had just hung in the air had been replaced with fear and confusion. Malcolm wanted to ask Bethany how she was doing. He wanted to ask if she knew what was going on. But he didn't want to break that eerie silence. He felt like if he had spoken, his voice would just fill that room; it was so quiet.

The silence was broken by what sounded like an elevator, that *whir* sound they make as they move up and down. Malcolm waited for the *ding* sound an elevator makes when it stops at a floor. The *whirring* noise stopped but no *ding*. He heard the very distinct sound of the door sliding open. The pitch-black room filled with the aroma of sulfur and wet dog. A spotlight illuminated a man, a very strange, not-quite-right-looking man. Flanking the man-like thing were three of those huge, ugly creatures. They looked almost giddy.

"Why are you humans so damn difficult?" the man-thing said, stepping further into the room. The spotlight and creatures followed its every move. "I will say, I am impressed by you all sticking together. You humans can actually come together sometimes. Which is hard to believe if you go look at your planet right now. We were not surprised that you all turned on each other so fast. You humans talk a good game about unity and 'doing the right thing,' but when the shit hits the fan, it quickly becomes every man for himself." The man-thing's skin rippled.

The room was still dark except for that spotlight. The creatures paced behind the man-thing, like they were really antsy about something. Or really excited about something. The man-thing's voice was robotic and seemed to fill the room more than it should have.

"Why do we keep these humans around?" the man-thing said, looking at one of the creatures. The creature smiled and shrugged. "I'll tell you why," it said, turning back to the room. "Because you fascinate us. We've watched and studied you humans for many millennia. You never cease to entertain, that is for sure. We wouldn't know what to do with our free time if we didn't have you humans to watch." The man-thing paused, and its skin rippled again. It chuckled to itself. "That's why we created reality TV—we thought you all might enjoy watching yourselves as well. And boy were we right!" It laughed. Its tone and demeanor quickly changed. "But you humans drive us crazy. We go out of our way to help you live on that beautiful planet, and all you do is destroy it. And you can't even agree on fixing it. Half of you humans don't even believe the planet is dying. The other half believes it but is too goddamn lazy to fight for saving the planet. Sometimes you humans make our blood boil." The creatures all grunted and snorted at that, as if in agreeance. The man-thing sighed. "Does anyone want to guess why you're all here?" it asked the room. Lights flicked on in the room, and the spotlight dimmed. No one raised a hand or said anything. "Come on now," it started. "There's a lot of very intelligent people in this room. *Someone* has to have a guess." Still just silence. "Well, I'm not answering the question unless I get some guesses. Come on, let's have a little fun here."

A young woman stood and raised her hand. Malcolm recognized her as Julia, one of the women from Las Vegas.

"I think you're holding us captive so you can do experiments on us," Julia said with a very shaky voice.

"No." The man-thing chuckled. "We created you. We don't need to do experiments on you. We already know what makes you all function the way you do. You're probably referring to abduction stories people tell, aren't you?" Julia nodded. "When we abduct people, we're not experimenting on them—we're repairing them. Or simply replacing their memories. Some of you humans are extremely intelligent, so much so that you stumble across us. Those few people need to be dealt with quickly. So we grab 'em, wipe 'em clean, and return 'em. Anyone else care to venture a guess? This is fun. Let's keep it going."

A man in the far back raised his hand and stepped forward. "You are going to eat us," he said.

"These guys"—the man-thing pointed at the creatures behind him—"have been known to nibble on you sometimes, but the rest of us won't. You humans taste awful. You know, fun fact, we did initially raise humans for food, but you became so aware and intelligent we just couldn't consume you. Plus, you're awfully gamey and a very tough meat. Besides, we have evolved into herbivores. We don't eat meat. Anyone else? I'm having fun here!"

Malcolm looked around the room. Everybody was looking at their feet or just looking around the room themselves. Malcolm saw a man step forward and raise his hand. "Is it because you can? You have the power and technology, so you just took us?" he asked.

"No, that's not it either." The man-thing made a sweeping gesture with his abnormally long arm, and the lights went out. Its spotlight got brighter. It put its hands behind its back and began to pace about the room, the creatures right on its heels. "I'll level with you," it began. "You all are here because almost all of you are the chosen ones. The ones we have chosen to start a new life on a refurbished Planet Earth. You were chosen because we feel like you all have the best chance of not fucking it all up so badly again. Do we have our doubts you won't actually fuck it up? Oh yes, we do. Every time we give you humans a new planet, you destroy it again. We have decided this is the last time, so we painstakingly handpicked all of you to repopulate the planet. Next time, we're just going to destroy the sun and watch you all slowly freeze to death. If I'm being honest here, giving you this one last chance was barely passed. One vote saved your planet this time. Nothing will next time." The man-thing pointed at Malcolm, and a spotlight hit Malcolm. "This man here is not a chosen. He just escaped his fate and somehow found his way here. That is why he was going to be destroyed. Now we are not totally without empathy for you humans, quite the opposite really. We love you, we really do, but goddammit, you infuriate us a lot of times. You all saved this man's life today. Your show of solidarity reminded us all of why you are the chosen. Keep sticking together, humans. We do want you to succeed."

The room went pitch-black again. The sound of the door sliding open and then closed filled the room, followed by the *whir* of the elevator. Once the *whirring* stopped, the lights in the room came back on. Julia and Dana grabbed Amanda and rushed over to Malcolm.

"Oh my god! Are you okay?" Julia asked Malcolm.

"Yes, I'm fine. This is Bethany," he said, putting an arm around her.

"Hi, I'm Julia, and this is Dana and Amanda." They all exchanged pleasantries.

The lights flickered three times. Malcolm looked around the room, confused.

"That means it's food time. Three times a day or night—or whatever the hell time it is—the lights flicker like that and then food appears over there," Julia said, pointing across the room. People were already lining up by the wall.

"How's the food?" Malcolm asked.

"Pretty good, actually," Dana piped in.

"The meat's a bit gamey. You can tell it's not beef or pork. Some other red meat," Julia said. "Reminds me of venison."

"That's surprising," Malcolm said. "I'm pretty shocked they not only feed everyone but feed 'em well from the sound of it."

"Let's get some food, babe," Bethany said. "I'm so hungry."

"Let's do it, babe," he said, taking her hand and heading to the food line. Dana, Julia, and Amanda followed.

The five of them found a quiet corner and all sat down on the floor to eat. It felt nice to have a meal with other people. Malcolm had been on his own and on the road so much he almost never ate with other people. Not counting truck stops where he ate next to someone, but that wasn't enjoying a meal with people you actually liked. Despite the circumstances, it was nice to have company. It was nice to be with genuine people. And most importantly, it was a tremendous blessing to have found Bethany again. He would not let her out of his sight no matter what.

As he ate and the women chatted to get to know each other, Malcolm wondered what that thing had meant that he was not a chosen one. How had they been planning on destroying him? Thank

God Bethany had been there. She had honestly been the one that saved his life. If she hadn't been brave enough to make a ruckus, who knows what would have happened? Amanda collected everyone's empty plates and returned them to where they had gotten them. The lights dimmed in the room, and people began to find spots to settle down. Malcolm snuggled into Bethany on the floor. It felt good to be held. The lights dimmed even more to a point where it was almost completely dark. Soon, he began to hear snoring and deep, rhythmic breathing throughout the room. Malcolm heard Bethany snoring lightly and drifted off to sleep in her arms.

*****

Billy came to in the back seat of Taylor's car. He looked around and noticed he was in the hospital parking lot. Billy slowly and painful climbed out of the back seat. Pete was nowhere to be found. Did Pete just abandon him in the parking lot of the hospital? He didn't know Pete all that well, but he didn't think Pete would do something like that. Billy limped to the driver's seat and slid behind the wheel with a groan. He put the car in gear and headed back to the mall. He was going to save Taylor or get mauled trying.

Billy's jaw hit his lap when he saw a military plane sitting on top of the mall's parking garage. The group of zombie-like people and creatures were still milling about on the bottom level. Billy drove up the ramp to the top of the garage; he just had to check out that plane. He parked behind the huge plane. The cargo door was open. Billy climbed out of Taylor's car and slowly approached the plane. Inside, he could see a woman passed out on the floor. He walked into the plane and gingerly kneeled beside her. Billy gently shook her shoulder. She groaned and stirred a bit but didn't open her eyes.

"You ok, miss?" Billy asked, shaking her shoulder again.

The woman rolled over to her back and blinked open her eyes. She looked around. Billy could tell she was dazed and confused.

"Are you hurt?" he asked her.

"No, I'm fine. Just groggy," she said, still looking around. She sat up quickly. "Hope!" she exclaimed. "Where's Hope?"

"Who's Hope?" Billy asked. "You're the only one that was in here."

"We gotta find Hope," Scarlett said, getting to her feet.

She frantically searched the plane. As Billy watched her search the plane, he noticed the weapons on board. He crawled over to them and tucked a pistol and a couple clips of ammo in his coat pocket. He picked up a shotgun. Billy filled his other pockets with as many shotgun shells as he could fit.

"I have to find Hope," Scarlett said to Billy. He wanted to say, "Don't we all?" but knew that would not be a good time for sarcasm.

"I'll help if I can," Billy said. "My friend is down there being held by those things. Maybe your Hope is too?"

"Take me there!" she said sternly.

Billy struggled to his feet; his ribs were killing him. Scarlett noticed he was in pain and gave him a hand to get to his feet.

"Are you okay?" she asked him.

"No, ma'am. One of things stomped on my chest, and I'm pretty sure it broke every rib I got," he said with a grimace. His breathing was raspy.

"My name is Scarlett. No need to call me ma'am," Scarlett said, guiding Billy out of the plane.

"I'm Billy. Nice to meet you, Scarlett."

"You too, Billy."

Scarlett helped Billy into the passenger seat of Taylor's car and then jumped into the driver's seat.

"Where to?" she asked.

"Just take that ramp down," he said, pointing out his window to the ramp off the garage. "They're right under us."

"God, I hope she is close. I can't lose anyone else," Scarlett said.

"I hope so too," Billy said.

Scarlett was shocked at what she saw when they got to the bottom level of the parking garage.

"That's her!" Scarlett shouted, startling Billy. "That's Hope right there!" she exclaimed, pointing at a young teenage girl.

"That's my friend Taylor over there by that young boy," Billy said.

"What's wrong with them?" Scarlett asked. "They look like zombies."

"I don't know," Billy said.

"How'd you know your friend was here?" she asked, looking over at Billy.

"Followed him here," Billy panted, trying to catch his breath again. "Me, Taylor, and this dude Pete were headed up to the mountain to where Pete's parents live when some cop car started chasing us. We knew it wasn't real cops chasing us, so we ran. We got off the main road to lose the car on the side streets. Then I saw a little boy just walkin' down the middle of the street. He looked dazed and totally out of it. Taylor almost ran the kid over! Taylor slammed on the brakes and got out to see if the kid was okay. As soon as he got out of the car, he looked totally dazed too. Then these lights came from the skies and creatures appeared. Pete wanted me to try to grab Taylor and pull him into the car as we drove past. But when I reached out to grab Taylor, a creature pulled me out of the car and stomped on my chest. It's all so crazy." Billy trailed off.

"It's all so unbelievable. If I hadn't seen and lived through what I just did, I wouldn't believe any of it. Shit, man, I flew here, wherever we are, with the president of the United States! In a military airplane! I saw fighter jets shoot a flying saucer out of the air!"

"Holy shit! Really? Damn, that's badass!" Billy said, smiling.

"It was terrifying, Billy, not badass. None of this is badass." Scarlett paused and looked at Billy. He kind of looked like he had just been scolded by his mother. She was done with the stories; she had to save Hope. "So how do you want to go about saving Hope and your friend?"

"I say we blast those nasty things. Maybe if we kill 'em, it'll release the trance the people are in."

"There's a lot of those things," she said, looking around. Across the street, she could see a gas station. "What about a diversion?" she said. "What if we could somehow blowup those gas pumps?"

"That may work," Billy said. "Think I could just blast the pumps with this shotgun?"

"Not from over here. Besides, the shotgun blasts would get the attention of those things. We have to be able to hide before the explosion. We gotta crash the car into those pumps."

"No way, Taylor loves this car!" Billy said.

"We don't have a choice. I think it's the only way to distract those things."

Billy noticed a big, jacked-up truck parked behind them, facing the gas station.

"Or if that truck back there has keys in it, we could use that. It's bigger."

"That'll work. Come on, let's go," Scarlett said, sliding out of the car. Neither the creatures or the people in the parking garage paid them any attention at all. The creatures had all their focus on the people, and the people were in that trance-like state; they had no idea what was going on.

Scarlett and Billy snuck over to the truck. The keys were in the ignition. There was a full gas can in the bed of the truck. Scarlett went to the flower beds along the side walk and found a big rock. She started the truck and put the rock on the gas pedal. The engine roared to full power. Billy doused the cab of the truck in gasoline and lit it on fire. He carefully reached in and forced the shifter into drive. Scarlett and Billy rushed back to Taylor's car and hid behind it. The truck took off like a cannon ball across the street. It plowed through both banks of gas pumps. The flames from the truck ignited the escaping gas and blew the whole place. The explosion shook the ground, and they could feel the heat from the fireball.

It worked; the explosion got the attention of the creatures. The creatures ventured out of the parking garage to investigate the explosion. As they did, Scarlett and Billy snuck in behind them. Billy found Taylor; he was still in a heavy daze. Billy grabbed him and pulled him back to the car. Scarlett found Hope and pulled her back to the car. Billy painfully pulled Taylor into the back seat with him. Scarlett loaded Hope into the passenger seat and ran around to the driver's side. The creatures had noticed what was happening and were running toward the car. Billy put the shotgun out the window and pulled the trigger. He hit one of the creatures in the leg, and it went down screaming. Scarlett threw the car into drive and peeled out of there. She had no idea where in the country she was, but she didn't need to ask Billy for directions. Any direction that took them away from those things was the right direction. With the tires squealing, she pulled onto the main street and sped away from the mall. The creatures quit chasing them as soon as they were out of the parking lot. Scarlett didn't slow down.

After about two miles, Taylor and Hope started to come out of their trances. They were both very groggy and extremely confused. Taylor wondered who the woman driving his car was and who was that girl up front with her. Why was he in the back seat with Billy? What happened to Billy? He was obviously badly injured. And where did he get a shotgun? Where was Pete? They were obviously running from something, so he decided to stay quiet for the time being. He didn't want to be a distraction with a bunch of questions.

"What now, guys?" Scarlett asked, slowing down a little. She figured they had put enough distance between themselves and those things.

"I dunno," Billy said, looking over at Taylor. Taylor shrugged. He was still wondering what in the hell was going on.

"I don't even know where we are. And by that, I mean what city? What state? You guys from around here?" Scarlett asked.

"Yeah, we are," Billy said. "This is Spokane, Washington. So where are you from?"

"Spokane, Washington, huh? I've heard of it. My parents were from Portland but decided city life wasn't how they wanted to raise their daughters. I grew up in Mosier, Oregon, but I've lived in Des Moines for almost twenty years now."

"So how'd you end up on the mall parking garage here?" Billy asked.

"That I don't know. We were supposed to be going to some base. Apparently, the base is fully functional. The president had to get there so they could launch an attack on those things. We obviously never made it. Last thing I remember is the president disappearing into a red light. Then Hope and I passed out, I guess." Scarlett was still driving but had slowed down considerably.

"Well, you guys were damn close to that base," Billy said. "And it's a damn good thing you never made it."

"Why is it a good thing? Those things took my daughter. Tell me how to get to that base. Maybe they can help us get up there—or wherever those things took my daughter."

"There isn't a base anymore. The aliens blew it up right after we left it," Billy said. "Besides, I don't think they would have been able to help. I got the impression they didn't know what they were doing there. If you saw the president disappear into a red light, then they have her," he said, pointing to the sky. "Pete said that happened to one of his friends."

"Shit! Those fuckin' things are hell-bent on destroying all of us!" Scarlett exclaimed. "And I know what the red light is—that's how they got my daughter. We need to find a way to get up there!"

"You seriously want to get abducted by them?" Billy exclaimed.

"I have to find my daughter and the president!"

"Not a good idea," Billy said.

"Okay, we are not going to purposely get abducted," Taylor piped in. "My grandma lives about five miles north of where we are now. Let's just go to her house, get some food and water, and then figure out our next step."

Scarlett reluctantly agreed to that idea. Taylor directed her to his grandmother's place. It was a quaint little place. The whole neighborhood was dark. Taylor's grandmother wasn't home; his parents had gotten her so she could be with them.

"We need rest too," Taylor said.

"We don't have time," Scarlett said. "We have to find my daughter! Those things have her, and I will fight every last one of them 'til I find her!"

"How?" Taylor asked. "I don't mean to be rude, and I am really sorry to hear about your daughter, but how exactly are the four of us going to fight an army of those things?"

"I don't know, but we have to."

"Look, I'm tired of running. I'm hungry and exhausted," Taylor said. "Billy is hurt—not sure what happened, but he's clearly injured."

"Creature stomped my chest, dude," Billy interjected.

"What we need to do now is rest and come up with a solid plan," Taylor continued. "Just tooling around hoping to get snatched or run into them isn't a good idea. I understand you wanting to find your daughter, but let's be smart about it. I saw things when I was with the creatures. They are way more intelligent and stronger than you can imagine. They know where we are and what we're doing. We gotta be careful."

Scarlett knew Taylor was right. She was starving and exhausted, plus they needed a solid plan. Taylor and Scarlett whipped up some canned food in the fireplace. They all sat down around the kitchen table to eat and devise a plan. They agreed to sleep for a couple hours. Regain some strength before trying to find Gwen and the president.

It took no time for Taylor and Billy, who had each taken a couch in the living room, to fall asleep. Scarlett lay in Taylor's grandmother's bed next to Hope, who had also fallen asleep quickly. Scarlett tried to fight falling asleep. She was worried that if she let herself sleep, she may end up sleeping longer than she wanted to. Sleep wasn't a priority to her, but she knew they all needed some rest. Scarlett couldn't remember the last time she had slept. It was a losing battle, and exhaustion finally won out. Scarlett drifted off to sleep.

CHAPTER 10

A New Planet

Pete found himself sitting in a room full of large tables and chairs. Two sides of the room were concrete walls with a door in the middle of one of the walls. The other two sides of the room were windows. Large floor-to-ceiling windows. Pete stood up and walked to the windows. The view he encountered was breathtaking. There, right outside those windows, was infinite darkness, dotted with bright stars. He could see the earth and the moon. The planet was dark but so beautiful. Pete had never imagined in his life he would get to see the earth from outer space. It was truly stunning. Pete stood there taking in the awe-inspiring beauty of his planet and its orbit.

"Beautiful view, huh?" a man's voice said from behind him. Pete was startled by the sudden interruption, and he spun around. There was a man; he looked like a bad drawing of a man. The man-thing was very creepy looking to Pete.

"Uh, yeah," Pete stammered. "It's great."

"No need to be nervous, Pete," the man-thing said. Pete did not like the way it had said his name. "We mean you no harm. If we had meant you harm, you wouldn't be standing here right now."

Pete didn't say anything; he didn't know what to say. God, that man-thing was so odd looking. It walked over to the windows, clasped its hands behind its back, and stared out the window. It looked over its shoulder to Pete and motioned for him to join it at the window.

"We sure are proud of that planet," it said, gesturing to Earth. "We miss it—that's why we visit so much. It's become our Disneyland. You humans are fun to observe." The man-thing turned to Pete and smiled. Its skin rippled. "I bet you're wondering why you're here."

"Um, yeah, I am," Pete responded, staring out the windows at Earth.

"It's your lineage. You come from a long line of strong, intelligent men. You have strong leadership qualities, even if you haven't figured that out for yourself yet. You have been blessed with exceptional genes, and we need men like you to repopulate that planet." It nodded to Earth.

Pete was confused. The man-thing looked over at him, its skin rippled again. Pete could feel tears welling up in his eyes. He didn't think that thing had the right guy. Pete didn't feel like he had any of those qualities.

"My lineage, huh?" Pete asked, quietly.

"Yup. You don't believe me?"

"Honestly, no. I don't see anything exceptional about me or my family. My dad is a lawyer, just like his dad and his granddad. Nothing special to me."

"Your great-grandfather was a mayor and brought his city out of the Great Depression, which we tried to steer you humans away from, by the way. He was an extraordinary leader and man. He pasted those qualities onto his son, your grandfather, who was a decorated military leader before becoming an attorney."

"How do you know all of that?" Pete asked.

"We know everything, Pete," the man-thing said.

"I don't feel like that's me. I think you have the wrong guy."

"Well, here's the thing: it *is* you or we dispose of you. We want the best of the best, but if any of you chosen ones become too difficult, we have zero qualms with eliminating you too. All of you question it. You humans get so gun-shy when you're asked to fulfill your destiny. We have saved you from the end of your world. You should be fuckin' grateful, not so cynical." The man-thing paused and walked over to the concrete wall next to the windows. It pushed a button Pete hadn't noticed, and a control panel popped out of the wall. "Watch this," it said and pushed a big green button.

The man-thing walked back over to Pete and pointed out the window. Within minutes, dozens and dozens of flying saucers broke through Earth's atmosphere and hovered just above the windows. Shortly after the saucers appeared, dozens of larger ships burst through the atmosphere and disappeared above the mothership.

"Pretty cool, huh, Pete?" the man-thing asked.

"Uh, yeah, I guess so. Why are you showing me all of this?"

"Good question, Peter. A lot of you chosen ones are just natural-born leaders who don't need any nudging ahead of time. But then there's you. We knew if we just dropped you back down there, you'd panic and fail. Just to be clear, when I say *you*, I mean you specifically, Pete. We really do want you down there when it's time to start over. We think between your genes and raw talent, you will help to populate a strong, new society. You're the kind of guy that needs to see everything to know what to do later. That's not an insult, just a fact of your personality right now. We know you can be a dynamic leader, Pete. You have it in you."

"So now what? You just take us back and we're on our own?" Pete asked. He didn't like any of what he had just heard. These things wiped out most of mankind and just kept a select few? None of it made much sense to Pete. This man-thing had just told him what they expected of him, but why had they done any of it? "Why do you even need to destroy anyone?"

"Let me answer the last question first because you have, yet again, destroyed that beautiful planet. It will all be explained shortly by President Cecilia Rodgers. We have put her in charge of the initial transition. To answer your first questions, yes and no. We will put preselected groups on seven different ships and drop the groups off on each continent. Anyone who decides not to play ball will not get to go back. In what will feel like just a few weeks to you humans but will actually be a couple hundred Earth years, you all will be home again. But before any of that, now that we have gotten all the chosen ones and everything else, we will need to create a new ecosystem. We need to destroy the rest of what you all damaged so badly. No more cities, towns, infrastructures—there will be nothing left. Then the rebuild begins. We will work endlessly to get that perfect planet thriving again and then return you and the others. We're hoping to see you all live long and happy lives. And hopefully you won't destroy it all yet again." The man-thing walked back to the control panel. "Now watch this," it said and pushed a big red button. "Watch the planet, Pete."

Pete looked out the window and saw the entire planet slowly light up in a brilliant yellow and orange glow. His eyes widened. He had a damn good idea what that was.

"Everything is gone again," the man-thing said with a hint of sadness to his robotic voice. "Sucks you humans make us do this so regularly. We just wish you would respect that wonderful world we gave you. Well, at least for our state of mind, this will be the last time we give you paradise. If—although most of the elders believe it'll be *when*—you humans destroy the planet again, we won't save any of you. We'll just blow up your sun and watch as you all slowly freeze to death. Either that or just move the planet closer to the sun and make it hotter than Venus. We haven't decided which would be more fun to watch. You humans do like to sunbathe—maybe we'll go that route." The man-thing chuckled and went back to the control panel. It pushed a button and the panel popped back into the wall. "You may stay for a bit and watch your planet burn," it said to Pete and headed toward the door on the far side of the room.

"Wait," Pete said. The man-thing stopped and turned to face Pete. "I just want to really understand everything you have just told me."

"What else is there to understand, Peter?"

"So, um, you guys will just watch us forever? And if we don't satisfy your expectations, you're just going to wipe us out?"

"Pretty much. At this point, you humans are like a sick old dog. We desperately want to save you, we want so many more years with you, but at some point, you just have to put it down."

"What's stopping us from fighting back?" Pete said with a shaky voice. He could feel himself shaking from nerves. He had never stood up to any kind of authority figure, not that he thought that thing was an authority figure. It still unnerved him because he didn't know what the man-thing would do to him.

The man-thing threw its misshapen head back and laughed. "Oh, you humans!" It laughed. "Every damn time, one of you says that to us. It'll never happen. Once we drop you back on that planet, you won't remember a damn thing. We will give you all happy new memories. It'll be like none of this ever happened."

"It's not fair," Pete said, still shaking.

The man-thing laughed again. "You're partially right, Pete, it's not fair. It's not fair to us that we work so hard to provide such a wonderful planet for you humans to thrive on and you just continually destroy it."

"Why not work together? Why do you stay so hidden until it's time to 'fix' Earth?" Pete asked, sincerely curious.

"You humans wouldn't be able to handle that. We make our presence known to the few special ones that we believe can handle knowing of our existence, and we hope they will lead appropriately. Most of the time, they don't. Corruption among you humans is so bad. You're so easily persuaded by money and status. If one of your beloved athletes wears a certain shoe, you gotta have it. If one of your movie stars drinks a certain kind of soda, that's the only soda you drink. You humans are so envious. You envy those who have more than you, while those who have more look down on the rest of you. We've tried to step in and help without resetting everything, but your pride and envy always gets in the way. You humans just cannot accept help from others. If you didn't ask for it, it's useless to you. You humans rebel. Rebelling never works out well for you all. That's why we do things the way we do. And that's also why we're never doing it again. We are at a point where we'd rather just turn that planet into an uninhabitable wasteland than deal with your shit much longer."

Pete felt his heart racing and his body tingle with rage. How dare that thing say human life is so unvaluable? That's essentially what it said to him. It sure did like to talk, but Pete understood the underlying message was, they were always going to be in control and they strongly believed the humans couldn't do a damn thing about it. Pete wanted to kill that man-thing. He had never had feelings like that before. He thought about how many lives had already been lost. He thought about how in another few hundred years, those things would probably just destroy all life on Earth, and he hated that idea. Pete knew he'd never live to see that, but he knew he'd have family that would. He couldn't imagine what it would be like to lose the sun or be pushed closer to it. What a horrific way for future generations to go out. The man-thing stared at Pete, waiting for some kind of response. Pete wouldn't say anything else. The man-thing raised its right hand to Pete. Pete felt his throat tighten as if someone had their hands around his neck. He felt his feet lift off the ground. His eyes began to bug out, and he couldn't breathe.

"You cannot defeat us. Not now, not ever," the man-thing said. Its eyes had gotten even blacker than before. The man-thing dropped its right arm, and Pete fell to his knees, gasping for air. "Again, just be grateful, you little prick! No more of this nonsense or we'll end it all now. And we'll start with your precious Amanda. We'll make sure you're there to witness her agonizing demise. You gonna play ball, Peter? Or are we going to have to make this even messier?"

"Uh-huh." Pete nodded, still gasping for air. "I'll play ball."

"Good." The man-thing waved its hand at Pete, and Pete passed out on the floor. The man-thing left the room, leaving Pete behind.

*****

John woke up to Serena shaking him. He blinked open his eyes and saw his wife looking down on him. As everything slowly came into focus, he could feel coldness along his back and legs. He sat up and looked around. They were in a decent-sized but cramped room. It looked like a laboratory, but not like any lab he'd ever seen. It was all so very foreign. There were shelves and shelves packed full of what looked like science projects. Jars filled with amber liquid with pieces and parts of God knew what floating in them. They were surrounded by shelves full of it. John was on what looked like an operating table.

"Where are the boys?" John asked her.

"I don't know, John. I just woke up lying on that table next to you a few minutes ago. We have to find them!"

"We will, baby," he said. "Let's get out of here first."

John got to his feet and was shocked that he didn't feel any more pain. He rubbed his hip and lower back; everything felt as it had before the wreck. Working most of his life on a farm had left him with mild, everyday aches and pains and that was all he could feel. He felt normal again, but how? He wasn't going to waste any time questioning it; they had to find their sons. John and Serena looked around the cramped room. They were appalled by what they saw. The jars had *human* remains in them. Each and every part of the human body, both male and female, was floating in a jar. John saw the terror in his wife's eyes and took her hand. They scanned the room for a way out but didn't see anything at first. That made it so they had to move about the room and take in more of the grotesque contents of those many, many jars. It wasn't a large room, but it seemed like it took forever to finally find the door. They expected it to be locked, but it swung open with no problem.

John and Serena, hand-in-hand, slowly exited the room. They stepped out into a narrow hallway. The left side of the hall was lined with doors that were equal distance apart for the entire length of the hallway. The other side of the hall was all windows. They stopped in shock and amazement as they stared out into the dark, starry universe. With mouths open, they slowly turned to each other.

"Let's keep going," John said and tugged on Serena's hand. She looked out the window again before heading down the hall with John.

They were approaching the end of the long hallway when a bell went off. It startled them and they stopped in their tracks. Every door that had lined the left side of the hallway popped open. Creatures like what John had seen in the window of the ambulance stepped out of each door. They all sniffed the air and quickly turned their massive heads toward John and Serena. John and Serena looked at the creatures for a split second and then took off running. They rounded the corner at the end of the hall, only to encounter another long hallway full of those creatures. They were surrounded. Nowhere to go. The creatures surrounded them. John's head started to pound, and his heart raced as sweat flooded from his hairline.

"Come with us," a robotic voice said in John's head.

The creatures all turned up the hall and guided John and Serena down the hall with them. John and Serena couldn't see anything but the creatures surrounding them. It felt like they were being led through a maze of hallways. Finally, the creatures stopped and made a path for John and Serena. There was another door, and it looked exactly like the door of the room they had just left. Had those things just led them back to that awful laboratory?

"Go through the door, John," the same robotic voice said.

John clenched Serena's hand a bit tighter, and they went through the door. On the other side of the door was a huge, open room full of people. There had to be thousands of people in that big, bright room. The room was very hot and smelled of body odor and urine. In fact, everywhere they had been thus far had smelled of urine.

"Mommy!"

It was Jeff. He and JJ rushed to their parents and hugged them tightly.

"Mommy, I was so scared," Jeff said, tears in his eyes and a hitch to his voice.

"You boys okay?" John asked.

"Yeah, Dad," JJ said. "We just been looking for you guys. Where were you?"

"I don't know, son," he said, hugging JJ. "It doesn't matter, we're all safe now."

"What is this place?" Jeff asked.

"I don't know that either, son," John said. "Let's just stick together and stay with all these other people. We'll just find a spot to ourselves and settle in for a bit."

They wandered around the room for a bit, looking for a spot they could sit down. That room had nothing in it except for people. No furniture at all. They found a spot against the cold metal wall next to a man and four women. The group were chatting away as if they all knew each other fairly well. The man and one of the women were holding each other; they were clearly a couple. John nodded to the man as he sat down, and the man nodded back. John sat closest to the group with the boys next to him and Serena on the other side of the boys. JJ leaned against his father, and Jeff cuddled into their mother. John scanned the sea of people. They all looked helpless and frightened. Everyone looked just as confused as he felt.

"Now what?" Serena asked John.

"I don't know, baby. We just wait, I guess. I don't want to be out there with those things. Seems safe in here."

"What things, Dad?" JJ asked.

"Never mind, son, it's not important now. Your mom and I will keep you boys safe no matter what, ok?"

JJ nodded.

"How did you boys end up in here?" John asked.

"I dunno," JJ said. "We just woke up here. I heard Jeff crying, and it woke me up. Then we just walked all around looking for you and Mom."

"How long ago was that?" Serena asked.

"I dunno. Seemed like a few hours, I guess," JJ shrugged.

"Well, boys, I think we're all safe now," John said, looking around the room again. He made eye contact with the man next to them again. "Hey," John said to the man, "can I ask you all a question?"

"Sure can," Malcolm said.

"Do you know where we are?" John asked.

"You want me to answer that in front of your kids?" Malcolm asked.

"Probably not if you feel the need to even ask that question," John said.

"Come on, then, let's have a little walk," Malcolm said, standing up.

John stood up and joined Malcolm. They introduced themselves to each other and the others in their respective groups. Malcolm and John wandered off toward the other side of the room.

"So to answer your question, we're on the mothership," Malcolm said.

"The mothership?" John asked and stopped to look at Malcom.

"Yup, sounds crazy, but this is indeed an alien mothership. Most of us that've been in here awhile have seen 'em. One of 'em in a bad human suit even spoke to us." Malcolm saw the look of utter disbelief on John's tired face.

"They speak out loud?" John asked.

"Yeah, sounds like a computer translator—probably is, in fact. Doubt they speak English regularly."

"I've heard 'em in my head but never out loud," John said, staring at the floor, trying to wrap his mind around everything.

"I'm sure it's just as creepy either way," Malcolm said.

"What did it have to say?" John asked, looking at Malcolm.

"Told us that we—well, everyone except for me apparently—are all the chosen ones. Those things are going to 'fix' the planet and put us back on it to rebuild and repopulate it. I don't know, man, it all sounded so crazy to me."

"It is all so crazy. Those things are big and scary."

"They are nasty things, that's for sure."

"How long have you been here?" John asked.

"My best guess is about two days now. I couldn't really tell you. There's no way to know what time of day it is. Three times a day, a door in that wall down there pops open and there's plates of food inside. Everyone gets one helping three times a day. Shortly after the third meal, the lights flicker and dim to almost complete darkness. Everyone settles onto the floor and tries to get some sleep. The amount of people in here is growing so fast that it's getting harder and harder to find space to yourself 'round here. The number of people has gone from a few hundred when I first got here to at least a thousand now," Malcolm said.

"Sure is crowded," John said. "Any troublemakers I should be aware of?"

"No, people are nice and respectful. My friends said a guy was harassing them about religious stuff and then he was somehow blown up. That's another thing—evidently we all have some sort of explosive device implanted in us that they can blow at any time."

"*What?*" John exclaimed. "Even my sons?"

"I'd guess so," Malcolm said.

"Holy shit," John said, shaking his head. "So at any moment, they could just blow any of us up?"

"Yeah, pretty much, but word is they will only do that if someone is being difficult or harassing other people. They made it pretty clear they want us all alive. You should feel good about being here, man. I woke up strapped to a metal table with tubes in me. I was lucky people came to my rescue 'cuz they were going to blow me up."

"Jesus, man. Holy shit."

"Yeah, that's about all that can be said about all this," Malcolm said, patting John on the shoulder. "All we can do now is ride it out, my man. Just wait 'til we're back home."

"From what you've told me, that seems like our only option, huh?"

"Yup, it really is. Hey, the accommodations ain't good, but we're still alive," Malcolm said.

"That's a good way to look at things right now. The only way in fact," John said. "Thank you for not saying anything in front of my boys. This is way too heavy for them to understand."

"I figured it'd be too much for kids to hear. I'd seen them wandering around—they looked absolutely terrified. People tried to help them, but your kids kept their distance from everyone."

"They're good boys," John said. "We taught them not to talk to strangers unless it was a fireman or cop. Thank you again for filling me in on everything. It is a tiny relief to know a little about what's going on."

"No problem, John," Malcolm said.

"One last question," John started. "You trust what those things told you?"

"I don't have a choice, do I?" Malcolm answered with a shrug.

"That's true. They got us by the balls, don't they?"

"They sure as hell do!" Malcolm said with a chuckle.

"Well, man, thanks again," John said, extending his hand.

"You bet," Malcolm said, shaking John's hand.

They headed back to their groups and settled back in. John reached behind the boys and put his hand on Serena's shoulder. The boys snuggled into John, and Serena relaxed against the unforgiving metal wall. They all sat there watching people mill about. Serena wanted to know what John had found out but knew that wasn't the time to ask about it. She knew if it was something bad, John would pull her aside and fill her in. Serena trusted John and if he was able to settle down and snuggle their sons, whatever he had just been told couldn't be that bad. She just wished she knew how long they'd be stuck there. Stuck on a spaceship in the middle of outer space. She knew exactly where they were; she just needed to know why.

*****

Scarlett woke up to the sound of Billy coughing and gagging. She rolled over to check on Hope, and she wasn't in bed. Scarlett rushed out to the living room to see Billy lying on his side, coughing up blood. The entire house was lit up from a bright light outside. Scarlett looked around for Taylor, but he was nowhere around either. She hurried to Billy and urged him to get up.

"I can't," he wheezed. "Hope, Taylor, outside." He coughed. "Leave, me."

"Not a chance," Scarlett said. "We're all a team now."

"I'm dying," Billy gurgled.

"The hell you are!" Scarlett exclaimed. "Come on, get up. We can get you help."

"I can't," he choked.

"I'll help. I got you, Billy." Scarlett put an arm under Billy and helped him to his feet. He coughed and wheezed the whole way up. Blood flew from his lips with each cough.

Scarlett was able to help Billy limp outside. The light hit them both like an avalanche. Scarlett saw Hope and Taylor standing in the middle of the street looking up at a huge aircraft. The aircraft was so low it just barely cleared the pine trees. Hope and Taylor were in that trance-like state again. Billy coughed violently, and Scarlett dropped him. He hit the ground with a thud and gasped for air. Scarlett knelt down to help him up.

"No. Get… Hope. Save…them." He coughed. "Please," Billy pleaded with her. She could see how scared he was, but he was clearly begging her to save Hope and Taylor.

Scarlett stood up and ran to Hope. As soon as she was ten yards away from Billy, that pulsing red light engulfed him, and he quickly vanished into it. Scarlett stopped and stared at the spot on the lawn where she had just left Billy. He was gone. She looked up at the large aircraft.

"Take us too!" she screamed.

The pulsing red light snagged Hope, then Taylor. Scarlett felt panic surge through her.

"You have my daughter! Please, I need to find my daughter!" she screamed at the top of her lungs. She heard laughter inside her head. Scarlett suddenly felt violently ill. It felt like she was going to vomit. The abdominal cramps made her double over in pain. Everything was spinning, and she fell to the ground. She could still hear that maniacal laughter inside her head. It was so sinister and evil sounding. It was them! They had taken everyone she knew and loved and now they were rubbing it in! She wanted so badly to scream, but she couldn't. She knew if she did, all that would come out of her would be vomit.

"*Sleep.*" A voice broke through the laughter in her head.

Clutching her midsection, she shook her head.

"*Sleep and we'll show you your daughter,*" the voice said. The laughter was gone.

"Please," Scarlett whimpered.

"*All you have to do is sleep.*"

"I just want to see my daughter," Scarlett cried. The sick feeling was subsiding.

"*You may regret that when you see her,*" the voice said. "*Sometimes it's better to remember them at their best.*"

"What'd you fuckers do to her?" Scarlett yelled.

"*ENOUGH!*" the voice screeched inside her head, making it feel like it was about to explode. "*Sleep,*" it whispered. It whispered "*Sleep*" over and over again until Scarlett did slip into a deep sleep.

*****

"Madam President Cecilia Rodgers, wake up," Eve Adams said, shaking Cecilia gently.

Cecilia awoke and sat up. She was still at the table in that restaurant area. Abby wasn't beside her anymore.

"Where's Abby?" Cecilia asked, frantically scanning the room.

"She's safe." Eve Adams smiled.

"I want to see her! You had her in that room where you prepared people for slaughter! I want to make sure you won't hurt that poor girl."

"We never had any such intentions, Madam President. The girl wandered off and got lost."

"Bullshit! She told me she woke up in there on a table! Kids too! You're killing and cooking up kids too?!"

"No, Madam President, we certainly are not. It is time for your speech." Eve Adams tried to hand Cecilia a tablet, but she wouldn't take it.

"I'm not doing you any favors until I see that little girl! I must know she's safe!"

"The more you annoy me, the less safe she will become. I assure you, Madam President, the little girl is fine and will remain that way. Unless you continue to fight me."

"Goddammit! I'm sick of this shit!" Cecilia exclaimed, getting up and approaching the grotesque woman. "You will go on and on about your plans but then be so fucking vague about what really matters!"

"I'm not being vague, Madam President. That little girl is safe. Now drop it."

"No, I won't drop it! You guys think you have us by the balls because you control whether or not we live through this, but the thing is, we don't care if we die here or not. I am a woman of faith, and I know I will spend eternity in heaven with my Lord, so do your worst!" Cecilia stared at Eve Adams.

Eve Adams threw her oversized head back and howled in laughter. "There is no God. There is no heaven. This is it, Madam President. If you die on this space craft, it's over. You humans *need* to believe there's something after your life, but let me assure you there is not. We're almost done with the planet. This is all almost over. Do you really want to just give up and die? Or do you want to be the hero you deserve to be? The woman who goes down in human history as the greatest leader of all time. You being the first female leader will rewrite the male/female dynamic that has plagued the human race for centuries. We have tapped a young man who comes from a long line of great leaders and strong genes. We can elevate him early and just do away with you, but I'm afraid that would end up creating another male-dominated society. You, and you alone, can change all of that right here, right now. So, Madam President, I guess you are correct—we do have you by the balls. What's your decision?"

Cecilia looked at her with anger and hatred. She knew she didn't have a choice but to go along with what they wanted. If she wanted to live, and she did, she had to do their bidding. Once they were put back on Earth, she could change the world for the better. Her legacy didn't matter to her as much as saving the human race. That's the thing about legacies: you don't live to see your own legacy. They did have her by the balls, and she had no choice but to play ball.

Cecilia sighed. "Fine. I'm in. What do you need me to do?" she asked, completely defeated.

Eve Adams handed Cecilia the tablet. "We have gathered all the chosen into one room. We want you to read that prepared speech. That is it. Read it verbatim and you will come across as the savior of the humans. We have had to interject and have had to tell some of the chosen our plans, but their memories of that will be wiped clean before you speak to them. They will all be very confused and probably upset. None of them will remember how or when they got here. You humans tend to panic when you don't have control over your circumstances, so the chosen ones will most likely be agitated. This speech should calm them down and make you look like the Queen Bee. You, Madam President, have just saved the human race from the evil extraterrestrials." She chuckled at that. "Fifteen minutes and we will bring you in to them." Eve Adams turned and left the room.

Cecilia sat back down at the table and began to read the speech. From sentence one, it was all lies. She shook her head and chuckled to herself throughout her reading of the speech. How would anyone believe any of that garbage? Even without any recollection of how or why the others were there, there was just no way any of that speech would be believable. Cecilia sat back in her chair and put her hands on her head. She smiled to herself. *They won't believe it,* she thought. *I can use that to my advantage.*

Cecilia hit the Edit tab on the tablet and began to rework most of the speech. She hoped if she dropped little nuggets of truth into the speech, it would be retained by those listening. If she could just somehow get people to understand what had really been going on, then maybe they would find a way to eliminate the aliens once back on Earth. It was at least worth a shot. Worst case scenario, the aliens would wipe everyone's memories again.

In the excitement of her plan, she forgot that the actual worst case scenario was the end of the human race.

*****

Billy woke up on an operating table in a small, cold operating room. The room was lit very dimly, and he was completely alone. His skin had goosebumps from the chilly air. As Billy began to sit up, he braced himself for the excruciating pain in his rips. There was no pain at all. He drew in a deep breath and nothing. He could breathe normally again and had zero pain. How was that even possible? The last thing he remembered was lying on Taylor's grandmother's front lawn, coughing up blood. Billy looked at his bare chest expecting to see surgical scars, but there weren't any. Someone, or some*thing*, had obviously fixed him up somehow. He knew he had had a punctured lung; that doesn't just heal without surgery.

It was all so perplexing, but he wasn't going to dwell on it. Billy felt better than he had in a long time. He got up off the table and searched the room for something to wear. All he was wearing was a pair of boxers that he didn't recognize as his own. That room was freezing; he needed to find clothes or at least a blanket. There was nothing in the room except for surgical instruments and medical supplies. Billy exited the double doors and found himself in a room full of stainless-steel tables with bodies on them. Every single table had a body on it. Men and women of all nationalities laid on those tables. They all looked to be very dead. The rank odor of death filled the room and his nostrils.

On the far side of the room, he saw an open closet with clothes strewn about. Still shivering, he rushed over to the closet and hurriedly sifted through the clothing. He found a pair of work pants and a hoodie. Billy dressed and got the hell out of that horrible room. His skin crawled from the smell and the sight of dead bodies. That room was by far the creepiest place he had ever been, and he had been to some creepy places before. Billy had been fascinated with ghost hunting and done several trips before the world had basically ended. On one trip, he was directly spoken to by the spirit of a young girl who had been killed in a house fire. That experience creeped him out and broke his heart, but that room he had just been in was far worse than anything else.

The room he entered after hurrying out of the dead body room looked exactly like the other room, stainless-steel tables with people laid out on them. Billy's heart sank. How many rooms were there like that? The new room didn't have the smell of death. Billy could hear what sounded like oxygen machines running in the room. He went to the first table, and the woman who was lying on it had her eyes open. Her eyes widened when she saw Billy. She didn't say anything, but her eyes were lit up with relief. Her eyes begged him to help her. He noticed an IV in her arm and touched it. The woman nodded to him with her eyes to pull it out. Billy gently removed the IV, and within minutes, the woman was moving her limbs. Billy unstrapped the woman, and she thanked him profusely. The woman got off the table and hugged Billy.

"We need to help everyone else!" she said, making her way to the next table.

The woman went down one side of the room, removing IVs and unstrapping people as Billy did the same on the opposite side of the room. There was a teenage girl on the last table on Billy's side of the room. Her eyes were closed, and she was unresponsive. Billy removed the I.V. in her arm, but nothing changed. Everyone else had come to right away and had regained strength and movement almost immediately, but not that teenage girl. People were leaving the room as soon as they had been freed. Billy gently shook the teenager and heard her groan. It was clear by the noise she had made that she was in some pain. The girl slowly blinked her eyes open and looked at Billy. Her eyes were bloodshot and distant. Tears rolled out of the corner of her eyes.

"Can you move?" Billy asked her.

The girl shook her head. Billy unstrapped her and picked her up. The room had already emptied out. Billy was irritated and frankly pissed off that everyone had just left. No one stuck around to help with the injured teenager.

Billy heard the door at the back of the room open. He turned around, and there was a woman approaching him. Billy knew instantly she was not human.

"You can set the girl down, Billy," the woman-thing said to him.

"Who are you?" Billy asked, still holding the teenager.

"That is not important, Billy," it said to him.

"If you want me to listen to you, I believe it's very important," Billy said rudely. He turned to leave.

"You're a chosen one," the woman-thing said. "Put the girl down."

"What? What's a chosen one?" Billy asked.

"Put the girl down and we'll tell you."

"She's hurt. I need to get her some help," Billy said, getting even more suspicious of that thing.

"She'll be fine," it said, stepping closer to Billy. The woman-thing smelled like sulfur and death. "We patched you up. We'll take care of her too."

"Like you took care of all those people in that other room?" Billy said, clutching the teenage girl closer to him. He didn't trust that thing.

"It was their time, Billy," the woman-thing said. "I think you better listen to me or maybe it will be your time too. Is that girl worth your life, Billy?"

Billy looked at the girl in his arms, and she looked a little better. Her eyes had more life to them. He could feel her move her arms and legs every once in a while. He could tell she was coming to.

"You're seriously going to make me chose my life over a child's?" he asked the woman-thing. "Look, I don't have a life. I'm twenty-nine years old and just moved out of my mom's basement six months ago 'cuz she kicked me out. My own mom was so sick of me that she kicked me out. I'm a loser. I've never had a long-term relationship. I've never had any real friends, except for Taylor—whom I'm sure you have also. So yes, she is worth my life. She is probably actually worth something. She probably has a mom out there somewhere who is desperately looking for her."

"She does, and you know her mom."

Billy looked at the woman-thing puzzled and in disbelief.

"Think really hard about it, Billy. You've only met one woman recently who has a daughter this girl's age."

It dawned on him, and his heart sank. He was holding Scarlett's daughter. That woman-thing wanted him to choose his life over Scarlett's daughter's life. Scarlett was a good woman and obviously a great mother. He could not let that girl get hurt anymore. He had to figure a way to save her.

"Figured it out, did you?" the woman-thing grinned at him.

"I ain't leaving this girl," Billy said. "Even if it costs me my life."

"So you'd rather it be both of you that perishes here?" the woman-thing asked.

"You just said she'd be fine. You said you'd fix her up like you did for me. Now you're threatening to kill her?"

"We will fix her up. We'll even reunite her with her mom, but you have to put her down, Billy. She doesn't concern you."

"I don't trust you," Billy said.

"And why should you? You haven't given us an opportunity to earn your trust." The woman-thing took a few steps closer and put her hand on Billy's shoulder.

Billy's body froze. He lost control of his arms and dropped Gwen. The woman-thing put its other hand out and guided Gwen to the floor. Everything went dark for Billy. Before long, images began showing in his mind. He saw his mother holding him as a baby. She looked so happy and joyful. Standing next to his mother was his grandfather, his mom's dad. His granddad had been a wonderful man. Billy had loved his grandpa with every bit of his heart. His grandad had passed away suddenly from a heart attack, when Billy was twenty-one. The sudden death of her father had devastated his mother. She went from a kind, loving woman to a depressed drunk. Billy had taken his grandfather's death especially hard and just isolated himself from everything and everyone. The next image that flashed in Billy's mind was of his granddad coaching his little league team. Grandpa Bill was a tough but fair and fun coach; he was a little tougher on Billy than the rest of the team. Billy's best childhood memories were playing baseball with Grandpa Bill. Billy had dreamt of being a major leaguer and giving his grandpa his first home run ball. The image changed to Billy's mom passed out in her lazy boy chair. Drool trickled from the corner of her mouth. Billy stood over her yelling at her about something. It was so odd to see himself like that. It wasn't a still photo in his mind, but it wasn't quite a moving picture either. The next image was of Billy on the balcony of his apartment, smoking a cigarette and scrolling dating apps on his phone. He could see himself swiping *yes* on every profile he came across. He'd swipe *yes*, but no women ever swiped for him.

Billy could feel rage boiling inside of him. Why were they showing him all of that? What was the point? To prove they had been watching him for his entire life? The images went away, and Billy could see again. He still couldn't move. The woman-thing took her hand off his shoulder, and he felt control return to his body. Billy looked to his feet where Gwen should have been, but she was gone.

"Hey! Where'd Scarlett's girl go?" Billy demanded.

The woman-thing put her hand back on Billy's shoulder, and everything went black again. An image of a large room filled with people popped into his head. In the center of the room, Billy could see Scarlett hugging Gwen. Next to Scarlett was Hope and Taylor. The woman-thing removed her hand, and Billy was back in the room with her.

"See, everyone's fine," it said to him.

Billy broke into tears. "Why are you doing this?" he sobbed.

"You're special, Billy," the woman-thing replied.

"I don't feel special, especially after what you just showed me. I am not a good person. My whole life revolved around video games and trying to get laid. Neither of which I was ever good at. So what's so fuckin' special about me?"

"Deep down you're a good man. The loss of your Grandpa Bill devastated you and your mom. Grandpa Bill was the only male figure you had in your life. He genuinely cared for you, and that love went away when he died. So you tried to fill the emptiness with meaningless relationships. And when that wasn't successful, you just kept trying. The more you were turned down by women, the more you wanted them. It became a vicious cycle. You craved validation and attention. Your mom crawled into a bottle and never came out, so you didn't get either from her. The person you became after your grandfather passed away isn't the real you, Billy. You are a good man, and you are a strong man. You're charismatic, and people like you. They listen to you. They may not respect the man you became, but you can get that respect back. We want dynamic people like you down there to repopulate that beautiful planet. We need strong people. You are one of the strongest, Billy."

The tears poured out of Billy's eyes. He knew that woman-thing was right. He had given up when Grandpa Bill died. Besides work and pot runs, he never left his mom's basement. When their fighting got so bad and she kicked him out, he wrote her off. Billy regretted that. He should have been there for his mom, not fought with her.

"Don't let this chance to be great go just because you are scared," the woman-thing said.

"What chance? What are you asking me to do?" Billy sniffled.

"We have destroyed the rest of the planet and now have teams down there repairing it and getting it habitable again. Once that is finished, we will distribute you humans throughout the world. We want the best of you to take charge and rebuild a world that won't end up in the dumpster again. You humans are disgusting creatures. We need people like you to take charge and lead the rebuild. You could become an immensely powerful and wealthy man, Billy. But I warn you, do not let that go to your head. No matter the spoils or the riches, always stay grounded and lead your people to a happy, healthy, sustainable life. You humans have failed at it every damn time we do this. Please, don't let that happen again. The consequences will be dire next time."

"Like wiping out civilization?" Billy asked.

"Yes, but we won't save any of you next time. This is the human race's last chance. It's up to people like you to not fuck it up again."

"What if we just destroy you guys?" Billy asked, feeling more courageous.

The woman-thing laughed. "I knew that was coming. You all always ask that. It's impossible—we own you humans. You have no feasible way of defeating us."

"That's what everyone told my baseball team when we reached the Little League world series, 'that scrappy little team from Spokane, Washington, has zero chance of winning the series.' Well, as I'm sure you know, we swept the other team and never allowed a run. Blanked 'em!"

"This isn't baseball, Billy, and we aren't a team of little kids from Dallas. We are the master race. We created you and we will eliminate you if we have to."

"My mom used to say that shit to me all the time, 'I brought you into this world and I can take you out of it!' She never did. I was an annoying kid, but she loved me. She would've never hurt me. I think you guys love us too much to ever actually eliminate us. Look, I'll do my part. I'm sick and tired of being the pudgy guy that has nothing. The guy who spends more time glued to a screen than anything else. Before all this, I worked—a late shift so I never had to get up early—came home, smoked a shit ton of weed, and played video games all night. Every damn day! I wasted my twenties hiding behind a game controller. I wasted my youth being angry. I lost my favorite man in the world, and I let that lead me to losing my mom as well. I want to repay society for being such a piece of shit for so long. I'm in."

"Perfect, Billy. We will have more instructions for you shortly."

"One more thing," Billy said, and the woman-thing nodded. "Can I see Taylor?"

"Sure. We'll make that happen." With that, she turned and left the way she had come in. Billy sat on the table he had found Gwen on. His heart was pounding, and his mind was going a mile a minute. Could he actually be that great leader? Could he actually help rebuild the planet? Would the aliens actually let them do it?

Billy suddenly felt exhausted. He couldn't hold open his eyes. He lay down on the table and was out cold.

*****

Malcolm sat against the wall holding Bethany. He sat there quietly, listening to the women chat. They were all getting along very well, and he was happy they had each other. Malcolm kept glancing over at John and his family. Seeing John hold his sons tight while he held his wife's hand made Malcolm a little envious. He wished he had had a family. It wasn't too late, or maybe it was considering everything that had happened to him. Malcolm was developing some strong feelings for Bethany and could tell she was falling for him as well. It felt great to have her, but they had just met. And no one knew what the future held for any of them. If, or when, those things put people back on Earth—which Malcolm was still struggling to believe any of what that man-thing had said—who knows if he'd even be placed with Bethany? The whole thing made Malcolm very anxious.

Looking around the room, Malcolm saw so many people that clearly felt the same way he did. It was written all over their faces and telegraphed by their body language. It was hard for him to wrap his mind around the fact that he and all these people were on an alien space craft. It didn't feel like that long ago he was in his truck delivering beer. God, a beer would have been great. Malcolm imagined having a beer with John and just shooting the shit. It's funny how people take the little things, like grabbing a beer with a buddy, for granted until it's taken away somehow.

The room went dark. They could hear that elevator sound again. The spotlight flicked on, and the same man-thing stepped into the light. There were two creatures and what looked to be a woman in the shadows of the bright spotlight.

"Humans," the man-thing started, "we have the President of the United States of America, Cecilia Rodgers, with us, and she has prepared a speech. We realize that not everyone in this room is American or voted for her, but she has made a great impact on us and has negotiated her butt off on your behalf. We have begrudgingly agreed to her terms and have allowed her to address you all. Madam President, the floor is yours." The man-thing stepped out of the spotlight and disappeared into the door they had all just came through. The creatures left with the man-thing.

Cecilia watched as the door closed on the man-thing and creatures. She heard the elevator whisk them away. Cecilia stepped into the spotlight.

"Ladies and gentlemen of Earth," Cecilia began, "we do not have countries anymore. We are now united as human beings." Cecilia could only see shadows of people; she couldn't make out any features in the stark contrast of the spotlight to the darkness of the rest of the mammoth room. "We are facing unprecedented challenges. No one in this room has ever encountered anything like where we now find ourselves, so we will go forward as one, united people. There is no more class divide, no more gender roles, no more national tensions. We start from nothing—together. This is our opportunity as people to change the past. We can move forward and build an all-inclusive society. I want equality for all moving forward. I want to see people treated with respect now and forever. If we do this right, we can erase all of the hate from our past. We need to eradicate envy and jealousy—those feelings lead us down dangerous paths. We need to remember we are all the same. We all have the same heart pumping blood through us. We will create a great nation where everyone has equal rights. We have all seen too much at this point to ever hate one another again. We now all have a common enemy that we must unite to protect ourselves from. These things say they love us and want what's best for us, but in the same breath, they threaten to wipe us out completely. They are far too advanced and powerful to defeat in any kind of battle. But we can defeat them in the way we live from here on out. By living positive and respectful lives, we can ensure they will never be back to harm us again. By respecting the planet and taking care of the ecosystem, we can ensure they will never interfere again. We must instill these values in every generation to follow. Our captors have assured me they only want what is best for that planet. They have given me their word that if we take care of Earth, they will leave us be. The only way we can do that is if we work together. If we let petty differences consume us again, we will lose the battle and ultimately lose the war. Everyone in this room will live out the rest of their lives on a brand-new planet set up just for us. I'm sure there's a lot of you in here with the mindset, 'Who cares about the future? I won't be around when they come back.' That's an attitude we cannot afford to have. What's even the point then? Why spend so much time and effort rebuilding our societies if we just set up future generations to fail? Might as well just give in now and let the aliens win. Anyone want to do that? I, for one, do not want there to ever be a possibility of the human race being wiped out. We are the superior race, and someday, we will have the technology to go toe-to-toe with these things. None of us will be around for that, but I like knowing it will happen if we do what needs to be done now. If we work together and raise generations of like-minded people, we will one day own the universe!"

The crowd erupted in applause. Cecilia knew she had gotten through to them, at least most of them. There would always be doubters and nonbelievers. That didn't matter; they would be dealt with later. An ear-piercing, high-pitched whistle noise filled the room. The applause stopped abruptly as people groaned and covered their ears. The noise was painful. The room filled with a blinding light, and people tried to shield their eyes and cover their ears. The bright light that filled the room began to flash, like a strobe light. It was dizzying and made everyone feel nauseous. Cecilia feared she had altered the prepared speech too much. She feared the aliens were going to end it all right then and there. The light went steady again and intensified. The high-pitched noise slowly faded out. The room had suddenly become overwhelmingly hot. Cecilia could hear people falling to the hard floor. Her head spun, and she tried hard to stay conscious. There was no way of hanging on, and she passed out and fell to the floor.

*****

The light went out, and the room returned to how it had been before the president had given her speech. Malcolm blinked his eyes and looked around the room. Every woman that had been in the room was gone. Any child that had been in the room was gone. Only the men remained.

"Serena! JJ! Jeffrey!" John shouted, jumping to his feet. "Where did my family go? Where did your friends go?" he asked Malcolm in a full panic.

"I don't know, John," Malcolm said, standing up. He was still dizzy and felt like he was going to pass out. "This shit happens all the time," he said to John, feeling a little steadier already. "That fuck-ing light illuminates the room, and people either appear or vanish. Must be their way of getting us in and out of here without being seen. It's hard to try to stop 'em from taking your people if you're incapacitated."

"We have to go find them!" John said, frantically searching the room with his eyes.

"I wouldn't know how to do that," Malcolm said. "Look, I want to find Bethany just as badly as you want to find your family, but I think we should stay put in case they are returned soon."

"I can't just sit here and wait!" John exclaimed. "We have no goddamn idea what they're doing to our loved ones, man. I have to find my family."

Malcolm was realizing John was right. It wasn't going to do any good to just sit and wait. "If we do this," Malcolm said, "we need to get every man in here to help us. They are surely missing people too. Those damn things can't stop all of us."

John nodded. He cupped his hands around his mouth and began to shout, "Gentlemen! We need to find a way out of this room! We need to find our women and children!"

Murmurs filled the room and then slowly grew into chants. The men in the room all seemed to be on board. The power of all those voices had filled that large room. The chants of 'Let's find them!' echoed throughout.

The room started to feel way too hot again. The chanting died down as everyone had begun to feel ill. The smell of sweat hung heavy in the room. The room became dead quiet. A mist had begun to fill the room. Men began to pass out and fall to the hard, metal floor. John watched as Malcolm's eyes rolled back into their sockets and Malcolm crumpled to the floor. John felt himself swaying back and forth. The room was spinning. An image of Serena and the boys flashed in front of his eyes as everything went dark.

*****

Taylor was being led down a long hallway by two of the creatures. The hallway had evenly spaced doors on both sides of it. The creatures were speaking to each other in a language Taylor didn't recognize. They stopped abruptly in front of a door. One of the creatures waved its clawed hand in front of a sensor next to the door. The door slid open, and the creatures stepped aside. They waved Taylor in. He stepped inside, and the door quickly slid shut behind him. The room looked like a hotel room. The furniture looked off, like it was made by someone—or something—that had never used that kind of furniture. The room was large, with three twin beds, a couple of chairs, and a little kitchen area. It smelled like cigarette smoke and stale beer. On the bed closest to the door, sound asleep, was Billy. Taylor rushed over to the bed and gently shook Billy awake.

"Taylor!" Billy exclaimed, hugging his friend tightly.

"I think that's the first time we've ever hugged," Taylor chuckled, giving his friend a squeeze.

"Who gives a fuck!" Billy said, releasing Taylor and sitting up fully on the bed. "I missed you, dude. I thought I'd never see you again."

"I missed you too, man. I thought maybe you were dead. You were injured so badly. How are the ribs feeling?"

"Great, dude. Feel like they never even got broken. Damnedest thing really," Billy said as he rubbed his chest.

"Weird, but glad to hear it," Taylor said, sitting down in a chair next to the bed. "Where you been, Billy?"

"Fuck, dude, everywhere, I guess. I woke up on an operating table feeling a hundred percent myself. They must've fixed me up somehow." Billy reached over to the nightstand and pulled open the drawer. He retrieved a pack of cigarettes, a lighter, and an ashtray. "Dude, they gave me cigarettes and beer!"

"Holy shit, I'd die for a smoke right now!" Taylor exclaimed.

Billy handed Taylor a cigarette and the lighter. Taylor lit his cigarette and inhaled the intoxicating smoke. He slumped into his chair with a look of total satisfaction. Billy got up and went to a mini-fridge on the counter next to a sink. He snagged two beers and returned to the bed. Billy handed Taylor an ice-cold beer and sat back down.

"Oh my god, man, this is awesome!" Taylor said after taking a long swig off his beer. "Shit, how did you get the high roller treatment 'round here? This is like a decent hotel room—you have smokes and beers. Damn, what creature did you suck off?" Taylor laughed.

"More like the other way, dude. Those things fuckin' love me. Evidently I am very important to rebuilding life on earth." Billy put his hand up to stop Taylor from commenting. "Don't even say it 'cuz I don't know either. Why they picked me is questionable, but I am happy to be in this position." Billy paused and drank his beer. "Dude, I wasted my best years so far. I was such a selfish tool for so long. Fuck, I even told you to not come a knocking when shit hit the fan. That was a dick move and I'm sorry."

"Shit, man, I thought we already cleared that up. I know you would've had my back no matter what. I know you still got my back no matter what."

"I do and always will have your back. You're all I have left, bro."

"Same here, bro. Hey, can I get another smoke? I've been jonesing for a smoke bad."

"Help yourself—they'll give me whatever I ask for 'round here."

"Sweet!" Taylor said, taking another cigarette and lighting it. "So what else happened? Did they just bring you here and set you up like a rock star?"

"No, not quite. So when I woke up on that operating table, I had no idea where I was. It hadn't occurred to me yet that I had been taken too. I wandered into a room that smelled like death. Dude, it was awful. There were tables and tables of dead bodies. So fucked up, bro. In the next room, I found more tables with bodies, but those people weren't dead. So I freed them, and they took off, except for this teenage girl who couldn't move. Guess whose kid it was? Scarlett's, dude! I found her daughter!"

"That's awesome, man. I was hanging with Scarlett and her girls. They were the only people I knew. Then the president gave us a speech. After the speech, I felt ill and passed out. Then I woke up in a small-ass room with two creatures. They made me follow them and brought me here."

"Shit, dude, this is all so crazy! I'm really glad you're here, Taylor."

"Me too, Billy. So finish telling me how you ended up here? I didn't mean to go off on my own tangent."

"No worries, dude," Billy said, getting up and grabbing two more beers. "So I had Scarlett's daughter in my arms…"

"Her name's Gwen," Taylor interjected.

"Okay, so I had Gwen in my arms—I was going to try to find her help. It looked like she was hurt bad. Then this really weird-looking woman came into the room. Dude, she looked like old, graying skin loosely wrapped around a skeleton. Like some fucked-up Halloween decoration. That lady-thing explained to me that I was a chosen one and wanted me to put Gwen down because she wasn't or sumthin' like that. I wouldn't do it—I didn't know what they were going to do to her. I couldn't just walk away from a helpless girl. I stood up to that lady-thing, dude. I was scared, but my give-a-shit was gone. Like, at that point, I didn't even care anymore. If they wanted to kill me, then fine, so be it. I had to at least try and save that girl. I'm glad she's safe with her mom now. Then it got really weird. That lady-thing put her bony hand on my shoulder, and everything went dark.

Then I saw images of my life flash inside my mind. I had no control over what my mind was doing. No thoughts, just emotions. It was so weird. I saw my Grandpa Bill and my mom when she was still sober. I saw a bunch of fun childhood memories. Then it went bad. Then I saw life after Grandpa. Me in my mom's basement surfing the web or playing stupid games. Me and my mom yelling at each other over every little thing. My mom kicking me out and telling me not to come back 'til I grow up. It was awful, dude."

"Holy shit, man," Taylor said, shaking his head. "So you're a chosen one?"

"I know, right? The human race is fucked!" Billy laughed.

"Oh, it was already fucked!" Taylor chuckled.

The door suddenly slid open. Billy and Taylor both quickly looked to the door. They could hear chatter in a language they didn't recognize. It was the language Taylor had heard the creatures speaking. Taylor and Billy looked at each other, puzzled. The chatter stopped, and they heard someone say, "You've got friends in there. We'll come get all of you when it's time" in English. They looked back to the door and watched as Pete walked in. His eyes lit up when he saw Taylor and Billy. The three men exchanged handshakes and excited hellos. Billy grabbed Pete a beer and invited him to sit down.

"Man, it's good to see you guys!" Pete said, opening his beer and taking a healthy sip. "How's the ribs, Billy?"

"Fine, dude. They fixed me up good," Billy said, patting himself on the chest. "How are you, Pete? Last time I saw you, we were following Zombie Taylor." He chuckled at that.

"I'm a little overwhelmed, honestly," Pete said. "Last time I saw you was in the ER parking lot. That's when they took me."

"I knew you didn't just abandon me there!" Billy exclaimed.

"I wouldn't do something like that, man," Pete said. "How are you feeling, Taylor? Do you remember anything from when you were in that trance?" He tried to shift the focus off himself. Pete wasn't ready to talk about what had happened to him.

"Oh, man, I remember everything," Taylor said, sliding a cigarette out of the pack. He offered the pack to Pete, but Pete waved him off. "It was like a dream, but not quite." Taylor paused for a second, searching for words. "It's hard to explain. I knew where I was. I knew I wasn't sleeping. I knew it wasn't actually a dream, but I was seeing things that weren't right in front of me. I felt like I was floating. I couldn't feel my feet hit the ground with each step. You know how when you're walking, especially on a hard surface like pavement, you can feel your feet hit the ground with each step?"

Billy and Pete both nodded.

"I couldn't feel that, but I *knew* I was walking. I *knew* where I was and where I was headed. I just couldn't see or hear anything. Or feel anything. I couldn't feel my clothes on my skin. I couldn't feel the air hitting my face." Taylor stood up and went to the mini fridge. The beers and cigarettes had already started to make him fell a little buzzed, and it felt amazing. He had thought he'd never feel that way again.

"Hey, grab us another one too, dude," Billy said to Taylor.

Taylor grabbed three beers and handed Pete and Billy each one on his way back to his chair. Taylor sat down with a relaxed sigh and popped open his beer. He looked at his friends and smiled. After everything that had happened and the fear of never seeing anyone who mattered to him, he felt very fortunate to have been sitting in that room, drinking beers and bullshitting with those two guys. He had no idea how long it would last, but he wasn't going to take one second for granted.

"Keep going with your story, dude," Billy said, popping open his own beer and tossing the beer cap in the small trash can next to the bed.

"So what I did see and feel were memories, but not memories I was recalling—they were like shown to me. It was like watching a movie of myself. It was like someone was showing me photos and, every once in a while, moving images. It started out good, like little snapshots from when I was a kid playing peewee football. Man, I remember thinking I'd play in the NFL someday." Taylor chuckled and shook his head. "I loved playing football. The images took me through my childhood into high school years and up until I started mechanics' school. Things got weird though. I saw my first love—you remember Samantha, Billy."

"Oh, yeah, I remember Samantha," Billy said, rolling his eyes.

"Man, I thought she was the one. I fell for her hard, as you know." Taylor looked at Billy, and he nodded. "She was my first kiss and my first everything else. I loved that girl so much. I saw her and I together forever. The many dates we had gone on, the dances we went to, the love letters we wrote to each other because she thought that was old school and romantic." Taylor looked at Pete. "Billy knows what happened to us. She cheated on me…" Taylor trailed off and sipped his beer.

"A lot," he added, pausing to collect himself.

"She turned out to be one nasty chick," Billy said to Pete. "I fucking hate her." He looked at Taylor. "You good, bro?"

"Yeah, man, I'm fine," Taylor said. "Anyways, as those images or dream—whatever it was—went on, I started to see Samantha with all those guys she messed around with. I mean full-on vivid images. I tried so hard to wake myself or think about something else, but it was like I didn't have control of my own mind. It was like someone hijacked my brain and was force-feeding me these fucked images. It was awful. I can still see it all so vividly. And the worst part was, Samantha was making eye contact with me in every image. She was with these other dudes but looking at me. It was like I was standing in the room and she knew I was there." Taylor shivered. "I don't wanna talk about it anymore."

"Shit, sorry about all that, dude," Billy said.

The room went quiet for a while. Reliving all of that had clearly upset Taylor but had also seemed to be a relief. It had been hard to talk about but had all just flowed out so easily. Taylor felt sad; he hadn't thought about Samantha in a long time. She had, at one point, meant the world to him. He thought she was going to be his forever girl. The cheating had absolutely devastated him; he wouldn't have ever even contemplated stepping out on her. Over time, he had learned that they were so young, and his feelings weren't as deep as he had once thought. He eventually realized he loved what they did together more than he had actually loved her.

After he broke up with Samantha, Taylor felt lost. He didn't date again for a long time. He couldn't hold down a job; it had really messed with his mind and his ability to trust anyone. Billy had always been a good friend, but at that time, he was dealing with his own loss. Taylor and Billy had both become depressed, and neither had the ability to deal with it. They had isolated themselves and ended up drifting apart for some time. After his dad had talked him into going to school, Taylor started to feel more normal again. Learning a good trade with a bunch of other like-minded people helped him to come out of his depression. It had felt great to learn something that he not only really enjoyed but was going to be a well-paying career. Taylor had learned a lot of life lessons in those years after Samantha. He even eventually tried dating again, but he didn't have much success. It had been really tough to fully commit to someone else, and he still had big trust issues, which made him a bit controlling. But he had grown to love his life and genuinely enjoyed the bachelor lifestyle. Taylor had hoped to someday meet the right woman and build a happy family life. That all changed with the invasion.

"Do you have a bathroom in here?" Pete asked.

"Yeah, dude, right by the front door over there," Billy said, pointing to the door.

"Thanks," Pete said and walked to the bathroom. He opened the bathroom door and stopped. "Whoa! You got a shower in here too?"

"Yeah, dude. And the water is hot!"

"Do you mind if I shower?" Pete asked.

"Hell no, I don't mind. Do it, Pete!"

"Cool, thanks, man."

"You bet, but don't thank me. I was put in here the same as you were. I ain't paying for none of this." He laughed.

Pete went into the bathroom and closed the door. It was a decent-sized bathroom with a full tub and shower. Like the furniture in the room, all the fixtures in the bathroom were a bit off. It looked like whoever—or whatever—built them had never used such fixtures. It was all functional, and Pete felt blessed to have a real bathroom to use. He undressed and turned on the water. The water was instantly hot. He stepped into the shower and just let that hot water cascade over his body. That shower felt amazing. Pete stood there and let his mind wander. He thought about Amanda. Pete knew he would probably never see her again. He wished he could have said goodbye. Pete had always wanted to tell Amanda how he felt about her but was now glad he hadn't. If she had similar feelings for him, that would have made what he was planning a lot more difficult to go through with. Sometimes, not knowing was better than knowing one way or the other. Amanda was a good woman, and she would find happiness with a good man someday. Pete had wanted to be that man, but he knew what he was about to do was more important than his feelings for Amanda.

Billy and Taylor heard the shower come on. Taylor took his shoes and socks off and put them next to the chair. He walked over to the center bed and sat down on it.

"I'm going to take a little nap," he said, stripping down to his boxers.

"Sounds good, dude. I'm going try to sleep again too."

They both crawled into their beds. They could still hear the shower running in the bathroom.

"Hey, Billy, what do you think of Pete?" Taylor asked from his bed.

"I like the dude a lot. He seems cool," Billy said, rolling over to face Taylor. "Why do you ask?"

"I dunno, man. He seems like a good guy, but there's just sumthin' about him that worries me. He's so quiet most of the time, like he's plotting sumthin'."

"What do you mean? He's had our backs from go. He let us escape the base with him, and that ended up saving our lives!"

"Yeah, and look where that got us," Taylor said.

"We're still alive, dude, and it sounds like we get to go back to a brand-new planet. We get to help rebuild and repopulate Earth!" Billy said, sitting up on one arm.

"I didn't consider that," Taylor said.

"He's a good dude, trust me. He wanted to save you from those things, and he took me to the hospital when he realized I probably had a punctured lung. Are you maybe a little jealous you don't have me to yourself anymore?"

"Shit no, dude," Taylor said. "Maybe I'm just being paranoid because of everything going on now. A little too paranoid."

"Maybe, dude. I don't think you have anything to worry about Pete. He's cool."

They heard the shower shut off. Taylor and Billy lay back down on their beds. After about ten minutes, Pete came out of the bathroom and looked at the other guys on their beds.

"Bedtime already?" Pete asked with a smirk on his face.

"Yeah, dude, nap time. Not much else to do 'round here but drink and sleep," Billy said.

"Do you get food?" Pete asked.

"They've fed me once, yeah," Billy said, sitting up on the edge of his bed. "It's been a while, though."

"Think they'll feed us?" Pete asked. "I'm damn hungry. I haven't eaten since the base, and who the hell knows how long ago that was."

"Yeah, dude, no idea how much time has passed since we've been here. There's no windows and no clocks," Billy said.

"I've seen out a window," Pete said. "I saw Earth from above, man. It was spectacular and scary as hell."

"Holy shit, really?" Billy said.

Taylor got up and dressed again. He went back to the chair he had been sitting in and lit another smoke. The room seemed to have some sort of ventilation system; despite how many cigarettes they had smoked, the room didn't get too smoky. After grabbing three more beers, Pete sat down next to Billy on his bed and handed out beers. The door slid open, and a cart of food rolled into the room, followed by the door closing again.

"Ask and you shall receive!" Billy laughed.

The tray had three platers of food on it. Each plate had the exact same thing: a steak, a baked potato, and a plain piece of white bread. The steak and potato had already been cut up into bite-sized pieces. Each meal had come with a spoon. The three of them looked at each other and then at the food. One by one they got up and grabbed a plate. They sat in silence as they shoveled the food into their mouths. The food wasn't great at all, all of it was cold and the steak was overdone and very chewy. None of them seemed to mind;

they were all pretty hungry and buzzed. Once they had all finished, they loaded their empty plates back on the tray and Billy pushed it to the door. He bumped the tray into the closed door a few times. The door suddenly slid open, and a creature stood outside. It looked at Billy and then at the tray. The creature grabbed the tray and rolled it into the hallway. The door slid shut again.

"Feeling better, guys?" Billy asked, returning to his bed. He plopped down onto his bed and lit a cigarette. Taylor was already smoking one.

"Yeah, man, that was decent," Taylor said.

"That was worse than hospital cafeteria food, but it hit the spot 'cuz I was so hungry," Pete said.

"Definitely not great, but hey, it's food," Billy said.

"That meat tasted funny. It didn't taste like beef to me," Taylor said.

"I doubt it was," Billy said. "Where would they raise cows up here? It's probably some kind of meat substitute. You know something that looks and kinda tastes familiar to us humans but is probably some kind of chemically made product."

"I bet you're right," Pete said. "I could see with their advanced technology them being able to grow crops, make bread and shit like that, but I don't see where or why they'd raise animals up here. Especially if they're only keeping us up here for a few weeks."

"How do you know how long they're keeping us up here?" Taylor asked. "Are you just speculating?"

"One of them told me it was going to *feel* like a few weeks to us up here," Pete responded.

"Shit, you both chatted with those things?" Taylor asked, surprised and, honestly, a tad jealous. Why were Pete and Billy so important they got briefings from those things? Why wasn't he that special?

"Yeah, I woke up in a room that had windows on two sides of it. That's where I saw Earth. Then this thing that kind of looked like a—"

"Chick?" Billy interrupted, excitedly thinking Pete had met the same human-thing he had.

"No, it kind of looked like a man. The skin looked like it had been loosely stretched over a skeleton, but not a human skeleton."

"What did it tell you?" Billy asked.

"It said that after they finish destroying Earth, they are going to replant it and create a new ecosystem and then they will put us all back to start over."

"Wait, they already destroyed the planet," Taylor said.

"Well, they finished it off. I saw it. A bunch of spaceships flew up from Earth and hovered just above this craft, and that man-thing made me watch as he hit a button and Earth went up in flames. Honestly, it was quite an amazing sight. Horrifying but pretty amazing," Pete said as he got up to get another round of beers. The fridge was stocked full; they would have plenty of ice-cold brews for the evening. Was it even evening? Who knew, but regardless, they were set.

"Okay, hold on a second," Taylor said. "So they blew everything up again? How is Earth going to be habitable in just a few weeks if it's completely destroyed?"

"Apparently time passes slower up here," Pete began. "That thing told me it would *feel* like a few weeks for us, but hundreds of years would pass on Earth."

"What the fuck, really?" Billy asked. "How is that possible?"

"They say astronauts on the Space Station age slower than they would on Earth," Pete said. "Look, we have no idea where we are now. After that thing talked to me, I passed out again. I seem to be doing that a lot lately."

"We all are," Billy said.

"Right, well, when I woke up, I was still in that room with the windows. When I looked out the window again, I couldn't see Earth anymore. There was nothing outside those windows except for stars and darkness. We could be anywhere in the universe right now."

"Fuck, dude, that's so trippy," Billy said. "Did you ever imagine yourself going to space as a kid? Growing up, I loved *Star Wars* and I dreamed about being in space, battling aliens. Now here we are!"

"Yup, here we are, except for the fighting aliens part," Taylor said.

"I just want off this damn ship," Pete said.

"I want to find a window," Billy said. "I want to see outer space."

"I will admit it was awesome," Pete said. "But at the same time, it's scary as hell, man."

"I think it's kind of cool, dude. Look at us," Billy said, motioning around the room. "We're set up like royalty, flying through outer space! This is once-in-a-lifetime shit right here."

"Once-in-a-lifetime shit that we will apparently not remember once returned to Earth," Pete said.

"What do you mean?" Taylor asked, exhaling a plume of cigarette smoke.

"That thing told me they would wipe our memories when they put us back on Earth, so we won't remember them. We won't remember any of this. Personally, I don't think any of this is cool. They've killed most of the human population. They clearly have no issue with killing us. They're so arrogant. They say they love Earth, and they want us to succeed down there. They say they have given us so many opportunities to thrive, and somehow, we always screw it up. Why do we have to live up to their standards? If they really did create us, why not just let us be? The human race will never thrive with those things meddling with us all the time. We'll never be good enough for them. We need to destroy them."

"Fuck, dude!" Billy exclaimed. "Don't talk like that! You know they gotta be listening to us right now. They picked us for some reason, talked to both of us about all this shit, and then put all of us together in this room. You think it's all just a coincidence? I don't! They're fuckin' plannin' sumthin'. Look, I don't like any of this either. I just ain't gonna cause any problems. I'm going to take advantage of this situation and ride this all out 'til I'm back on Earth. Then it's every man for himself as far as I'm concerned. I got your backs, guys, but other than that, I don't care."

"That's the kind of attitude that's going to get us wiped out, Billy. We have to work together to fight them. The human race will never survive as long as they are around," Pete said. Pete was scared, but he wasn't going to let that stand in his way. The way he saw it was no matter what, his life was over as he had known it. For some reason, he had been tapped to lead the rebuild, but what was the point of rebuilding anything if those things were just going to come back and wipe it all out again? In Pete's opinion, the human race's only chance of survival was going to be to get rid of the aliens. How that would be possible, Pete didn't know, but he did know it had to happen.

"You are both too worried about all of it," Taylor said. "They chose us to repopulate the planet, and that's what we should do. We ain't going to live long enough to be wiped out by them. What does it matter? In my opinion, we're fucked no matter what. From what you have said, it sounds like we're going to be dropped off in the wilderness or sumthin' like that. We're going to spend the rest of our lives building a community and having kids. Our other option sounds like death. I vote for a new life on Earth. I don't wanna start any shit with those things."

"See, that right there is why we're here now. That mindset is what drives people apart. We could be the superior race if we could just all work together, but people are far too concerned about themselves to see anything else. Look at what happened after they attacked us. People didn't come together to fight for our planet. Instead, they fought each other. Killin' and lootin'. It was a disgrace, guys, but honestly not a surprise. You're right—we won't live long enough to see the planet destroyed again, but our families will. Our descendants will. You really want that to be our legacy? You just want to do what they tell us to do? We have a chance here to be heroes. We have a chance to literally save the human race."

"That's exactly why we're here," Billy said. "We are the chosen ones, remember? Everyone on this ship is a chosen one or we wouldn't be here."

"Chosen to go back to Earth and eke out an existence until they decide they're done with us. I, for one, believe we all deserve to thrive without Big Brother watching and waiting until we fuck up again."

"We really should stop talkin' about this shit," Billy said, looking around the room. "I don't want to be eliminated before we even get a chance to start over. Personally, I welcome the restart. My life was fucked, and I'm looking forward to a fresh start. For a chance to be a better person and leave a lasting impact on the new world."

"Me too," Pete said. "But I'd like my impact to be the guy that fought for humanity, not just someone who rebuilt a society and then died. Look, guys, we have a chance to be the saviors of the human race."

"Wait, you just said they're going to wipe our memories," Taylor said. "How are we going to fight them if we don't even remember they exist?"

"We gotta do it before they wipe our memories," Pete said.

"How?" Billy asked. "How exactly do we do that?" Pete's intensity and confidence was becoming infectious. It had made Billy forget about the potential of being listened to.

"I don't know yet. It's not going to be easy."

"Obviously not," Taylor said. "How do we destroy them without destroying ourselves in the process? They have us by the balls here."

"I don't know that either," Pete said. "But there has to be a way. There's always a way."

"I knew you were badass from go, Pete, but you're really surprising me here," Billy said.

"Honestly, I'm surprising myself too. When all this first happened, I just wanted to get to my parents' place and hide out. Ride it out with them. But obviously, that wasn't the plan for me. Then, for a moment, I wished I was dead. Now I'm embracing my role in all of this. I'm at a point now where I'm willing to sacrifice my life for the betterment of all human life."

Taylor and Billy looked at each other. Pete was so passionate about everything they couldn't help but be pumped up by what he was saying. Was there really a chance to defeat those things and save the human race? They both knew no matter what they, or anyone else, did moving forward, those things would eventually just wipe them all out. Billy stood up and went into the bathroom. As he stood there using the bathroom, he thought about his life and how he had wasted it. His whole adult life had been focused on girls and trying to get with them. He had never wanted a real, meaningful relationship;

he had just never wanted to open himself up to someone that way. Billy had always been afraid to let people in, especially after losing his grandfather. He thought if he could just hook up and move on, he'd somehow be happy. Deep down, he had always known that wouldn't have ever been the case. This was his chance to do something to better the lives of everyone else. To give mankind a chance at a long, productive existence. It would most likely lead to his demise, but that was okay with him. He was surprised that he was, in fact, okay with that. It was time to truly grow up and become a man. He had always put himself first; now he could put humanity first.

Billy returned to his bed and sat down. Taylor was asking Pete what they should do next. Pete, again, said he didn't know yet. They heard a noise outside of the room.

"Shit, they heard us!" Billy exclaimed. "Fuck, guys, they're going to kill us!"

"Calm down, Billy," Pete said. "We don't even know what that noise was."

The room door slid open, and a woman walked into the room. They all instantly recognized her as the president of the United States.

"Young men," Cecilia began, "I have been brought here to tell you guys to abandon any thoughts or plans to try to fight our hosts. They truly mean us no harm, and we must all work together to move the human race forward. As long as we all live in harmony with the land and each other, we will never have issues with them." She looked at the three of them and winked, as if to say, 'I'm only telling you what I was told to say, but carry on.' The look on her face and that wink had been clear as day to the men. President Rodgers was on board with their ideas; she just couldn't say it out loud. "Now they have told me we will soon be split into large groups and placed on smaller crafts for the trip back to Earth." She paused and looked at them with wide eyes that were pleading with them to pay attention and read between the lines. She needed them to listen to her body language more than her words. "This mother ship will not make the trip back to Earth." Cecilia paused again and gave them an encouraging look. "Their soldiers will take us to Earth and then return here. They have assured me they will give us centuries before they even begin to think about interfering with us again. Gentlemen, we have been given a second chance. We have all been chosen to live. That is something to be grateful for, not to question." The three men could tell it made her sick and angry to say these things. It was written all over her face. She dropped her head and spoke a little more softly. "They have also assured me that if you continue to talk about such things, they will not be returning you to Earth. In their words, shut up or die."

"Yes, ma'am," Taylor said. "We're sorry. We're just talkin' shit over beers. Sorry 'bout the language, ma'am."

"No worries, no need for formalities anymore, gentlemen. Heed my advice, please. We need every able body we can get down there. They said they will be scattering us all over the planet, so our groups will be small. We must all work together." Cecilia winked at them again. She looked at the three of them hanging on her every word. She could tell she had gotten through to them. She could tell they knew what had to be done. "Thank you for your time," Cecilia said. She turned and walked out of the room. The door slid shut behind her.

Billy, Taylor, and Pete looked at each other in shock.

"Shit! I knew they were listening," Billy said.

"Good," Pete said, "I'm glad they're listening because I want them to know we heard them loud and clear. We will play by the rules. We will not try anything. We are sorry we even discussed it."

Pete grabbed an empty beer bottle and motioned for the others to follow him. He led them into the bathroom and shut the door. Pete turned the shower on to its hottest setting. He could tell Billy wanted to say something, but he just kept hushing him. After a few minutes, the mirror above the sink fogged over. Pete smashed the beer bottle on the edge of the sink. Pete held up the broken beer bottle, and with his finger, he wrote, "Bottles are weapons" in the condensation on the mirror. He then wrote, "We'll hide out. Wait 'til the drop. Attack." He wiped the mirror clean with a towel and waited for it to fog over again. Pete then wrote, "Attack from inside. Destroy ship."

Taylor and Billy looked shocked but nodded in agreement. Pete shut off the shower and headed out of the bathroom. Billy and Taylor followed. Pete grabbed three more beers and handed two of them to the other guys. Pete walked over to the far bed and sat down. He looked around the room and smiled.

"Well, guys, it's been a long day. I think I'm going to go to sleep after this beer," Pete said and winked at them.

"Good idea, dude," Billy said and winked back.

Taylor popped open his beer and sat down on the middle bed. He didn't say anything.

"We fucked up," Pete said. "The president is right—we should be grateful to have been saved. So many lives lost, and although we're here and scared, at least we are alive."

"I agree," Billy said. "We were just scared. I want to apologize as well for the nonsense."

Pete stood up and went into the bathroom. All those beers had made him have to go to the bathroom badly. As he stood there doing his business, he looked around. He noticed a large vent above the shower. It looked like it was big enough for all of them to crawl through. That was it! That was their way out of that room. Pete was excited and rushed back into the room. He motioned for the other guys to follow him into the bathroom again. Billy and Taylor got up from their beds and went into the bathroom with Pete. He showed them the vent, and they all smiled.

As Taylor was looking at the vent, it slowly dawned on him that he wouldn't be making it off that ship alive. His smile faded. He really wanted to do the right thing, but was what they were planning the right thing? At least the right thing for him? He was shocked that Billy was so gung-ho about all of this. His oldest and only friend left had never been the kind of guy who gave two shits about anyone but himself. Taylor knew that to be true from personal experience. Neither Taylor nor Billy had had any brothers, so when they became friends in middle school, their relationship grew into more like brothers than just friends. They annoyed the hell out of each other, but there was an unconditional love and bond that was unbreakable. This new side of Billy was impressive and admirable, but Taylor feared when push came to shove, Billy may freeze up. Shit, Taylor was afraid he would freeze up too. They had no godly idea what they were in for. No idea how to fight those things. What, they were planning to use broken beer bottles? Taylor saw a .22 round basically bounce off one of those creatures in his apartment courtyard. Not a very powerful round, but a .22 would put a human on the ground. Now their only plan was to use broken beer bottles and climb around a ventilation system? Taylor didn't like any of it, but he wasn't going to abandon his friends. He considered Pete a friend at that point. Any doubts he had had about Pete were dashed over the past several hours. The guy was indeed a badass.

Pete turned the shower on again and waited for the mirror to fog up. Once it was, he wrote "more bottles" and looked at Billy. Billy left the bathroom and returned with more empties. Pete took them one by one and smashed them on the side of the sink. He handed a broken bottle to Billy and Taylor. Pete put his finger on the mirror and wrote, "now." Billy and Taylor nodded. Pete reached up and pulled off the vent cover. One by one, they all climbed in.

CHAPTER 11

Earth

Scarlett, Gwen, and Hope were in a long line of people. They didn't recognize their surroundings and couldn't remember how they had gotten there. The line was slowly moving through a long hallway, into a large doorway. Scarlett was holding Gwen's hand, and the girl was trembling. Gwen was afraid they were being led back to that awful room she had been in. She didn't say anything to her mother or Hope about where she had been and what she had seen. Her mom was already clearly terrified and stressed out. Gwen didn't want to add to her mother's worries. She knew even if they were being led back to that room, there was nothing any of them could do about it.

After what felt like at least an hour, they made it through the hallway to the door. They went into a pressurized room and then through another door. They found themselves in a large room filled with rows of what looked like airplane seats. Everyone was being led to a chair by people who looked to be in a trance and instructed to strap in. The fear and panic dropped as they sat down. Scarlett looked around. The room was quickly filling up with people, all kinds of people. Men, women, and children. There was one thing she noticed right away: there wasn't anybody in that room older than fifty, if even that old. She thought about that for a moment and slowly realized if these were the people that were headed back to Earth, it would make sense to the creatures not to bring older people back. If these were the people tasked with repopulating the planet, older people honestly wouldn't be much help. It saddened Scarlett greatly that she not only got that point but she understood it as well. She tried to convince herself that no one was going to remember any of this, so all the many lives lost wouldn't be an issue going forward. That thought hurt her as well, but there really wasn't any other way of thinking at that point in time. They didn't have any control over anything. Although horribly tragic, the massive loss of life didn't change anything. Selfishly, Scarlett was just thankful she and the girls were alive and together.

The room had filled up, and they heard the large door slam shut. The lights in the room dimmed. A voice filled the room as a large screen came down from the ceiling in the front of the room.

"Make sure you are all buckled in," the robotic voice said. "This ride will get bumpy, although you won't be awake to experience any of it. Please direct your attention to the screen. We appreciate your cooperation and wish you all luck in your new lives."

The room went dark, and images of what had to be Earth started to flash across the screen. Beautiful, crystal-clear lakes and streams. Tall, strong trees showed on the screen. Short videos of animals prancing about flashed on the screen. The room seemed to fill with a fog. The air got really heavy and acidic. Scarlett had a bitter taste in her mouth all of a sudden. The room began to shake. Scarlett grabbed Hope and Gwen's hands. She held them tightly as the room bounced more violently. The images on the screen began to repeat, as if they were on a loop. The images started flashing faster and faster. Between the bouncing and those rapid images, everyone began to feel dizzy. The bouncing suddenly stopped, and it felt like the room was completely still again. The images on the screen slowed back down, and the acidic feel to the air was gone. Scarlett relaxed her grip on the girls' hands but didn't let go of them. Those pictures on the screen were so beautiful, it looked like it could have been a pine forest in Northern America, but nothing like what she had seen before. Growing up on the Columbia River, in Oregon, Scarlett had seen some of the most beautiful nature the world had to offer, but nothing compared to what she was seeing on that screen. It looked like the days of city life were over. The gridlocked traffic, daily office life, grocery store runs, happy hour at the local pub, all of it appeared to be over with. It all seemed like a distant memory already. The faces of her coworkers had already blurred. The sights and sounds of living in a city were faded. Scarlett couldn't even remember what her own car had looked like. It was all fading away—and fading quickly at that. All those day-to-day city life memories were being replaced with the images on that screen.

"Mom, are we going home?" Gwen asked.

"I think so. It won't be the home we were used to, though," Scarlett answered and squeezed her daughter's hand.

"That's okay," Gwen said. "Anything would be better than this place."

"I agree," Scarlett said. "To me, it doesn't matter where we are, as long as the three of us are together."

"Me too," Gwen said.

"Me too," Hope said. "I miss my mom, though."

"I know, honey, we all miss her," Scarlett said and gave Hope's hand a loving squeeze.

They sat in silence for a moment, watching the images on the screen. The pictures had been burnt into their memory as all their other memories continued to fade. The images suddenly disappeared, and the screen ascended into the ceiling. The lights in the room came on. The same robotic voice filled the room.

"Your attention, please," it began. "The president of what was the United States of America, Cecilia Rodgers, has an announcement."

The room hushed, and people looked around. Cecilia stood up from a chair in the front of the room. She turned and faced the packed room.

"Ladies and gentlemen, I am happy and honored to be here with all of you. We are all so very fortunate to be here right now. In case some of you haven't figured it out yet, we are currently on an aircraft back to Earth. Our gracious hosts have set up a paradise for us down there. We have everything we will ever need to not only survive but to thrive!" Cecilia paused and began to pace in the front of the room. She had her hands folded at her waste and looked out over the crowd of people. All eyes were intently on her. "I have to be honest," she began, pausing again, "at first, I was very skeptical and, frankly, rebellious of our hosts. I didn't trust them, and why would I? It was not only an internal mistrust. I vocalized my doubts to our hosts. I told them we humans would not bow down to their demands anymore. I told them we would rise up and fight for our planet. I told them we didn't need them interfering with us anymore." Cecilia paused again. She stopped pacing and stood still, facing the room. "I was wrong. Flat out wrong," she said to the room. Cecilia could see people start to look around at each other. She knew what was going through their minds. They were surely wondering what happened to our tough, take-no-shit president. At least that's what she *hoped* was going through their heads. "Look," she continued, "it's not only okay to admit when you're wrong. It's noble and the sign of a strong leader. None of us are perfect. That's how we learn: we make mistakes and correct those mistakes. Our hosts aren't perfect either. The way they handled all of this was brutal and uncalled for. I've had many conversations with them by now, and I have convinced them there is no need for lives to be lost like this again. They have agreed to let us have the planet outright. They have agreed to leave us alone from here on out. We struck a deal—they can visit and take needed resources as long as they don't meddle anymore. I feel that is a fair deal. We are now allies instead of master and subordinate." Cecilia looked around the room. Everyone looked like they were in disbelief and very confused. "People, this is a good thing! Our species is finally one hundred percent safe from any outside interference. Now we only need to worry about ourselves."

The room erupted in applause. People unbuckled their seat belts and rose to their feet. People hooped and hollered. It felt as though all of the stress and uncertainty since the initial attacks had been replaced with optimism and relief. Scarlett stood in front of her seat, clapping. She had a huge smile on her face for the first time in a very long time. The president's speech had confused her at first and, honestly, upset her. Scarlett had always looked up to Cecilia as a strong, powerful woman. At the beginning of that speech, though, the president sounded almost weak and defeated.

Cecilia winked at the crowd and smiled. Scarlett's own smile increased; she knew without a doubt the president had some sort of trick up her sleeve. That wink made it very clear Cecilia had said what she wanted their captors to hear but she had other plans in the works. Scarlett's admiration for Cecilia grew a bit; that badass woman was still there—and stronger than ever.

"Thank you all!" Cecilia shouted over the applause. The applause died off, and everyone returned to their seats. "I know this has all been so scary and stressful. We have all lost people who were extremely close to us and that is a tragedy. We are on the back end of all this, and we will take time to mourn our loved ones once we are settled. For now, we must soldier on. We must all come together and work as a team. Myself and a handful of others have been chosen to lead the rebuild process, but it doesn't have to be that way. I will not govern you. I will work hand in hand with everyone. No single person is greater than the whole. We have the opportunity to build a society without class division and envy. Human history has taught us that envy and greed was the downfall of every great society. That all ends with us!" Again, the room erupted in applause, everyone except for one man in the front row stood and cheered Cecilia. She took notice of the man still seated. He looked angry. "You, sir," she said to him, "do you not agree with that?"

"No, I do not," he said, standing up. The applause had quieted, and all eyes were now on him. "Why do we need to follow you? We didn't put you in charge—they did."

"You don't have to follow me. That's the point I'm trying to get across here. We don't need an all-powerful leader. We don't need kings and queens or dictators or even presidents. This is our chance to create an infallible society."

"That's impossible," the man interrupted. "We as humans are not infallible. We are incapable of not being envious or greedy. It's human nature to want more. It's human nature to covet what some-one else has, whether it's money or status. What you are suggesting sounds like socialism, and socialism has never worked. The people at the top always end up with everything while the rest of us get the scraps. We get our basic needs barely met while you fat cats live it up on our hard work. I, for one, want no part of a society like that."

"Well, sir," Cecilia began.

"Call me John, please," he interrupted again. "My name is John Henderson. I was originally from Hastings, Nebraska. I did not vote for you for president, and I had no intention of voting when you ran for a second term. You and the rest of the Democrats have tried for decades to turn the US into a socialistic dictatorship. I don't want anything to do with you or your new ideas." John was trembling a bit. He could feel every person in that room glaring at him. He knew there had to be a number of people who agreed with him, but they were all too scared to say anything. John figured someone had to say something, and he knew at that point, he had nothing to lose. His family was still missing; he hoped he'd find them once they were all back on Earth, but he feared that there wasn't much chance of that.

"Well, John, I appreciate your honesty, and I respect your opinion," Cecilia said. "We haven't even made it back to Earth yet. We still don't know what to expect down there. I am simply trying to get everyone to work together, to live as a unit instead of divided. John, we survived Armageddon. We are all fortunate to be alive and have all been given the chance to survive and live long, fruitful lives. But we won't be able to if we can't work together."

John looked at Malcolm, who was still seated. Malcolm looked away from John. Malcolm didn't want any part of what John was saying. In fact, Malcolm was pretty shocked by John at that point. He had gotten the feeling from the small amount of time he had spent with John that John was a pretty conservative man. Malcolm knew if they had met back in the old world, they would have had very opposing views on politics and the world in general. John's feelings and opinions hadn't surprised Malcolm, but John standing up to the president like that did surprise Malcolm. He hadn't figured John to be the kind of person to make a scene like that. Malcolm could tell by the hushed murmurs of the room that John was pretty much alone in his feelings. Malcolm got the feeling that most of the people in there with them were probably sick and tired of the old ways of life. He could tell a vast majority of the people in that room had been hardworking people who probably voted when it was time to, but outside of that, politics had little to no effect on their daily lives. Malcolm hoped most people shared his current feelings; no more government would be better than anything else humans had ever tried. The problem would be guys like John. People who wouldn't want to go along just because they didn't like the president or anyone else that may take on a leadership role. They weren't even back on Earth and there were problems arising already. Malcolm feared the worse. It all made him miss Bethany even more. She was so close but still too far away for comfort. He had seen her seated with Julia, Dana, and Amanda as he and John were led to their seats. He wished he could have sat with her and held her hand. He just wanted to be with her; he didn't need or want any of this drama.

"We can work together without being a socialistic society," John said. "We need a hierarchy to survive as a society. We need class division. Everyone in this room is going to want to be the doctors and the teachers and the farmers. No one will want to be the sanitation worker. No one wants to deal with the waste of their fellow man. But you need those people in a society. How long do you think a guy is going to shovel shit when he's getting compensated the same as everyone else? Or vice versa. How long do you think you'll keep doctors around when they are tasked with saving lives for the same as what a guy shoveling shit gets? It's never worked and never will."

"John, I was never referring to a socialist society. I have always been against that. You are right—socialism doesn't work because people can be very envious and greedy. I ran on that philosophy. But this is different. We aren't trying to rework an existing government. We aren't trying to change a nation from one way of operating to a different way. We are starting fresh. We have a clean slate. We don't know what resources are down there for us. We don't know where we will even end up down there. We could end up in the north and have to deal with inclement weather. There are so many factors still to be sorted out. The last thing I want, and I feel I speak for everyone else also, is to start out divided. Come on, John, we have a chance for a beautiful thing down there. Forget about me and my politics of the old world. This isn't about any of that. We don't have a United States of America anymore. Shit, we don't even have an America anymore as far as we know. We are all humans, and that makes us all equal in my eyes."

"Sure, for now," John said. He turned to the crowded room. "People, she's right. We do need to work together to survive, but we don't need a socialist leading us. We need someone to lay down the law. Someone who won't just guide us—we need someone who will *direct* us!" He turned to Cecilia. "I'm sorry, ma'am, but I don't agree with the direction you're planning to take us. I have said my piece and I will sit back down. For now, we will ride this out and see what awaits us down there."

"John, I appreciate your candor. We will just have to see what happens when we get down there." Cecilia turned her attention to the rest of the room. "Ladies and gentlemen, I appreciate your attention and your patience. I guess you really didn't have a choice." She laughed, looking around the room. "I appreciate someone having the courage to stand up and state their opinions on matters. I want to be a community that can engage in healthy debates. I disagree with John that we need a hierarchy. I don't believe we need to be governed if we can govern ourselves. No government in human history has ever worked for more than a couple hundred years. Let's take the rest of this trip to rest and try to relax because we really don't have any idea what is in store for us down there. Thank you all for your time and attention." Cecilia sat back down in her seat and shook her head. This was going to be quite the adventure.

*****

Pete, Taylor, and Billy crawled through the ventilation ducts. Billy was a bit larger than the other two and barely fit. He was struggling to keep up with the guys. They had no idea where to go or how they would carry out their plan. The ducting was made of a strong, very solid, metal, something they had never seen before. The air in the ducts was thick and heavy, making it difficult to breathe. Billy's left elbow slipped as he put his weight on it, and he slumped forward. As he fell forward, his left arm grazed the broken beer bottle in his right hand, cutting him. The cut was mostly superficial, but it bled pretty badly.

"Guys, I need a minute," Billy panted.

Pete and Taylor stopped. They all took a few moments to catch their breath. Billy took the broken beer bottle and cut the sleeve off his shirt. He tied the sleeve around his cut.

"Okay, guys, I'm ready," Billy said.

Pete started moving first, followed by Taylor and Billy. As they got going again, everything shook violently for a moment. They all instinctively hunkered down.

"What was that?" Billy asked.

"I think it was a ship undocking from the mothership. Guys, six more of those and we can destroy this bitch!" Pete said excitedly.

"How do we do that, dude?" Billy asked.

"Not sure yet," Pete responded.

"That's what you keep sayin'. We need a plan, dude," Billy said.

"Then come up with one. I'm all ears," Pete said.

"Dude, this was all your idea. We could be on one of those ships back to Earth right now, but instead we're in this fuckin' cramped, smelly vent with nuthin' but broken beer bottles to protect us. I'm getting a bad feeling about all of this," Billy said.

"Me too," Taylor added.

"Guys, we will figure this out. We will destroy this ship and save the rest of the humans."

"What about the ships taking people back to Earth?" Taylor asked.

"They won't last long without the mothership. I bet they're probably fully automated and they'll just die without the mother-ship. Maybe they'll fall to Earth and the people down there can steal the technology for the new world. Who knows? And who cares? We won't be around to see any of it."

"That's the part of this mission I don't like," Billy said.

"We'll be heroes," Pete said. Everything shook violently again. "Five more, guys."

"How do you even know what that is? And how do you know there will be seven?" Billy asked.

"That man-thing told me they were splitting people up into seven different ships and dropping them off on each continent," Pete answered.

"Okay, so how do you know that shaking is a ship taking off?" Billy asked.

"Shut up and listen. I thought I heard it the first time. Sounded like a ship undocking to me," Pete said.

The three of them stopped crawling and just listened for a bit. It had gotten extremely hot in the ducting. They were all dripping with sweat. Everything shook again, and that time they all heard what could only be the sound of a ship releasing from the mothership. They must have been close to where they were taking off from.

"We have to find a vent, guys," Billy panted. "I can't fuckin' breathe."

"Yeah, neither can I," Taylor said. "Those things must be pumping heat through. They know we're in here."

"These are heating ducts, of course it's goin' to be hot up here," Pete said. "But I don't think they know we're here. Did you guys have a feeling like you were being watched ever since we've been here?"

Taylor and Billy both said they had.

"I don't have that feeling anymore," Pete said. "Do you guys?"

Taylor and Billy thought about it for a moment. They both realized that feeling was gone.

"I don't think they can track us up here. I think we're safe," Pete said.

"You just have all the answers, huh, Pete?" Billy said, sounding irritated. He was irritated, not with Pete but just in general. He was way too hot and exhausted, and his whole body ached from crawling through that ducting.

"I'm trying to figure this shit out as we go," Pete said, ignoring Billy's irritation. He knew Billy was just hot and tired. Pete didn't want to get into any arguments with those guys. He needed them level-headed and alert, not angry and distracted. Pete started crawling again; they did need to find an air vent.

Taylor and Billy didn't say anything else; they followed Pete as he started to move again. They came to a T in the ducting. Pete stopped and looked left, then right. To the right looked like the ducting either ended or led to another T. To the left, it looked like there was no end to the ducting. Pete didn't know what to do. He sat there for a moment trying to hear anything from below. That ship had to have some kind of engine compartment or engine room. Pete had seen the ship right before they had taken him, and it was gigantic. So there had to be a huge engine of some sort powering that thing. Finding it from the ducting was going to be next to impossible. Pete took a deep breath and turned left. He glanced behind him and watched as Taylor and Billy both stopped at the T, looked right, and then followed him left. Pete was nervous; he had no idea where they were or where they were headed.

About a hundred feet down the ducting, Pete saw an air vent. He stopped and put his face to it. The smell of death filled his nostrils, and the air coming up through the vent was cold. Pete looked through the vent. They were above what looked like a morgue. The room was full of tables with bodies under white sheets on them. He couldn't see anything else in the room except for those tables and bodies. The cool air felt good on his sweaty face, but that smell was too much. Pete got moving again. Taylor stopped at the vent and gasped. He didn't linger long and started after Pete. Billy stopped at the vent and peered through it. He'd seen a room just like that one before. It could have been the same one; he couldn't tell for sure. Billy looked up at Pete and Taylor. They were crawling away from him. Billy shook his head and got moving again too. What had he gotten himself into? Billy didn't think this would turn out the way Pete thought it would. He knew one thing for sure, though: he would never make it off that ship alive.

Pete stopped at another vent about fifty feet from the last one. He could feel hot, humid air seeping into the ducting from that room. Pete peered through the slats of the vent. The room was filled with grow lights and beds of vegetables. That was where they had grown all the food. Pete could see small gray creatures down there tending the garden. He turned to the others and put his finger to his mouth, making the *shush* gesture. Pete slowly and as quietly as possible started to crawl again. Both Taylor and Billy stopped to look through the vent and then quickly moved on. Pete was starting to feel good with his decision to go this direction at that T. They had already found two rooms and he was hopeful they'd find more. Hopefully, the engine compartment. The whole ship shook again, followed quickly by another shake.

"That's five gone!" Pete said. "Two more and home free!"

"No, everyone on those ships is home free. We're on a suicide mission," Billy panted as he wiped the sweat from his face.

"Billy, that's enough!" Taylor snapped at him. "I don't like this either, but we all agreed to do it. Now it's too late to back out, so there's no reason to keep bitchin' about it. Man up, dude."

Billy stopped crawling and stared at the back of Taylor. He smiled to himself and got moving again. Billy loved how easygoing Taylor was until he was pushed too far and just snapped at him like that. Billy respected that about his good friend. And he knew Taylor was right; they had all agreed to that wild and stupid mission, and complaining about it was not helpful. It was actually completely useless. Billy had to get those fears and doubts out of his head. He couldn't let them get in his way when the time came to act.

Pete stopped at another vent. This one had cool air coming through it. There weren't any smells or sounds. He looked through the vent and saw a small room full of weapons. He had never seen weapons like that before, but they were clearly weapons. The room couldn't have been any bigger than 10 × 10. There were shelves and racks lining all four walls with guns and knives on them. Pete could see a door on the far side of the room from where they were in the ducting. He could see the entire room, and besides all the weapons, it was empty.

"Guys, there's a shit load of guns and knives in this room," Pete said, pointing to the vent. "We gotta get down there and load up. Ditch these beer bottles."

"Don't you think they'll be guarding that room?" Taylor asked.

The whole ship shook violently again. The shaking had gotten more and more intense as they had been moving in this direction.

"I doubt it. They got the humans off the mothership as far as they know. Who would they need to guard against? Besides, I can see the whole room. There's nothing down there but weapons."

"One of those things could be posted up right outside the room," Billy said. "If they hear us in there, they'll come in after us."

"Then we'll blast 'em!" Pete said, fidgeting with the vent cover.

Pete was able to remove the vent cover. He set it down inside the ducting just in front of him. Pete wiggled forward a bit and kicked his legs out of the vent. He slowly lowered himself to the ground. Taylor looked like he was going to follow Pete into the room, but Pete motioned for him to stay up there. Pete started grabbing guns and handing them up to Taylor. Pete found three large knives in sheaths. He handed those up to Taylor as well. Pete looked up at the vent; it seemed a lot higher than it had when he dropped down from it. The air in that room felt so good on his hot, sweaty skin.

"Come on, Pete," Taylor said, sticking his head out the open vent.

Pete nodded at Taylor. He looked around the small room one more time. A large crate in one of the corners of the room caught his attention. Pete walked over to it. The crate was full of what looked like hand grenades. He smiled and grabbed an arm load. Pete handed the grenades to Taylor and went back for more. Pete was in the middle of handing Taylor more grenades when he heard something right outside of the door. It was voices. He couldn't understand what they were saying, but they were just outside of that door. Panic washed over him. The whole place shook again. The last ship had finally departed. Pete heard the voice slowly get quieter, as if they were moving away from the door. Pete looked up at Taylor and put his arms up to have Taylor help him climb back into the ducting. Pete put a foot onto the shelf against the wall and grabbed Taylor's outstretched hands. He pushed himself up, and Taylor helped him climb into the ducting. Pete grabbed the vent cover and put it back in place. He heard the door slide open and froze. Pete stared through the slats of the vent cover and watched as one of those small gray creatures walked into the room. It was carrying two large guns. The guns were as long as that thing was tall. The creature placed the guns on a shelf and looked around the room. It sniffed the air with its noseless nostrils. The creature said something in a language Pete didn't recognize, and another creature came into the room. The second creature looked a lot like the first one, but Pete could tell the difference between the two. The first one said something to the second one and pointed around the room. The second creature walked around the room, examining the shelves and racks. It walked back over to the first one and said something to it in their language. They both stood in the middle of the room, talking back and forth and looking around. They each grabbed a handgun off one of the shelves and left the room in a hurry. The door slid shut behind them.

Pete glanced back at Taylor and Billy and gave them the "Be quiet" signal. Pete started stuffing guns and grenades into his pockets and the waist of his pants. He then slowly started crawling forward. Taylor followed right behind Pete. Billy was trying to situate his guns so he wouldn't have to carry them. He sat there on his hands and knees watching as Pete and Taylor crawled away from him. Billy was starting to feel overwhelmed. He was stuck in that hot, cramped metal ducting and was beginning to feel very claustrophobic in there. He was soaked from head to toe in sweat. Breathing had become exceedingly difficult. Billy just wanted out of that damn metal tube! He had made himself come to terms with dying on that ship, but he did not want to die in that ducting. It certainly felt like he was going to die up there. He sure hoped Pete would get to wherever it was he wanted to find. Billy didn't know how much longer he would last up there. Billy sighed and made himself move again. They had been stopped in that duct for so long at that point; his joints had gotten tight. He shook his head, he was only twenty-nine, but in that moment, he felt like he was seventy. Everything ached and hurt. He just wanted to get the mission over with and die already.

*****

Cecilia Rodgers woke up on a hard, lumpy bed. She sat up and looked around. She was in a small room with the bed she was on, a nightstand next to that, a dresser on the other side of the bed, and a desk across the room. There was a candle and matches on the night-stand. Early morning light creeped into a window on the other side of the room above the desk, but it was still fairly dark in the room. Cecilia grabbed the matches and lit the candle. The room was freezing cold, and she was only wearing a nightgown. She walked around the bed to the dresser. She started pulling open drawers. The dresser was full of all sorts of clothing, underwear, pants, shirts, sweaters, and even shorts. Cecilia got dressed in the warmest clothes she could find. She picked up the candle and left the room. Everything around her was built out of wood and mortar. There were several other rooms around hers. The doors were all open, so she peeked into the rooms as she walked by. There was a woman close to her age asleep in one of the rooms and two teenage girls sleeping on bunkbeds in another. Two young women were bunked together fast asleep on separate beds in the next room and another young woman was asleep alone in the last bedroom.

Cecilia made her way into a large kitchen. The kitchen was stocked with pots and pans, plates, bowls, and glasses. There was a huge wood stove in the middle of the room with a brick chimney. Counters and cupboards lined the back wall of the kitchen. Cecilia looked around for the sink, but there wasn't one. On the other side of the wood stove was an open area with couches and a dining room table with seven chairs. The place was immaculate. Everything looked brand new. The entire place smelled like fresh timber.

Cecilia looked at the front door; hanging on hooks next to the door were seven coats and hats in various colors. She blew out the candle and set it on the wood stove. She grabbed the black coat and put it on. Under the coats was a shoe rack with boots that matched each coat and hat. Cecilia slipped on the black boots; they fit perfectly. She opened the front door and headed out into the early morning light. Cecilia turned around to check out her new dwelling. It was a good-sized log cabin that looked as if it had just been built. The cabin was sitting on a hillside overlooking a small community. She could see many more log cabins—they all looked to be identical to hers—in a large circle. The cabins surrounded a small town.

There were quite a few buildings lining the main street. Everything appeared to be brand new, but somehow it was all so familiar to her.

"Cecilia?" a tired voice said from the doorway of the cabin.

Cecilia turned around and saw the other woman that was about her age. She knew the woman; she recognized her right away. But what was her name? Cecilia knew she had known the woman's name; it had just slipped her mind.

Scarlett! That was her name! The two teenage girls were Hope and Gwen, Scarlett's girls. Cecilia couldn't remember the other young women's names at the time.

"Yes, Scarlett," Cecilia said.

"What sounds good for breakfast?" Scarlett asked.

"I hadn't thought about breakfast. I was too confused to even think about eating," Cecilia responded.

"Confused about what?" Scarlett asked, grabbing her coat and boots. She stepped outside and joined Cecilia in the front yard.

"Where we are. How we got here. I don't remember any of it."

"Are you serious, Cecilia?" Scarlett asked with a grin.

"Yeah, aren't you wondering the same thing?" Cecilia asked, kind of offended by the smile.

"No, we've been here for months. You're the mayor of this town. You have got to be messing with me, right?"

"I'm the mayor?" Cecilia asked, confused. "How long have I been mayor? Why does the mayor live in a house with so many other people?"

Scarlett looked at Cecilia in complete disbelief. How could Cecilia not remember any of it? She had to be fooling around. She did like to joke around, but she seemed genuinely confused. Scarlett looked past Cecilia at their small town. She could see people starting to move about the main street. Scarlett knew Cecilia needed to get to her office shortly.

"Come with me to gather eggs," Scarlett said. "I'll humor you and tell you what's going on." She motioned for Cecilia to follow her to the back of the cabin.

"You don't need to humor me, Scarlett. I genuinely don't remember anything since the ship."

Scarlett stopped and turned to face Cecilia. "The ship?" she asked. "What ship?"

"The mothership. You don't remember being on that damn ship with those things?" Cecilia asked. Scarlett was looking at her like she had lost her mind. Cecilia was beginning to feel like she *had* lost her mind.

"Mothership? What things? Are you okay, Cecilia? Is the stress and high expectations of running our town getting to you?"

"I'm fine, Scarlett!" Cecilia snapped. "I feel like yesterday we were all on that damn ship and now I'm waking up here. But you're telling me we've been here for months. I've somehow been mayor for months and don't remember a second of it? How in the hell did I go about my daily business running a town and I don't remember any of it? I was the president of the United States and now I'm the mayor of some small mountain community? None of this makes any sense at all."

Scarlett stared at her in shock. United States? What the hell was that, and where did Cecilia come up with that? And why did she keep talking about some ship? The lake and streams nearby weren't big enough to facilitate a ship; their small boats and canoes were plenty big enough. Cecilia must have had some crazy, vivid dream that she hadn't fully awaken from yet. Ships, United States, "things"—Scarlett feared her friend and boss was going mad.

"Where do I even begin?" Scarlett asked her. "What is the president of the United States? What are the United States?"

Cecilia looked at Scarlett, thoroughly confused. This was the same woman she had met in Des Moines, wasn't it? The same woman that had looked at her with such admiration and awe at first but was now looking at her like she had two heads. How could she remember everything so vividly and Scarlett couldn't? Was she actually going insane? Had she somehow imagined or dreamed all of it? They stood there in the cool morning air, studying each other.

Cecilia sighed. "Forget about all that. The United States is clearly not relevant anymore. Please, in your words, humor me and tell me how we all ended up here. Pretend like I just got here and explain daily life to me. Maybe I hit my head and I had a strange dream. Now I have forgotten reality."

"Cecilia, you're worrying me. You have always been such a level-headed, strong woman, and now you're talking nonsense. As your deputy mayor and friend, I feel I can say such things. You know I respect you and you respect me, so I will always be honest and blunt with you."

"I appreciate that, I really do, but please tell me what the hell is going on around here," Cecilia said.

"Follow me, I really do need to get breakfast going." Scarlett turned and started for the back yard again. Cecilia followed her. "Where should I start?" she asked as they walked.

"The beginning," Cecilia said. "How we ended up in this small town?"

Scarlett stopped at the chicken coop. "You really don't remember, do you?" she asked, opening the gate to the coop. She picked up a basket and began filling it with eggs.

"No, that's why I need you to explain it to me," Cecilia said, watching Scarlett collect eggs. The chickens were running around, squawking.

"We broke away from Henderson and began building this place a year ago. We lived in tents and Teepees for months. Every last one of us worked basically around the clock to get this town built before winter. We just completed the dam and should have electricity throughout town in a matter of weeks now. We did all of this, Cecilia. You were so proud of this place. That's why I'm so shocked you don't remember any of it." Scarlett left the chicken coop and closed the gate. She looked at Cecilia and headed back toward the front door.

"Why'd we break away from Henderson? What is Henderson?" Cecilia asked, following Scarlett back to the cabin.

"Henderson was awful," Scarlett said. "If you truly don't remember Henderson, then you should feel lucky about that because it was horrible. That's why we're here and doing things the right way now. Everyone equal and working together instead of against each other."

"Tell me more about Henderson," Cecilia said. "What was so awful about it?"

"Does that really matter now?" Scarlett asked, heading into the cabin. She set the basket of eggs on the kitchen counter and then took her coat and boots off. Cecilia removed her coat and boats as well and joined Scarlett in the kitchen. "We got away from the oppression and violence. We don't need to relive it."

"I think it does matter. How can we make sure it is not repeated here if we don't understand what happened there? You may remember it, and it clearly bothers you, but I don't remember. If I am going to be a successful mayor and leader, I need to understand what drove us out of that town," Cecilia said, watching as Scarlett stoked the fire in the wood stove.

Scarlett grabbed a big mixing bowl and flour. She mixed the flour and eggs and added some butter from a dish sitting on the counter behind the stove.

"Do you remember John at least?" Scarlett asked.

"I remember a man named John who debated with me a bit on the ship. Is that the same John?" Cecilia asked.

"Again, what ship? I don't know if it's the same John because I know nothing of this ship you keep referring to. I'm going to try to forget about this ship talk and just tell you about Henderson and John." Scarlett was mixing the batter in the bowl as she spoke. She grabbed a cast-iron skillet and placed it on the stove. "Henderson was named after John's family, or so the story goes. John ran the city. He was a firm believer that any society or community needed a hierarchy in order to thrive. In his opinion, there had to be a leader, although he acted more like a ruler than any kind of leader. John surrounded himself with like-minded people, all of whom were also male. John constantly told stories about his lost family. No one knew what he meant; that town had been built by his family. He was an incredibly angry, bitter man. You and John never got along and never once saw eye-to-eye on anything. He very obviously did not like you, and from what you said in private to me, the feeling was mutual." Scarlett started putting scoops of the batter onto the hot skillet.

"I generally don't dislike people, so that seems a bit out of character to me," Cecilia said. The sizzle from the cold batter hitting the hot skillet was a soothing sound to her. It was also making her feel quite hungry.

"I know that about you, but no one outside of his circle liked him," Scarlett said, flipping the pancakes. "You know how you get a feeling about certain people? Sometimes you can tell someone was a good person at one point in their lives but something happened to them and whatever that was had changed them? That was John. I could tell from interactions with John that he had been a good man at some point in his life. Something horrible must have happened to him because the John we knew was not a good man. He was an evil man. And he hated women. His hatred for women made a lot of other men also hate women. Especially strong women like us. You tried to compromise with him. You tried to make Henderson a safe place again, but he was far too arrogant to reason with. So we decided we would just create our own community. It didn't take much convincing to get a lot of people to come with us. Most people living in Henderson back then hated it as much as we did. And now we have Washington. It was your idea to name our little town that. None of us know what it means or where you came up with it, but we all thought it sounded good." Scarlett smiled at Cecilia. She grabbed a plate and loaded it with pancakes. She spooned more batter into the hot skillet.

"Tell me this, how did I become mayor of this town? Was it simply because I was part of creating the town? Or because I came up with the name?" Cecilia asked. She grabbed a pancake and rolled it up. She ate the pancake as Scarlett answered her.

"We all appointed you. You said we didn't need a government or any kind of hierarchy. You said we should learn from the oppression we all suffered in Henderson and we should all live in harmony with each other and nature. Although that sounds good in theory, we all knew it would never work in practice. No matter how all-in people are, there still needs to be rules in place and consequences if rules are broken. We needed some form of government to create and enforce the rules of a community. You fought us for a bit, but we were able to convince you that we as a whole not only needed rules but *wanted* them as well. People can only coexist for so long without law and order."

"I'm honored you all chose me. I wish I could remember all of that," Cecilia said with a sad look on her face.

"You were—still are actually—a badass, Cecilia. You are a fair, honest, and intelligent leader. You were clearly born with great leadership skills. It's like you've done it before." Scarlett chuckled at her last statement.

"I have," Cecilia began, grabbing another pancake. "I started my political career as the youngest and first female mayor of Houston, Texas. Then I ran and won a Senate seat. Served the Senate for years before running for president. I was elected in a landslide victory against a sexist, racist businessman. You should know this. You told me in the past life you had voted for me."

"What past life? Cecilia, you're not making any sense again. Senate? President? Of what?" Scarlett looked at Cecilia like she had lost her mind. Cecilia was not herself. For the first time ever, she looked scared and lost. Cecilia never looked that way; she always had the utmost confidence in everything she said and did.

"Never mind," Cecilia sighed. "Just another weird dream I guess." She knew it wasn't a dream. For some reason, Scarlett had no recollection of the time before. How could she not remember everything they had been through?

"Maybe that weird lightning last night made you have weird dreams. We are all so connected to the Earth. Things like that can affect our bodies and our minds," Scarlett said, cooking up the last of the pancake batter.

"What weird lightning?" Cecilia asked, perking up a bit.

"It was the strangest thing I've ever seen. There were no bolts of lightning, just bright—*really bright*—lights flashing in the sky last night. It looked like an explosion, honestly. Very strange. All of us, except for you, began to feel ill and we all went to bed. You said you would go to bed after the lightning stopped. That's all I remember of it. As soon as my head hit my pillow last night, I was out." Scarlett walked to the hallway and shouted, "Breakfast, ladies!"

"Weird lightning, huh?" Cecilia said, putting her finger to her chin as she contemplated it.

"Yeah, maybe the electrical field that lightning created caused you to hallucinate. It sure made the rest of us feel sick and dizzy."

"I bet that's it," Cecilia said. "Sorry to be so weird this morning. I think I am going to go lie down for a bit. Maybe some rest will help me feel like myself again. Maybe I will remember things again."

"I hope so. I'll let the others at City Hall know you're not feeling well today, and I'll handle any business at hand," Scarlett said, giving Cecilia a smile. "But don't worry, I won't tell anyone about your memory loss. I'm sure it's just temporary."

"Thank you, Scarlett," Cecilia said and smiled back.

Hope, Gwen, and the three young women Cecilia didn't recognize all said good morning to her as she passed them in the hall. The girls were all still very groggy and shuffled passed Cecilia to the kitchen. Cecilia went into her room and closed the door. She changed back into her nightgown and crawled into bed. Cecilia closed her eyes and tried to fall asleep. She hadn't felt rested when she had woken up that morning. She really wanted to get some sleep, and hopefully, she would wake up herself again. Nothing about what Scarlett had told her seemed accurate or even possible. None of it felt real. This wasn't her life. Cecilia could clearly remember being president of the United States of America. Then there was a big gap in her memory, with little flashes of running from something or running to somewhere. The last thing she did remember for sure was being on some sort of ship. She remembered being in a lot of meetings with people about the future of mankind and what kind of society to build. Why would they need to build a new society? What was wrong with what they had in America? Everything was wrong with it, she guessed. Maybe that was why they had moved on from America. She didn't remember abandoning America, but she also didn't remember anything that Scarlett had told her. What was that lightning Scarlett told her about? Was that what had scrambled her memories? Maybe she had read stories about some place called America and then she had dreamt about those stories. Maybe she had never been president; maybe all of that was just a dream too. It all seemed so real, though, but that was how dreams could be sometimes, especially the really vivid ones. You wake up from dreams like that wondering if any of it had really happened or not. The more she pondered it all, the less vivid everything became. Those vivid, oh-so-real memories of what she had called the United States became hazy. The ship she thought she had been on was fading away. When she woke up from her nap, she was going to look through all her books and find the one that had caused those random memories. She was now convinced it had to have been something she had read. She had probably been reading the book before the lightning storm. The lightning storm then disoriented her, and she fell asleep confused and ill, causing her to dream all those random things. She needed to figure it all out—and quickly. Cecilia didn't like the way Scarlett kept looking at her. She didn't want Scarlett or anyone else thinking she had lost her mind.

Cecilia pushed all of that out of her mind and made herself relax. She made herself not think about any of it. She needed sleep. Cecilia finally fell asleep.

Scarlett sat at the dining room table with the girls. They were all devouring the pancakes she had made.

"Ladies," Scarlett started, "Cecilia is acting very strange today. I won't go into details, but it seems she has lost her memory, or at least she is remembering things very differently. We need to give her some space and let her rest. Hopefully, some good rest will help her to feel normal again. I think it has to do with that strange lightning last night."

"She didn't look right for the brief moment I got to see her this morning," Julia said. "That lightning last night was strange and made me feel like shit."

"Me too," Dana said.

The other three girls all agreed that it had made them feel sick as well.

"That's what I'm thinking caused Cecilia to feel off today. She will be fine, ladies," Scarlett said.

They all nodded and kept plowing through their pancakes. Everyone stayed quiet while they finished up breakfast. Once they were all done, the girls all thanked Scarlett for breakfast and returned to their rooms to get dressed for the day. Everyone had their own chores and responsibilities. Hope and Gwen were responsible for tending to the animals. Dana and Julia both had jobs in town at the general store. Amanda took care of the cabin. She kept the place clean and organized, washed the dishes daily, did all the laundry. Everyone worked well together and, with the exception of Amanda and Gwen, there was hardly ever any fighting or jealousy. They all enjoyed their share of the responsibilities.

"Hope! There's a hole in the pigpen!" Gwen shouted to her friend. "Some pigs got loose. We gotta go find them!"

"Shit!" Hope shouted back from the chicken coop. "I'll be right there!"

Hope closed up the chicken coop and headed toward Gwen. The girls grabbed some rope and set off toward the wood just behind the animal pens. They knew the pigs had run off into the woods; this wasn't the first time they had had pigs escape. The pigs almost always went to the same clearing in the woods to graze.

"What do you think is going on with Cecilia?" Hope asked, as they walked into the woods.

"I dunno," Gwen responded. "It's gotta be a pretty big deal if my mom felt the need to bring it up to all of us at the table."

"I think adults worry too much sometimes," Hope said, swinging the rope in her hand.

"Yeah, me too. They seem to be stressed out most of the time," Gwen said. "Hey, what's that?" Gwen asked, stopping and pointing to their right.

"Looks like a tree fell," Hope said, squinting her eyes in that direction.

"That looks like more than one tree fell," Gwen said. "Let's check it out."

"Maybe that lightning hit them," Hope said.

Gwen and Hope headed toward the downed trees. As they got closer, they noticed the trees were all blackened from fire. There was no smoke in the air and no signs of fire anywhere else. Several large pine trees had fallen over in a circular pattern. Everything else that wasn't impacted by those trees was completely undisturbed. The girls had to climb over one of the downed trees to get to the center of the circle the trees had created.

"What in the fuck is that thing?" Hope said, looking over at Gwen.

"I have no idea, but we found the pigs," Gwen said, pointing at the pigs that had escaped.

The girls stood there staring at a huge metal object sticking out of the ground. The pigs were milling around the object, eating a green ooze and something that looked like leather. A gray/brown, dingy leather. The metal object didn't look remotely like anything they had ever seen before in their young lives. Hope started to walk toward it.

"What are you doing?" Gwen asked.

"Gonna check it out," Hope said.

"We should go get my mom. We don't know what that thing is or if it's dangerous."

"And you think your mom would know?" Hope said, rolling her eyes. "Come on. Let's just check it out and get these damn pigs back before they eat too much of that green shit off the ground."

Gwen reluctantly followed Hope over to the large object. As they got to the thing, they could smell sulfur and wet dog. It was an awful combination. The pigs were going to town on the green ooze and leathery stuff. Hope leaned down and picked up a piece of the leather. It was cold and slimy. She held it up to Gwen.

"What the hell?" Hope said to Gwen.

"Who knows, but don't touch it!" Gwen snapped at her.

"Too late for that!" Hope said back. "Whatever it is, it smells horrible!" she exclaimed and tossed it away. Two of the pigs hurried over to it and started ripping it to shreds, devouring it.

"Fuckin' gross!" Gwen said. "We shouldn't let them eat that shit."

"They're fine," Hope said. "Pigs can eat anything."

"I know that. But then we eat them, so we will end up eating whatever that shit is too."

"That's not how it works," Hope laughed.

"Why aren't you scared?" Gwen asked her.

"Nuthin' to be scared of really." Hope shrugged.

"Are you kidding me? Look around! What the fuck is that thing? And what are our pigs eating? None of this scares you?"

"It's weird, I'll give you that. But no, I don't feel scared at all. I'm fascinated and honestly a bit excited. We live the most *boring* life possible. This"—she pointed to the large metal thing sticking out of the ground—"is the most exciting thing that has ever happened to us. Embrace it, sister!"

Hope walked closer to the thing and touched it. The metal was fire hot and burned her hand instantly. She screamed out in pain and yanked her hand off the thing.

"Holy shit, that's hot!" she cried, holding her wrist and looking at her burnt hand. "Fuck, it hurts!"

"Are you okay?" Gwen said, rushing to Hope.

"No! It hurts so bad!" Hope had tears streaming down her cheeks.

"Let's get you home. We have to tell my mom!"

"She'll be mad, Gwen," Hope sobbed.

"No shit she will! We should have gone and gotten her right away. We shoulda never approached that thing."

"It hurts. Oh, shit, it hurts so bad!" Hope bawled.

"Come on," Gwen said and helped Hope over the fallen trees.

Gwen led Hope back to the cabin. Dana, Julia, and Scarlett were all gone. Amanda was scrubbing the kitchen floor on her hands and knees. Amanda stood up when she heard Hope and Gwen burst through the front door. Hope was bawling.

"What happened?" Amanda asked.

"There's this thing out there in the woods and Hope touched it. It burnt the shit out of her hand. We need cold water—now!"

Amanda rushed out of the cabin and ran back in with a bucket of water. She set the bucket on the dining room table, and Hope stuck her whole hand into it. The cold water instantly soothed her throbbing hand.

"What thing?" Amanda asked.

"Dunno," Gwen panted, still trying to catch her breath. "It's a huge metal-looking thing. It's buried into the ground. A bunch of trees fell over around it. I dunno, Amanda, it's all too weird to explain. Where's my mom?"

"What? A metal thing? Who around here could afford metal? How would a metal thing even be in our woods?" Amanda was shocked beyond belief by what Gwen had just said.

"I don't fucking know!" Gwen snapped. "Where's my mom?!"

"She's in town at work. You should know that she goes there every fuckin' day, remember?" Amanda snapped back.

"Hey, don't give me any shit!" Gwen said, stepping to Amanda. "I'm not in the mood for your shitty attitude today!"

"My attitude was fine until you spoke to me like that! Just 'cuz you're freaking out doesn't give you the right to snap at me, understand?" Amanda said, stepping to Gwen.

"Get out of my face!" Gwen snarled. "I gotta help Hope. I don't got time for your bullshit!"

"Again. You started it!" Amanda said, stepping closer to Gwen. Amanda loved everyone in that house and was very appreciative to have such a wonderful place to live, but sometimes Gwen got on her nerves. Gwen had an attitude because she was Scarlett's daughter. It seemed like she felt she was better than the rest of them.

"Just back off, Amanda!" Gwen growled. "I don't wanna fight with you!"

"Then show some fucking respect for me! I work my ass off to keep this place clean and tidy for all of you! No one seems to give a shit!"

"Oh, so is this now the Amanda pity party? We all work our asses off! I think you better go cool off somewhere, I need to help Hope." Gwen stepped away from Amanda and returned her attention to Hope.

"Typical," Amanda said, shaking her head. "It's always your way around here."

"Enough!" Cecilia yelled, walking down the hall to the kitchen. "What in the hell is all the yelling about out here?"

The girls all quieted quickly and looked to the floor.

"What is going on?" Cecilia asked again.

"Me and Hope found this metal thing in the woods, and Hope touched it, burning her hand. When we got back here, Amanda started arguing with me and giving me attitude," Gwen said softly.

"That's not true!" Amanda cried out. "She started in on me. I was just standing up for myself."

"I don't give two shits about your little argument. Just knock it off," Cecilia said. "Now, Gwen, what metal thing?"

"Some huge metal thing buried in the ground out in the woods. A bunch of trees fell over around it. It stinks so bad, and there's a green ooze and leather fragments all around it. We've got a few pigs who escaped down there eating whatever that stuff is," Gwen said, still looking at the floor.

"Take me there," Cecilia said.

"What about Hope's hand?" Gwen asked.

"Let me see it," Cecilia said. Hope pulled her hand out of the cold water. The skin was red and beginning to blister. "It's burnt pretty badly. Amanda, help Hope bandage that hand and put some ointment on it. Gwen, take me to that metal thing—now."

"Yes, ma'am," Amanda said and led Hope down the hall.

"Yes, ma'am," Gwen said. "Follow me."

Gwen led Cecilia out of the cabin and out to the woods. Gwen kept her head down and stayed quiet for the entire hike. Once they reached the metal thing, Cecilia stopped in her tracks and just stared at it. She looked around at the fallen trees and then looked at Gwen.

"How did you girls find this?" Cecilia asked Gwen.

"I noticed some pigs escaped, and whenever they escape, they always head for the woods back here. I noticed a tree had fallen over, so we went to check it out. Then we saw that thing." Gwen pointed to the huge metal object sticking out of the ground.

"Grab that rope right there and get those hogs out of here. We don't need them eating any more of whatever that green stuff is. Quarantine them. I don't want them penned up with the other hogs. We'll probably end up having to destroy these hogs, but I want to observe them first," Cecilia told Gwen.

"Yes, ma'am," Gwen responded, picking up the rope. "How do you think that thing got here?" she asked Cecilia.

"I don't know," Cecilia said, climbing over the fallen tree to take a closer look. "Just get these hogs out of here, please."

"Yes, ma'am, will do," Gwen said and climbed over the fallen tree.

Gwen tied the pigs together and led them back toward the cabin. The pigs were very familiar and comfortable with Gwen and followed her lead without issue. Once she got them back up to the cabin, she tied them to a tree away from the pigpen. Gwen gathered food for the pigs and scattered it on the ground around them. She wanted to go back to the woods with Cecilia, but she knew she'd just be told to go home. Gwen knew Cecilia well enough to know she wouldn't want Gwen around while she tried to figure that thing out. Gwen didn't want to go in the cabin and have to deal with Amanda again. She liked everyone they lived with, but Amanda was always so moody toward her. Amanda was the closest girl to her and Hope's age, so she had had high hopes of becoming good friends with Amanda, but that didn't materialize. Gwen just tried to avoid Amanda as much as possible and just go about her daily business. Gwen decided she better fix the pigpen fence before they lost any more pigs. That way, she could avoid Amanda and Cecilia while getting some work done. She hoped if she buried herself in a project, she would be able to keep her mind off everything that had happened.

As Gwen fixed the fence, it turned out to be a much easier fix then she had first thought it would be; she decided she'd head into town and tell her mom what had happened. She wanted to tell her mom about how Amanda had treated her as well. Cecilia was the mayor of the town, and from the outside, she was the head of their household, but in reality, it was her mom that ran everything. Gwen hoped she could convince her mom to get rid of Amanda. She'd even take over the household chores if it meant getting rid of Amanda. Gwen put the finishing touches on the new section of fence and headed into town.

Cecilia walked around the metal object. It was gigantic. A third of it was buried into the earth. What in the hell was it? Cecilia examined the thing closely. The materials it was made of were so foreign. She had never seen anything like it before. The part sticking out of the ground had to be at least ten feet, maybe even twelve feet, high. It was about eight feet wide. On the opposite side from where they had come in, there were lights. The lights weren't lit up, but she knew they had to be lights. She didn't know how she knew that, but she did. Under the cluster of lights, half buried in the ground, was a circular opening. Cecilia got down on her hands and knees. She couldn't see into the opening—it was too dark inside—but it was definitely a door. Too much of the door was buried, and she couldn't get inside. Cecilia got to her feet and headed back to the cabin. She retrieved a shovel and her candle. It might not be the best idea, but she was going to crawl inside that thing and see what she could find.

Cecilia got back to the metal object and began digging out the door. The ground was soft, and it didn't take long to dig a bigger hole. She lit her candle and peered into the interior. It smelled so bad in there she had to quickly pull her head outside. Cecilia coughed and gagged. She held her breath and stuck her head back inside. Everything in there was destroyed. She couldn't tell what anything was in there. It wasn't anything she had ever seen before. There were buttons and knobs that were far more advanced than anything people could have made. That whole thing couldn't have been made by people. They just didn't have the materials or the technology to build something like that. So where did that thing come from? Maybe there were people in other parts of the world that did have the technology and materials to build such a thing? But if that was the case, how did it end up here?

Cecilia thought she heard someone walking through the woods toward her. She stood up and looked around. A man was walking toward the downed trees. He was still too far away for her to know if she recognized him or not. Of course, she might know him and wouldn't be able to remember anything about him. Her memory was still so foggy and discombobulated. As then man got closer, she did recognize him. She couldn't remember his name, but his face was familiar.

"Hello, Cecilia," the man said. "What is that thing?" He pointed at the metal object.

"I don't know," Cecilia responded, climbing over the fallen tree. She stood next to the man. "I don't mean to be rude, but could you remind me your name? I am suffering from some memory loss."

"No worries, I'm Malcolm," he replied. "My wife, Bethany, and I live in the next house down from you guys. She works at City Hall with you."

"Thank you, Malcolm. I do recognize you. I just can't remember names. What brings you out this way?"

"I was gathering firewood out behind my place and saw the downed trees. I figured the trees had probably been struck by that lightning storm we had last night. But when I saw you head out here with a shovel, I thought I'd come see if you needed any help." Malcolm glanced at Cecilia as he spoke, but mostly he stared at that metal thing. He had never seen anything like it. He knew no one had.

"I appreciate that," Cecilia said. "I don't know what to do from here, so I'm not sure if there is anything to help with right now."

"Were you trying to dig it out?" he asked.

"No. There's an opening on the other side that was half buried. I dug that out to try and get inside, but it smells horrible in there. Plus, there's not really anywhere to stand up in there. I was afraid if I did brave the smell and climb in, I may not have been able to get back out."

Malcolm nodded. "Could you at least see inside of it?"

"Yes, and it's nothing I've ever seen before. Crazy, out-of-this-world shit inside that thing."

"You mind if I check it out?" Malcolm asked.

"No, go right ahead," Cecilia said, handing him her candle.

Malcolm climbed over the fallen tree and walked around the metal thing. He saw the opening and got down on his belly. He lit the candle and slowly poked his head into the opening. Cecilia wasn't exaggerating; the smell in there was horrendous. Malcolm held his breath and wiggled further into the thing. He looked around with wide eyes. Everything was metallic. There were buttons, levers, and switches covering a large counter—at least it looked like some sort of counter to him. He had never seen anything like it, so he didn't even know what to call it. In front of that counter thing was a chair. The chair was large and was covered in black leather. Who would waste leather by covering a chair with it? It was all so confusing. Malcolm took a breath and regretted it immediately. He coughed and quickly held his breath again. The candle flickered as he coughed, but it didn't go out. Malcolm felt something soaking through his shirt. He looked underneath him and saw a trail of green ooze. The trail went from the seat all the way out of the opening. Malcolm backed out of the opening and stood up. He was a bit dizzy and nauseous. That awful smell lingered around him. He blew out the candle and handed it back to Cecilia. That smell just wouldn't leave his nose.

"What do you make of it?" Cecilia asked him. The smell from that thing was all over Malcolm; he must have spent too much time in there.

"I haven't a clue," Malcolm responded, still feeling dizzy. And that smell, it seemed to be everywhere now. "Did you see the leather chair in there?" he asked.

"No, I couldn't stay in there long—that smell was too much for me," Cecilia said. She was beginning to feel nauseous.

"Hopefully since you dug out that entrance, that thing will air out now. We really should try to at least get that leather. Seems like a waste to cover a chair with leather," Malcolm said.

"I agree. It's a lot of work to make leather. I think we should take everything out of that thing. Maybe we can figure what in the hell it is," Cecilia said. She was realizing that Malcolm smelled like the inside of that thing. She looked at him and noticed his shirt was soaked in a green liquid. "What's that on your shirt?" she asked, pointing to the wet stain.

"I don't know. There was this green ooze streaked from that chair all the way out of the opening. I didn't notice it until I had already been lying in it for a while."

"I think that's what smells," she said as politely as possible.

Malcolm pulled his shirt to his nose and sniffed it. He gagged and almost threw up. That was most definitely the source of the smell.

"I am goin' to head home and change out of this shirt," Malcolm said. His eyes were watering.

"Good idea. I'd burn that shirt if I were you," Cecilia recommended.

"I plan on it. I think a bath is in order too."

"We don't know what that green ooze is. You better wash it off as soon as possible. Who knows what it could do to your skin?"

"That's the plan," Malcolm said. "Should we meet back here in a couple of hours?"

"Yes, I think we should. I'm going into town to get some supplies. I want to try to get rid of that ooze and smell. There's no way we can work in there with that ooze."

"Sounds good," Malcolm said. "I'll see you later."

"Okay, Malcolm, see you in a bit." Cecilia said.

Malcolm headed back to his place. Cecilia turned and went back to the cabin. She went inside to find Gwen. Amanda was cleaning the dining room, and Hope was lying on one of the living room couches with her bandaged hand raised in the air.

"Where's Gwen?" Cecilia asked Amanda.

"I don't know. I thought she was still with you," Amanda responded.

"No, I sent her back up here an hour ago," Cecilia responded. "Are you fine here by yourself?" she asked Hope.

"Yes, ma'am, I'm fine. I'm just really tired," Hope responded.

"Okay." Cecilia turned back to Amanda. "You come with me. We're going to town to fetch supplies.

"Okay, ma'am." Amanda said and took off her apron.

Cecilia led Amanda out the front door. It was only about a ten-minute walk to town.

"Do you know where City Hall is?" Cecilia asked Amanda.

"Yeah," Amanda responded, confused by the question. The mayor should know where City Hall was.

"Take me there first. I want to talk to Scarlett."

"Okay, ma'am," Amanda said. She walked ahead of Cecilia and showed her the way to City Hall.

They got to City Hall and went inside. A woman sat at a desk just inside the front door.

"Madam Mayor, are you feeling better?" the woman asked.

"I feel fine," Cecilia said. "Where's Scarlett?"

"She's in her office," the woman replied.

"Take me to her, please," Cecilia said.

The woman gave her a confused look. Why would Cecilia need her help finding Scarlett's office? The woman didn't say anything; she stood up and led Cecilia to Scarlett's office.

"Thank you," Cecilia told the woman.

"You're welcome," the woman said. She returned to her desk.

Gwen was sitting across from her mom. Scarlett was looking through some paperwork spread across her desk.

"Cecilia! It's good to see you," Scarlett said, setting aside her paperwork. "Are you feeling better?"

"I feel fine," Cecilia responded. "Would you please excuse us? I need to talk to your mother in private," Cecilia said to Gwen.

"Of course," Gwen said, standing up and leaving the room. As she turned toward the reception area, she could see Amanda standing by the front door. Her mom had told her she would not ask Amanda to leave the cabin. That had pissed Gwen off. The sight of Amanda standing there made her even angrier. Gwen didn't say anything to Amanda or Bethany; she just walked by the both of them and straight out the front door. Bethany had looked up from her desk to say something to Gwen but saw the look on her face and decided to keep quiet.

"Scarlett, we need to talk," Cecilia said, closing the door and taking a seat across the desk from Scarlett.

"What about?" Scarlett asked.

"The girls found something out in the woods behind our place," Cecilia began.

"Gwen told me about that," Scarlett said. "What do you think about it?"

"I don't know what to think about it. It's not anything I've ever seen before. It doesn't look like anything man-made," Cecilia said.

"What in the world could it be if it's not man-made?" Scarlett asked.

"That's just it, I have no earthly idea what it could be," Cecilia said.

"What do you want to do about it?" Scarlett asked.

"Our neighbor, Malcolm, has volunteered to help me go through the thing and salvage whatever we can. He said there's a chair inside covered in leather. We sure could use that leather with winter coming soon."

"Malcolm is a good man," Scarlett said. "He and Bethany are both good people. I'm not surprised he offered to help. Besides the leather, what else is salvageable?"

"I don't know that either. Everything about that thing is so alien to me. That thing is made from materials you couldn't even imagine. They're certainly materials we have no access to. But maybe we can repurpose some things."

"I want to check that thing out when I'm done here. I will help you and Malcolm however I can."

"I appreciate that, Scarlett. We do need to be careful—that thing burned Hope pretty badly," Cecilia said.

"I heard about that too. Gwen had a lot to tell me." Scarlett rolled her eyes. She loved her daughter with every ounce of her being, but that girl could be overly dramatic about things. Scarlett figured it was just her age; teenagers did tend to take everything too personally. Scarlett had been extremely disappointed in Gwen for fighting with Amanda and then demanding that she be asked to leave the household. She told Gwen that was not and would never be an option. Everyone in that household was important and had a home forever there. "I also heard about the argument between Gwen and Amanda. Gwen wanted me to kick Amanda out of the house. I told her that would not happen. I talked to her about her attitude and that she needed to treat everyone with the same level of respect. I plan on talking to Amanda as well."

"Nice work, Scarlett. I really appreciate you handling such matters. I do not have the patience for that nonsense. Amanda is out in the reception area if you'd like to chat with her now," Cecilia said, standing up. "What kind of tools do we have at home?"

"We have a little of everything. Hammers, screwdrivers, saws. Why?"

"I'm going to the general store to get supplies for working on that thing out there in the woods. I don't even know what we would need to take that thing apart. Can you tell me where the general store is? My memory has not come back yet." Cecilia opened the door.

"It's across the street and down a block. Take Gwen and I'll send Amanda that way after I talk to her."

"Thank you, Scarlett. I'll send Amanda your way on my way out. I'll see you back at home later."

"Thank you. I'll see you later," Scarlett said.

Cecilia walked to the front door and told Amanda to go see Scarlett. Cecilia could see Gwen standing in front of the window just outside of the front door. She went out and told the girl to come with her to the store. Julia was behind the front counter of the general store. She said hello to Cecilia and Gwen as they entered.

"I need tools, towels, and probably some buckets," Cecilia said to Julia. "Can you show me to those things?"

"I can have Dana show you. I need to stay up front," Julia replied. Julia called out to Dana, and she stepped out of an aisle.

"Hey, what brings you in here?" Dana asked.

"I need tools and towels. Lots of towels. I want some buckets too," Cecilia said.

"No problem, let's go get what you need," Dana said with a smile. "Is it for that thing in the woods?" she asked Cecilia.

"Yes. How do you know about that?" Cecilia asked. "You were gone before we found it."

"Mr. Abrams was in here not too long ago looking for a sledgehammer. He said there was a big metal thing in the woods behind his place. I guess he wanted to smash it up," Dana told her.

"Is Mr. Abrams's first name Malcolm?" Cecilia asked.

Dana looked at Cecilia puzzled; she should have known Malcolm wasn't Mr. Abrams's first name. Everyone in town knew Mike Abrams.

"No, his first name is Mike," Dana said. Cecilia was acting so strange. She seemed like a stranger, not at all her normal self.

"I only saw Malcolm out there. Did this Mr. Abrams say when he saw that thing?"

"No, but he said he was investigating it right before he came here. That was about an hour ago."

"I was out there in the woods an hour ago. I would've seen him if he was out there too." Cecilia's overall memory was shot, but she remembered everything from that day clearly. Malcolm was the only other person out there with her. "Was Mr. Abrams out there when you girls found that thing?" she asked Gwen.

"No. No one else was around, ma'am," Gwen answered.

"What else did he say about what he saw out there?" Cecilia asked Dana.

"He said there was blood around the thing but nothing else. He assumed someone else had found it first and somehow cut themselves up pretty badly. He said there was a lot of blood."

"Human blood?" Cecilia asked.

"That's what Mr. Abrams said it was. What other kind of blood could it be?" Dana asked.

"Could be animal blood. Did he see any green ooze? Or say anything about an awful smell?" Cecilia asked.

"No. He didn't mention green ooze—I would have remembered something like that. He didn't mention any smells either. He was only in here for a few minutes. We don't have any sledgehammers in stock right now. Several people came in first thing this morning and bought every sledgehammer we did have. Mr. Abrams said he would just borrow one and left. What's going on? I'm very confused now," Dana said.

Amanda walked up to them and stood behind Dana, as far from Gwen as she could get.

"I don't know, but I'm confused too. Can someone take me to Mr. Abram's place?" Cecilia asked.

"I can," Amanda answered.

"Perfect. Gwen, get as many towels and buckets as you can carry and take them to that thing in the woods. Wait there for me," Cecilia said to Gwen. Gwen agreed to do it and took off to get the towels. She knew the store well and didn't need any assistance finding what they needed. "Thank you, Dana. Let's get going, Amanda."

"You're welcome," Dana said as Cecilia turned toward the front of the store.

"When you two are done here, I'll need your help with that thing in the woods. We will need as many hands as possible to deal with it," Cecilia said to Dana.

"Okay, we will be off in a couple of hours," Dana said.

"Perfect. See you then." Cecilia walked to the front of the store and told Julia the same thing. She and Amanda then left the store and headed to Mr. Abrams's property.

Cecilia knocked on the front door of Mr. Abrams's cabin. The exterior of the cabin was identical to the one they lived in. A woman with an apron on over her dress answered the door. Cecilia could tell the woman recognized her and was surprised to see her on the doorstep.

"Hello, ma'am. Is Mr. Abrams available?" Cecilia asked.

"Hello, yes, he is out back in the woods. He stumbled upon something quite strange back there," the woman politely replied.

"May we go back and see him?" Cecilia asked.

"Oh, yes, of course you may. Please, let me show you the way," she said and stepped out the front door. Cecilia paused and let the woman get a little bit of a head start. She grabbed Amanda's arm and held her up.

"Do you know her name?" Cecilia whispered to Amanda.

"It's Kim Abrams," Amanda whispered back. "Mike's wife."

"Thank you," Cecilia whispered.

Cecilia and Amanda followed Kim around the back of the cabin. Kim led them around a big vegetable garden, toward the woods. Cecilia could see more downed trees. She could smell the charcoal odor that lingers after a forest fire. As they marched further into the woods, Cecilia could hear banging.

"Mike's been pounding away at that thing for over an hour now," Kim said to Cecilia. "I don't think he's having any luck. He'll give out long before that contraption will." She chuckled.

They climbed a small hill and saw Mike hammering away at a large metal object that looked exactly like the one they had found behind their cabin. Cecilia stopped and stared. What in the holy hell was going on?

"Mike!" Kim shouted. "The mayor is here. She'd like to talk to you."

Mike stopped what he was doing and looked up at them. He dropped the sledgehammer and walked toward them.

"Hello, Madam Mayor," he said once he had reached her. He put out his hand, and they shook hands. "What brings you out to our place?"

"That thing you're pounding away at over there," Cecilia said, pointing at the huge metal object.

"I know, pretty weird, huh?" he said, wiping sweat from his brow with a red handkerchief.

"We've got one in the woods behind our place too," Cecilia said. "May I go look at yours?"

"Yes, of course, follow me." Mike said, turning toward the contraption. "I've been hammering away at that thing and nothing. I may have put some minor dents in it, but I can't get anything to break free. It's like hitting a boulder."

"That doesn't surprise me," Cecilia said. "Whatever that thing is made of is nothing like we have ever seen."

Cecilia walked around the metal object in awe. Everything about this thing was exactly like the one she had checked out at her place, with one exception, no foul odor. She noticed the blood Dana had mentioned. There was a pool of blood just outside of the opening of this one. A trail of blood led into the woods.

"Did you follow that trail of blood there?" Cecilia asked, pointing to the ground.

"No, ma'am. I didn't want to encounter whatever got injured. I assumed an animal was investigating this thing and somehow cut itself up pretty good," Mike answered.

"I'm going to follow it. What if it was a person, not an animal?" Cecilia asked.

"I'll come with you," Mike said, picking up the sledgehammer. "I'm going to take this with us just in case."

"Good idea, Mike," Cecilia said. "Amanda, stay here with Kim. We'll be right back."

Amanda nodded. Cecilia and Mike headed off further into the woods, following the blood. They walked for at least a hundred yards before stumbling across what had left that trail of blood. Lying against a large pine tree, barely breathing, was a young man. He was clutching his side. The young man was covered in blood. Cecilia rushed over to him.

"What happened to you?" she asked as she knelt beside him.

"I don't know," he muttered.

"How did you get injured?" she asked.

"I don't know," he wheezed.

"Mike, help me get him out of here," Cecilia said to Mike, standing up.

"I've got a hay trolly back at my place. Let me run and get it. We can wheel him out of here," Mike said, not waiting for answer.

Mike took off in a full sprint back toward his place. Within minutes, he returned with a long, empty trolly. Mike and Cecilia carefully put the man on the trolly. They slowly wheeled him out of the woods.

"We should take him to the doc," Mike said.

"Yes, we should. Lead the way, Mike," Cecilia said. "Amanda, get home and let Scarlett know what is happening."

"Will do, ma'am!" Amanda said.

Amanda ran off toward their place. Cecilia followed Mike back toward town. The young man on the trolly winced and grimaced the whole way. He was bleeding badly; Cecilia was amazed he was still alive. They got him to the doctor's office, but it was closed.

"I'll go fetch Doc!" Mike exclaimed, taking off again.

The man started coughing. Blood splattered out of his mouth with each cough. Cecilia knelt beside the trolly and held the man's free hand. He was still holding his side with the other hand. He squeezed her hand.

"We'll get you help," Cecilia told him.

"We got 'em," he wheezed. "We fuckin' got 'em!" Tears rolled down his face. He coughed several more times and closed his eyes. His chest slowly stopped heaving. He let out one last raspy breath and died.

"Young man! Wake up!" Cecilia said, shaking him gently. There was no response; he was gone.

Cecilia stood up. She was shaken up; she had never watched someone die before. Or had she? She couldn't remember if she had. It felt like maybe she had seen someone die, or maybe even a lot of people. Cecilia didn't want to dwell on whether or not she had ever seen anyone else die. The young man's last words echoed in her mind. "We got 'em." What did that mean? And where did this guy come from? He was probably a local man and she just couldn't remember his face. He must have been messing around with that thing in the woods and hurt himself. There had been an awful lot of blood pooled up beside the entrance to that thing. Maybe he had crawled inside and somehow jabbed himself in the side. All he could do at that point was crawl away in pain.

"Are we too late, ma'am?" Mike asked, looking down at the young man on the trolly.

"I'm afraid so," Cecilia responded. "He passed away right after you left."

"That's so sad," Mike said. "He was so young."

"I'll check him out and make a declaration," the doctor said.

"Thank you, Doctor," Cecilia said.

Cecilia and Mike stepped away from the trolly. Doctor Richards opened up his office and wheeled the trolly inside.

"Shall we head back to that thing in my woods?" Mike asked.

"I will be returning to my place. I have one of those things in the woods behind my place as well. I appreciate your time and your help with that young man," Cecilia said.

"My pleasure, ma'am. Well, minus the poor man passing away."

"Did you know him?" Cecilia asked, figuring Mike should know him, especially since the man had been so close to Mike's cabin when he was injured.

"No, never seen him before. Must be new to town. Poor fella just moved here and then dies? It's tragic." Mike looked at his boots. Seeing that young man so severely injured had really gotten to Mike.

"Death is always tragic, Mike. Again, I would like to thank you for all you've done today. And I also appreciate you letting me look at the metal object in your part of the woods."

"Again, my pleasure, ma'am. I hope to see you all again real soon." Mike tipped his hat to Cecilia.

"I hope so too, Mike. And please, if you discover a way to break that thing apart, let me know. Or if you discover anything new about it."

"I will. And you do the same, please."

"Absolutely," she said. Cecilia gave Mike a little smile and turned back toward her cabin.

"Bye for now," Mike said, heading off toward his property.

Cecilia headed straight to the metal thing in the woods behind her cabin. As she approached, she saw everyone from her household and the woman from the town hall standing just outside of the downed trees. They were all looking at the metal object. Cecilia approached them.

"Well, Ladies, what do you all think of that thing?" Cecilia asked the group.

"I have no idea, Cecilia," Scarlett said. "Malcolm is inside that thing right now."

"*What?*" Cecilia exclaimed. She took off toward the object.

The smell was awful; it seemed worse than before. Cecilia got down on her belly and looked into the opening. She could see candlelight flickering inside. The smell was so bad it made her feel sick.

"Malcolm!" she called out. "You in there?"

"Yeah, I'm in here." His voice was muffled. "This thing is pretty big, ma'am."

"How can you stand this smell?" she asked.

"I tied a handkerchief around my mouth and nose. It helps a bit, but it still stinks like hell in here. And it's so hot inside," he responded.

"What are you seeing in there?" She still couldn't see Malcolm, and it was difficult to understand him.

"A lot of things that I do not recognize. It's all so strange looking," he responded. Malcolm stood up and could see Cecilia looking in through the opening. "I'm going to climb out. It's too damn hot in here. I got the leather cut off of that seat." He handed her the leather.

Cecilia took the leather and stood up. As she waited for Malcolm to get out of the contraption, she studied the leather. It looked and felt like leather, but it was definitely not made from cow hide. Malcolm pulled himself out and got to his feet. He was dripping wet with sweat. He removed the handkerchief and caught his breath.

"Damn, it's hot in there. It feels like a woodstove," Malcolm said, wiping sweat from his face with his shirt sleeve.

"Did you examine this leather at all?" Cecilia asked, looking away from the leather and at Malcolm.

"No, not thoroughly," he responded. "It was too dark in there, even with the candle."

"It doesn't look like it was made from cow hide," she said.

Malcolm took the leather and examined it closely. His eyes got wide, and a look of disgust came over his face.

"I've worked with leather a lot, ma'am. I've tanned many hides in my day. All kinds of animal hides. You name an animal and I've worked their hides into leather. This is not made from any animal I know of." He still had a shocked and disgusted look on his face.

"What could it be then?" Cecilia asked.

"This is going to sound morbid and out there, but I think it's human."

"Human?" Cecilia asked, confused. "Are you telling me you think this leather was made from human skin?"

Malcolm hesitated. "Yes, ma'am, I think it was. I'm not sure of course, and I hope like hell I'm wrong, but I really think it's human skin."

"What in the fuck?" Cecilia exclaimed. "What in the holy hell is going on around here?"

"Cecilia!" Scarlett shouted from behind the fallen trees. Cecilia looked up at her. "Doctor Richards is here. He said he found something inside that young man you and Mike found."

"Inside?" Cecilia shouted back. "I'll be right there." She turned to Malcolm. "Your theory about what that leather was made from stays between us, okay?"

"Yes, ma'am," Malcom replied.

Cecilia headed back up to the group. Doctor Richards was standing beside Scarlett; he was dressed in surgical gear.

"What did you find, Doctor?" Cecilia asked.

"I was in the middle of performing an autopsy, even though it was quite clear the young man had succumbed to that wound in his side, when I found this at the base of his skull, just inside the muscle wall. I rushed right over here with it." He held out a small, round metal object. It had a tiny wire sticking out of one end of it. The thing looked like it was made of the same metal the large object in ground had been made of.

"What is that?" Cecilia asked the doctor.

"I don't know, ma'am. I've never seen anything like it. Especially inside of someone's neck! I sanitized it—you can take a closer look if you'd like."

Cecilia took the object and rolled it around in her hands. It was very smooth and cold. Freezing cold. Malcolm had joined the group. He looked at what Cecilia had in her hand.

"Hey! I found something exactly like that while I was inside that big thing," he exclaimed, pulling it out of his pocket. He handed it to Cecilia. The two small objects were identical.

"Is there anyone in town who could figure out what in the hell we have here?" Cecilia asked the group.

"Greg would be the only person I could think of," Scarlett responded.

"Who's Greg?" Cecilia asked, which confused everyone except for Scarlett. Everyone in town knew Greg well.

"Greg O'Sullivan, the town electrician and mechanic. He's the one who designed the dam and is starting to install electricity in everyone's homes," Scarlett told her. "Greg knows everything there is to know about electricity and mechanics."

"Well then, someone go fetch Greg!" Cecilia demanded. "We should have had him on site this whole time!"

"He's probably at his shop," Malcolm said. "I'll go get him." Malcolm headed off toward town.

"I'll leave that thing with you, Madam Mayor," Doctor Richards said. "I am going to get back to my office and finish the autopsy. Should I prep him for burial when I'm done?"

"Yes, Doctor, I think we should bury him. We need to get word out to the town, see if anyone knew him. It would be nice to have a name for the young man," Cecilia responded.

"I'll get the word out," Doctor Richards said. "Would anyone here being willing to help me?"

"Amanda, you go with the Doctor," Cecilia commanded.

Amanda agreed and walked off with Doctor Richards.

Malcolm returned with Greg. He brought Greg to Cecilia, and she handed the electrician those odd metal devices. Greg turned them over in his hands and studied them. He was both confused and intrigued by those things. Greg had worked with every piece of electrical equipment that had been invented; in fact, he himself had invented several electrical devices. Those things were like nothing he had ever seen before.

"Any idea what those could be?" Cecilia asked Greg.

"No, ma'am," Greg replied. "I've never seen anything like this before. Malcolm told me they looked like they could be electrical devices, and they certainly are, but nothing I have ever encountered. Where did they come from?"

"Malcolm found one of them inside that thing over there, and the doctor found the other one inside a young man's neck," Cecilia answered.

"Inside his neck?" Greg slowly asked in disbelief. "How would something like this end up inside someone's neck?"

"We don't know that, but maybe if we could figure out what those things are, we could figure out why and how one ended up in a man's neck," Cecilia said. "Could you examine them more closely?" she asked Greg.

"I sure can. I would love to, in fact—I am so curious about these things now." He looked at Cecilia. "Can I take them back to my shop?"

"Of course," Cecilia said. "There's more you should see first, though. That thing over there has all kinds of foreign electrical devices and lights. None of it seems to work, though."

"I'd be happy to look. I was over at Mike's place earlier today inspecting a similar object behind his house. It is all very foreign. The thing at his place had technology that shouldn't exist. There's wiring and switches made of material that we don't have access to. I'd like to get access to it, though—it's amazing material. I took some samples from his object and was in the process of doing some tests on it when Malcolm came and asked me to come here. I can't tell you what any of this is or where it came from, but it is all so very intriguing and exciting. If I could figure out a way to replicate it, it would be a game changer for us," Greg said as he and Cecilia walked over to the metal contraption. "Yup, this is exactly like what Mike has at his place. May I crawl in there and take more samples?"

"You sure can, but there is an awful smell in there," Cecilia said.

"I can already smell it." Greg pulled a handkerchief out of his back pocket and tied it around is nose and mouth. "I'll brave anything at this point to get my hands on more of that technology. I want to steal this technology, but I also want to figure out where this came from and how in the hell it got here."

"So do I, Greg," Cecilia said. "Go ahead and go get whatever you want out of that thing. I am going to go rejoin the group."

"Yes, ma'am. Thank you. I'll be a while. You all can go on and get some supper while I work here. No need to wait around for me, I'll come find you when I'm done, if that's okay."

"Yes, of course that is okay. I think we could all use a break from this thing. Thank you, Greg."

"My pleasure, ma'am."

Greg dropped down to his hands and knees and shimmied himself into the thing. It did stink like holy hell in there. Cecilia headed back to the group and told everyone to get some dinner. Malcolm and Bethany headed home. Cecilia and her household headed for their cabin. Cecilia didn't like the idea of leaving Greg alone inside of that thing, but she figured he'd be okay for a few minutes. She would check on him after a bit.

Greg pulled tools from the tool belt he was wearing and began removing anything and everything that was electrical. He was shocked by how lightweight and workable everything was. Greg was lying awkwardly on his back, underneath what he thought was a counter but was more like an electrical control panel. So many wires running under that thing. Despite the horrible smell, he was almost giddy. That wiring was phenomenal and would help him power the whole town. Greg had to hammer and pry the bottom of the panel apart; none of his screwdrivers matched the screws on that thing. He didn't want to ruin the sheet metal—how anyone had access to that much metal was beyond him—but he wanted all of it. The hammer slipped free from the metal and hit Greg in the head. The impact dazed him for a bit. Greg was dizzy, drenched in sweat and starting to gag from the smell. He powered through all of it; he had to have that wiring. He finally got the sheet metal out of the way and began pulling wires. Most of the wiring pulled free easily, except for a thick black wire that ran the length of the panel. For leverage, he used the claw of his hammer. Greg placed the claw over the wire and pulled. He moved out of the way so he wouldn't end up with the claw buried in his chest when that wire broke free. It finally pulled free, and the whole contraption shook. Greg could feel everything shaking around him. The shaking intensified, and the whole panel fell on him, pinning him underneath. Greg yelled for help but knew it was of no use; everyone had left. He could smell smoke. The shaking kept intensifying. Something was not right. That thing should not have been shaking like that.

The metal contraption Greg was trapped inside of exploded. Pieces of it blew into the air and scattered about the forest. What had once been a huge, seemingly unbreakable object was reduced to tiny metal fragments. The explosion was so great it shook the cabin. The women and girls all ran out to the woods. They all stood there in shock, looking at the hole in the ground where that contraption had been. Lying just outside of the crater was a boot; there was part of a leg sticking out of the boot. Cecilia stared at the boot; she knew whom it had belonged to. Anger and sadness washed over all of the women. Cecilia didn't remember Greg, but she could tell he was a good man. The town had just lost one of their own and in a horrific way. Everyone was in shock and didn't say anything about what they were looking at; there was no need to in that moment.

Another large explosion shook the ground. From their backyard, they could see the fireball and debris. It had come from Mike's place. Was Mike still working on that thing when it blew? And why were those things suddenly exploding? They all rushed to his cabin. Malcolm and Bethany had already come out of their cabin and joined the group on their way to Mike and Kim's. They found the couple standing out back, staring at the hole in the ground where their metal object had been.

"I was just out here twenty minutes ago. Kim made me come in for supper," Mike said softly. "She saved my life." He said this with tears in his eyes. Mike put his arm around Kim and pulled her close to him.

"I'm glad you're okay, Mike," Cecilia said. "I'm glad you're both okay."

Another explosion rocked the ground, followed by another. They were further away, but still close enough to feel. Fire, smoke, and debris could be seen above the tree line.

"What the hell?" Scarlett said, breaking the stunned silence.

"We should get to town. Folks will begin to come around to see what's going on," Cecilia said.

Everyone agreed and they headed off toward town. It was early evening by that point, and everything but the town's only tavern was closed. They all headed inside the tavern. The owner and bartender, Bob, greeted them as they all filed in. He offered a round of drinks, everyone except for Cecilia and the teenage girls accepted a drink. A drink sounded good to Cecilia, but she wanted to keep her mind clear. They needed to come up with a plan of action. She wasn't sure what, if anything, could be done at that point. Clearly there had been more than just the two contraptions she had seen. Those other explosions couldn't have been anything else but more of those things blowing up.

Once people started sipping on their drinks, they seemed to loosen up a bit. Everyone was chatting among themselves. The conversations all revolved around everything that had happened that day. Cecilia took a seat at the bar and motioned for Bob to come to her.

"What have you been hearing about what's going on today?" Cecilia asked Bob. She knew people treated bartenders like therapists and confided in them.

"People have been talkin' about it all day," Bob replied. "I've had a couple of people tell me they found large, strange metal objects in the woods behind their place. Mallory Turner was in here a little bit ago asking if I could help her find some men to dismantle that thing for her. I said I'd ask around. No one knows what they are, and most people don't want to go near them."

"Did Mallory Turner say anything else about the thing in her back woods?" Cecilia asked. She had no idea who Mallory was, but she didn't need to know right then. What was more important at that moment was what the woman had said about what was in her part of the woods.

"Not much, she was pretty damn confused about it. She said it was huge and extremely hot to the touch. She burnt her hand touching the thing." Bob paused and thought for a moment. "She did say she found this strange green ooze in and around the thing. Said it smells awful, the worst smell she's ever encountered."

"I know that smell and that ooze," Cecilia said. "Bob, could I get a water?"

"Sure thing, Mayor," he said and poured her a glass of water.

"Anyone else say they found one of those things? By the number of explosions, I know there were at least four of those things."

"No, ma'am. People have talked about seeing them, but I haven't heard anything about where the fourth one was."

"We'll have to ask around," Cecilia said. "We need to figure out the locations of each one of those things. But first, I'd like to talk to Mallory about what she saw. Things have been so crazy and stressful today that I've been having trouble keeping everyone and everything straight. Could you point me in the direction of Mallory's place?"

Bob looked at Cecilia with a confused look. Mallory ran the only barber shop in town; she cut everyone's hair. She was well-known and liked by all; Cecilia should have known how to find Mallory.

"She just walked in. She's right over there talking to Scarlett," Bob said, pointing across the room.

Cecilia turned around on her barstool. She found Scarlett standing across the room with a drink in her hand talking to a plump middle-aged woman. Mallory was in tears and shaking badly. Scarlett put her arm around Mallory. Cecilia got up and walked to them.

"Mallory, are you okay?" Cecilia asked.

"No, I am not," Mallory sobbed.

"Bob told me about what you found in the woods," Cecilia said. "Did it just explode?"

"Yes," Mallory cried. "My dog was out there sniffing around it. I kept hollering at her to come back inside, but she wouldn't leave that thing. She was right next to it when it exploded. She's gone." Mallory cried harder, tears flowing from her eyes like a waterfall.

"I am so sorry for your loss," Cecilia said. "We have lost a couple of fine men today too. Something out of this world is going on around here."

The tavern had been slowly filling up with townsfolk. Cecilia didn't recognize anyone, but she knew she should have. She imagined most of the town was now in the tavern. Bob was busy pouring drinks, and the tavern was getting louder as people began chatting with one another. Cecilia decided this was a fine time to address the town. She went to the front of the bar and called for the attention of the crowd. The tavern slowly quieted down.

"Folks," Cecilia began in a loud, commanding voice. She wasn't yelling but was speaking loud enough to be heard. "By now we all know what was found in the woods around town. I personally saw two of those things, and I have no earthly idea what they are. No one I have spoken to today has any idea either. We know there was one behind Mallory Turner's place. Anyone know where the fourth one was?" A man raised his hand. "Go ahead, sir," Cecilia said to the man.

"There was one behind my place," the man said. "It just blew up too."

"So that explains the four explosions," Cecilia said. "Anyone else have these things in their woods?" Everyone in the room said no. "Okay, it sounds like there was only four of them. That's at least good to know. No more surprises." She paused and took a sip of water. "We had hoped to maybe salvage what we could from those contraptions," Cecilia continued. "But now that's obviously not an option. We have had a long, stressful, and heartbreaking day." She paused again and sipped her water. She wanted to tell the townsfolk about Greg, but that was harder than she had thought it would be. She knew they would take the news hard. Cecilia sighed and addressed the crowd again. "With a heavy heart, I can inform you all that we lost Greg O'Sullivan today." The crowd was clearly shocked and greatly saddened by that news. Greg had been loved by all. He had been a great man and worked on every home in town at one point or another. Murmurs went around the room as people took in the sad news. "We will mourn Greg. He was a good man." Cecilia didn't know that for sure but had gotten the impression from the crowd's reaction that he was well-liked. "He will be missed. But for now, we need to gather whatever debris we can from those things. We need to bury it all and bury it deep. I do not want anyone else hurt or killed by what's left of those things. First thing tomorrow morning, I want everyone to meet at town hall. Get the word out to folks who are not here with us now. This is an all-hands-on-deck situation. All other town business will be shut down until we have handled this situation. We need to clean up this mess and get back to regular life. We are more than just neighbors—we are family. So are we all in agreeance, tomorrow morning we will come together and clean up this mess?"

The crowd shouted out that they were all in agreeance with Cecilia and her plan. Everyone in that tavern wanted to put this whole saga behind them, and they would do whatever it took to do just that.

"Great!" Cecilia exclaimed. "I appreciate everyone coming together for the common good of the town. Eight a.m. tomorrow morning at town hall. For tonight, let's all have a drink in memory of Greg and the young man. Losing our neighbors is heartbreaking. Let's make sure we honor them."

The crowd raised their glasses and shouted, "For Greg!"

"Thank you all again. I will see you all in the morning," Cecilia said.

Cecilia walked back to Scarlett. People thanked her and told her they'd be at town hall in the morning as she walked through the crowd. She was proud of her little town. It was everything she had ever imagined a community should be. A great community puts the town and what's best for all above themselves. There had to be sacrifices to have a healthy, thriving society. No one person was greater than another.

"Who was the man that raised his hand earlier?" Cecilia asked Scarlett quietly.

"That's Ron Davidson. He and his son are carpenters. They have the large property just north of town," Scarlett responded. "You still haven't gotten your memory back?"

"No. At this point, I'm not sure I ever will," Cecilia responded.

"It'll come back in due time. Once we get all of this handled and your stress level goes down, I bet your memory will come back."

"I hope so," Cecilia said to Scarlett. "I am heading home. I need rest. You stay here as long as you'd like. Enjoy an evening with our neighbors."

"Will do," Scarlett said. "Thank you for bringing us all together on this. We will clean up those woods, and it will be as if none of it ever happened."

"Yes, we will. I'll see you later."

"Would you mind taking Hope and Gwen back home with you?" Scarlett asked. "There's not much for them to do around here."

"No problem, Scarlett," Cecilia said.

Scarlett told the girls to go home with Cecilia. Gwen argued for a moment, but Scarlett made her go. Hope was happy to go home; her hand was killing her, and she was exhausted. Ever since she had touched that thing, she hadn't felt well. Hope assumed it was from the trauma of the burn. Her entire body was hot, and she had a funny tingling sensation throughout her body. Her head was pounding, and her guts churned. Hope just wanted to crawl into bed and sleep it off. She figured she'd feel better in the morning.

Cecilia, Gwen, and Hope left the tavern. It had gotten loud in there again as people milled about, talking. Cecilia still had a headache and just wanted to sleep. The next day was going to be very busy. Cecilia hoped the townsfolk wouldn't be out too late; she needed everyone well rested for the next day. When they got back to the cabin, Cecilia said good night to the girls and went to her room. She got ready for bed and climbed in. She pulled on the covers and drifted off to sleep.

Gwen waited for Cecilia and Hope to fall asleep and then she left the cabin. She wanted to go back to the tavern and be with everyone else, but she knew her mom would just send her home again. Gwen was upset with everyone she lived with, even Hope. Cecilia had taken charge and was bossing everyone around. Her mom was going along with Cecilia and that irritated Gwen. She understood that Cecilia was the mayor, but she didn't feel like that gave her the right to be so bossy. Gwen used to really like Cecilia; she had saved them all from that horrible town of Henderson, but Cecilia was acting so differently today. She wasn't her normal, easygoing self, and that annoyed Gwen. Then there was Amanda—she hated Amanda. Gwen never had liked Amanda much, but things had gotten a lot more tense between them recently. Amanda had started to become controlling and would complain about everything Gwen did. Worst of all, she constantly tattled on Gwen to Scarlett. Gwen wished her mom would just listen to her and kick Amanda out of the cabin. She didn't understand why Amanda even lived with them. Her mom had always told her that Amanda had nowhere else to live and that she was a vital member of their household. No one was vital; any one of them could leave and the household would continue to run smoothly. She would get rid of Amanda one way or another. Gwen was cool with Dana and Julia being around; they were funny. But they didn't do much around the house. It seemed like just because they had jobs in town, they felt like they didn't have to work around the house at all and that frustrated Gwen. Gwen felt like she worked her butt off taking care of the animals and the garden, no one except for Hope ever helped her out. She cared for and fed every animal they had. She slaughtered them when it was time. It was the dirtiest job around there, and no one seemed to appreciate that. Hope helped a little, but when it came to the gross jobs like cleaning manure or slaughtering an animal, Hope was nowhere to be found. Hope loved feeding the animals and interacting with them, but when it came to any other job, she disappeared. Gwen loved Hope like a sister, but that girl annoyed her to no end sometimes. Her mom had told her she adopted Hope when she was quite young after both her parents died of an illness. Maybe that was why her mom seemed to favor Hope over her; she felt bad for Hope. Gwen didn't care about any of that. She and her mom were the only ones actually related in that whole house and she was treated the worst. Gwen hated it there most days.

Gwen walked around to the back of the cabin. It was pretty late, but the full moon lit up the backyard. She stopped dead in her tracks. The pigs they had found down by that metal thing were all dead. Their skin looked like it had melted off. Their guts laid in a putrid pile next to their bodies. All their teeth had fallen out. Their eyes were missing. She hesitantly approached the pigs. Gwen got a few feet closer and stopped again. The smell coming off those pigs was horrendous. It was so bad it made Gwen vomit. She ran back around to the front of the cabin. She thought about waking up Cecilia but decided not to. Gwen decided to go see Doctor Richards. Amanda hadn't come home yet, so she assumed they were still at his office working on that dead man. She didn't want to deal with Amanda, but she didn't know what else to do. She hoped the doctor would check out the pigs and have an idea of what had happened to them. Gwen jogged off toward town.

Amanda had followed Doctor Richards back to his office. She was nervous about helping him with a dead body; she had never seen a dead body before. Amanda hadn't had any intention of volunteering to help, but when Cecilia tells you to do something, you do it. No one ever argued with Cecilia, except for Scarlett from time to time. Cecilia and Scarlett ran their household, and they expected a lot out of everyone. Amanda had nothing but respect and admiration for them. She cared for both of them greatly and appreciated a nice place to live. Amanda got along well with everyone, except Gwen. She despised that spoiled little brat. Gwen drove her mad. If she hadn't needed a place to live so badly, she would've beaten Gwen by then. In her opinion, Gwen deserved a good-ass beating. Amanda could feel herself getting angry, so she pushed thoughts of Gwen out of her mind. She needed to be clear headed to help Doctor Richards.

They arrived at his office, and he escorted her inside. He took her to a back room. The room was bright and cold. Everything in that room was spotless. In the middle of the room on a table was the young man. He was dressed in a suit that looked to be at least two sizes too big. Amanda walked up to the young man's body. She didn't know why she had, but she just needed to get a closer look. Her chest tightened when she saw his face. He was a very handsome young man. He looked to be her age. Amanda felt weird and gross for thinking a corpse was handsome, but there was no denying the fact that he was. A terrible sadness came over her. Amanda burst into tears. She stood there next to the young man and just sobbed.

"Amanda, it's okay," Doctor Richards said and put his arm around her. "Death is always sad."

Amanda stared at the man on the table and cried. She missed him so much. She couldn't explain why or how she missed him, but she did. Amanda had a feeling like she had known that young man for years, but she knew she had never seen that guy before in her life. Except she had seen him before; she knew that too. How could she be so certain she knew him but also be so aware of the fact that she had never met him before? Maybe he just had one of those faces that seemed familiar even if you had never seen it before? But that wasn't it, and she knew it.

"Amanda," Doctor Richards began, "I don't mean to sound rude or insensitive here, but are you going to be able to help me tonight? I understand seeing death firsthand can be very overwhelming and emotional, but I need a helper who can focus. Again, I'm not trying to be rude. We just have a lot of work to do."

"I'm sorry." Amanda sobbed. "I don't know what came over me." She turned away from the table and walked to the other side of the room. She found some tissues and wiped her face. "It wasn't seeing a dead body that got me," Amanda said as she approached Doctor Richards. "It was seeing *his* body that overwhelmed me. I know him somehow."

"Well, that's great news. So you know who he is? Do you know his family as well?"

"I don't know him like that, Doc," Amanda said. "I don't remember his name or his family. I feel like I *knew* him at one point in my life, but I have no idea who he is. I do know I cared for him greatly, though. I feel like I loved this man at one point in my life." Doctor Richards looked at her, utterly confused. "I know it sounds nuts," she said, looking up at the doctor.

"It sure sounds out there," he responded. "I know that when a person experiences death up close and personal like you just have, it can take an emotional toll on that person. I think you have internalized this, and you are feeling things you've never felt before. That may be causing you to feel like you knew him."

"I don't know," Amanda said, returning her attention to the young man's body. "I just know for a fact I knew him at some point. I can tell by his face. I loved this man; I know that without a doubt. The more I look at him, the more I know I knew him. I have feelings for him I've never had before. I realize he is gone, but I think I feel his presence with us. I know this all sounds so crazy, but I feel him here with us. He's telling me everything will be okay now. He says we don't have to worry anymore. We don't have to worry about them." Amanda looked at Doctor Richards, he was staring at her with an extremely concerned look on his face. "What them?" she asked the room. Amanda tilted her head back and forth. She looked at Doctor Richards again. "He won't say what 'them' means. He just says we're all safe now. Life will go on forever now. He just keeps saying we're safe." Amanda suddenly felt dizzy and lightheaded. The entire room was spinning. Her eyes rolled back in her head, and she fainted. She fell to the floor. As she passed out, she heard the young man say goodbye and that he loved her.

Doctor Richards picked up Amanda and carried her into one of the exam rooms. He laid her on the exam table and checked her vitals. Everything was normal. He went out to a supply closet and got a blanket. Doctor Richards put the blanket over Amanda and left the room. She would be perfectly fine; she just needed rest. He could tell from everything she had said that she had been under a lot of stress that day. The whole town had been through so much. He returned to the young man's body. Doctor Richards was appalled by what he saw as he approached the body. The man's skin was melting off of his skull. His nose hung askew. His eyelids were gone, exposing his eyeballs. Doctor Richards stood there in shock and watched as the young man's eyes turned to goo and slowly vanished into his skull. The doctor was so taken aback; he didn't even hear or feel the first explosion. Or the second one. Moments later, he did hear and feel the third and fourth explosions. The last two were awfully close to his office. The loud explosions snapped him back to reality, and he rushed out of the office, totally forgetting about Amanda passed out in the examination room. He saw townspeople out on the street. They were all headed for the tavern. Doctor Richards, still very shaken up, went to the tavern as well. It looked like the whole town was there. Mayor Rodgers was giving instructions on what needed to be done next. He had wanted to show her the young man's body, but she left abruptly after her speech. He found Scarlett and asked her to come back to his office with him. Scarlett told him whatever was happening could wait for the morning. The town couldn't handle any more bad news that day. She assured him she would come by in the morning. He pleaded with her to go right then, but she refused. Angry and offended, Doctor Richards left the tavern and went back to his office. The young man's body was nothing but a skeleton in a cheap suit at that point. Doctor Richards went to his office and began going through his medical books; there had to be something that had caused that man's skin to melt off like that. He spent the rest of the night reading those books. He had to find an answer.

Doctor Richards was interrupted by a light knocking on the front door of his office. He got up and went to the door. Scarlett's daughter Gwen was standing on his doorstep. She looked terrified and ill.

"What is the matter?" he asked her.

"Some of my pigs died," Gwen said. Doctor Richards was confused as to why she would come to him about that and, frankly, a little annoyed by it. "Their skin melted off their bones and their guts are all over the ground."

"What?" Doctor Richards exclaimed. "Are you sure? How long have they been dead?"

"Not long. They were fine this morning. They got out and me and Hope found them chewing on something by that metal thing in the woods. Cecilia told me to isolate them from the rest of the pigs, so I did. I just went to check on them and found them dead without skin. It's so gross."

"Take me to them!" he demanded, rushing out the front door.

Gwen took Doctor Richards to the dead pigs. They could smell them before they even got close. The doctor pulled his shirt over his nose and went to the dead pigs. They looked just like the young man's body. No skin, no eyes, just guts and bones. The smell was the rotting guts; he had no doubt about that.

"What did this?" Gwen asked, with a hitch in her voice.

"I don't know," he replied. "I am going back to my office to do some research. I'd recommend cleaning up the guts, though—they'll attract predators."

"What should I do with them?" Gwen asked.

"Bury them, and bury them deep," he said. "I'll be in touch as soon as I know anything." Doctor Richards said goodbye and hurried back to his office.

The whole office stunk of decay. It was overpowering. There was no way he could work with that smell. He remembered Amanda was still in an exam room and went to wake her. She was gone. His heart skipped a beat, and he ran to the autopsy room. He hoped he would not find her in there, she did not need to see what had happened to the young man's body. Luckily, she was not in there. The suit was drenched in blood and bile. The smell was beyond sickening. Doctor Richards went back to his office and grabbed all his medical books. He took off toward home, locking up the office on his way out.

As Doctor Richards headed across town toward home, he could see people leaving the tavern. Everyone seemed to be in good spirits.

The alcohol had surely helped to make them all feel better, but he knew Cecilia's speech had put everyone at ease too. She had been right; they needed to bury the remnants of those metal things and move on. He needed to get to the bottom of the rapid decaying of the young man's body and the pigs. That rate of decomposition shouldn't be possible, even in the harshest of environments. He had stood there and watched as the young man's skin rotted from his face. It was all so confusing. He wouldn't stop until he found an answer.

Doctor Richards entered his cabin and headed straight for his home office. He lit some candles, spread out his books on the desk, and began reading. After a few minutes, he went to the kitchen and boiled water for tea; it was going to be a long night.

CHAPTER 12

The Mothership

Pete decided not to tell the other guys about the creatures he had seen in the weapons room. He didn't want to stress them out anymore, especially Billy. Pete had had about enough of Billy's complaining. He understood the man's complaints; he was feeling the same way, but he was sick of hearing about it. Yes, they did need to find their destination. Yes, they needed to get out of that ducting; it was horrible up there. Pete could smell himself, and it wasn't pretty. Three grown men crammed into a hot, metal tube was starting to get ripe. Pete could hear Billy and Taylor panting behind him.

Pete came across another air vent and looked through it. His heart skipped a beat. It was a large open room full of the little gray creatures. All but one of them were sitting down. The one standing was talking to the room in their language. It kept gesturing wildly and pointing at the ducting. Every creature in that room was armed. They knew the guys were still on the ship, and it appeared as though they knew exactly where. Pete's heart rate tripled.

"Come on guys! Let's keep moving," Billy called out.

Pete turned his head toward Billy and shushed him. That clearly angered Billy. Pete pointed to the vent and hushed Billy again. Pete got moving and the others followed. Pete was panicking. He assumed if those things knew they were there, then they probably also knew why. Those things were obviously coming up with a plan to find them and kill them before they could carry out their plans. Pete feared they would be guarding the engine room and any other vulnerable places on that ship. He had always known they would die carrying out that mission, but he hoped they wouldn't get killed before they had a chance to destroy the ship.

Pete came to a four-way crossing in the ducting. He turned his body and slid into one of the sections of ducting. Pete directed the other guys to stop for a minute. They all found a spot to stop and face each other.

"Those things know we're here," Pete told them.

"Shit," Taylor said.

"Of course they do!" Billy said. "You think they don't know everything that goes on around here? They knew as soon as they went to our room to get us and we were gone."

"Regardless of how long they've known, the important thing is that they do know. And I'm pretty sure they know we're up here."

"Fuckin' A, dude," Billy said, shaking his head. "We're fucked now."

"Not necessarily," Pete said. "We can still carry out our mission. We just gotta hurry up."

"Hurry up how?" Billy asked. "We're stuck in this goddamn ducting and don't even know where the hell we're going. This is bullshit, dude."

"We may need to split up," Pete said. "We would have a better chance of finding the engine room if we split up."

"Oh, fuck that shit, dude!" Billy exclaimed. "That's a death sentence for sure."

"This whole fuckin' mission is a death sentence, Billy! We don't have many options at this point. If we don't find a control room or engine room before they find us, then this whole thing was for nuthin'!" Pete was pissed. "We've given up everything for this mission— we cannot fail!"

"Honestly, we didn't give up much," Billy said. Billy lowered his voice and tried to calm the situation down. He could see he had pissed off Pete. "Our lives as we knew them were already over. Who knows what was in store for us on Earth? I am fine with dying for this mission, but I don't think we should split up. We have a better chance if we stick together. I have a good feeling we're close. I can't explain it—I just feel like we're close."

"What do you mean a feeling?" Pete asked.

"Like I said, I don't know how to explain it, but once we stopped, I got a feeling we should go that way," Billy said, pointing down the ducting behind Pete.

"What if they gave you that feeling and it's a trap?" Pete asked.

"What if it's not?" Billy asked. "We should at least check it out. But we should stick together."

Pete sighed. "Okay, let's go." He turned around and headed down the ducting behind him.

That section of ducting went on forever. Pete couldn't see an end to it. As they crawled along, they began to hear a whirring sound. The sound got louder and louder as they crawled. Pete was getting excited; that sound could be the engine. If that was the case, they were getting close. After what felt like miles of ducting and that sound becoming almost deafening, the duct ended. There was an air vent at the end of the ducting. Pete peered through the slats and saw the engine room. He was ecstatic! He removed the vent and climbed out of the ducting. Taylor and Billy followed him out. They had made it!

"This is it, guys," Pete said smiling.

"Now what?" Billy asked.

"We blow this bitch up!" Pete exclaimed, pulling a grenade out of his pocket.

"Whoa! Whoa, we need a better plan than just throwing grenades around," Billy said. "What if blowing this room up doesn't destroy the ship? We need an escape plan."

"You're right," Pete said, looking around the room. "I may have gotten a little too excited."

"Over there," Taylor said, pointing at a door behind them. "We can blow the room and escape out of that door."

"Good idea," Pete said. He walked over to the door and it slid open.

"Well, dude, it was nice knowing you," Billy said to Pete. "Taylor, I love you, man. You've been my best friend for years, and I appreciate you and your friendship more than I could ever put into words. Thank you for always having my back even when I was an asshole to you." Billy had tears in his eyes. Everything had just gotten real. He thought he had come to terms with dying, but now that it was staring him in the face, he was petrified.

"I love you too, man," Taylor said and hugged Billy. "You were and are my truest friend. I have always appreciated you and your candor. You've always been a hundred percent real with me, and I love that about you. I wouldn't have wanted you any other way." He let go of Billy and turned to Pete. "I'm glad we met, Pete. You're a good dude, and I consider you a friend. I appreciate everything you have done for us."

"Thanks guys," Pete said. He could feel tears welling up in his eyes. Seeing Billy and Taylor tear up made him feel even more emotional. He had been so focused on the mission that he hadn't really given himself any time to come to terms with the fact that he was indeed going to die on that ship. "You guys have become friends to me as well. I appreciate you helping with this mission. I have nothing but respect for you guys, and I'm proud to be your friend. There isn't anybody else in this world I'd want to be with in this moment." The tears escaped his eyes and flooded down his red checks.

All three of them stood in the doorway crying. The weight of what they were about to do had really sunk in. They knew those creatures were looking for them, and as soon as they detonated those grenades, those things would know exactly where they were.

Pete looked at the grenade in his hand. He studied it, turning it in his hand. He was trying to figure out how to detonate it; there wasn't a pin to pull. On the top of it was a numbered dial. Maybe it was a timer? Pete turned the dial, and the grenade started to tick. It must be a timer!

"Guys, these things have timers. Let's set them around the room and get the hell out of here!" Pete exclaimed, rushing back into the room.

They set the timers on the grenades and placed them around the room. As they left the room, Pete stopped in the doorway and said, "This is for you, Amanda." They ran down a hallway. Minutes later, the grenades went off. The explosion shook the entire ship so hard it knocked all three of them off their feet. Lights and sirens started going off.

"Have your guns ready, guys!" Pete shouted over the siren. "They're gonna be coming for us!"

They got to their feet and pulled guns out of their belts. The ship was rocking and bouncing. It was exceedingly difficult to stay on their feet. The hallway behind them was now engulfed in flames. The fire was gaining on them. They got to the end of the hallway and ran around the corner. Running toward them were six of the small gray creatures. Pete raised his gun and fired at them. The guns didn't shoot bullets; they fired lasers. He held the trigger down. Pete hit one of the creatures in the chest, and it went down; green ooze spurted out of its chest. Billy opened fire on the creatures as well. He hit another one, and it went down. The creatures returned fire. Billy got hit in the shoulder, spinning him around. Billy fell to the ground. Taylor stepped over him and fired at the creatures. Pete had hit another one. Taylor had hunted with his dad and uncles his entire life; he was a damn good shot. Taylor hit the remaining three creatures in the head. He turned and helped Billy to his feet. The three of them set off down the hall, jumping over the dead creatures. They knew there would be more.

The ship shook violently again. They could hear and feel more explosions going off all around them. They smiled at each other as they ran down the hall. To their surprise, they didn't encounter any more creatures. They could hear and smell the fire, but it wasn't right behind them anymore. The hallway they were running down ended in a T. They stopped and looked to their right, then to their left. To the right was another long hallway, and to the left was a shorter hallway that led to a large, open room. They could see those gray creatures inside the large room. A lot of creatures. They were frantically running around the room, shouting at each other in their language. The guys turned and ran to their right. The hallway was lined on either side with doors. Every door they passed slid open as they ran by.

"Should we hide out in one of these rooms?" Taylor panted. He could feel his heartbeat in his temples.

"Let's!" Pete agreed and ran into the next open door.

The door slid shut behind them. They were in a room like the one they had started in. Three beds, a couple of dressers and night-stands, and a bathroom. They stood in the middle of the room, desperately trying to catch their breath.

"What now?" Taylor asked after he had caught his breath.

"I don't know," Pete said, wiping sweat from his forehead.

"Let's wait it out here," Billy suggested.

"For a bit at least," Pete said. "We're trapped in here if they come looking for us again."

"We're dead anyways, dude. If that door opens and those things are out there, I say we blast 'em 'til they get us."

"What if we could escape the ship?" Taylor asked.

"What? How?" Billy asked.

"Find one of the smaller ships and fly it out of here," Taylor said.

"Do you know how to fly a spaceship?" Billy asked him.

"No, but…" Taylor began.

"Neither do I!" Billy interrupted. "I like the idea of not blowing up with this ship, but I don't see how we could fly out of here. Even if we could find a smaller ship and figure out how to fly the damn thing, we wouldn't know how to land it! Shit, we don't even know where we are or where Earth is. I'm dying right here on this fucker!" Billy said, sitting down on one of the beds.

"Taylor has a pretty good idea, actually," Pete said, rubbing his scruffy chin. "What if we could do it? Destroy those things and survive it? I'd like to at least try. There is someone on Earth I'd like to try to find. At least I assume she's on Earth."

"You guys are talkin' crazy talk!" Billy said, standing up. "*If* we could even find a ship and *if* we could figure out how to fly the damn thing, how do you plan on finding one person on Earth? Those things scattered people all over that planet. How would you even know where to go if we could even find Earth itself?"

"I would know," Pete said. "I know my heart would guide me."

Billy burst out in laughter. "Sorry, dude, I don't mean to laugh, but all of this is so ridiculous. We made the choice to not go back to

Earth. We made the decision to stay here and destroy those things and their mothership. That's what we need to do!"

"We did that," Pete said.

"Did we? We're still here. Those things are still here. We saw 'em in that room back there. We destroyed a room, but it doesn't look like we've destroyed the ship itself. I still have a grenade. I say we go back and throw it into that room full of those ugly motherfuckers! I'm sick and goddamn tired of this shit!" Billy exclaimed, pulling a grenade out of his pocket.

"Why did you keep one?" Taylor asked.

"I thought setting off five in one room would be sufficient, and it was. I figured if we didn't immediately blow up, having another grenade may come in handy. And it looks like it has. I'm going to go blow those things to bits!" Billy said and walked toward the door.

"Wait!" Pete shouted. "Enough of this back-and-forth arguing! We need a plan!"

"We have a plan! Destroy this ship and those things! That's what I'm going to do. You two can go find a ship or whatever."

"Billy, wait," Taylor said and grabbed his arm. "I think we should find an escape ship first then destroy the rest of them."

"I agree with Taylor," Pete added. "I would like to at least try to get back to Earth if at all possible."

"Who's down there, dude?" Billy asked Pete. "What happened to us going down with the ship? We'd be heroes, remember?"

"Her name's Amanda. Why do we have to die up here if there's a chance to escape?" Pete asked.

"You've mentioned her name before," Billy said. "You love this girl?"

"Yeah, man, I do. I love her very much," Pete said quietly.

"Was she your girlfriend?" Billy asked.

"No, but I wanted her to be. I was never sure if she felt the same way I did. We were close friends, and God, I wanted more, but I never had the balls to pursue anything else. I want that chance now. I want to at least try to find her." Pete began to tear up again.

Billy looked at Pete and then at Taylor. He stood there looking back and forth at them for a moment. Billy didn't want to die on that ship either, but he just couldn't imagine them being able to fly one of those ships. He didn't even know how to drive a car with a manual transmission; how would he be able to fly an alien aircraft? No matter what they ended up doing, he didn't believe they would ever make it back to Earth. He sighed and looked at Pete and saw tears in Pete's eyes. Billy felt for him; he really did. He knew if he had someone down there that he loved, he would want to do whatever possible to try and find them.

"I love you guys," Billy said. "You guys find a ship outta here. I'm going to go murder some aliens."

"Fuck that, Billy! You're coming with us!" Taylor said.

"No, I'm not," Billy said coldly. "I will go create a distraction for you guys."

"You don't have to do that. Please come with us," Taylor pleaded.

"I feel like I do," Billy responded. "Taylor, help get Pete to his girl. I'll make sure this damn ship is destroyed. You can't talk me out of it."

"Thank you, Billy," Pete said as tears rolled down his cheeks. "You're a good man and a hero."

"Yeah, yeah. Save it for the statue you're going to make in my honor." Billy chuckled. "Good luck to you guys," Billy said.

"Good luck to you too, man," Taylor said.

They hugged each other one last time and left the room. Billy headed back the way they had come from, while Taylor and Pete headed off in the opposite direction. The ship was still shaking violently, and lights were still flashing in the hallway. The sirens had stopped. Billy could feel tiny explosions under his feet. Hopefully, those little rumbles were the ship breaking apart. Billy got to the T and paused. He could see into the room from there. It was still full of those creatures. Billy smiled to himself and set the timer on his grenade. He walked toward the room and chucked the grenade into it. The creatures stopped milling around and talking when the grenade hit the floor. They all looked out of the doorway at Billy. He smiled and waved at them. The grenade exploded. Parts and pieces of the creatures blew out into the hallway. The room caught fire, and Billy turned down the hall. Those tiny explosions under him were beginning to intensify. Billy stood at the T and looked back the way they had originally come from. The fire was out, so he decided to head back that way. He hadn't told the other guys, but he still had one more grenade. Billy wanted to find another room full of those creatures or another control room. He was going to destroy that ship one way or another. He hoped Taylor and Pete found a way off the ship first.

Billy could tell the fire had been put out by something. Then he saw what had most likely put the fire out: a couple of the gray creatures were inside the engine room they had blown up. They had fire extinguishers—not any kind of extinguisher he had ever seen, but he knew that's what they were. The creatures were bantering back and forth at each other, completely oblivious to Billy approaching. He grabbed his gun and shot them both in the back. They fell to the floor screeching. Billy jogged into the room and shot them both in the head. The grenades they had set off in that room had done the job, that room was obliterated. The ceiling, including the vent they had crawled out of, was gone. Billy knew that ship was built to withstand pretty much anything, but he could tell blowing that room up had delivered a crippling blow to the ship's functionality. He smiled and nodded as he looked around the crumbling room. For a moment, he considered setting off his last grenade in there, just to finish the room off for good, but he decided to save it. The extent of the damage already done to that room was beyond repair. Those engines and controls would never be operational again. Billy left the room, extremely proud of what they had done to it. He stood in the doorway for a bit, plotting his next move. He didn't want to go back the way he had come from; he didn't want to risk running into Pete and Taylor. Billy loved those guys and hoped they would get off that ship, but he didn't want to see them again. It had been hard enough to walk away from them. It had been so tempting to try and find an escape ship with them. But he knew damn well they never would. He knew it was better for everyone if he just went his own way. Billy didn't want to get killed trying to escape; he wanted to die as the man who destroyed the alien ship. He wanted to be a hero. Billy decided since he wasn't going to head back where he had come from, his only choice at that point was to head down the opposite hallway. He had no idea where it would take him, but he had no idea where any of the hallways would take him. Billy set off down the hall, gun in his right hand and the grenade in his left.

Taylor and Pete ran through a maze of hallways. That ship was ridiculously huge. The ship rocked forcefully, as if it had been hit by something. It felt like the ship had been struck just outside of where they were. They looked at each other, puzzled. Just ahead of them, a door slid open and a huge brown leathery creature walked out of the door. Steam slowly rolled into the hallway behind the creature. Pete and Taylor raised their guns and blasted the thing. It never even saw it coming. The creature crumpled to the floor, screeching as green ooze spurted out of its many gunshot wounds. Taylor and Pete slowly approached the creature; it was barely hanging on. Pete shot it in the head.

"Holy shit, dude!" Taylor exclaimed. "It's a fuckin' ship!"

"What? What is?" Pete asked, turning toward Taylor.

"This," Taylor said, pointing into the door the creature had just walked out of.

"Holy shit, it is! We did it, man! We found one!" Pete exclaimed.

They could hear many feet running toward them. A large number of creatures were obviously approaching them.

"Come on, man, we gotta go!" Pete shouted.

"There's only room for one of us in there, dude," Taylor said. He was upset that they both wouldn't be able to escape, but he knew he had to let Pete take that ship. "You go," he told Pete.

"What about you?" Pete asked.

"I'll find my own ship, shouldn't be hard now that we know what they look like. Go, dude! Go find your girl!" Taylor said, pushing Pete into the ship.

Taylor saw a group of the gray creatures round the corner at the end of the hall.

"Thanks, Taylor. See ya down there," Pete said from inside the ship.

"Yup, see ya down there," Taylor said, knowing full well he'd never see Pete again. Shit, he'd probably be dead before Pete even figured out how to fly that damn thing. Those creatures were getting close. "Close the door! Get the hell out of here!"

Pete hit a switch, and the door slid shut with a small thud and then a loud click. There was a large leather-covered seat in front of a huge control panel. Behind the control panel was a wall of windows. Everything outside of the windows was pitch black. *Hopefully, spaceships have headlights,* he thought to himself and chuckled. For as advanced as the technology was, the controls looked to be simple enough. Pete figured if those big, dumb creatures could fly that thing, he should be able to as well. Pete sat in the seat and studied the control panel. Everything was labeled, but it was all written in some funky language of letters and symbols. The letters were not English or any other human language, but he knew they were letters. The symbols were fairly easy to decipher. Pete felt confident he would actually be able to fly that thing. He started flipping switches, and the ship roared to life. The vast emptiness of outer space was now illuminated. Pete hit a button, and the ship jerked free from the mothership. He grabbed the yoke and steadied the ship. It was very responsive and surprisingly easy to control. The control panel was lit up with little lights. Pete pulled the yoke toward him and felt the ship fly up. He pushed the yoke away from him, and the ship descended. He pulled it right then left, and the ship responded by moving in each direction. An LED screen popped out of the center of the control panel. The screen had pictures of planets displayed on it. Pete reached out and touched the photo of Earth. The ship lurched forward and spun around. It took off into the darkness. The LED screen flashed. He looked at it and saw there were three other ships following him. They kept pace with him. Pete's hands shook on the yoke. There was no going back. If those other ships shot him then so be it, at least he had tried to get back to Earth.

A huge explosion went off behind him and sent his ship out of control. No matter what he did, he could not right the ship. The LED screen blinked out, and the control panel went dead. Pete yanked on the yoke, and nothing happened. He was spinning and flipping out of control. Pete figured this was the end for him, but he was happy. He knew without a doubt that explosion was the mothership. Billy and Taylor had done it. No matter how it ended for Pete, they had succeeded in saving humanity. Pete burst into tears, tears of utter relief and happiness. Pete released the yoke and sat back in the captain's seat. He looked for a seatbelt, but there wasn't one. The energy from the mothership exploding had pushed Pete's now dead ship toward Earth, and he knew he was in for a devastating crash landing. The ship hit Earth's atmosphere, and Pete was certain that ship was going to blow apart. He braced himself for impact. Trees were the last thing he saw. The ship slammed into the ground and flung Pete into the control panel. He hit the panel so hard the yoke pierced his side, splitting him open. Pete passed out from the pain.

Pete came to and started mashing buttons. The door to the ship slid open, and holding his side, he crawled out. Every move sent pain throughout his entire body. He was having trouble breathing. Pete was surrounded by trees. Nothing but trees as far as he could see. He had thought he'd never see Earth again, but there he was, back on the planet. He knew he would never live long enough to find Amanda, but at least he had tried. Maybe, if the mothership hadn't exploded so soon, he could've made it to Earth in one piece, but even then, it would've been next to impossible to find Amanda. Pete couldn't crawl anymore. He perched himself up against a tree and waited to die. He was content. Pete could tell Amanda was safe. He knew without a doubt she had survived the transition and was currently living a happy life. That made him happy and proud. He wasn't sure how he was so certain Amanda was safe and happy, but he just knew it. He could *feel* it. He could feel her. Pete closed his eyes and waited for death to come get him.

*****

Taylor heard Pete get the ship started. He knew his new friend was off to find Earth and hopefully his girlfriend. Taylor knew that would probably never happen. How would Pete be able to find one person somewhere on the planet Earth? It was a ridiculous idea, but he admired the man for trying.

The creatures came to a stop when they saw Taylor standing in the hallway. Taylor raised his gun and opened fire on the creatures. He hit one after the other, but there were just so many of them. The creatures advanced on him, returning fire as they did. Taylor stood tall and just held the trigger down. He was hit in the stomach, then the leg, then his chest. He fell to the floor. Blood gushed out of his wounds. His body went limp. He looked up and saw a creature looking down at him. The creature pointed a gun at Taylor's face and smiled. Taylor smiled back at it and waited for the kill shot. The creature pulled the trigger and ended Taylor.

Billy made his way through narrow hallways. He could hear generators—at least that's what he thought the noises were. He followed the sound. The sound kept getting louder, and he was almost certain it was generators. He was getting close to their backup power! This was it! If he could find those generators, he could finally destroy that ship. The noise had become deafening; he was so close. Billy rounded a corner, and there it was, a huge room full of loud motors, all of which were running at full tilt.

Movement from down the hall caught his attention. A large group of the gray creatures was running toward him. They all had guns pointed at him. Billy ran into the large room full of generators. He set the timer on the grenade and put it in his pocket. The creatures ran in behind him. Billy put his hands up.

"Hey, guys, don't shoot!" Billy shouted over the engine noise. "You got me." The grenade was vibrating in his pocket. The creatures slowly approached Billy and surrounded him. Billy smiled. This was it. He was going to blow up their backup engine room and take a bunch of them out with him.

The grenade exploded and obliterated Billy and the creatures. The engine room exploded into a huge fireball, blowing the entire ass end of the ship off. The explosion caused a chain reaction, and the entire mothership blew up. The explosion lit up the darkness of outer space. The debris and dust cloud looked like an atom bomb had been detonated. Debris flew past Pete's ship and burned up in Earth's atmosphere. It would have been an absolutely beautiful and terrifying sight from Earth.

CHAPTER 13

Empty Skies

Scarlett directed a group of townsfolk in the woods behind Mike's place. Cecilia was working with a group of people in the woods behind their cabin. Malcolm had taken a group to clean up behind Mallory's place. A fourth group of townsfolk worked on the cleanup behind Ron Davidson's place. Ron had thrown out his back raking up debris and was resting inside his cabin. All the townsfolk had come together; some people were busy digging holes as others gathered fragments of the metal contraptions. Pieces of the metal things were embedded in trees and the ground. They rounded up what they could and buried it. There wasn't anything left that was salvageable. Cecilia had hoped they could find something they could use. Those things were solid metal and metal was hard to come by, but the explosions had completely destroyed whatever those things had been. Cecilia was taking a break from the cleanup to come up with a plan to move forward from this mess. It had really stressed the whole town out, and she needed a way to calm everyone down. The cleanup process was going smoothly, but she knew that wouldn't be the end to all that had happened. People would still be stressed and confused. People would want answers eventually. Cecilia didn't think she, or anyone else, would ever have answers for what they all had just been through. Two people had already died because of those things, and she didn't want to lose anyone else. Cecilia was deep in thought when a voice from behind startled her.

"Madam Mayor?" Doctor Richards said, approaching Cecilia; he could tell he had surprised her. "I did not mean to startle you, ma'am," he apologized.

"It's okay, Doctor. I was just lost in thought. I was really hoping we could salvage some of the materials from these things, but it's all too far gone now. Were you able to identify the young man?" she asked him.

"No, ma'am, I wasn't. Um, that's partially why I'm here, though. I'd like you to come back to my office with me. Something strange and honestly not possible has happened to the young man's body," the doctor said quietly.

"What happened?" she asked, her curiosity piqued. She was at a point that nothing was going to surprise her anymore.

"I'd rather not say around others. I don't want to worry people just yet. Please, come to my office and I'll explain everything in private."

"Okay, Doctor, lead the way," Cecilia said. She let the others know she was going with Doctor Richards and she would return shortly.

Cecilia and Doctor Richards got to his office, and he escorted her inside. The smell of death and decay hit her like a punch to the face. Doctor Richards handed her a handkerchief to tie around her mouth and nose. The handkerchief smelled like lavender.

"The smell is awful," he began. "I soaked my handkerchiefs in lavender to help block out that smell. I've been a doctor for a long time, and as you know, I've processed numerous dead bodies. There is always a smell, but never anything remotely like this. And I've never seen what happened to the young man's body." Doctor Richards shook his head.

"What happened, Doctor?" Cecilia asked.

"Follow me." He led her to the autopsy room.

Cecilia walked into the room and was appalled. Lying there on a table in the middle of the room was a full human skeleton. The smell in that room was so strong she could smell it through the lavender-soaked handkerchief.

"What is this?" she asked, shocked and curious as to why the doctor decided to show her that.

"That's the young man you found in the woods yesterday," Doctor Richards replied.

"*What?*" Cecilia exclaimed, looking from the skeleton to the doctor. "I'm no doctor, but I do know it takes longer than one day for a body to rot like that. How is that even possible?" she asked, looking back to the young man's skeleton.

"That, ma'am, I do not know. I stayed up all night pouring through every medical book I have and found nothing that could explain this. Even if he died in those woods and was never found, it would take months, possibly even a year or more, for him to decompose like this. Even if scavengers and insects got to him, it wouldn't happen this fast. I'm baffled."

"What the hell is going on around here lately?" Cecilia asked.

"I don't know, but it has me worried," Doctor Richards replied. "Gwen came to me last night and said three of your pigs died and their skin melted off as well. I went to check them out, and the smell was putrid. They had decomposed just as quickly as our young friend here."

"Gwen didn't say anything to me about that. I didn't see any dead pigs this morning," Cecilia said. "Our backyard has reeked since that metal thing showed up, so I didn't think anything about the smell this morning."

"I told Gwen to bury the pigs and guts. She must have done just that. Whatever caused this isn't anything I've ever seen, and evidently, no one else has either. This is something that would have been written about it if had ever happened before. We're dealing with something that we know nothing about."

"What should we do now, Doctor?" Cecilia asked.

"I'm going to bury the young man. He needs a proper resting place, and I need to sterilize this entire place. Aside from that, I guess we just wait until someone or something else dies to see if it happens again," Doctor Richards said.

"Wait, did Gwen say anything about which of our pigs died?" Cecilia asked the doctor. Some of the puzzle pieces were starting to come together for her.

"Yes, she said they had gotten out of the pen and she had found them down by the metal thing in your woods." It was starting to click with him as well.

"The pigs were around those things in the woods. The young man had obviously been inside the other one at some point. Greg O'Sullivan was inside the one behind my place when it blew. We kept finding bones while we cleaned up out there, but I just assumed his flesh had burned off in the explosion. But what if his skin melted off like the young man's and the pigs?"

"It has something to do with whatever those metal contraptions were!" the doctor exclaimed.

"Every one of us has been in contact with those things now. This could happen to all of us as we die," Cecilia said, shaking her head. "Doctor, do whatever you can to figure it out. I know that's a tall task, but you will have my full support and every resource available to you. We will spare no costs trying to figure this out."

"Yes, ma'am, but unfortunately, I think at this point, I will need a freshly deceased body to study. I can't determine anything from bones."

"We will let the town know if a loved one passes. You need to examine the body immediately. I want to be a vague as possible, though. We don't need to stress these good people out any more than they already are. Keep this between us, please." Cecilia turned toward the door. "Thank you, Doctor."

"You're welcome, ma'am. I will keep this between us, but Gwen saw the pigs and Amanda may have seen the young man after he decomposed," Doctor Richards said.

"Okay, I will speak with them as well. Thanks again. Keep me updated," Cecilia said and headed toward the door. The lavender-soaked handkerchief wasn't helping with the smell anymore, and she had to get out of that room.

"I will. Thank you for your time, Madam Mayor," Doctor Richards said and walked Cecilia to the front door.

"You're welcome, Doctor. We will talk soon," Cecilia said and left the office.

Cecilia walked slowly back toward the cabin. She needed to figure out a way to tell the girls to keep quiet without saying too much as to why. For the most part, they were good girls, but sometimes they could have attitudes. Cecilia didn't want to deal with any of that. She stopped walking and looked around. It had just dawned on her that she hadn't seen Gwen or Amanda all morning. Cecilia had been so busy and focused on orchestrating the cleanup that she had completely forgotten to find the girls. As she started walking again, she figured they were probably with Scarlett helping behind Mike's place. Cecilia changed course and headed for Mike's place.

"Madam Mayor!" someone shouted from behind her. She turned and saw a younger man jogging toward her. "We found a skeleton in the woods behind our place." The man panted once he had caught up to her.

"Where is your place?" she asked. The man looked somewhat familiar; she was sure she had seen him at the tavern the night before, but she didn't know his name.

"Just north of town," he said, pointing over his shoulder. "We were back in the woods cleaning up the debris from that thing and came across a skeleton. It looks pretty fresh, ma'am."

"Is that the Davidson property?" she asked.

"Yes, ma'am," he replied.

"Did you guys examine the contraption at all before it exploded?"

"Yes, ma'am. My dad and I tried to dismantle it for the metal," the man replied. "But we couldn't get anything to break free from that thing."

"Did you find any blood in or around it before it exploded?"

"No, just this awful-smelling green ooze," he replied.

"Anything else?" she asked him.

"There were pieces of what looked like brown leather but really old, wrinkly leather."

"And where is that leather now?" she asked him. "Did you touch any of that?"

"No, ma'am. My dogs took off with the leathery stuff. I hollered at them to leave it alone, but they didn't listen," the man said. He was starting to look confused.

"I know I'm asking a lot of questions here, so I appreciate you answering them. There is something really fishy going on around here, and I'm trying to gather as much information as possible. Let's go get Doctor Richards and check out that skeleton," Cecilia said.

Cecilia and the man went to Doctor Richard's office and told him about the man's discovery. Doctor Richards gave Cecilia a concerned look before following the man back to his place. The man led them several hundred yards into the forest behind his cabin. Lying in a small clearing was a human skeleton. Doctor Richards knelt beside the skeleton and studied it.

"Do you have any idea who that could be?" Cecilia asked the man.

"I don't have any idea, ma'am," he answered. "I can tell you this wasn't out here two days ago. I was out in this part of the woods two days ago hunting rabbits, so I know for a fact this was just put here. Why would someone put a skeleton in the woods behind my place?" he asked, shaking his head.

"The doctor and I will figure it out," Cecilia told the man. "Why don't you get back to what you were doing, and we'll let you know what we come up with?"

"Okay, ma'am," he said. The man turned and walked away.

"What can you tell me about the bones, Doctor?" she asked Doctor Richards after the man left.

"I can tell you they're female. I estimate she was about fifty," he said, looking up at Cecilia. "These bones are very fresh, ma'am. I think it's safe to say that whatever happened to the young man's body happened here too."

"Shit, I figured as much," Cecilia said. She felt like she was going to burst. The stress, frustration, and anger were boiling up inside her. "Any idea how she died?"

"No, ma'am. The bones are all intact. No signs of any trauma to the skull. There aren't any teeth marks from scavengers. These look like the bones of a perfectly healthy middle-aged woman. Without tissue and organs, I cannot figure out a cause of death."

"We need to figure out who she is then. Maybe that will shed some light on the situation," Cecilia said.

"Shouldn't be hard, someone in this small town has to be missing her," Doctor Richards said, standing up. "I will delicately ask around. But first I want to get these remains back to my office."

"Sounds good, Doctor," Cecilia said.

They heard someone running toward them. They both looked behind them and saw Scarlett running at them in a full sprint.

"Doctor Richards!" she panted. "I need you to come look at Hope. She is very sick!"

"What seems to be wrong?" he asked.

"I don't know. She is burning up and vomiting. Come quick, she has deteriorated quickly." Scarlett said, turning back toward their cabin. "And now Gwen is saying she doesn't feel well either."

Cecilia and Doctor Richards followed Scarlett back to the cabin. Hope was lying on the couch with a cold cloth on her head. Gwen was lying on the other couch, moaning. Doctor Richards went to Hope and examined her. Her eyes were dull and distant. Her body was covered in sweat. He checked her vitals, and they were normal. She was obviously very ill, but he didn't think it was anything too serious, just a bug.

"Hope, how do you feel?" Doctor Richards asked. He knew she felt awful just by looking at her, but he wanted to get her to talk to him.

"I feel horrible," she whimpered. "Everything hurts. I can't keep food or water down."

"I think you have the flu, dear," Doctor Richards said. He walked over to Gwen and examined her. "How about you, Gwen? What seems to be ailing you?"

"Same as Hope, Doc. Everything hurts. I'm not throwing up yet," Gwen whined.

"I think you girls caught a bug. Just stay inside and rest. Try to hydrate if you can keep it down. I'll check back on you later."

Doctor Richards, Cecilia, and Scarlett went back outside.

"You really think it's just a bug?" Scarlett asked. She was terribly concerned about her girls.

"I do," he responded. "It is that time of year. Keep an eye on them and make sure they stay hydrated. Just make them rest—that's what they need right now. How long have they been feeling sick?" he asked Scarlett.

"Hope started feeling sick yesterday. I asked Gwen to stay with Hope today because she kept trying to wander off. She's been so out of it. Now Gwen is acting the same way."

"They're probably a bit out of it because of the high fever. As you know, a high fever can make a person delusional. Just keep an eye on them. I'm confident they'll make a full recovery in a day or so."

"Okay, Doctor, thank you," Scarlett said.

"I'm going to head back to the office and then go get the skeleton," he said to Cecilia.

"All right, keep in touch," Cecilia responded. Doctor Richards headed off toward town.

Scarlett shot Cecilia a confused look. "Wait, what skeleton?" she asked Cecilia.

"The Davidson kid found a skeleton in the woods behind their place. The doctor and I checked it out. It's a middle-aged female's remains."

"Holy shit!" Scarlett exclaimed. "What the hell is going on around here? I don't know how much more of this shit I can handle!"

"Just stay here with the girls and try to relax a bit. All of this is overwhelming and stressful. Take advantage of a little downtime, please," Cecilia said to Scarlett. "I'm going to go around and check on the progress of the cleanup."

"Okay, Cecilia." Scarlett sighed.

"Everything will be okay, Scarlett," Cecilia said.

"I'm sure it will, but I'm really worried about the girls. I raised those girls. I've seen them sick before but never anything like this. It seems like more than just a flu bug."

"Well, I trust the doctor. Just keep an eye on them. I'm sure they'll be fine." Cecilia turned toward the back of the cabin. "Make them some tea and give yourself a little break from all of this," she said to Scarlett, waving her arms in the air.

"I will. Send for me if you need me," Scarlett said.

"Hopefully, I won't need you. I'll come back shortly to check on you and the girls."

"Thank you, Cecilia."

"You're welcome," Cecilia said and headed off behind the cabin.

Scarlett watched Cecilia disappear behind the cabin. She went back inside and closed the front door. Scarlett started the woodstove and placed a kettle of water on to boil. There was a knock on the front door. She went to the door and found Malcolm standing on the doorstep. Scarlett invited him inside.

"How are you, Malcolm?" Scarlett asked. "Would you like some tea?"

"No, thank you on the tea. I'm overheated as it is—I don't need any hot tea," Malcolm said. "I am worried, Scarlett."

"About what?" she asked.

"Bethany," he said, sitting down in one of the kitchen chairs. "She hasn't been feeling well today and she's not acting like herself."

"Uh-oh." Scarlett said, sitting down across the kitchen table from Malcolm. "There seems to be some sort of bug going around. Both of my girls are quite sick."

"This ain't no bug," Malcolm said. "She's not physically ill." He paused for a moment. "We haven't told anybody yet." He paused again. "Bethany is pregnant."

"Oh my! That is great news!" Scarlett exclaimed, smiling ear to ear.

"It is," Malcolm said with zero enthusiasm. "We are both very excited but also nervous. As you know, we lost the first pregnancy, and that's why we haven't told anyone yet."

"I remember, that was devastating. I'm sure this time will be different," Scarlett said.

"I am too, at least I'm extremely hopeful it will be. We have been trying for so long now."

The tea kettle whistled on the stove, and Scarlett got up to fetch it. Malcolm joined her by the stove. Scarlett began to make three cups of tea.

"I know you have. Bethany and I have had many conversations about that. This will all work out well," Scarlett said. She went to give the girls their tea, but they were both asleep. She didn't want to wake them. Scarlett took her cup of tea and returned to the kitchen table. Malcolm joined her. "You said she has been feeling ill lately. Is it morning sickness?"

"No, she's hasn't had much of that. Like I said, it's not a physical illness. It's in her head. It's hard to explain, but she has been having memory loss and has been talking about some weird shit the last couple of days," Malcolm said. He was clearly flustered. "I wanted to talk to Cecilia about all of it, but she's been acting weird too."

"Yes, she has. Don't repeat this to anyone," Scarlett said, giving Malcolm a stern look. "But Cecilia doesn't remember anything before yesterday. Nothing at all. I could tell she even struggled to remember my name."

"Same thing with Bethany," Malcolm started. "She remembered me and bits and pieces of things, but I had to remind her she worked for you guys. I had to remind her of your names."

"She did seem a bit distant yesterday at the office. She kept asking me when Cecilia would be in, when did I expect her. I saw her studying the painting of Cecilia in the hall. She must have been trying to make herself remember Cecilia's face so she could act like she knew her when she showed up."

"She told me when she got home yesterday that she did a good job pretending that she knew everyone. It's got me so concerned, Scarlett," Malcolm said.

"Me too, I thought it was just Cecilia." Scarlett could tell Malcolm was hot and probably thirsty. She stood up and got him a glass of water. He thanked her. "What else has she said?"

"Crazy shit," Malcolm said and took a big sip of his water. "She talked about being a waitress. She talked about being taken. I asked who took her and she just said, 'You know, them.' I told her, 'No, I don't know, who's *them*?' She couldn't explain any of that. She said I was there with her. She said I saved her from them."

"Did she mention a ship?" Scarlett asked.

"Um, yeah," Malcolm replied, confused. "How'd you know that? I wasn't going to mention that because it's so crazy."

"Again, do not repeat any of this to anyone. Cecilia mentioned a ship frequently yesterday morning. She was certain we had all been on some ship."

"So was Bethany!" Malcolm said, shaking his head. "At first, I just chalked it up to pregnancy hormones or something like that, but the more she went on about it, the more worried I became. Then interacting with Cecilia and having to remind her who people are around town made me realize that it couldn't be related to the pregnancy. Something else is going on around here."

"I thought it had something to do with that lightning storm the other night. Everything was normal the day before that. I wonder if anyone else has memory loss?" Scarlett said, getting up to refill her tea.

"Throughout this clean-up process, I've interacted with almost everyone in town, and they all seem normal. No one else seems to be off like Bethany and Cecilia. They both just *seem* like different people. I can still feel and see the love Bethany has for me, but she's not the same person I married."

Scarlett sat back in her chair and sipped her hot tea. She thought about the last couple of days. She hadn't encountered any other townsfolk that seemed to be off like Cecilia and Bethany either. She had known Bethany wasn't right the day before at the office, but she had just assumed the woman was stressed about those things in the woods, like everyone else was. Scarlett thought back to her conversation with Cecilia the morning before. The two things that had really stood out to her was how many times Cecilia had mentioned a ship and her referring to something called the United States.

"Did Bethany say anything about *United States*?" Scarlett asked Malcolm. He gave her a confused look.

"No. Why? What's that?" he asked her.

"Cecilia said she was the president of the United States. It made no sense to me, still doesn't. I was just wondering if Bethany had said something similar. I thought Cecilia had just had one of those crazy, realistic dreams and was blurring the dream world with the real world," Scarlett said, sitting forward again.

"Bethany didn't say anything about a United States, but she did say she was from Las Vegas." Scarlett gave Malcolm a puzzled look. "I know," he said. "Those aren't even words, 'Las Vegas.' I asked her what the hell that meant, and she said that's where we met."

"*What?*" Scarlett asked, stunned.

"I know, right? Crazy talk. We obviously met in Henderson when I started working for her dad on his dairy farm. She knows that! I had to win her dad over before I could even start dating her. It's all so strange and out of this world." Malcolm put his head in his hands and sighed heavily.

"It sure is," Scarlett said, sitting back in her chair again. "That lightning storm and those metal contraptions have to have something to do with all of this. Women like Cecilia and Bethany don't just go mad overnight. I am hoping once we have all of the debris cleaned up and buried deep, things will go back to normal. I'm hopeful we'll get Cecilia and Bethany back to the way they were."

Gwen started coughing and crying out to her mom. Scarlett jumped up and rushed to her daughter. She glanced over at Hope on the other couch. Hope was awake and looking around the room. Hope looked quite a bit better. Gwen looked worse. Seeing an improvement in Hope made Scarlett feel better. Gwen was getting worse, but she had come down with whatever they had after Hope, so she should start to improve soon also. Gwen said she felt like she was going to throw up. Scarlett ran and got her a bucket. Gwen vomited several times and laid back down. She was burning up from head to toe. Scarlett was sympathetic but now felt less stressed out. The girls had just come down with a bug, and it looked like they would be just fine in a couple of days after all.

"Are the girls going to be okay?" Malcolm asked after Scarlett returned to the table.

"Looks like it," she replied. "I wasn't sure at first, but it seems like it now. Hope looks way better than this morning, so I'm hoping they will both be fine in a day or so. Doctor Richards said it was just a flu bug."

"Well, that's good," Malcolm said. "The last thing we need around here now is some kind of superbug."

"Ain't that the truth!" Scarlett exclaimed.

"Well, Scarlett, I better get back to Bethany. Thank you for talking to me. I was so worried about her—I just needed to talk to someone about it. You made me feel a lot better. It helps to know that Bethany isn't the only one experiencing whatever it is." He paused and leaned closer to Scarlett. He dropped his voice and asked, "Isn't it weird they both mentioned a ship?"

"Yes, very," Scarlett replied quietly. "I'm not sure what to make of that."

"Neither am I," Malcolm said, standing up. "Well, let's just keep humoring them and see if they regain their real memories."

"I sure hope they will soon. I'm worried about Cecilia. She has jumped right in and led the town in this cleanup process, but she's just not herself. I want my old friend back." Scarlett nervously chuckled.

"And I want my wife back," Malcolm said sadly. "Again, thank you for the talk. I will see you later."

"You're welcome. And congratulations on the baby." Scarlett smiled.

"Thank you, we are so excited and happy about it." Malcolm walked to the front door and opened it. "Talk to you soon."

"Bye, Malcolm," Scarlett said, and he disappeared out the front door.

Scarlett sipped her tea. Talking to Malcolm had made her feel better. At least it wasn't just Cecilia acting strange. That made her theory about the lightning even more plausible. She was sure there were more people experiencing what Bethany and Cecilia were; they just weren't talking about it. Some people had a greater connection to the Earth and were affected differently by natural phenomena like lightning. Scarlett had known Cecilia for a long, long time, and she knew Cecilia was sensitive to the environment around her. Cecilia had a special way of connecting with the natural world around her. Scarlett figured Bethany must be the same way.

Scarlett got up and checked on the girls again; they were both sleeping peacefully. She freshened her tea and stepped outside onto the front porch. The air was cool and felt nice against her face. Scarlett sipped her tea and tried to push all the stresses and worries aside for a bit. She looked out over their small, happy town—well, a little less happy those past couple of days. Scarlett felt a sense of pride bubble up inside of her. The entire town had come together without hesitation to handle the cleanup process. No one bitched and moaned about any of it. Cecilia, even in her current state of mind, had orchestrated a hell of a response to the situation that had unfolded in front of all of them. Leadership like that was special, and Scarlett was honored to be a part of it.

The fresh air and warm tea helped to soothe Scarlett. She was less worried about the girls. Kids got sick; it was a fact of life. It was always heartbreaking to watch your children feel so crummy, but she could tell they were already on the mend. Gwen still had to face the worst of it, but Hope looked way better than she had just a few hours earlier. Scarlett let herself enjoy some downtime; it felt like she never got any sometimes. Part of her felt bad she wasn't out helping with the cleanup, but she pushed that feeling aside too. Her girls were more important than some hunks of metal in the woods, and she needed to stay close to them. Scarlett took a couple more deep breaths of the clean, crisp air and went back inside to check on the girls again. They were both still sleeping. Scarlett quietly tidied up the kitchen as the girls rested.

*****

Doctor Richards had the remains from the woods on a table next to the remains of the young man. He studied both of them closely. The young man's ribs were broken, but that was obviously from whatever had impaled him. The woman's skeleton was almost perfect. He could tell she had broken her right arm at some point, but besides that, she had obviously been an extremely healthy woman. That was puzzling. What had caused her to die? Doctor Richards knew it could have been a number of things: a heart attack, a brain aneurism, kidney failure. But if she had died of natural causes, how did she end up so far into the woods? He had to be missing something.

Doctor Richards got out his bone saw and cut out a section of her leg bone. He did the same with the young man. The bones splintered as he cut through them. Their bones were hollow and soft. There was no way they would have been able to walk on those fragile bones. One step on those legs and the bones would have snapped. Doctor Richards started dissecting more bones from the remains. Every bone was the same. That seemed impossible, but everything he had seen with those bodies had seemed impossible before he saw it with his own eyes. He took a cross section of the leg bone from each of them and studied it under a microscope. Doctor Richards gasped at what he discovered. Tiny, microscopic, almost robotic-looking insects were feasting on the bones. Thousands of them. That had to explain the rapid decomp too. If these tiny insects could destroy bone that quickly, they'd have no problem with flesh and organs. It wouldn't take long for those insects to get through that bone.

Doctor Richards rushed over to the cemetery. He needed Kevin, the town's mortician, to prepare two burial plots. Doctor Richards wanted to get the remains buried before they were reduced to dust. He also wanted to bury those bugs with the remains.

Kevin and his crew had just dug a burial plot for Greg and were waiting for the rest of his remains to be gathered from the woods. He got his crew back together, and they dug two more graves. Doctor Richards hadn't fully explained why it had to be done so quickly and quietly. The doctor had told him that they would perform services graveside sometime in the next couple of days. He explained to Kevin that the town had to finish the rest of the cleanup before they could have any funerals, but those bodies needed to get in the ground as soon as possible. Kevin said he could preserve the remains until it was time for a service, but Doctor Richards told him that was not an option. The doctor had been quite forceful with Kevin, and even a tad on the rude side. Kevin brushed the doctor's attitude off as stress and exhaustion. He could tell Doctor Richards hadn't slept in quite some time. Kevin understood the whole town was wound up. The typically happy-go-lucky vibe of the town had changed to a sad and confused vibe. People had been snapping at each other, and everyone seemed short-tempered. The stress level was higher than Kevin had ever seen, even higher than when they had all moved there. That first month of living in tents and teepees had been so hard on everyone. Some people even gave up and returned to Henderson. That was the last place Kevin ever wanted to be again. Everyone else pulled together and built a strong, thriving community. Kevin hoped the events of the last couple of days wouldn't erode what they had all built. He had faith that it wouldn't, but he also knew people wouldn't stay put if they didn't feel safe anymore. The mayor needed to hold a town hall meeting and settle everyone back down. The town was full of great people, but even the best person can only put up with so much before they would seek out other opportunities.

Doctor Richards and Kevin had a moment of silence before they filled in the graves. A small feeling of relief came over Doctor Richards as he headed back to his office. Amanda was standing outside of his office. She looked tired, dirty, and depressed. She gave him a weak smile as he approached her.

"Amanda, are you okay?" he asked.

"I'm okay," she quietly responded. "Could I see the man's body again? I just want to say goodbye and pay my respects."

"Kevin and I just buried him," Doctor Richards replied.

Amanda stared at the doctor with a hint of anger behind her eyes. Why would they just bury him without a funeral?

"Why didn't you have a service first?" she asked, sounding insulted.

"Amanda," Doctor Richards began. He unlocked the door to his office. "Come inside, I'll tell what I can."

Amanda followed him into the office. He motioned for her to sit down in one of the waiting room chairs. The whole place smelled like death. Doctor Richards sat next to Amanda.

"The young man's body decayed rapidly." Doctor Richards started as gently as possible. "I found microscopic insects devouring his remains." Amanda began to cry. Doctor Richards wanted to give her answers, but he didn't know how to do so without being so graphic. "I'm sorry to just lay it out there like that, but I don't know any other way to explain it. We found a woman's body out in the woods today, and she had the same insects. These insects were breaking down the bodies like I've never seen before. I wanted to get our deceased friends buried before they were totally devoured by those insects. I also wanted to get those damn bugs in the ground. I'm sorry you weren't able to say goodbye. You can go see Kevin, and he will gladly show you to the young man's grave. You could say your goodbye and pay your respects there."

Amanda wiped tears from her eyes and stood up. She said "Okay" and left the office without another word. Doctor Richards stood up and looked out the front window. He watched as Amanda walked toward the cemetery. He felt bad for her, but he had had no other option. Doctor Richards went down the hall to the autopsy room and began to disinfect it from wall to wall and floor to ceiling. Every inch of that room was going to get the most thorough cleaning he had ever performed. In fact, his entire office was going to get the scrubbing of a lifetime.

Kevin led Amanda to the freshly dug graves. They stood over the graves for a moment in silence.

"Which one is his?" Amanda asked after a bit.

"That one is the young man's," Kevin responded, pointing at the grave to their left.

"His name is Pete," Amanda said, tears welling up in her eyes.

"So you knew him?" Kevin asked in surprise.

"I did, a long time ago," she said softly.

"Do you know his family? I'd like to reach out to them," Kevin asked.

"No, his family is long gone," Amanda said. "Could I be alone with him, please?"

"Yes, of course," Kevin said. He wanted to find out more about the young man, but he could tell Amanda didn't want to talk to him about any of it. She needed to be alone. He would leave her be and talk to her about all of it at a later time.

"Thank you," Amanda said.

"You're welcome," Kevin said and set off toward the funeral home.

Amanda dropped to her knees in front of Pete's grave. Tears poured down her cheeks as she sobbed. She knelt there crying for a while.

"Pete," she began after a bit, "as soon as I saw your face, I recognized you. I know you were special to me. I'm sorry I didn't get to say goodbye sooner. Everything has been a mess around here lately. No one knows what's going on. I miss you, Pete." She began to cry harder again. "I spent the night in the woods where they found you. I was drawn to that tree. I sat there most of the night, crying. Exhaustion must have taken over because I did end up falling asleep under that tree. You sure did pick a beautiful tree to spend your last moments under. I had a dream, a very strange and vivid dream. I dreamt you and I were in a huge building with a lot of people our age. Everyone was dressed up in clothes I have never seen before. There was loud music playing. And boy, it was weird. I've never heard anything like it. People seemed to be really enjoying it, though. Everyone was dancing. You and I danced together. You held me so lovingly. I felt safe in your arms. I felt like nothing bad could ever happen to me as long as I had you. We were both nervous, but we were having so much fun! You never stopped smiling. You looked at me like I was the only person in that room. I could see the love you had for me in your eyes. Oh, Pete, you had such beautiful eyes. You were a kind man. I know that for sure. I'm sorry I shunned you back then. I'm sorry I didn't let you love me. I missed out on a beautiful thing, and I will take that regret to my grave." She paused and caught her breath. "I wish I could have been there for you. I wish I could have saved you from this awful fate. I wish I could have been your one and only. I wish I hadn't been so selfish back then. I wish I would've told you that I loved you too. I still love you, Pete, and I always will. I hope you are in a better place. I hope you rest peacefully." Amanda stood up and wiped tears from her cheeks. "I love you, Pete. I will visit you often."

Amanda walked away from the graves. She didn't go back to see Kevin again; she knew he'd have a million questions for her. She headed back to the woods and the tree she had spent the night under. Amanda had gotten such a peaceful and calming feeling under that tree. She felt love there. She could feel Pete's presence there. His soul had stayed with that tree.

Amanda curled up under the tree. It was a bit chilly, but that didn't bother her; she just pulled her arms inside her coat. Amanda closed her eyes. The stress and the constant crying had exhausted her. She wanted to fall asleep. She wanted to find Pete in her dreams again. Maybe they could dance again? His arms around her had felt so safe. Holding him in her arms had felt natural, like he belonged there. Like he had always been there.

Amanda did find Pete in her dreams. She was on the shore of a large lake. A long wood dock jutted out over the lake. Standing at the far end of the dock, overlooking the beautiful lake, was Pete. He turned and motioned for her to join him. Amanda walked to Pete, full of excitement and love. Pete was smiling at her, and she could see the love and admiration he had for her. She joined him on the edge of the dock, and he took her hand in his. The water was so calm it looked like glass. The sun was shining, and she could feel the warmth on her skin. That's when she realized she was no longer bundled up in a coat. She was wearing a pretty floral-patterned sundress, and Pete was dressed in nice shorts and a white T-shirt. Amanda closed her eyes and breathed in that warm, clean air. She exhaled the breath of air and opened her eyes. She looked at Pete and smiled. He smiled back at her. It was a genuine, full-of-love smile. Amanda released Pete's hand and put her arm around his waist. She pulled him to her and gave him a kiss. He kissed her back. They stood on that dock, kissing in the warm sunshine. Pete pulled away from Amanda and gave her another smile.

"I love you," Pete said.

"I love you, too," Amanda said, smiling. They kissed again. "I wish I didn't have to eventually wake up. I wish I could be with you forever." Tears welled up in her eyes.

"You could be," Pete said. The sight of tears in Amanda's eyes made his heart hurt. "Don't cry, my love." He pulled her to him. "Come with me. Be with me forever."

"How?" she asked. "I want to, oh, I want to so badly. But how?"

"Let go," he said.

"Let go of what?" she asked. Did he mean let go of him?

"Life. Let go of life as you know it. If you do that, we can be together in the new world forever." His tone was so confident, like it should have been obvious.

"How do I do that?" she asked.

"You're already so close," he said. "You're almost there."

"What do you mean, Pete?" she asked him. Pete seemed so calm and collected. He was speaking as if that should have all been a no-brainer.

"Release yourself from your body and follow me."

"Again, how?"

"You know how, baby. You're just scared. Take a moment and think about it. All the answers are inside of you—you just have to listen."

Amanda turned slightly from Pete and looked out over the lake. It was so big; she couldn't see the end of it. The water was so still it didn't even look real. In fact, everything looked fake. It felt like they were standing in the middle of a painting.

"Close your eyes and let go," Pete said to her. "Come with me."

Amanda closed her eyes. The warm sun faded away. The smell of the lake disappeared. She could feel cool air all around her. She could smell pine trees. Pete was gone. Everything was dark. She kept her eyes tightly closed. She feared if she opened them, she'd be back in the forest and Pete would be gone again. He was so real in her dreams. She could feel his skin on hers when they embraced. She could taste his lips when they kissed. A light slowly began to appear before her. Pete was standing in that light, smiling at her. He had his hand out to her. Amanda stood up. All she could see was Pete and that light. She had no peripheral vision. It was as if she was looking into a tunnel with a spotlight at the end of it. She walked toward Pete. The light washed over her. It was very warm and welcoming. Pete was still wearing his tan shorts and white T-shirt. As she walked to him, her coat and house dress changed back to the pretty sundress she had been wearing at the lake. The nauseous feeling and the headache she had been dealing with all day vanished as she approached Pete. The nervousness of the past couple of days went away as well. She felt a calm and peace she had never experienced before. Love and acceptance engulfed her like a warm, fuzzy blanket.

Amanda stopped and glanced behind her. She heard Pete's voice say, *"Don't do that. Keep coming to me."* His voice was inside her head. She looked anyway. Amanda could see herself lying under that tree. Leaves and pine needles blew around her on a light breeze. She had pine needles stuck in her hair. Her coat was dirty. She got the overwhelming feeling that she had to go back. She must turn around and go back to her body.

"Baby, there's nothing left for you there. Come with me, we'll be happy together forever. It's perfect here," Pete said, inside her head again.

Amanda turned back to Pete. That feeling to go back was literally pulling her away from him. Or was he retreating? *"We'll never see each other again if you go back,"* he said. *"I want you here with me, Amanda."*

She looked behind her one last time. A dog was sniffing at her body under the tree. Amanda looked at Pete; he was still smiling at her and still had his hand out. She wanted her hand in his. She wanted his arms around her. She wanted his kisses. Amanda began walking to Pete again. As she got closer to him, the beautiful light surrounded them. He put his arms around her and hugged her tight. There wasn't anything else around, just the two of them and that warm light. Amanda closed her eyes and cried. She cried tears of joy and relief. Those tears washed away all the pains of her life. Pete pulled her closer to him. She could hear him sobbing softly. They stood in that light and held each other.

It was perfection. She had made the right decision.

CHAPTER 14

The Request

Doctor Richards stood outside his office, puffing on a cigar and sipping a stiff drink. He had taken a break from scrubbing his office, a well-deserved break. He saw Cecilia headed his way and he put his cigar out. Cecilia walked up to him. She looked exhausted and fed up.

"Hello, Cecilia," Doctor Richards said to her. "You look like you could use a drink."

"I sure could," Cecilia said, "but I will pass for now, too much going on."

"Maybe later?" he said. "Please don't tell me you're here because you found another body."

"No, Doctor, that is not the reason for my visit. But I do think we figured out who the woman from the woods could be. Did the remains show signs of a broken right arm?"

"Yes, they did. Looked to be an old fracture that wasn't set right. She would have had some pain in that arm. Who do you think it was?" he asked her.

"Denny Roberts went to check on Mallory. No one had seen her all day. Most people assumed she was just depressed from losing her dog. Mallory wasn't home, and it looked as though she hadn't been home since yesterday. Denny and Malcolm went into the woods looking for her. They found the dress and coat she had been wearing at the tavern last night, but no signs of her. I asked Denny if she had

had any medical issues or if there had been any trauma to her bones at any point in her life. When they found her clothes, I knew the remains had to be her, but I wanted to see if there was any way to be sure. You've confirmed it. A skeleton of a middle-aged woman with a previously broken right arm—that has to be her."

Doctor Richards dropped his head and sighed. "That is terrible news," he said, taking a sip of his drink. "Mallory was a good woman, and she was well loved by all. This is heartbreaking."

"It is terrible news, Doctor, but she is gone. We can't bring her back now. So now, we just need to try and figure out what happened to those bodies." Cecilia felt for the doctor; it was clear that he had really cared for Mallory.

"I may have figured that out, Cecilia. I took sections of their bones and studied them under the microscope. I found microscopic bugs devouring their bones. Their bones had already been hollowed out. I've never seen anything like it. I had Kevin bury the remains. I wanted to get them and the insects into the ground as soon as possible. I wanted them to have a proper burial before they were reduced to ashes."

"Good call, Doctor. Great work. I appreciate it," Cecilia said. Doctor Richards thanked her. He looked so defeated and sad. "You know what, I think I will take you up on that drink after all."

"Okay, great," he replied with a smile. "Why don't we head inside. I gave the whole place a thorough cleaning—it doesn't stink anymore."

"Sounds great," Cecilia said and followed the doctor inside.

Doctor Richards led Cecilia to his office. He poured them both a drink, and they sat down. Cecilia sipped her drink. It was strong, but it hit the spot.

"Two things occurred to me on my way over here," Cecilia started, setting her drink down on the doctor's desk. "First, did you find another one of those small metal contraptions in Mallory's remains?"

"No, I didn't. With everything going on, I honestly forgot about the one I found in the young man," Doctor Richards replied.

"I will take that as good news," Cecilia said, picking up her drink and taking a small sip. "The other thing that has me puzzled is how did Mallory end up way out in the woods? And why was her clothing found so far away from her body?"

"My best guess is that she was ill, like Scarlett's girls, and wandered off into the woods. If she had a fever like they do, it would have made her delirious and overheated. I think it's a really good possibility she got too hot, stripped her clothing off, and kept wandering. She then probably succumbed to the elements and died. That's the only thing that makes any sense at this point. And without being able to do a full autopsy, we'll never know for sure."

"That makes sense to me, Doctor," Cecilia said. "Scarlett's girls were very out of it. I could see someone suffering from the same illness wandering off like that. It's tragic." She shook her head. "I will check on the girls as soon as I return home."

"That would be a good idea. Keep an eye on those girls," Doctor Richards agreed. "It's all so tragic. Our little town has experienced quite the upheaval the last couple days." He paused and took a drink. "Do you know if everyone else is accounted for? I'd hate to discover any more bodies."

"I do. I have been all around and everyone else is alive and mostly well, except for Amanda. No one has seen her since she went with you yesterday. I have people out looking for her," Cecilia said.

"I saw her earlier today," Doctor Richards began. "She is convinced she knew the young man we found in the woods. She wasn't happy that had him buried without a funeral. I told her to go see Kevin at the cemetery and she could pay her respects there. She's probably still there."

"She knew him?" Cecilia asked, surprised. "That's good news, we can find his family. I'm sure someone is looking for him."

"She didn't know him like that. It was all so puzzling, honestly. She told me she knew him at one point in her life. She said she had loved him."

"If she had loved the man, she has to know who he is and who his family is," Cecilia interjected.

"That's what I thought too, but she said she doesn't even remember his name." Doctor Richards sipped his drink. "Honestly, Cecilia, I think the girl is delusional. I think she is overstressed and seeing a dead body for the first time just pushed her over the edge. That young man was her age. I suspect seeing someone her age, laid out dead on an autopsy table, frazzled her. She then subconsciously made up a story to make herself feel better. Maybe in her mind, if she convinced herself she had known and loved that man, it would make her feel better about what she was looking at."

"Everyone is stressed out and frazzled," Cecilia said, taking a sip of her drink. "I'm glad to know she is around. We'll give her some space so that she can come to terms with what she saw. I strongly believe once we have everything cleaned up and get back to normal life, people will settle down and we can all get past this."

"I agree," he said. "You said people are mostly well. Are there more people who have become ill?"

"Denny told me his wife hasn't been feeling well, but she doesn't have a fever, so I think she'll be fine," Cecilia said. "Everyone else is just exhausted and ready to be done with cleaning up that damn debris. We have pretty much completed the cleanup process. We'll be totally done by sundown. I have instructed everyone to just head home tonight and stay put. I am holding a town hall meeting tomorrow afternoon at the tavern at one o'clock. I would like you to speak to the town about your findings."

"I can do that. Do want me to tell them everything or give them an abbreviated version?"

"Tell them everything. The town deserves to know. We're all grownups here, Doctor. The more information that is given, the better prepared everyone can be."

"Okay, will do, Cecilia."

"Thank you, Doctor. I am going to return to my place and help get everything tidied up. I'll see you tomorrow," Cecilia said and stood up.

"Sounds good. I'll see you tomorrow, and thank you," Doctor Richards said, standing up. He walked Cecilia to the door.

"Get some rest, Doctor, you need it."

"I will. I'm beat. Have a good evening."

"You too." Cecilia left the office, and Doctor Richards closed the door behind her.

Doctor Richards went back to his office and grabbed his drink. He went out front and relit his cigar. He thought about heading home, but there was nothing he could do there. Doctor Richards decided he'd stay put at his office in case anyone needed him.

Scarlett had finished up in the kitchen and went out to the living room to check on the girls. She noticed Hope had sat up on her couch and was watching Gwen sleep on the other couch. Hope looked so much better. Scarlett checked on Gwen, and she was asleep.

"How are you feeling?" Scarlett asked Hope.

"I feel fine," Hope answered. "What happened to Gwen?"

"She's sick. Just like you were," Scarlett answered. She went to Gwen and touched the girl's forehead. Gwen was still warm but not as hot as before. Gwen stirred a bit when her mom touched her.

"I feel fine," Hope said again. "I don't remember being sick."

"Well, you were, and you were very sick," Scarlett said.

"I don't remember any of it," Hope repeated.

"That's probably a good thing," Scarlett said. "I'm not surprised—you had an extremely high fever and you mostly just slept. I'm glad you're feeling better, dear."

"Thanks," Hope said. "I'm so hungry."

"I bet you are. You haven't been able to keep anything down for a couple of days now. Let me make us some dinner." Scarlett walked to the kitchen and stoked the fire in the wood stove.

Gwen started coughing; it was a violent, wet, and raspy cough. She rolled over to the edge of the couch and hung her head off the side. The bucket from earlier was sitting there next to the couch. Gwen spat blood into the bucket and rolled back over. The coughing fit continued, and Gwen had to spit more blood into the bucket. Scarlett rushed over to her daughter. The high fever and vomiting had had Scarlett worried, but watching her daughter cough up blood put her into a panic.

"Hope! Go out back and get Cecilia!" Scarlett exclaimed.

Hope slowly stood up; her legs felt weak. Her whole body felt weak. Hope headed out the front door. She went around to the back and found Cecilia at the wood line, talking to Malcolm. Hope slowly approached Cecilia.

"Excuse me, ma'am," Hope said shyly. Hope liked and respected Cecilia, but at the same time she was a little timid around her. Cecilia had a big personality and was a tough woman.

"Yes, dear?" Cecilia said. "You must be feeling better. It's great to see you up and about!"

"Thank you. I am feeling better. But Gwen is really sick. Scarlett wanted me to come get you."

"Okay, dear. Let's go." Cecilia turned back to Malcolm. "Thank you for everything you have done today. It is greatly appreciated and will be remembered. I will see you tomorrow at the town hall meeting."

"You're welcome, ma'am," Malcolm said. "I'll see you tomorrow." He turned to Hope. "I'm glad to see you're feeling well."

"Thank you, sir," Hope said.

Cecilia and Hope headed back to their cabin. Cecilia could hear Gwen coughing as they entered the house.

"Gwen's coughing up blood!" Scarlett exclaimed as Cecilia entered the room.

"Oh, shit, that's not good!" Cecilia said and rushed over to Scarlett and Gwen.

Gwen's eyes were glazed over, and she looked to be completely out of it. Scarlett was rubbing her back. Cecilia could see the sheer panic on Scarlett's face. Gwen stopped coughing and rolled onto her back. Her eyes slowly closed, and she was out again. Her breathing was deep and peaceful. Scarlett looked at Cecilia.

"Should we go get Doctor Richards?" Scarlett asked Cecilia.

"It's getting pretty late," Cecilia started. "Let's keep an eye on her for a little bit first. If she starts coughing like that again, we'll go get him."

"She was coughing up blood. I'm terribly worried about her," Scarlett said, standing up.

"I am too, but at this point, what could the doctor do for her? He'll tell us to keep an eye on her and try to keep her hydrated, which is what we're already doing."

"Yeah, you're right. I just feel so damn helpless. I hate it when my kids are sick." Scarlett put her hand on Gwen's shoulder.

"I know. I don't like seeing them ill either," Cecilia said. "Scarlett, she'll be fine. We should let her rest."

"Okay, but I'm not leaving this house for any reason until she is well again," Scarlett said. Scarlett sighed. "I was about to fix some dinner when she started coughing." Scarlett headed to the kitchen.

"Why don't you let me handle that tonight?" Cecilia said. "You sit with Gwen. I'll whip up something to eat."

"Thank you, Cecilia," Scarlett said and sat down on the couch across from Gwen. Gwen was in a deep sleep.

"No problem," Cecilia said and went to the kitchen. She began cooking.

"Have you seen or heard anything about Amanda?" Scarlett asked Cecilia.

"Yeah, Doctor Richards said she took seeing that young man's body pretty hard. He said she was at the cemetery. I suspect she'll be home any time now. I bet she's hungry too," Cecilia said, from behind the stove.

"In all the madness of today, it never dawned on me that I hadn't seen her in a while. I know her and I just assumed she was out there helping with the cleanup. I'm glad she's accounted for at least," Scarlett said.

"She's fine. She'll come home when she's ready," Cecilia said as she cooked.

"I know she will. I just wanted to know if you had seen her today."

"Not personally, but she's out there and she's fine."

Scarlett knew that last statement was Cecilia's way of saying "Drop it." Scarlett knew Amanda would be fine. Amanda was a full-grown woman, and if she needed some space to deal with everything that had gone on, then she should be able to take some time to herself. But at the same time, she needed to keep up with her responsibilities. It was getting to a point where Scarlett was starting to worry a bit. She knew there wasn't much reason for concern; Amanda was a fairly responsible person.

The cabin had fallen quiet, except for the sounds of Cecilia cooking. Scarlett couldn't tell from the couch what Cecilia was cooking, but it sure smelled good. Smelling food cooking made her realize how hungry she was. It dawned on her that she hadn't eaten all day. Cecilia asked Hope to set the table. Once the table was set, Cecilia set out dinner. Scarlett, Hope, and Cecilia sat at the table and ate dinner. They were all starving and plowed through dinner without any talking.

Gwen suddenly sat straight up on the couch and screamed. Scarlett got up and ran to her daughter. Gwen's eyes were wide and full of fear. She was drenched in sweat. Tears flooded down her cheeks. Gwen blinked her eyes and looked around the room.

"Are you okay, honey?" Scarlett asked, rubbing Gwen's back.

"Yea, I think so," Gwen panted. "I had a weird dream. It was so scary."

"How are you feeling?" Scarlett asked. Gwen looked normal to her. Not even an hour ago, her daughter was coughing up blood, and now she seemed completely fine.

"I'm fine, Mom. I just had a scary dream. Why am I sleeping on the couch?" she asked, still a bit dazed from her dream.

"You've been sick. You and Hope were both very sick," Scarlett replied, so confused by neither one of them remembering they had even been sick. They had been so ill; they should have remembered feeling that badly.

"Oh. I don't remember being sick," Gwen said. "Something smells amazing. I'm so hungry," she said, swinging her legs over the side of the couch.

"Go sit at the table. I'll get you a plate," Scarlett said.

Gwen sat at the table next to Hope. She smiled at her friend and Hope smiled back.

"Do you want to tell us about your dream?" Scarlett asked, handing Gwen a plate and silverware.

"Sure," Gwen said, piling food onto her plate. "Mom, you, me, and Hope were at this weird house. It was huge and not made out of wood like the cabins around here are. There were other houses just like it, but different colors, and some of them were on fire. There were big metal things with black wheels on the bottom and glass windows all around the top. Kind of like wagons but made of metal and glass. Very weird." Gwen was shoveling food into her mouth as she spoke. "I think it was nighttime because it was really dark outside." She paused and sipped her water. "Something blew up, and I was hit on the leg with glass, I think, and I fell to the ground. The whole sky was lit up super bright, like brighter than the sun. It was a really strange and unnatural light. Like a million candles." She stopped again and drank more water. She was shaky and her throat felt tight. "Then, this…" She trailed off. She sat back and sighed.

"It's okay, honey," Scarlett said. She could tell her daughter was flustered and the dream had upset her. "It was just a dream. None of it was real."

"I know, Mom. But it *seemed* so real." Gwen took another drink of water. She took a deep breath and continued, "I was lying on the ground. My leg hurt so bad, and I was bleeding. All of a sudden, something appeared over me. I have no idea what it was, some creature thing. It was huge and brown. Its skin looked like leather. Its head was big and long. It had beady black eyes and rows of pointy teeth. It was the scariest thing I have ever seen. It sniffed me and then stepped away from me. Another light appeared from the sky. Everything was so bright I couldn't tell where these lights were coming from, even though I was looking up at the sky. That second light was red, and it was kind of flashing. More like pulsing, really. It was weird. That red light went around me…"

She paused again and took a moment to compose herself. As she talked about the dream, all the feelings from it came flooding back. The fear, the panic, the uncertainty, all of it. With a big sigh, she continued, "The red light was warm, really warm. I could feel sadness and anger in that light. I know that sounds weird, and I can't explain it any better than that. All I could see was that red light. Then I couldn't see anything. Everything was dark. I couldn't move or talk. I felt something messing with my leg. It hurt so bad, and I was terrified."

Gwen stopped again and looked around the table. She took a deep breath and went on with her dream. "Then I was alone. You and Hope were gone. I was tied to a metal table in a room that looked like it was made out of metal too. That room was so cold. There were no windows or doors. I didn't know where I was or how I even got there. How do you get into a room without a door? Then I heard voices and people moving around quickly. I still couldn't move my body. I was so scared, Mom. I didn't know where I was or what happened to you and Hope. A man came to me and untied me. I started crying. He asked if I could move and I shook my head. He picked me up and started to move. Then there was a lady in the room, a really weird-looking lady. The lady called the man 'Billy.' The lady wanted Billy to put me down, but he wouldn't. He said he wouldn't let them have me. He wanted to keep me safe and get me help. He kept looking at me in his arms, and he looked scared and mad. The lady touched him, and he dropped me. I sort of floated to the floor. Then everything went black again. Next thing I know, I'm in a tiny, metal room. No windows or doors in that room either. I put my head in my hands and cried. I heard a *swoosh* noise and looked up. Part of the wall had opened somehow. There was no door there, just a door-shaped hole in the wall. The air that came through it was hot and smelled really bad. I can't describe the smell because I've never smelled anything like it before. Two of those really tall, ugly creatures walked through the door." Gwen paused again to catch her breath. Everyone at the table were staring her. They were all fascinated.

"Are you okay, honey?" Scarlett asked. She could tell Gwen was getting upset talking about her dream.

"Yeah, I'm fine, Mom. The next part of the dream is hard to talk about." Gwen sipped her water. She wanted to be done talking about her dream, but she could tell by everyone's faces that they wanted to hear the rest of it. As she sat there collecting herself for a moment, she began to realize talking about that dream was starting to make her feel a bit better. Hearing herself tell the story was starting to help her realize how ridiculous and far-fetched the whole thing was. "Okay, so after the creatures came in, a smaller one came in. The smaller one was dressed like a person, but I could tell it wasn't a person. It had those same beady black eyes. The little one talked to me in a weird voice—it didn't sound like a person's voice. I can't explain it—it just sounded fake. It told me that I was a chosen one and I was going to be okay. It said that my mom and sister would be okay too—they just had more work to do before they could join me. It never said where I was or what being a chosen one meant. All it said was that I'd be okay and I would see you and Hope again soon. Then it left the room, and those huge ugly things followed it. After a few minutes, I got up and walked out of the room. I was in a long metal hallway. It was so bright. I heard a scream and what sounded like flesh tearing. I looked down the hall, and I saw one of those big, ugly things tearing a lady apart. That's when I woke up." Gwen sat back in her chair and sighed. She felt better. She didn't feel as frightened as she had felt upon waking from that dream.

The table was quiet. Scarlett, Cecilia, and Hope looked at each other and then back to Gwen. Listening to Gwen talk about her dream, Cecilia could tell it had been a realistic and vivid dream. The way Gwen had talked about smells and lights, strange metal rooms, and especially the creatures worried Cecilia. It sounded more like Gwen was recalling memories than talking about a dream and that was how Cecilia had felt the last few days. Scarlett had insisted that what Cecilia thought were memories were simply weird dreams. But the perplexing thing about that theory was, Cecilia didn't remember dreaming those things; she truly felt like she had *lived* it. No one knew much about dreams or why people even had them, but some theorized that people's brains told them stories at night while they slept. They could never answer the question why their brains did that, but everyone did indeed dream. Cecilia wasn't comfortable just chocking it all up to weird dreams. All this madness had begun when those metal contraptions had appeared in the woods. It had to be related somehow. Cecilia hoped they would one day figure out what those things were, but for now, there were far more questions than answers.

Scarlett got up from the table and started lighting candles. She thought it was odd that Gwen and Cecilia had had similar dreams, but at the same time, it made her feel better. The things Cecilia had said the day before had worried Scarlett. She had chocked it up to a crazy dream and now she was certain that was all it had been. Everything was starting to make sense to her. Gwen had just finished a book called *Sky People* that Cecilia had read and highly recommended. Cecilia had picked the book up at the store, thinking it was about people's theory there was a life after death. That people went to live in the sky with the Creator after they died. Cecilia had told Scarlett the book had nothing at all to do with life after death but that it was a good book anyway. A quick and easy read, filled with nonsense and craziness. She had told Scarlett that the author must have one of the most overactive imaginations ever. That's all Cecilia had told her about the book and added she should just read it; even if it was nonsense, it had still been entertaining. Scarlett hadn't read the book yet, but Gwen had told her a lot about the book. It was a fantasy saga about a large nation of people that were visited by people from the sky. Gwen didn't go into a whole lot of detail. She didn't want to spoil anything, but she had mentioned to Scarlett that the "sky people" were big, ugly-looking things. Those things took people into the skies with them. Gwen said after they took people the book got really creepy but oh so good. Scarlett wanted to read the book for herself. Cecilia and Gwen had been the only ones in the household who had read the book and, coincidentally, the only ones who had had strange creature dreams. Scarlett was going to start the book that evening. She had to know what else was in that book.

Gwen got up from the table and said she was going to heat water for a bath. As Gwen went about her task, Cecilia announced she was going to head for bed. Hope said she was going to do the same. Scarlett took the *Sky People* book and headed for her room. It was still fairly early. Scarlett wasn't quite ready for sleep, even though she was tired. She also wanted to wait up for Amanda. She was beginning to worry about Amanda; it wasn't like her to be gone for so long. Scarlett knew Amanda had been through a lot, but hell, they all had. No one else had just disappeared. She was concerned about

Amanda but also a little annoyed with her. It was awfully selfish to hide out like Amanda had done. None of them had asked for any of it, and none of them wanted to have to deal with it all, but they all came together and did what needed to be done. Everyone except for Amanda. The more Scarlett thought about it, the more upset it made her. She cared for Amanda, but sometimes her attitude frustrated Scarlett. She wanted Amanda to feel like she was family, but she didn't believe Amanda had any right to be so rude, especially toward Gwen. Those two seemed to always be in some sort of a tiff with each other. Scarlett knew it was all derived from jealousy issues. Amanda was jealous of Gwen being Scarlett's daughter, and Gwen was jealous that Amanda had been accepted as a daughter. Scarlett would talk to them about it, and things would be fine for a few days. But it never lasted. She knew it was a temporary situation; Amanda was at the age where she would be dating and getting married within the next year or so.

Scarlett had just settled into her reading chair when she heard the front door open. She heard Dana and Julia enter. They headed straight for their room. It was normal for them to miss dinner; they were dating brothers and would have dinner with their boyfriends almost every night. Dana and Julia were great housemates; they were rarely around, and when they were home, they were very respectful and helpful. They worked a lot at the general store and contributed to the household. They all had a good thing going, and Scarlett enjoyed their living arrangements. Scarlett cracked open the book and began reading. She only got a few pages in before she fell asleep. The excitement and hard work of the day had exhausted her. She slept for a few hours. When she awoke, she put the book down and went to see if Amanda had returned home. She hadn't. That frustrated Scarlett. She figured Amanda was still upset with Gwen and saddened by seeing the young man's body. Amanda was probably staying at her friend's place. Her friend, Leah, had her own place across town. Amanda had thought about moving in with Leah, but Scarlett had talked her out of it. Amanda had spent many nights with Leah and always returned in the morning to do her chores. Anytime she was upset with Gwen, she'd run off to Leah's for a bit. Scarlett settled into bed and tried to let go of the stress and annoyance of that day. One more busy day and then they could all get back to their normal routines. Scarlett was looking forward to getting back to the office and taking care of town issues. She was really looking forward to putting all the craziness behind them.

*****

Scarlett was awoken the next morning by someone pounding on their front door. The loud knocking woke the entire household. Scarlett opened the door, and Marcus Riley, the sheriff from Henderson, was standing on their doorstep. He looked panicked and haggard.

"Marcus, what brings you to our little town?" Scarlett asked.

Marcus looked past Scarlett and saw everyone else standing just behind her.

"I need to talk to Cecilia," he said. "I'd rather talk in private, though."

"We can talk outside," Cecilia said, stepping forward, "but Scarlett will join us."

"That's fine," Marcus said, stepping away from the door. Cecilia and Scarlett put their coats on and joined Marcus outside. Dana, Julia, Gwen, and Hope all went back to bed.

"What's going on?" Cecilia asked. The man looked familiar, and she knew she should remember him, but she didn't. Scarlett had called him Marcus, so at least she knew his name.

"Henderson is a mess," Marcus began. He pulled a cigar out of the front pocket of his coat. "Do you mind if I smoke?"

They both said they didn't mind at all.

Marcus lit his cigar and took a couple of puffs. "Where do I begin?" he asked aloud.

"Start at the beginning," Cecilia said. It was quite chilly that morning, and she wanted to spend as little time as possible standing outside with this man. She didn't have the patience for him to stand there and dilly dally.

"Okay, well, as you know, we were doing great when you all left. As far as we were told, we were thriving. Turns out John hid a lot of shit from us. He was not a good leader at all. He was a vindictive, selfish man. He ruled our little town like a tyrant. You all weren't the only ones who left Henderson to start their own community. John ran off more than half of our townspeople." Marcus paused and puffed on his cigar. Neither Scarlett nor Cecilia smoked, but that cigar smoke smelled really good to them. It had an extremely sweet aroma to it.

"That doesn't surprise me one bit," Scarlett said.

"It surprised John," Marcus said. "He couldn't understand why so many people were leaving. He honestly believed he had created the perfect society—that's what he always called Henderson, a society, not a town. He hated it when people would refer to Henderson as a town."

"No offense, Marcus, but let's cut to the chase," Cecilia said. She was still in her nightgown and house slippers. She was getting colder by the minute and less patient. "Are you here to ask if you can move here with us?"

"No, ma'am," Marcus said. "I am here to ask you to govern Henderson as well as this fine town. I have spoken to the townspeople of Williamsville, just north of here, and they'd like you to govern their town as well."

"I think John would have some objection to that," Scarlett said.

"John's dead," Marcus said. Cecilia and Scarlett looked at each other shocked and confused. "He got violently ill and died the night before last. His entire inner circle has fallen ill and are dying. They have all probably passed on by now. The town needs some strong and fair leadership. You're the only person any of us can think of to be that leader."

"So you're here to ask me to run three towns?" Cecilia asked. "I don't see how that would be logistically possible. How can I be in three places at once? In order to be the leader you want me to be, I'd have to be hands on, and I can't do that from here."

"We understand that, ma'am," Marcus said. "From what I've been told—I've stayed in touch with Malcolm—you two have created a thriving community here. Your town sounds like it treats everyone equally and everyone seems so happy."

"They are all very happy. We've had some strange things occurring around here the last couple of days, but we've made it past all that," Cecilia said. "I am honored to be asked to govern your town as well, but I just don't think that's possible at this time."

"Would you excuse us for a moment?" Scarlett asked Marcus. "I'd like to discuss this with Cecilia in private."

"Sure thing," Marcus said.

Cecilia and Scarlett went back into the cabin.

"Cecilia, you should do it!" Scarlett exclaimed. "Imagine the resources we'd have from three towns."

"It would be nice to triple our potential resources, but how am I supposed to be in three places at once? How is one person expected to run three towns by themselves?"

"You don't do it by yourself. Our town could be home base for you as it is now, and you could periodically travel to the other towns. They aren't that far away, a half-day trip at most. I can run our town while you're away, and you can appoint deputy mayors in the other two towns to handle the day-to-day business when you're not there."

"Scarlett, that sounds like a logistics nightmare." Cecilia shook her head.

"At first it will be," Scarlett said. As they talked, Scarlett was heating water for tea. "There are five towns around us within a day's trip. You could end up governing all of them at some point. You are a strong and passionate leader, Cecilia. You should do this."

"Why?" Cecilia asked. "What do we get out of this besides a hell of a lot more work? We are run pretty ragged just running our little town. Now we're talking about possibly running five more? It's crazy talk."

"No, it's not," Scarlett said. The water had boiled, and Scarlett was fixing three cups of tea. "We're talking about being the leaders of our corner of the world. If we ran all the towns, there would be no more need for trading and bartering over basic supplies. Everything would belong to everyone. If Henderson needed something that we had in abundance, it would be theirs just as anything we need from them would be ours. I think once we establish a chain of command and set out the rules we have implemented here, we would all thrive."

"Why do we even care about these other towns? We fled Henderson for a reason. We didn't just move to a different town—we built our own. We must have done that for a reason as well. I'm going to sound selfish here, but seriously, why do we even care?" Cecilia sipped her tea. Scarlett sure knew how to brew a delicious cup of tea.

"Because eventually, these other towns are going to want to branch out and take over more land. Someday, there will be fights over land. Just in the past year, three new towns popped up around here, including ours. People are raising families, and these towns continue to grow in size. If we can incorporate all the towns into one large community, we can avoid any potential future altercations. Think of it as one community with several towns that are mostly self-sufficient. All of which is governed by you." Scarlett was excited by the idea and it showed.

Cecilia sighed and sipped her tea. "Invite Marcus inside." Cecilia took a seat at the dining room table.

Scarlett went outside and invited Marcus in. She gave him a cup of tea and told him to join them at the table. He took off his hat and coat and sat at the table.

"How soon do you need an answer about all of this?" Cecilia asked him.

"I was hoping to get one today while I'm here," he replied, sipping his tea.

"That seems a bit rushed to me," Cecilia said. "What you are asking of me is a huge, life-altering decision. You can't honestly expect an answer right away. I need time to process this and to determine if it's even possible."

"I do understand that, ma'am. It is a big decision, but it is a time-sensitive one. You see, John had ruled Henderson with an iron fist. Everything was his way or get the F out. A lot of people were fortunate to get out, but there are a lot of good people left in Henderson. Now these fine people are lost. No one in that town was allowed to make a move without John's okay. He literally ran everything, and we are now dead in the water. We need direction, and we need it now."

"Can you give me at least a day?" Cecilia asked. "Scarlett has some ideas for how this could work out. We need at least today to discuss this and come up with a plan. Again, I am very honored to be asked to do this, and I don't want to sound ungrateful or uninterested—I am interested—but I need time to make sure it can be done. You can understand that, right?"

"Yes, Ma'am, I can. Malcolm has offered me a place to stay, so I can give you today to decide, but I do need to get back to Henderson by tomorrow. The town has quickly become a mess since John died. I'll level with you. No one—and I mean no one—was sad to see that man go, but none of us know how to rebuild that town. The only thing we all have been able to agree on is that we are going to change the town name. Totally erase that son of a bitch from our lives."

"Okay, Marcus, I will have an answer by tomorrow morning," Cecilia said, standing up. "We are holding a town meeting today at one, in the tavern. You are welcome to join us."

"Thank you," Marcus said and stood up. "I'll be there. I look forward to it. Marcus put his hat and coat back on. "Thank you for your time, and thank you for considering my request. I hope everything will work out well for all of us. We really do need you, Cecilia."

"Things will work out how they are meant to. Thank you for the kind words. We will talk more later."

"Yes, ma'am," Marcus said and tipped his hat to her.

Marcus let himself out and headed for Malcolm's cabin. Malcolm had been one of Marcus's deputies back in Henderson and had begged Marcus to leave with him. John was Marcus's uncle, and Marcus had been terrified of him. He knew if he had left his uncle's town, John would find him and kill him. He had seen John kill men who disobeyed his wishes. John had been a bad man and an even worse leader. Marcus was glad his uncle was dead.

"You're going to do it, right?" Scarlett asked Cecilia after Marcus had left.

"Most likely," Cecilia said with a sigh. "I don't know how yet, but I also don't see any other option. You're right—we will eventually end up battling the other towns for resources. If we all become one society, we will avoid that unfortunate reality. We both know there are more men out there like John, and I'd hate to see any of them gain any power. If we can run those other towns the way we have run this one, we will have a happy, thriving society of equal and like-minded people. That's how a society should be."

"That's great news!" Scarlett exclaimed. "I know it will be a tough, exhausting transition, but it will all be so worth it in the end. I'll be by your side through the entire process. This is going to be good, Cecilia!"

"I hope so. I hope we're aren't getting in over our heads." Cecilia put her cup down on the counter in the kitchen. "I might take a bath and work on my speech for the town hall meeting this afternoon. I want you to brainstorm some ideas on how we will govern six towns instead of just one. If we're going to do this, we need to start working on it immediately."

"Will do, Cecilia! I'm excited about this!" Scarlett poured herself another cup of tea. She placed it on the dining room table. She grabbed a pencil and some paper and settled down at the table.

As Scarlett scribbled away on her paper, Cecilia thought about warming up water for a bath. She remembered a time when all you had to do was turn on a faucet and hot water would pour out. Cecilia hoped they could find that technology again. Boiling water for a bath was so time consuming, and it never stayed warm enough. Cecilia fixed a cup of tea instead; she didn't want to fuss with bath water. She took her tea to her room. Dana and Julia were up and making themselves some tea and breakfast.

Cecilia tried to focus on her speech for the town hall meeting, but she couldn't get Marcus's request out of her head. What an utterly daunting task it would be to govern six towns. She'd be traveling all the time. She would have to be in six different places at the same time. One town would need one thing, while another would need something completely different. Any time there were any problems anywhere, she'd have to pick up and go. Trying to nail down the logistics of it all was making her head spin. Cecilia was glad she had Scarlett; she would come up with some great ideas. The only thing Cecilia could really come up with in that moment was she would have to move out of their town. They would have to set up some kind of unincorporated little place in the middle of all of the towns. Somewhere central where she and her staff could live and work. Something like a capital building and a few homes. Their new society would need to figure out a way of combining their currency to make value equal. As it was now, each town decided what value was placed on their currency. That made it so towns had to barter and trade for goods instead of just outright buying what they needed. The more she thought about all that would need to be done, the less enthused she felt about it all. She knew she would eventually become more excited about it. That was just the sort of challenge she enjoyed taking head on.

Cecilia headed back to the kitchen for more tea. She made herself stop thinking about any of it—the potential new society, the townhall meeting, all of it. She needed to just clear her mind and relax before she made herself go mad. She could feel a huge ball of stress growing in her stomach. She took her fresh cup of tea outside. She sat down in one of the chairs on the front porch and looked up to the sky. Cecilia did some deep breathing and was able to relax. She kept her mind clear and just enjoyed the cool, morning air. It was going to be another long, stressful day. She sighed; she now had an endless number of long, stressful days ahead of her.

Cecilia and Scarlett left their cabin to head to the tavern with Hope and Gwen. The girls both said they felt great. Neither of them even remembered being so sick. The delirium from the fever must have made them forget all about being sick. They arrived at the tavern about forty-five minutes before one. The place was already quite packed. Bob's tavern was the only meeting place in town and was more than big enough to accommodate a town-wide gathering. Cecilia took a seat at the bar. Scarlett and the girls found a table toward the back of the room. Cecilia hadn't prepared a speech; Marcus's visit and request had thrown her for a loop. She decided she would just wing it. She knew exactly what she wanted to tell everyone, and she figured a less-prepared approach would be better anyway. It would lead to more interaction with the townsfolk.

Cecilia saw Marcus enter the tavern with Malcolm and Bethany. She went to Marcus and asked to speak to him privately out front. He agreed, and they exited the tavern.

"I will do it," Cecilia said to him.

"Oh! That is great news, Cecilia! Oh my, that makes me incredibly happy! Everyone in Henderson will be so excited to hear the news." His excitement was written all over his smiling face.

"There's something I want to ask you," Cecilia said.

"Yeah, anything," Marcus replied.

"Did you all find any large metal contraptions in the woods around Henderson?" Cecilia could tell by the confused look on his face that they had not.

"No, ma'am," Marcus responded. "Why do you ask?"

"We found some in the woods around our town. It's a long story that isn't of much importance right now. I was just wondering if there had been more in the area."

"We didn't find any metal contraptions, but one of my deputies was called out to a body in the woods. We have no idea what it was, but it was not human or any kind of animal we have ever seen. John immediately took over the investigation and had his top men bring the body to city hall. He fell ill that same night and died shortly thereafter. His top guys, as I said earlier, have all fallen ill as well. After John's death and his men all headed home to recuperate, I went to investigate that thing, but it was gone. I don't know what they did with that body, but it's nowhere to be found now. My deputy was the only one outside of John's circle that saw the thing. He said it was hideous."

"Did your deputy describe the thing?" Cecilia asked.

"Yea, he told me it was huge, at least eight feet tall. He said it was brown with leathery skin. He said it had the biggest head he'd ever seen, bigger than a moose. Black, beady eyes and large, pointy teeth. Sounded like something out of a fantasy book."

Cecilia stared at Marcus in shock. He had just described the same thing Gwen had described from her dream. The same thing she herself had dreamed about. How was that even possible? What in the world were those damn things? Maybe a new species of animal that had migrated their way? That would explain how it ended up in the woods outside of Henderson, but it didn't explain how they ended up in her and Gwen's dreams.

"It's gotta be some kind of animal we haven't discovered yet," Marcus said. "Although, based on how big my deputy said that thing was, I don't know how we haven't discovered it yet."

"Must be," Cecilia said just to agree with him. She knew it wasn't any animal. She had no idea what it was, but she was certain it was not an undiscovered animal. "We'll have to alert the hunters out your way."

"We should. John kept it all very secretive. No one in Henderson knows anything about it except for the man who called it in, my deputy, and myself. I was thinking of leaving it that way, but now that I think about it, we should warn the townspeople. I'd hate to have someone come across one of those things without any warning. That would end terribly."

"Yes, Sheriff, it sure would," Cecilia said. "I need to get back in that tavern and give my speech. We'll discuss all of this further at a later date."

"Sounds good, ma'am," Marcus said.

"One last thing," Cecilia began, "I want you to be an integral part of all of this moving forward. I would like to see you take over the law enforcement side of things."

"Oh, my, thank you, ma'am! I would be honored. It would be my pleasure. Thank you so much."

"You bet, Sheriff, you're definitely the right person for the job," Cecilia said, opening the door to the tavern. "We'll hammer out details later."

"Thank you again, ma'am," Marcus said and followed Cecilia into the tavern.

The tavern was loud but quickly quieted down after Cecilia entered. The townsfolk were clearly anxious to hear what she had to say. Everyone took a seat, and all eyes were on Cecilia.

"Hello, all," Cecilia started. "Thank you for coming out this afternoon. I know we have all had a long couple of days, so I want to make this as brief as possible. I will take questions. I can't promise

I'll have any answers—none of us know what has gone on around here. But maybe together we can come to some sort of conclusion. Regardless, I want to thank you all for your hard work yesterday, and I am proud and honored to be a part of this beautiful town and community. You all are absolutely wonderful and amazing people."

The crowd of people erupted in applause and shouted out thanks to Cecilia.

"Now none of us know what those things in the woods were, but they're mostly gone now, so I say we just put it behind us. It was a bitch of a cleanup process, but we got through it. Great job everyone!"

The crowd applauded again.

"Now," Cecilia began after the applause stopped, "on to the sad news. As I'm sure most of you know by now, we found the remains of a young man in the woods. He has yet to be identified. My best guess is he was from a neighboring town, and we will eventually find his family." She paused and looked around the room. She saw sadness on everyone's faces. The crowd knew what she was going to say next. With a heavy sigh, Cecilia continued. "We also found the remains of Mallory. It appears she was quite ill and wandered off into the woods in a fever-induced panic. Unfortunately, our fine doctor was not able to perform an autopsy, so we don't know for sure how she died. A flu bug seems to be going around. People suffer from extremely high fevers that cause them to become delusional, and that's what Doctor Richards and I believe happened to Mallory. She will be greatly missed. She was a lovely woman and an important part of our community. Let's take a moment of silence." Cecilia bowed her head, and the crowd did the same.

Cecilia lifted her head and looked around the room. Almost everyone still had their heads down. Cecilia made eye contact with a young girl. The little girl smiled at Cecilia. She recognized the little girl immediately. The girl's name escaped her, but she knew that little girl somehow. Those blond pigtails and sparkly blues eyes were unforgettable. And the little girl obviously knew Cecilia well. The little girl was sitting with a young couple at a table in the middle of the tavern. She was holding the woman's hand. Cecilia smiled back at the little girl.

Slowly people started to raise their heads and look at Cecilia. Almost every eye in that room had tears in it. The mood in the room was very somber. People had loved Mallory very much, and she was sorely missed by all. Cecilia wished she could remember Mallory; it was clear by the town's reaction she had been a wonderful lady. The town had lost two great townspeople over the last couple of days; it was going to take a while for people to come to terms with the loss. People would never fully get over it. It's one thing to lose people to natural causes, but to lose them the way Greg and Mallory had been lost was devastating.

Cecilia didn't know what else to say. She stood there just staring at the faces in the crowd. Everyone was waiting on her. Cecilia's heart started to race, and she felt nervous. She had never been nervous speaking to a crowd of people. The longer she stood there trying to figure out what to say next, the more nervous and anxious she became. She should have prepared a speech!

Doctor Richards could tell Cecilia was struggling with what to say next. He stood up and asked if he could have the floor. Cecilia quickly agreed and he watched as the nervousness drained from her body. Cecilia took a seat at the bar.

"Now, folks, Greg and Mallory were great people and even better neighbors. They will be tremendously missed by every one of us. I'm sure that young man we found was a good man as well and someone is missing him too. We need to mourn our fellow brothers and sister, but we also need to focus on the future. We will be holding services at a later date, but for now, let's move on with town business."

Doctor Richards paused and looked around the room. It didn't appear as though he had offended anyone with his comments. He honestly didn't give a shit if he had. He was tired and, frankly, over all of it. "I never got a chance to examine Greg's body, but the other two decomposed at an alarming rate. The rate of decomp should have been impossible. That is why we were not able to nail down a cause of death for Mallory. The young man died from being impaled in the side by a blunt object. It would have hurt like hell. But I don't need to dwell on such matters here. I mention that only to say this: if we lose anyone else, I need to examine their body immediately. I don't know much about this rapid decomp, but I believe it has to do with microscopic insects I found on the remains of both Mallory and the young man. I hope like hell we don't lose anyone else anytime soon, but if we do, I need to know right away. You all know where to find me."

The crowd nodded at him.

"I didn't mean to be so blunt about everything, but I don't know any other way to communicate what I need to. Are there any questions?" Quite a few hands went up around the room. "And don't ask me what those damn things in the woods were, because like the rest of you I have no idea." Most of the hands that had been raised lowered. "Denny, what's your question?" Doctor Richards asked Denny, who had kept his hand raised.

Denny stood up. "Do you think animals will decompose as rapidly as our Mallory and the young man did? I'm curious if this could affect our livestock and the butchering process."

"I can't say for certain," Doctor Richards began. "Three of Cecilia's pigs died, and they did decompose rapidly, to be completely honest—it looked as if the pigs' skin melted off. But those pigs had been in contact with the metal contraptions and ate some of that green ooze that was found around those things. I am no expert on any of this, but I am hoping that the pigs' rapid decomp was because they had had direct contact with those contraptions, the same as Mallory and the young man. I wish I had a better answer for you, Denny, but all I have right now are guesses. Same as everyone else in the room. Only way we'll know for sure is to butcher an animal and see what happens. Hopefully, our livestock hasn't been affected."

Denny thanked the doctor and sat back down. Mike had his hand raised, and Doctor Richards called on him. Mike stood up.

"This question is more for our mayor," Mike started. Cecilia got up and stood next to Doctor Richards. "What do we do now?" Mike asked her. "Where do we go from here?"

Cecilia looked at Marcus, then to Scarlett, as if to ask if she should tell the town about what she had agreed to with Marcus. Both

Scarlett and Marcus excitedly nodded at Cecilia to go ahead and tell everyone the news.

"Thank you for your question," Cecilia started, and Mike sat back down. "For now, we get back to business as usual around here. We've basically had this town shut down for two days now." The nerves were completely gone, and she felt like the confident leader she had been before all the madness of the past few days. She was excited to tell the townsfolk the news, but she knew a few of them probably wouldn't like it. "Again, I want to thank you all for your hard work in getting the debris cleaned up and buried. It was a lot of work. Now that we have that behind us, it's time to get our town humming again. We need to keep an eye on each other and our animals. I need to be informed of any abnormalities that occur going forward. I am happy we can put this chapter behind us, but we still don't know the full impact of it all." She paused and looked at Marcus. "Now I'd like to invite Sheriff Riley up here."

Marcus stood and joined Cecilia. Doctor Richards returned to his seat.

"I'm sure you all know the sheriff of Henderson, Marcus, here."

The room all nodded. They had all known Marcus well back in the Henderson days. Almost everyone in that room had begged him to leave Henderson with them. "Marcus came to me to share some news from Henderson and to offer me a new position."

Hushed murmurs floated through the tavern.

"I'm not going anywhere, folks," Cecilia said. "At least not on a permanent basis. Marcus informed Scarlett and I that John Henderson has died." The hushed murmurs turned into surprised whispers. No one in that tavern had liked John one bit; that disdain for him was why everyone was in that tavern at that time. The townsfolk were not saddened by the news, but they didn't celebrate it either. "Marcus also informed us that all of John's city officials have fallen ill and are not expected to recover. Losing their entire government has put Henderson in a tough spot. I have been asked to run Henderson as well as several other neighboring towns. I have accepted the position, and I am looking forward to the challenge."

The townsfolk all started to chatter among themselves. Cecilia stayed quiet for a moment to let the people digest what she had just told them. After a few moments, the room quieted, and people began to raise their hands. "I know there are a lot of questions right now," Cecilia continued, "but please wait until I'm finished here. I hope to answer a lot of those questions right now."

Everyone put their hands down and gave Cecilia their full attention.

"Logistically, it is going to take some time and a lot of energy to make this all happen. It most likely will not be a smooth transition, there's just so much that will go into making all of it happen. I am honored to have been asked, and I am looking forward to bringing all of our towns together into one society." Cecilia paused and looked around the room. She could see the looks of confusion and trepidation on the faces of the townsfolk.

"May I say something real quick, Madam Mayor?" Marcus asked her.

"Yes, of course, Sheriff," Cecilia said and stepped back so Marcus could have the room's attention.

"I just want to let you all know that I have spoken to the people of Henderson, and they all want to merge our towns. We have resources that you all do not and vice versa. This is going be a good thing for all of us. I am personally very excited about this. My Uncle John was an asshole, we all know that. I am going to be frank here, do I miss the man? Hell no. He ruined what was once a nice town. You all came from Henderson. We're all still friends and family. I am excited to get back to a fair and equal society with my friends and neighbors. We couldn't think of anyone better suited to lead all of us than Mayor Rodgers. Getting everything ironed out will be a lot of work for us, but you all can just go about your daily business and reap the benefits of this adventure. Thank you all." Marcus looked around the room. Everyone looked a bit relieved. He turned to Cecilia and nodded at her. He stepped back and gave Cecilia the floor again.

"Thank you, Sheriff," Cecilia said. She turned to the crowd of people. They all looked happy and content but also still a bit confused. "I know we have just hit you all with some big and unexpected news. I will be honest—I was seriously considering turning it down so I could continue to focus one hundred percent of my attention on our great little town. Scarlett brought up a good point that led me to my final decision to indeed accept this new responsibility. She pointed out that as we and the surrounding towns grow, we will all need more land and resources. That need could, and most likely would, lead to altercations between towns. If we are all one united nation, there would be no need to fight over land and resources—we would all already share it. I gave myself plenty of time to think about this, and I am convinced this is the best thing for all of us. For every single town in our little corner of the world. This will give us the opportunity to grow and eventually become a great society. A society of acceptance and inclusion. A nation of people who are united for the greater good."

She paused and looked around the room. The little blond girl was still smiling at her. The little girl sat in a chair next to her mother, swinging her feet in the air. "Take this young girl here," Cecilia said, pointing to the blond girl. "We now have the opportunity and the resources to make sure she, and all of our children, grow up in a community without violence and animosity. To grow up in a world where everyone works together and looks after each other. Where everyone is equal. I keep saying equal because that matters a lot to me. I remember a time where people boasted about being equal, but no one really was. I remember a time where status and riches mattered more than character. I remember a time when someone would be denied basic human rights for the color of their skin or whom they loved. I don't ever want to be a part of a society like that again. I don't want our children growing up with hate in their lives. I don't want to see anyone discriminated against because they are somehow different than others. I don't ever want to see a man like John get the kind of power he took again. We can raise our children in a society where that mindset and behavior has been eradicated."

The feel of the room was becoming electric. Cecilia could feel the excitement and joy the townsfolk were beginning to experience. She knew she had made the right decision and they were going to build the best society imaginable. "We can all unite and live happy, healthy, and fulfilling lives, together as one nation!" The crowd erupted in applause. Everyone was whooping and hollering. Cecilia smiled at the crowd. Everyone stood and gave her a standing ovation.

Cecilia's gut reaction to Marcus's request had been to say no. She was now glad she hadn't. Looking at that tavern full of her townspeople clapping and cheering made her happy. Cecilia felt happy and excited for the first time in days. She knew without a doubt she could lead a thriving community no matter how large it was. She was proud and honored to be these people's leader. She would spend the rest of her life working her butt off for her people.

The crowd settled down, and everyone took their seats again.

"I am putting Scarlett in charge of our town here while I'm away working with the other towns. I have decided to officially appoint her mayor." The crowd erupted into applause again. Scarlett stood up and smiled at everyone. "I will call myself the governor, and I will appoint strong leaders to be mayors of each town. We will get this new, united community up and running, and then in the future, we will hold elections to elect mayors and town officials. But for now, we need to incorporate several towns into one nation, and that will take a lot of hard work. I will be going to Henderson with Marcus when he returns and start there." She paused and looked around the room. "Any questions?"

Everyone in the room shook their heads. She knew a lot of questions and concerns would arise over time, but for now, she could tell the townsfolk were excited by what they had heard. "We will always be outright and honest with everything we do from here on out. Thank you all for your time and diligence over the past few days. You are all greatly appreciated! Now let's have some drinks and enjoy the rest of this beautiful day!"

The crowd jumped to their feet and applauded. People were shaking each other's hands and excitedly patting each other on the back. The tavern was abuzz with excitement. Drinks started flowing and the chatter got louder. For the first time in days, everyone was relaxed and enjoying themselves. They all had the feeling that everything was going to be okay again. Life would get back to normal. It was a great feeling. The entire town celebrated that overwhelming feeling of relief and optimism well into the evening.

Cecilia went to Scarlett, and they hugged. They were both very excited and happy about how the town hall meeting had turned out. As they stood there and chatted about the day, they were interrupted by Amanda's friend Leah.

"Where's Amanda?" Leah asked, looking around the tavern.

"We thought she was with you," Scarlett answered, quickly growing concerned. Scarlett and Cecilia scanned the room, looking for Amanda. They knew if she wasn't with Leah, she wouldn't be anywhere in that tavern.

"I haven't seen her in a couple of days," Leah said. "I'm really worried. You know we do lunch every day. I didn't think much about it the first day she didn't show up because of those things in the woods. I assumed she was busy helping you guys. But when she didn't come by yesterday or today, I knew something was wrong. Has anyone seen her lately?"

"Yeah, Doctor Richards and Kevin both saw her yesterday. She was at the cemetery," Cecilia said. "Let's find Kevin and ask him if she said anything." Cecilia and Scarlett looked around the tavern for Kevin. Cecilia hoped Scarlett would find him because she couldn't remember what he looked like.

"Why was she at the cemetery?" Leah asked.

"She was paying her respects for the young man we found in the woods. She thinks she knows him, and from what the doctor said, she was terribly upset by all of it," Cecilia replied.

"There he is," Scarlett said, pointing to the bar. Kevin was standing at the bar chatting with Doctor Richards. They all headed over to the two men.

"Excuse me, Kevin," Scarlett began. "Have you seen Amanda back at the cemetery since yesterday?"

"No, ma'am," Kevin replied. "I am surprised I haven't, though. She was so upset yesterday. I thought for sure I'd see her out at the young man's grave again today."

"Did she say anything to you about the young man?" Cecilia asked. "Doctor Richards told me she was convinced she had known the man."

"That's what he and I were just talking about," Kevin replied. "All she said to me was that his name was Pete, and his family is long gone."

Everyone was quiet for moment. Then Scarlett turned to Leah and asked, "Did she ever mention a Pete to you?"

"No, never," Leah replied. "And if she had been interested in someone, she would have definitely said something to me about it. We talk about that sort of stuff often."

"What sort of stuff?" Cecilia asked. She knew she should have known Amanda better, but with her memory loss and the confusion of the past several days, Amanda seemed like a complete stranger to her. She wanted to try to understand the woman better; it would probably help them to find her.

"We talked about men a lot. We are both at the age where we are ready to settle down, get married, and start families. The thing is, there isn't really any suitable guys around here, so if she had met someone that she was into, I would have known right away," Leah replied. "This isn't like Amanda at all."

"It certainly is not," Scarlett said.

"Has she ever said anything about having a spot she goes to when she's upset?" Cecilia asked Leah.

"No, not really. I know she likes to go on hikes in the woods when she's frustrated or upset." Leah paused and looked at Scarlett. "She'll do that when she's mad at Gwen."

"Those two do get into a lot," Scarlett said, shaking her head.

"I know, I hear about it every time," Leah said. "I've invited her to move in with me and my sister, but she said she didn't want to abandon you two."

"Has she ever told you where she hikes?" Cecilia asked, completely ignoring Leah's last statement.

"She just heads into the woods behind your place. There's a trail that snakes through the woods behind Mr. Abrams's place, and eventually, the trail comes out near my place. She'll make that hike and then come over for lunch and talk about whatever had upset her that day," Leah said.

"Mike Abrams's place, right?" Cecilia asked.

"Yea, Mr. and Mrs. Abrams are my neighbors. Amanda and I have hiked that trail a lot—it's a beautiful hike. And the Abramses don't mind us walking behind their place."

"What if she went out to hike those woods and got hurt?" Cecilia said. "We need to go search those woods for her now!"

"We'll come with you guys," Doctor Richards said. Kevin nodded in agreement. "That way we can split up and cover more area."

"Thank you, gentlemen," Cecilia said. "Take us to that trail," Cecilia said to Leah.

"I'll get Hope and Gwen to come with us," Scarlett said.

"Perfect, let's do this," Cecilia said.

"I hope she's okay," Leah said softly.

"I hope so too, dear," Scarlett said.

They all headed for the woods. Gwen gave her mom a bit of attitude about having to go look for Amanda; she wanted to stay at the tavern and chat with people. Gwen figured Amanda was fine and was just having one of her episodes, and honestly, she didn't want to be around Amanda when they found her. Scarlett told Gwen it wasn't up for debate. One of their own was missing, and they were all going to go look for her. Scarlett told her daughter that if she was the one missing, she'd want everyone looking for her.

Leah took everyone to the trail behind her place. Scarlett told her to stay put in case Amanda showed up there. The rest of the group split up. Scarlett and Cecilia followed the trail back to their cabin, Gwen and Hope went into the woods behind Mike's place, and Kevin and Doctor Richards headed off behind Malcolm's place.

"Why does Amanda always get so much attention?" Gwen complained.

"She's been missing for like a day now," Hope said. "Maybe she's hurt—we should be looking for her."

"She ain't hurt!" Gwen snapped. "She's having one of her pity party episodes. She's so dramatic!"

"She's not that bad, Gwen," Hope said softly. She didn't want to upset her friend anymore, but she didn't like it when Gwen complained about Amanda. All it did was lead to more animosity toward Amanda.

"Are you guys like besties now or sumthin'?" Gwen asked with a tone of jealousy.

"No, I just don't think Amanda is as annoying as you do. She's always been cool to me."

"She's a tattletale! She's always running to my mom and telling on me for shit. Usually made-up shit!" Gwen's annoyance was turning to anger.

"You guys need to work it out. It's kinda annoying to the rest of us when you guys are fighting all the time," Hope said. Hope loved Gwen like a sister, but she could be so petty and rude, especially when it came to Amanda. Gwen seemed too hyper focused on anything Amanda did or said, and every little thing made her mad.

"I'll do that!" Gwen exclaimed. "Whenever she decides to come back, I'm just gonna ignore her."

Hope chuckled and rolled her eyes at that last statement.

"*What?*" Gwen snarled.

"There's no way you'll ignore her. She gets on your nerves too much. I think you enjoy—"

The girls both stopped dead in their tracks. Shock and fear engulfed them. Lying right in front them, under a large pine tree, was Amanda. She looked peaceful. Her eyes were closed, and she had a smile on her face. For a split second, Hope and Gwen thought she may have been sleeping, but they quickly realized she was dead. The girls panicked and ran back toward their cabin to try to find Cecilia and Scarlett. They were bawling and out of breath. They were a mess.

Scarlett and Cecilia were searching the woods back behind their cabin, shouting Amanda's name as they wandered around. Hope and Gwen heard them shouting and ran to their voices. The girls were hysterical by the time they found Cecilia and Scarlett. The women knew instantly that the girls had found Amanda and that what they had found was the worst possible scenario. They didn't even ask the girls any questions; they just told the girls to take them to what they had found. Gwen refused to go back. Hope didn't want to go back either—she didn't want to see Amanda like that again—but she took Scarlett and Cecilia to the tree anyway. Gwen crumpled to the ground and bawled. She felt sick to her stomach. Her head was spinning, and her face was covered in tears.

Hope led Cecilia and Scarlett close to the tree and then pointed them the rest of the way. She just couldn't let herself see the body again. She already knew she would never get that image out of her head. She certainly didn't need to see it again.

Cecilia and Scarlett stood under the tree in shock. The same tree they had found the young man's body under. That struck Cecilia as an extremely odd coincidence. They had never even considered they may find Amanda dead. Utter sadness and confusion washed over them. Amanda looked so peaceful, even happy. Her hair was messy and had pine needles in it. Her face still had a little pink to it from the cold air. Her clothes were all intact. It looked as if she had just fallen asleep there and never woke up. They had to stare at her for several minutes before they even realized she was indeed gone. Scarlett began to cry and fell to her knees. Cecilia put a hand on Scarlett's shoulder. Cecilia squeezed Scarlett's shoulder before turning away from Amanda. She walked over to Hope and told her to head toward Malcolm's place and find Doctor Richards. Hope did as she was asked. Cecilia went back to Scarlett. She was still crying but had stood up again.

"What do we do now?" Scarlett sobbed.

"I told Hope to go get the doctor. I don't know what else we can do at this point." Cecilia was heartbroken, but she knew they had to carry on the best they could. Losing such a young woman was devastating and would have a lasting impact on the entire town. She had already decided to put off her trip to Henderson.

Doctor Richards and Kevin came running up to them. Doctor Richards stopped and gave Cecilia a look. It was a "We've been here before" look. He didn't want to panic anyone any further, so he collected himself before saying anything.

"Oh my." Doctor Richards sighed. "What in the hell is going on around here?"

"I don't know, but we don't need any more of this," Cecilia said.

"No, ma'am, we do not," Doctor Richards responded. "Kevin, go ask Mike if we can use his hay trolley. We need to get Amanda to my office." Kevin nodded and headed to Mike's place. Doctor Richards went to Amanda and knelt next to her. She was very cold to the touch, but he couldn't determine how long she had been dead. "I'm worried it'll happen again before I can examine her. I can't tell how long she's been gone."

"Let's hope that's not the case this time. We need answers," Cecilia said. "Can you and Kevin handle this, Doctor?"

"Yes, Ma'am." Doctor Richards replied.

"Thank you. We have some very upset girls that need our attention. We will be at our place if you need us or find anything out."

"Sounds fine, ma'am. I will be in touch."

"Thank you again, Doctor."

"You are welcome, and hopefully, this is the last time we have this sort of conversation in a very long time."

"Let's hope," Cecilia said. She took Scarlett's hand, and they headed back toward their place.

Kevin returned with the trolley. The two men loaded Amanda onto the trolley and wheeled her to Doctor Richards's office. After Kevin helped Doctor Richards get Amanda onto the autopsy table, Doctor Richards told Kevin to go to the cemetery and prepare a burial plot. He told Kevin to make sure it was next to the young man's grave. Kevin agreed and took off.

Doctor Richards quickly prepared Amanda's body for autopsy. He wanted to examine her before she decomposed. Her skin was firm, and he could tell rigor mortis had already begun to set in. That was a good sign to him; maybe she wouldn't decompose as rapidly as Mallory and the young man had. He began the autopsy. Her organs were all intact and looked very healthy. He had to work hard to break through her ribcage. Her bones were not at all brittle. Mallory and the young man's bones had crumbled in his hands. He took a section of bone and flesh to his microscope. Both looked normal for a woman in her age. He didn't see any of the bugs that had been feasting on the other two bodies. Doctor Richards sighed in relief and continued with the autopsy. Everything seemed to be perfectly normal and healthy. He had no clinical idea of what had killed the young woman. It was as if she had just fallen asleep and never woke up.

Doctor Richards cleaned himself up and got a drink. He went out front and lit a cigar. He stood in front of his office and puffed on the cigar as he watched townsfolk mill about. Everyone was in high spirits, going from shop to shop. Mingling with one another. Smiling and laughing with their fellow townspeople, all completely oblivious to what had just been found under that pine tree. He hoped word of Amanda's death wouldn't get around too soon. The town needed a little break from bad news and death. Besides, he really wanted to find a cause for her death before he had to tell people about it. A healthy woman Amanda's age dying suddenly for no apparent reason was big news—and frightening.

As Doctor Richards was scanning the crowds of happy people, he noticed Cecilia walking toward him from the direction of her place. He took a few more puffs off his cigar and then put it out.

"Hello, Cecilia," he said when she got to him.

"Hello, Doctor," Cecilia responded. Neither of them were very upbeat. "Any news on Amanda?"

"Well, she didn't decompose like Mallory and the young man—maybe I should just call him Pete—so that's at least good news," Doctor Richards said. "Come inside with me."

"That is good news, I guess," Cecilia said, following Doctor Richards inside the office.

"I cannot see any obvious cause of death," he began, leading them into his office. He refreshed his drink and poured one for Cecilia. "All of her organs—her heart, her brain, skin, muscles, bone—all normal. She was an extremely healthy young woman."

"We all knew she was a healthy young woman," Cecilia responded, taking a sip of her drink. The liquor burned her throat going down but really hit the spot. "Do you have any guesses to how she may have died?"

"The only things I could come up with so far are maybe she came down with that flu bug or she was so upset and distraught. I'm leaning more toward the flu because I should have been able to see stress to the heart if she had died from stress and anxiety. I've never seen it myself, but I have read that a panic attack or someone who is overly stressed can die from it, but it usually looks like a heart attack after. I didn't find any stress to the heart, but that doesn't necessarily mean she didn't die from being too distressed and anxious. I've seen it referred to as dying of a broken heart. Your heart obviously can't physically break, but stress and trauma can cause someone to die."

"The flu sounds most reasonable to me. She had been around Hope and Gwen right before they got sick. It's probably the same thing that happened with Mallory—she fell so ill that she was delusional and succumbed to the elements and her illness."

"I am going to examine her one more time, just to be certain I didn't miss anything. If I don't find anything the second time, I will most likely officially state her cause of death as flu related. It's the only plausible answer at this point." He sipped his drink and sat forward in his chair. Even though they were alone, he lowered his voice and said, "How strange was it that she was under that tree?"

Cecilia sat forward in her chair. "So strange. I couldn't believe it at first. Shit, I still can't really believe it. But you know what, so many strange things have been going on that nothing surprises me anymore. I just hope we don't have any more people die on us. This town can't take much more of this."

"I agree. I think we should keep this to ourselves for a day or so. Let these good people enjoy their day. Everyone is in such good spirits since the town hall. I just really don't want to bring everyone back down so soon."

"I couldn't agree more, Doctor."

"I still have a lot to do with her remains. I had Kevin go ahead and prepare a grave for her just in case she decomposed as rapidly as the others had. I say we hold a service for all four of them in a couple of days. And hopefully we can finally move on as a town and get past the nightmare of these past few days. Maybe having some form of closure like a service will help people to get over all of it. You know, give them a chance to pay their respects and mourn our fallen friends."

"Yes, I think that would be a good idea. I have already told Scarlett and the girls to keep quiet about Amanda. My only concern is her friend, Leah. She will be asking a lot of questions. I think I will have to tell her. I don't want her out in the woods looking for Amanda. We can't risk losing her too." Cecilia finished her drink and stood up.

"I think you should tell her. Leah's a good kid. She will respect our wishes to keep it quiet," Doctor Richards said as he stood up.

"I will go talk with her now. Thank you, Doctor. Please keep me updated," Cecilia said as she walked to the front door.

"You are welcome, and I certainly will be in touch often. Bye for now."

"Goodbye," Cecilia said and left the office.

Cecilia went to Leah's place. She delicately broke the news to Leah. Leah burst into tears. She had feared that Amanda wouldn't be found well. She knew her friend, and it wasn't like Amanda to just disappear. Cecilia tried to comfort her. She invited Leah to come stay with them, and Leah accepted. Cecilia gave Leah some time to compose herself and gather some clothes and personal belongings. This was all so overwhelming. The stress and sadness of everything had really weighed on Cecilia. The last several days had been a roller-coaster of emotions. She just wanted it to all be over. She hoped like hell Amanda's death would be the last devastating thing to happen to her town. She didn't know what she would do if anyone else died.

Cecilia and Leah got to the cabin. When the girls saw Leah, they rushed to her and hugged her. The three of them stood in the dining room, crying and holding each other. Gwen hadn't gotten along well with Amanda, but she had always liked Leah. She often wondered why Leah was such good friends with Amanda but never let that influence how she felt about Leah. Hope had always gotten along well with Leah. Scarlett was glad Cecilia had brought Leah home with her. She knew it would be good for all of the girls to be together. And she knew it'd be easier to keep Amanda's death quiet if everyone who knew about it was together. All they had to do next was tell Dana and Julia when they got home. They would also take it awfully hard; they had been very close to Amanda.

Cecilia asked Scarlett to step outside for a moment. She told Scarlett what Doctor Richards had said.

"I just knew he wouldn't find anything," Scarlett said, shaking her head. "Amanda was too happy and healthy to pass away from natural causes. I'm terribly saddened and angry about it, but a part of me is relieved that Gwen and Hope got over their flu without any complications. I don't know what I would've done if it had been one of them. Don't get me wrong—I loved Amanda dearly and I'm heartbroken by this, but those are my girls."

"No need to explain, I totally understand. Anyone dying so young is a tragedy, but if it had been one of your girls, it would have been even more devastating. I loved Amanda too, and she will be greatly missed. But we can honor her death by moving on and creating a society that she would have been proud of. I don't want it to seem like I'm brushing all of this aside, but I do need to get to work on this merger with the other towns."

"I don't feel like you're brushing anything aside. Death is toughest on the living. Amanda is gone and, as you said, will be dearly missed, but we do have to keep living and working. Our world can't stop just because we lost someone so dear to us. Amanda would want us to carry on." Tears rolled down Scarlett's cheeks as she spoke. "I loved that young lady."

"Me too," Cecilia said. "She was a great young woman. It pisses me off that her life was cut so short. I hope if there is a life after this one, she is happy. I hope she has moved on to a better place."

"I believe there is life after this one. I believe we get to live in peace and harmony in the afterlife. I believe Amanda is happy wherever she is now," Scarlett said. She looked down the path to town and cried. She cried for Amanda and Mallory. She cried for Greg and the young man. She cried for all that the town had been through. She looked back to Cecilia and saw that she was crying as well. She couldn't remember a time she had seen Cecilia cry like that.

"I hope so," Cecilia sobbed. "It's nice to think this life isn't all we get? I like the idea that once we die, we don't just rot in the ground. I like the idea of moving on to a better place."

"I have to believe this isn't it," Scarlett cried. "I just have to."

Cecilia went to Scarlett and put an arm around her. Scarlett put her arm around Cecilia. They stood there looking down toward town and cried. The pain and stress of the last day flooded out in those tears. Their love for Amanda and the heartbreak of finding her dead cascaded down their cheeks. They sobbed and held each other.

They stayed outside for quite a while. They were in no rush to get inside or get back to real life. They needed that break. They needed to just cry. The next several days, weeks, probably even months were going to be a whirlwind of travel and work. They would need to plan Amanda's funeral, but that could wait until the next day. They would need to coordinate with the other towns, but that too could wait. At that moment in the fading light of dusk, they just needed to cry. That was it, just let themselves have emotions. If they didn't, they'd probably go insane.

Cecilia woke up the next morning to the sounds of chatter and cooking coming from the kitchen. She could tell by the voices that everyone in the house was up and in the kitchen. The voices sounded chipper and jovial. Cecilia was happy to hear them all sounding so relaxed. She knew everyone was still reeling from the news of Amanda's death, but it was good to hear them out there enjoying each other's company. Cecilia got up and dressed. She sat down at her small desk and began writing out a speech to the people of Henderson. Marcus had headed back to Henderson without her the day before. He was going to send for her in a few days. The people of Henderson were desperately in need of leadership, but Marcus had assured Cecilia that the townspeople would understand the circumstances she was dealing with and would be able to wait on her. Cecilia wanted to hold a service for all three of the recently lost townsfolk and the young man. She hoped having a funeral would give the rest of the town some sort of closure and they could all move on. Doctor Richards had told Cecilia he would have Kevin preside over the services so she wouldn't have to. She was relieved to not have to deliver a funeral service. She felt like she needed to distance herself from that.

Cecilia was struggling with her speech. She knew she would have to address everything that had happened in their town, but she didn't want to go into too much detail. None of it was of much concern to Henderson. Cecilia wanted to focus solely on her plans for the mergers and her plans for the future. She got up from her desk and headed out to the kitchen to get a cup of tea. Everyone said good morning to her, and she responded with good mornings back to them all. They all really did seem to be in good spirits. That had surprised Cecilia. They had all been so upset the night before. None of them even talked; everyone had just cried. Now they all seemed so happy, almost like nothing had happened.

"You all seem to be in a good mood this morning," Cecilia said as she made a cup of tea.

"We are," Scarlett began. "We all talked about it this morning, and we figured Amanda wouldn't want us to mope around for days on end." The rest of the house mates all nodded in agreeance. "We aren't going to forget her ever—she was a huge part of all of our lives. She was loved by us all. We just know she would want us to celebrate her life, not mourn her death." The mood of the room got a bit sadder at the word *death*. "She would want us to be happy and to live our lives."

"I believe you are right—she wouldn't want us to mope around about it. We can still miss her dearly, but she would have wanted us to move on," Cecilia said.

"Breakfast is just about ready," Scarlett said. "Will you be joining us?" she asked Cecilia.

"No, I am not hungry. I am going back to my room to work on my speech for Henderson. Thank you though. You all enjoy." Cecilia headed back to her room.

Despite everyone acting so happy, there was a heaviness to the cabin. Amanda's presence was sorely missed. The vibe in the house was a good one, but everyone felt as though a part of them was missing. No one talked about Amanda. No one told stories or shared fond memories. They would eventually end up doing that, but that morning wasn't the time or place. The wound was still too fresh.

Scarlett served breakfast and then excused herself. She told the young women that she was going for a walk. She really needed to clear her head. The last few days had been a whirlwind of stress, anger, and utter sadness. Scarlett had not had a single moment to herself in a long time. She *needed* to be alone for a little bit.

Scarlett went behind the cabin and headed for the trail. The morning air was cool, but it felt great to be outside and alone. She walked and let her mind wander. As she passed behind Malcolm's place, she saw him outside tending to his garden. She waved at him and hoped he wouldn't try to engage her. Scarlett thought very highly of Malcolm and liked him quite a bit, but she didn't want to chat at that moment. She had always loved their conversations, but she knew if they talked that morning, the conversation would revolve around everything that had been going on. Scarlett just wanted to be alone and try to forget about all of the madness for a few minutes. Malcolm did call out to her and started walking toward her. She felt a bit of dread as he approached. It had made her feel bad that she dreaded an interaction with him, but she really didn't want to talk to anyone right then.

"Good morning, Scarlett!" Malcolm exclaimed as he got close to her.

"Good morning," she replied.

"How are you doing?" he asked. "How's the family?"

Ugh, small talk, Scarlett thought to herself. She had put on a brave face and acted happy for her house mates and her daughters, but she was actually still terribly upset. She certainly was not in the mood for small talk that morning, even if it was with Malcolm. But she didn't want to be rude to him either. She hoped they would have a quick neighborly exchange and she could get on her way.

"Despite everything, we are all doing well," Scarlett answered. "How are you and Bethany? Is she feeling any better?"

"We are good, and yes, she is feeling much better. Thank you for asking. She's still acting a bit strange—you know, out of character—and her memory hasn't come back yet."

"Well, I'm glad you're both well. I'm sorry to hear she hasn't regained any memory yet, but Cecilia hasn't either. I'm still hopeful that in due time they will," Scarlett said. She shuffled her feet to hint that she wanted to get moving again.

"I hope so too. Between you and me, I'm damn tired of hearing about that Las Vegas place she's now always talking about. She said people just called it Vegas. Apparently, it's some kind of party town. People would come from all over the world to gamble and party there. I don't know how people from all over the world would get to one location just to party, but I don't ask questions when she talks about it. I don't want to encourage it."

"That's probably a good idea," Scarlett said.

"Does Cecilia talk about random, made-up places like that?" Malcolm answered.

"No, she hasn't actually talked about anything out of the ordinary since that one morning after the lightning storm. I think she's just been far too busy with everything that has been going on. And like you, I don't ask questions," Scarlett replied.

"I wish Bethany had some things to distract her. She just works herself into a little frenzy over all of it. She's so confused about how we got here. She keeps saying the last thing she remembers is leaving Vegas in a truck and then being on a ship. She says she has no idea how we ended up in the eighteen hundreds, whatever the hell that means. She's really worrying me, Scarlett."

"I am worried about her too. You should have her talk to Doctor Richards. Maybe the pregnancy is affecting her psyche," Scarlett said. "What's a truck?"

"Shit, I don't know. I didn't ask her either," Malcolm replied. Scarlett could tell he was stressed out by all of it. "I think talking with Doctor Richards is a great idea. I will have her get in touch with him. Thank you, Scarlett."

"You are welcome. I am going to excuse myself and continue my walk. It was nice to see you, Malcolm."

"It's always nice to see you. Enjoy your walk, and I hope you have a good day."

"Thank you, and I hope you have a good day as well. I hope Bethany can get some help from Doctor Richards. Keep me posted," Scarlett said and began to walk again.

"Thank you and I will. See you later," Malcolm said.

"See you later," Scarlett said with a wave and headed down the trail again.

Scarlett was really worried about Bethany. Cecilia had mentioned some really weird things that morning after the storm but hadn't said anything since. The fact that Bethany was still going on about it was quite worrisome. She hoped it was just related to the pregnancy. Scarlett knew personally that pregnancy hormones could really affect a woman's psyche; she had experienced it. She had faith that Doctor Richards would be able to help. He was a great doctor.

It began to rain, and Scarlett turned around toward home. The cold rain hit her exposed face like tiny needle pricks. She picked up her pace a bit. She had wanted to take a longer walk, but that rain was too much; it was really starting to come down. The gloomy, rainy weather made her even more depressed. Scarlett missed how things had been just a few days before. Hell, she even missed Gwen and Amanda fighting all the time. It had annoyed her, but she knew it all came from a deep love for each other. Gwen and Amanda had just been too much alike, so every little thing one of them did or said annoyed the other. Scarlett wished she could hear them bicker just one more time. She wished she could give Amanda one more hug. Scarlett began to cry. She stopped under a tree and let the tears flow. She didn't want to go back to the cabin crying. She knew that would have set off a chain reaction of tears.

Death was natural—no one lived forever—but it was always so hard. She never thought she would lose one of the girls. She had always believed they'd all outlive her. She had heard from folks who had lost children that it was the toughest thing you would ever have to go through. Losing an elderly loved one whom you know is close to dying is difficult enough, but to lose someone so young and so suddenly was almost beyond comprehension. Scarlett knew life would go on and they all would eventually get back to normal—their new normal at least. But she would never fully get over losing Amanda like that. And the worst part, not knowing how or why she died so young. And finding her out in the woods like that, under *that* tree. The events of the past few days had all been so crazy and unnatural that she shouldn't have been surprised by anything. But

Amanda wandering off and dying alone in the woods under the same tree they had found the young man had been shocking. It was all too much. Just too damn much.

The woods were dead quiet except for the sound of rain. The wind had picked up. Scarlett huddled closer to the tree to try to stay somewhat dry under the branches and leaves. The wind whipped past her. She thought she heard a voice on the wind. No, that couldn't have been possible. It was just her imagination. Her emotions were getting the best of her.

"Stop crying for me. I am happy and at peace. I am with the love of my life."

Nope, she didn't hear that, no way; it was her emotional brain playing tricks on her.

"Please, Scarlett, stop crying for me. This was my decision, and I'm happy now. I love you."

The air had gone freezing cold around her. She began to shiver. The tears rolled down her cheeks and soaked the collar of her coat. Scarlett wiped her face with the back of her hand. She took several deep breaths to try and calm herself. She refused to let herself think that she had heard a voice in the wind.

"It's real, Scarlett. It's really me. I wanted to tell you I'm okay and you don't need to cry for me anymore."

Scarlett began to sob. She couldn't control her emotions. Everything else seemed to have vanished. It felt like it was just her, that tree, the rain, and the wind. And Amanda. No, it couldn't be Amanda; it was her imagination. The lack of a good night's sleep and the stresses and overwhelming emotions had made her go a bit mad. She had heard of people becoming delusional from lack of sleep and a lot of stress. She had even heard those things could kill a person. Scarlett was not going to let herself believe that Amanda was somehow communicating with her from beyond the grave. No way in hell. It wasn't possible.

"It is possible. I don't have much energy left. I must go now. I love you. You were like a mom to me. Goodbye, Scarlett, I will miss you. But I am happy and at peace."

Nope, didn't hear that either. The coldness left her. The wind went away. Scarlett walked away from the tree. The rain had died down a bit. She wasn't ready to go home yet. She still didn't want everyone to see her so upset. Scarlett changed course and headed for town. She was going to go talk to Doctor Richards. Maybe he could help her cope with her feelings. Maybe he could prescribe something to help her sleep better so she wouldn't get delusional again. Maybe just talking to someone outside her house would help.

After a couple of hours of writing, Cecilia had finished her speech. She was incredibly happy with what she had come up with and she planned to use that same speech to address all of the towns. Cecilia had been vague but forthcoming in regard to the events that had rocked her little town. Her main focus in the speech was to address the future of all six towns. She tried to hammer home that a merger would be beneficial to all. Cecilia wanted people to walk away from her speech feeling confident and validated. She wanted people to know she wasn't going to rule over them; she wanted to assure them they all had a voice in the governing of the newly united towns. Cecilia wanted to make sure they all understood that the old ways of doing things would be gone forever. She wanted to enter a stage of government that was inclusive and equal. Cecilia knew that kind of governing would lead to disagreements and arguments amongst people, so she wanted to be clear in her speech that that was normal and a good thing. Peaceful disagreements made for a better society. She wanted to make it clear that any violence would be met with swift and strict punishment. No one person was greater than another. This was going to be a great society, and all would thrive, but everyone would have to work together. Cecilia believed her speech would fire people up. She hoped it would show people that they could all work—and live—in harmony without being ruled by a tyrant.

Cecilia was excited to get the ball rolling. She knew she had to wait at least a day, probably two. They had to hold the services for the four people who had died, and as the town's first and only mayor, she had to be present for the funerals. It wasn't that she didn't want to be there for them; she just wanted to get moving on the next chapter of her life-and the town's life. There would always be bumps in the road. She was just overly anxious to get going because she knew it was going to be a long process, and it wasn't going to be an easy one. Cecilia hoped she wouldn't be met with much pushback. It sounded like all the towns were already on board for the merger, but she knew from personal experience that there would be a few folks who didn't want to go along with it. That's where she hoped her speech would ease their trepidation.

Cecilia got up from her desk and headed out to the kitchen. The house was empty. Dana and Julia had gone to work at the general store, and Cecilia could see Hope and Gwen out back, tending to the animals. She assumed Scarlett had gone into the office in town, and Leah had probably headed home. Cecilia made herself a bit of food and a fresh cup of tea. She headed back to her room with her lunch and tea to read over her speech one last time.

Life seemed like it was already beginning to return to normal. The only thing missing was Amanda cleaning the cabin. Cecilia wasn't concerned about the cleaning; it just reminded her again that Amanda was gone. The older women were at work, and the teens were out back doing their chores, and it really hit home that one of their own was gone forever. Cecilia sat back in her chair and took a moment of silence for Amanda. She had never been as close to Amanda as Scarlett had been, but she had still deeply cared for Amanda; she had been a wonderful young woman. Sadness and confusion were a normal part of losing someone so suddenly, but it wouldn't bring them back. Cecilia knew that she could honor and remember Amanda but that she would have to do so while she moved on. Amanda wouldn't have wanted any of them to stop living their lives just because she had left them. Amanda was the type of person who would have wanted to be celebrated, not mourned. And that's exactly what Cecilia planned to do. Henderson needed a new name, and Cecilia was going to pitch the name Jamison, Amanda's last name, in honor of the young woman. What better way to let Amanda's legacy live on forever? Cecilia was confident the people of Henderson would be totally on board with that idea.

Cecilia was happy with her speech and proud of her idea to rename Henderson in honor of Amanda. She got up from her desk and changed clothes. She had decided to go meet with Kevin to plan the services. The sooner they held the funerals, the sooner they could all get back to normal day-to-day life. And the sooner she could move forward with merging the towns.

*****

Scarlett sat across from Doctor Richards in his office. She was in tears and was having difficulty explaining to the doctor what had just happened to her. She knew it was just her overly tired and over-worked brain playing tricks on her. It was her mind's way of trying to give her closure.

"It seemed so real," Scarlett sobbed.

"I'm sure it did," Doctor Richards replied. "Our mind is a pow-erful tool, way more powerful than we even know. Our brains have a way of playing tricks on us."

"That's what I assumed, but I'm telling you it just felt real. I heard her voice," Scarlett said, wiping tears from her face as more tears escaped her tired eyes.

"I'm sure it sounded like her voice, but you've heard her voice daily for years. It was your brain's way of making it seem more real to you. It was just a memory of her voice," Doctor Richards said. "Amanda was like a daughter to you—we all knew that—so it is no surprise that this is so hard on you. It's normal, in fact. It should be hard on you—you loved her dearly."

"It is so hard," Scarlett cried. "I have been trying to be strong, you know, for the girls especially, but it's just so damn hard to be strong. I am always the one who has to be strong. I am always the one comforting everyone else in that damn house. I'm the one that puts out the fires. I'm the one who soothes everyone else. I am the one that cleans up all of the fucking messes they get themselves into. No one is ever there to help me through a tough time. No one is ever there to give me a fucking break! I am responsible for every damn thing in that household, and I am the one responsible for most of the town too." Scarlett paused and caught her breath. "I just want a damn break, Doctor."

"You deserve a break, and you should take one. There is no crime in taking some personal time. You had the right idea this morning when you set out for a walk. It sounds like you didn't get much of a chance to decompress before Malcolm laid his stresses on you. No dig to Malcolm—he was just confiding in a friend and had no idea what you were going through. I think you should make taking walks a daily thing. Just you. Don't think about what's going on that day, just walk. Try to keep your mind clear and just be a part of the natural world. It is an incredibly freeing thing to do. I can tell you are beyond overwhelmed, and that would explain what happened out there today. I think if you keep taking walks and clearing your head, you will not have any other episodes like today."

"Thank you, Doctor," Scarlett said. She still had tears in her eyes, but the sobbing had stopped. She felt better. She knew it was her mind playing tricks on her, but it made her feel better to have Doctor Richards confirm that. Of course, it was just her mind's way of coping. What else could it have been? It certainly wasn't actually Amanda's spirit talking to her. "I appreciate you taking the time to talk with me, and I'm sorry I am such a mess."

"You are welcome, Scarlett. And never apologize for being human and having emotions. You are allowed to feel pain too. You don't always have to be the savior."

That made Scarlett cry harder again. She knew he was right, but she also knew her position in life at that moment in time would never allow her to be anything but everyone else's problem solver. Scarlett knew she would eventually get past this episode and would go back to being there for everyone else. She also knew that no one would be there for her again. She was solidly cemented in as the go-to person of the household and town, which left her with no one to go to when she needed an ear.

"I am always here for you," Doctor Richards said. "I will be your problem solver and an ear to voice your concerns and grievances."

"Thank you again, Doctor," Scarlett sobbed. "I feel a lot better. I'm still wiped out, but I feel better about what I thought happened out in those woods this morning. You're a good man, Doctor, and I appreciate your advice."

"You are welcome, Scarlett. I'm glad I could be of some help. And again, I am always here for you and anyone else. If anyone comes to you with their problems and it feels overwhelming to you, please don't hesitate to send them to me. I care for every person in this town, but I don't have the same level of love you have for a lot of them, so I am able to distance myself from the problems they may be dealing with. You are a good woman, but I feel like you take too much on yourself. These people are fine folks and are capable of dealing with their own issues. You don't always have to be the savior. Take care of yourself and your girls first."

"Thanks again. That is good advice, and it's what I needed to hear. I have felt that way from time to time, and it feels good to have someone like you tell me it's ok to feel that way. I appreciate that, and I will send folks your way in future if I cannot handle it myself." Scarlett stood up. "I am going to try and take that walk again. I am going to ignore everything for a couple of hours."

"That's a great idea and exactly what I think you should do," Doctor Richards said as he stood up too. "Take care of yourself, Scarlett, and come see me anytime."

"Thank you, and I will. Take care," she said as she headed for the front door. "I'll see you soon, Doctor."

"See you soon. Enjoy your walk," he said with a smile as he walked her out of the office.

"I will. Bye for now," Scarlett said as she left the building.

"Bye," Doctor Richards said as she left. He closed the door and went back to his office.

CHAPTER 15

A New Normal

Over the next couple of days, things had begun to get back to normal around town—until the day of the funerals. The town had taken the news of Amanda hard. She had been so young. Amanda had been a fixture around town; people loved her. The entire town gathered at the cemetery. Not one person was missing. Sheriff Riley from Henderson showed up. He had known Mallory, Amanda, and Greg quite well from their time as residents of Henderson. Marcus had also shown up to escort Cecilia to Henderson after the services. He had assembled all the leaders from the neighboring towns in Henderson to get the ball rolling on the merger. Marcus, although terribly saddened by the deaths of Greg, Mallory, and Amanda, was excited to get going on uniting the towns. He knew the distraction of doing so would be good for all. The news of the four deaths had spread to all of the other towns and had upset everyone. Especially the people of Henderson who had all known Mallory, Amanda, and Greg. No one knew who the young man that had died was, but it had still been incredibly sad—a life lost so young was difficult to process no matter the circumstances.

Kevin gave a beautiful eulogy. The entire town had been reduced to tears. Everyone cried for their fellow townsfolk. The tears brought the closure everyone had needed. They all came together that day to remember and mourn their friends. Amanda, Greg, and Mallory had been loved and respected by all. It was an extremely sad and painful day. Four people now lay in the ground, gone far too soon. All four of them had so much life in front of them, and to have that cut short was devasting and a sobering reminder to how short life really was. Kevin reminded everyone that it was okay and normal to be upset, but he also reminded them that their fallen brothers and sisters would want their lives to be celebrated. He told the town to go forth and be happy. Remember how short life can be; work hard but play harder. Enjoy each other. Always love and respect your fellow townsfolk because you never know how much time you will have together. He told everyone they were family, not just neighbors and co-workers. They were all in this together.

Kevin's words had brought tears to all, but they had also made everyone feel so much better. He was right: they were a family. They did need to move on in remembrance and celebration of the lives lost that week. Those that were no longer there would want the town to get back to normal life. They would have wanted everyone to be happy again. Death doesn't affect the dead. The dead have no more worries or desires. The living were the ones burdened with death, not the dead. The living had to find a way to move on. Losing people that were greatly loved and respected wasn't easy at first, but it would always get easier with time. New life moments would come; babies would be born; friends would marry; birthday parties would happen. Each new life milestone would slowly erase the sadness of the deaths. The dead would never be forgotten, but the pain would go away.

After the services, most of the town gathered at Bob's Tavern for drinks, food, and fellowship. The crowd at the tavern was in good spirits despite how sad the funerals had been. Holding those services had been the closure the town needed. People were able to openly mourn their deceased neighbors. They were able to come together and celebrate the lives of a few great people—well, Mallory, Greg, and Amanda, they knew had been great people—no one knew anything about the young man. Kevin had explained in his eulogy that Amanda thought she had known the young man and that she had called him Pete. Having a name for him helped a little bit; it gave the townsfolk a way to mourn the man that had suddenly shown up and died in their town. Pete was the main buzz around the tavern that night. Who was he? Where had he come from? How did he end up in the woods with a hole in his side? All questions no one had answers to. Theories about the Pete guy and liquor flowed throughout the tavern.

Malcolm and Bethany had gone home after the services; she couldn't drink so she didn't even want to be at the tavern. Malcolm was content to just stay home with her, but she insisted that he go have a few drinks and unwind. He told her he didn't need to unwind and was perfectly happy spending the evening at home with her.

"Baby, I'm so tired. I am just going to go lay down anyway," Bethany told him. "Please, go, have fun."

"Okay," Malcolm agreed. "I'm not going to stay long though."

"Stay as long as you'd like. I want you to be with your friends right now. I am just going to be sleeping."

"Okay, baby. I love you."

"I love you too." She smiled. "Have fun!" She put her arms around him and hugged him tight. They kissed goodbye, and Malcolm set off for the tavern.

Malcolm had wanted to go the tavern. He had wanted to have drinks and just chat with people. The heaviness that had hung over the town that past week was gone. People were more relaxed again. Malcolm missed just socializing with people. It had only been a few days, but with everything that had happened, it had felt like months. It felt good to be returning to normal life. Malcolm felt so bad for Scarlett; he knew how much she had loved Amanda. Scarlett was the type of person who kept her emotions to herself, but he knew she had to be reeling from the loss of Amanda. Especially considering the odd circumstances surrounding the young woman's death. Malcolm didn't know all the details—no one in town did—but he knew there was more to it than she just fell ill and passed away. He didn't know how he knew that to be the case, but he was certain there had to be more to the story. Malcolm hoped Scarlett would be at the tavern so he could talk to her. He didn't want to pry; he just wanted to be there for his friend. He knew she wouldn't talk much about it, especially in public, but he hoped he could at least make her feel better just being there for her. Over time, Scarlett had become like a sister to him; he loved and respected her so much. She had been and always would be there for him; he needed to return the favor. Or at least try to.

The tavern was packed by the time Malcolm got there. Almost everyone in town was there. It was a great sight to see. People were talking and laughing. A buffet of delicious food was laid out. There was just an air of fun and excitement in that tavern. Malcolm knew it was the town's way of trying to forget what had happened, their way of forcing themselves to move on. Sometimes all people could do was just pretend nothing had happened, at least for a bit. Take one night to just enjoy each other's company and party. Malcolm scanned the room and didn't see Scarlett anywhere. He wasn't surprised she wasn't there; the tavern was probably the last place she wanted to be after burying Amanda. Malcolm saw how upset Scarlett had been at the funeral. He had never seen her like that. No one had. Honestly, it was nice to see her let herself have big emotions about something. She had always been everyone else's shoulder to cry on. Malcolm knew Scarlett held a lot of feelings in so she could be the strong person in town. He knew she liked being the go-to person in town.

Malcolm found a seat at the bar. Bob came over to him, and Malcolm ordered a drink. Bob poured Malcolm's drink and set it in front of him.

"Thanks, Bob," Malcolm said.

"You're welcome. How are you and Bethany? Where is Bethany?" Bob asked, looking around the room.

"We're good, thanks for asking. We found out she's pregnant. Doctor Richards just confirmed it, so since she can't drink, she stayed home tonight. Plus, she was pretty tired after the services today."

"Congratulations!" Bob exclaimed. "That's great news. I'm happy for both of you."

"Thank you. We are very excited too. As you know, we've been trying for a while now," Malcolm said and took a sip of his drink.

"I know you have been, so this is great news. Besides tired, how has she been feeling?" Bob asked.

"She's had some sickness with it, but overall, she's been fine. She's starting to show a little bit already." Malcolm was excited about the pregnancy, but he was worried about Bethany's mental state. He wasn't about to share that with Bob, though.

"I'm glad she is mostly well. Make sure to tell her I said congratulations."

"I will, thank you again."

"You're welcome. If you could excuse me, I have some drinks to make. Again. Congrats, my friend," Bob said.

"No worries, Bob, we'll talk again soon." Malcolm grabbed his drink and stood up.

Bob wandered off to make drinks, and Malcolm set off into the crowd of people. He mingled and chatted for a while. It did feel good to be out socializing. He had missed it more than he had thought. Malcolm still wanted to check in on Scarlett, but he wasn't going to bother her that night. He would give her some space for a day or so.

Malcolm finished his third drink and headed for home. He had a slight buzz and was feeling good. Bethany was in bed, asleep. She awoke when he came into the room and sat up.

"How was the tavern, babe?" she asked, rubbing sleep from her eyes.

"It was fun," Malcolm said as he began to undress to change into his night clothes. "Bob sends his congratulations on the baby."

"Oh, that was nice of him," Bethany said. "So we're telling people now?"

"Yeah, I thought that's what we agreed after Doctor Richards confirmed it." Malcolm put on his night clothes and sat on the bed.

"I suppose it won't hurt anything at this point." Bethany sighed.

"We can't be afraid to lose this one, baby. We need to celebrate it. Let's not dwell on something that the doctor said wasn't even likely. He said everything looked great." Malcolm put his hand on his wife's shoulder. "I'm excited about it. I want to share our good news with everyone."

"Me too, baby, but I'm scared." Bethany had tears in her eyes. "I barely remember last time. I know it was the worst thing that has ever happened to us, but aside from that, I don't remember much else."

"That's all you need to remember, love. Again, let's not dwell on the past. Let's move forward and get ready to welcome our child into the world." Malcolm pulled Bethany to him and held her. She cried into his shoulder.

"I know, I shouldn't focus on negative things, but sometimes I can't help it. They just creep in." Bethany lifted her head from Malcolm's shoulder and looked at him. He was such a strong, kind, caring man. His beauty made her fall in love with him more every time she looked at him. His kind spirit made her heart skip a beat. Malcolm was everything she had ever wanted in a partner and more. "I love you, baby," she said.

"I love you too. So much, baby," Malcolm said and kissed her. "No matter what life brings our way—good, bad, or indifferent—we will handle it all together. I am always going to be your rock, love. I will do whatever possible to keep you safe and happy." Tears flooded down Bethany's face. Seeing her cry made him cry as well. "You and me forever, babe." He pulled her to him again and held her as they both cried.

After a bit, Bethany pulled away from Malcolm a little and asked if he would get her a cup of tea. Malcolm wiped his face and said he would. He went to the kitchen and prepared tea for the both of them. Bethany had changed out of her night dress into something a little more fun. Malcolm was taken aback at first but enjoyed the surprise. He set the cups of tea down on the dresser and approached the bed. He crawled in bed with his bride and embraced her. Nothing would come between the two of them. They were in life together until the end.

*****

Cecilia was in her room packing for her trip to Henderson. Marcus was waiting for her at the tavern. She paused what she was doing; she could hear Scarlett crying. Cecilia left her room and knocked on Scarlett's bedroom door. Scarlett invited her in.

"Are you going to be okay?" Cecilia asked, sitting down next to Scarlett on her bed.

"Someday, hopefully." Scarlett sobbed.

"I know it's so overwhelming right now, but it will get easier," Cecilia said as gently as possible.

"That's what everyone keeps saying, but it doesn't feel like it ever will," Scarlett cried.

"I promise you it will. It has affected us all, but we need to honor them by living our best lives. This has been a stark reminder that life is short. None of us have much time here. We can't squander what little time we have being sad."

"Why not?" Scarlett asked, slightly irritated. She wasn't irritated at Cecilia, just annoyed in general. Everyone kept saying that same thing, "The deceased would want us to move on and be happy." Or what Cecilia had just said about life being short, it was all starting to agitate Scarlett. "Why can't I be sad that Amanda is gone? Not just gone, she's fucking dead! A bright, energetic young lady gone forever. And for no reason. She got the flu and died? Seriously? Gwen and Hope both had it and they survived. What if it had been one of them? Would you all still tell me to just move on? Would you all still tell me that life is short, and I shouldn't be so sad if it was my daughter that had died? I hope not! Amanda was like a daughter to me, the same as Hope. I didn't give birth to either of them, but I took them in as my own. I think I deserve to be upset right now. We literally just buried one of our own! I'm tired of people telling me it will be okay. Or that life is short, I shouldn't waste it being sad. We just fuckin' buried her! I should be sad!" Scarlett stood up and paced her room. She was getting more and more angry.

"No one is saying you shouldn't be sad or you shouldn't mourn her. All we are trying to do is make you feel better. We're trying to remind you that you are still here. You need to move on when the time is right. No one is trying to make you get over this in one night. It will be a long process for all of us." Cecilia was trying to calm Scarlett down, but she could see it wasn't working.

"I will never get over this! And I shouldn't have to. She was my family, and she's gone forever. She didn't just move out or move away, she's fuckin' dead! Dead, Cecilia!" Scarlett stormed out of her room. Cecilia got up and followed her.

"Scarlett, I know she is, and I understand why you're so upset—we all are," Cecilia said when she caught up to Scarlett in the kitchen.

"Are you? Everyone else in town is down at the tavern living it up like nothing happened!" Scarlett shouted. "You're packing to go to Henderson. Tomorrow I will have to be at work putting out fires again. I'll have to put on my brave face and pretend like I'm not torn apart by all of this so that I can be the sounding board for everyone else's problems. Dana and Julia will be back to work at the store tomorrow. Hope and Gwen will be back to their chores. Life will go back to normal, just like everyone wants it to. And slowly we will forget about Amanda altogether. Poof, like she was never here!"

"We will never forget her, Scarlett. Never. She was part of our family, and she always will be. Just because we return to our—quote, unquote—normal lives doesn't mean we have to forget her. But we do have to return to our normal day-to-day responsibilities. It will just be a new normal," Cecilia said.

Scarlett looked furious. The sadness that had been all over her face moments ago was gone. Now her face was painted with anger and disdain. Cecilia knew Scarlett wasn't angry at her, so she remained calm. Cecilia was more than willing to let Scarlett vent at her.

"Yeah, a new normal without her!" Scarlett growled.

"Scarlett, she's not coming back, so yes, a new normal without her. We all need to come to terms with that."

"I don't want to!" Tears exploded from her eyes. Scarlett buckled to the floor and wailed. Cecilia knelt beside her and put an arm around her dear friend's shoulder. Scarlett nuzzled into Cecilia and bawled.

Cecilia didn't say anything else; she just let Scarlett cry. She knew that's what her friend needed the most, a shoulder to cry on. A friend to lean on. The two women stayed on the hard kitchen floor until their knees were screaming in pain. Scarlett's sobbing had quieted, and she seemed more collected. They stood up. Scarlett put water on the stove for tea.

"I don't ever want to forget her," Scarlett said softly.

"You won't," Cecilia responded. "This is how life works, unfortunately. Loved ones pass away and we are tasked with trying to figure out how to live without them. They are gone. They can't help us feel better. That's why people always say they would 'want us to move on and be happy.' We don't know that for sure. That's our way of coping with the loss. It's our way of making ourselves feel better because we *have* to move on. We feel guilty because we are still here and living our lives, so we convince ourselves that that's what they would want. We don't know if that's true or not, but I do believe if we could ask them, they would say, 'Yes, please move on. Always honor and remember us but move on and be happy.' At least that's how I'd feel. If I died tomorrow, I would absolutely want you to move on and live a happy life. You could mourn me and be sad that I'm gone, but I would want you to live your best life."

"I know all of that, and I agree with it all. I just want to be allowed to be sad. That's it," Scarlett said as she fixed tea for the both of them.

"No one is saying you can't be sad," Cecilia said.

"It feels that way sometimes," Scarlett said. "Speaking of moving on, don't you have to get to Henderson?"

"I can push that back a day," Cecilia responded.

"Don't," Scarlett said.

"I think I should. I want to be here for you."

"I'll be fine, Cecilia. This is important. We really need to get the ball rolling before the towns start changing their minds. If we keep putting it off, they're going to start to think we aren't reliable."

"Are you sure?" Cecilia asked.

"Absolutely. And honestly, I wouldn't mind being alone for a bit. Leah said the other girls could stay with her tonight. I really need to just be alone and get my emotions right. I need to mourn Amanda my way." Scarlett paused and took a sip of her tea. "I don't need a babysitter. I just need a friend, and you've been that for me."

"Well, I do agree that we need to get the ball rolling on the merger. You're right about the other towns. They may indeed start wondering if we're reliable. Thank you, Scarlett."

"No problem. I feel better already. I think I just needed to get a few things off my chest. I just needed a sympathetic ear, and you gave me that, so thank you for listening." Scarlett put down her tea and gave Cecilia a hug. "It felt good to just vent."

"You are welcome. Do you need anything else before I get going?" Cecilia asked.

"No, I'm good now." She did actually feel a lot better. She was still devastated, but venting had helped her compartmentalize everything. Cecilia had, in her own strange way, helped Scarlett realize it was okay to be sad. It helped her realize she could be sad and still move on with life. Moving on didn't mean forgetting Amanda; it was something she *had* to do. Life without Amanda would never be the same, but that was to be expected.

"Okay, then. I will head out and see you in a few days," Cecilia said.

"Sounds good," Scarlett replied. "Good luck, Cecilia. I hope this all works out well for everyone. Hopefully, you are met with town leaders who are as optimistic and excited as we are about this."

"I am confident that will be the case. From what Marcus has said, the other towns are biting at the bit to get going with this." Cecilia turned and headed to her room. She returned moments later with her bags. She put on her coat and a hat. "Goodbye, Scarlett. Thank you for holding down the fort around here while I'm gone."

"My pleasure, Cecilia. Have a safe trip." Scarlett walked Cecilia to the door. They said goodbye one last time, and Scarlett watched as Cecilia disappeared toward town.

Scarlett closed the front door. She grabbed her tea from the kitchen counter and went into Amanda's bedroom. Scarlett sat down on Amanda's bed and looked around the small room. Amanda had always kept her room so clean and tidy. The young woman had been fairly neurotic about cleanliness; that was why she had made for such a good housekeeper. Scarlett knew it was her imagination, but she swore she felt Amanda's presence in that room. It was probably because she was surrounded by Amanda's belongings and personal affects. They say people leave an imprint of themselves on their belongings. The feeling Scarlett had wasn't eerie or frightening; it was calming. She felt calm and almost happy in that room. Scarlett felt closer to Amanda in that room.

Amanda's nightdress was laid out on her bed. Scarlett set down her tea on the nightstand and picked up Amanda's dress. She held it tightly to her. It smelled like Amanda. Scarlett lay down on the bed. As she clutched the nightdress, she began to cry again. That was the closest she would ever be to Amanda again. Eventually, they would have to remove Amanda's belongings from that room. Scarlett assumed that either Dana or Julia may want that room at some point. It did not make sense to have a bedroom in the house that was full of Amanda's stuff and therefore unusable. It saddened her to think that this last part of Amanda would soon be gone as well.

Scarlett let herself relax a bit. Her tears slowed again, and she felt sleepy. She thought about getting up and going to her room, but she didn't. Scarlett let sleep take over and slowly drifted off, clutching Amanda's nightdress.

*****

Dana, Julia, Gwen, Hope, and Leah all sat around Leah's dining room table, playing cards and drinking tea. Leah's sister had gone to bed already. She had been born with what doctors called a "crooked spine," which caused her a great deal of pain. That night, she was in more pain than usual after being on her feet at the funerals for so long. She had told the ladies to have a fun night and not to worry about her; she'd be asleep in no time.

The young women were all giggling and laughing at the silliness of the card game they had just invented. Dana and Julia had had a few drinks back at the tavern and were both a bit buzzed. Hope and Gwen were not old enough to be served alcohol yet, but Dana and Julia had snuck them a couple of drinks, getting them buzzed as well. Leah wasn't a drinker and never had been, but she did have one drink in honor of her best friend. She knew Amanda would have done the same for her. The ladies had all been so incredibly sad all day that all they wanted to do that night was be loose and silly. They wanted to laugh and enjoy the company of friends. It was proving tough to stay jovial though. Every once in a while, someone would say, "Amanda would have loved that" or "Amanda would've thought that was funny too," and the mood would go somber again. It was impossible to not be reminded of Amanda. She had touched every one of their lives so deeply. Even Gwen's disdain for Amanda had been born out of feelings of love for each other. It was hard to hate someone that had been accepted into your life as family, even if you didn't particularly like them. Gwen was old enough to understand that her feelings for Amanda had been because of her jealousy toward Amanda. It made her feel horrible that she had treated Amanda the way she had for so long. Listening to the stories from the other girls at the table slowly made her realize she had missed out on being friends with a great girl.

Gwen kept quiet when the others told stories about Amanda. She had complained about Amanda to everyone at that table, except for Leah, countless times. She knew she had no place to reminisce about Amanda. She did find herself missing Amanda, though. Gwen wished she could have had a chance to apologize to Amanda for the way she had treated her. She knew Amanda would have accepted her apology and apologized for her role in their tumultuous relationship. Gwen vowed to herself in that moment that she would never let herself feel that way toward anyone else ever again. She never wanted to make someone else feel like they were less important than herself.

Leah was excited to have company after the day she had had. She had known all these ladies most of her life. She had never been close to any of them, especially Gwen. Amanda and Gwen hadn't gotten along since they had all moved away from Henderson. Dana and Julia were good people, and she had always enjoyed being around them, but they had never become what she thought as good friends, just friendly. Hope had always sided with Gwen, so Leah had never had an opportunity to become close to Hope either. But she was glad they were all together that night, even Gwen. Especially Gwen, in fact. She could tell by Gwen's demeanor that she felt terrible about everything. It made Leah realize that Gwen probably wasn't as bad as Amanda had made her out to be. Leah knew there was always two sides to every story, and she had only ever gotten Amanda's side. She wasn't naïve enough to believe that everything had always been Gwen's fault. Leah knew her friend well and knew Amanda could be difficult sometimes. Amanda had a chip on her shoulder for some reason. She had always carried herself as if she were better than everyone else. Amanda had come from the same humble beginnings as everyone else in town. Amanda hadn't grown up privileged, so it had always confused Leah as to why her friend had thought she was so much better than everyone else. Leah just shrugged it off as being part of Amanda's character. She loved Amanda like a sister, nonetheless.

"Let's spike these teas, ladies!" Dana said, pulling a bottle of booze out of her purse.

"Hell yeah!" Julia exclaimed. "Let's keep this party going!"

"I don't know if we should drink anymore. My mom would kill us if we got drunk," Gwen said.

"You won't even see your mom until tomorrow. She'll never even know," Dana said. "Besides, we don't need to get drunk, let's just have a couple drinks and keep playing cards."

"I'll have some," Leah said. That shocked the table; everyone else knew Leah never drank. "Come on, this is the type of situation that calls for drinks," she said in response to the surprised looks she had just gotten.

"Leah's right!" Julia said.

"I'm in too," Hope said, looking at Gwen.

"Fine, me too." Gwen sighed. She had seen Dana and Julia come home from the tavern drunk numerous times. Her mom never said anything to them, but she could tell her mom didn't like it. Her mom would have come unglued if she had found out Gwen and Hope had drunk too.

Dana dribbled some booze into everyone's tea. Leah took a healthy sip of her now spiked tea and got up. She went to the kitchen and started another pot of tea. They were going to need more tea to spike. Leah looked over at the table from the kitchen and smiled. Amanda would have loved this. She would have been excited to see them all enjoying themselves in her honor. Tears crept into Leah's eyes, and she blinked them away. That wasn't the time for tears. If any one of them had begun to cry at any point, the rest would automatically follow suit. Leah missed her friend terribly and was beyond sad, but in that moment, those were tears of happiness trying to escape her eyes. Happiness and content to have friends gathered in remembrance of her best friend.

The girls all drank and laughed late into the night before slowly dispersing and going to bed. Gwen and Hope turned in first, followed by Leah. Dana and Julia had one last drink outside after the others had gone to bed.

"What a day," Dana said, sipping her spiked tea.

"What a week!" Julia added.

"Could you have ever imagined anything like it?" Dana asked, looking up at the starry night sky.

"No way. Who would?" Julia asked, staring at the sky as well.

"I can't believe Amanda is gone," Dana said, shaking her head.

"I know. It doesn't feel real," Julia said, sipping her spiked tea.

"No, it doesn't. None of it seems real. Like those things in the woods. What the fuck were those things?"

"Who knows, but shit got real weird 'round here after they showed up."

"No kidding. Normal, everyday life one day, and bam, shit hits the fan the next." Dana looked over at Julia. "I hope it's all over with now."

"Me too," Julia said, looking over at Dana. "Me too."

They stood there outside of Leah's cabin and stared up at the clear night sky. The moon was just a crescent but provided a little bit of light. Just enough to make the late night seem a tad creepy. Dana looked back over at her best friend.

"I love you. I just want to make sure you know you are my best friend in the whole world, and you mean everything to me. I don't know what I'd do without you," Dana said, getting a little choked up. Both Dana and Julia had been fairly close to Amanda but nowhere near as close as they were to each other. Being graveside at Amanda's funeral that afternoon had made Dana realize how important family and friends were to her. Dana wanted to make sure she reminded Julia how much she and her friendship meant to her.

"Aw, thank you!" Julia responded. "I love you too. You are my best and truest friend, and you also mean the world to me. I wouldn't want to live a life without you." Julia hugged Dana.

"I know with you by my side, we can conquer anything," Dana said as they hugged.

"Totally. We have a great thing. This friendship is special and unique," Julia said.

"It makes me feel so bad for Leah. Amanda was her Julia," Dana said as they returned their eyes to the sky.

"I know, it's so sad. *Sad* isn't even a strong enough word for it. I was glad to see her enjoying herself tonight, though. It's gotta be hard to try to move on from something like that. Just knowing that you never get to see your best friend again would be more than devastating. I hope she can continue to heal and move on," Julia said, tears welling up in her eyes.

"She'll never fully move on. I wouldn't be able to if I ever lost you." Dana said with tears in her eyes as well.

"I wouldn't either, but the depressing thing is you have to. That would be the hardest part. Leah and Amanda had lunch together almost every day. Now every time she eats lunch alone, she'll be forced to think about Amanda. That's going to be so heartbreaking. Poor Leah." Julia dropped her head as tears leaked out of the corners of her eyes. She didn't want to cry again; she had been crying so much that week, but she couldn't help it. Putting herself in Leah's shoes made the reality of it all hit home so much harder.

"I can't imagine the heartbreak of that. Right now, she has the love and support of the town. Right now, she has us here with her to distract her from things for a bit. But all of that won't last long—the rest of us have to return to normal life too. Soon, she'll be alone and forced to face her loss head on. It's going to crush her over and over again," Dana said as tears began to roll down her cheeks as well. She had just wanted to remind Julia of how much she meant to her. She hadn't intended on bringing up the pain of losing each other. Putting themselves in Leah's position was not what she had wanted to do, but maybe it was important to feel those emotions.

"It will," Julia said. "I think it will crush us all over and over again. We lost some great people this week. They were all loved and important people. But I feel like we forget that we lost them sometimes because we were so much closer to Amanda."

"I agree with that," Dana said. "Even that Pete guy. No one knew him or how he got here, but he was still a person. Someone somewhere is missing him. Worst of all, whoever is out there missing him doesn't even know he's dead. They still have hope that he'll come home. I think that would be even worse than just knowing he's gone."

They were both staring up at the night sky again. The stars seemed brighter somehow. A shooting star cut through the dark sky. They both gasped at its beauty and sudden appearance. The first one was followed quickly by three more shooting stars, all of which were just as brilliant and sudden as the first. They slowly turned to each other with looks of shock on their faces before quickly returning their gaze to the sky. There were no more shooting stars.

"This may sound crazy, but what if that was them?" Dana said slowly and quietly. "What if that was them telling us they're okay?"

Julia looked at Dana for a moment. That thought had never even crossed her mind. No one knew much of anything about what was in those skies, but they had seen shooting stars before. No one knew what they were or where they came from, but they had all seen one at some point. The mysteries of what was above their heads were endless. They only had theories. Some believed they had a creator up there somewhere. Something that had created the world they occupied and had even created them. Some believed there was nothing up there but the stars and moon at night and the sun during the day. That was the belief most had. It didn't make much sense to most that there was some being that had created the world. How would that have even been possible? Those that believed in a creator would always just say anything is possible. They knew so little about their own world that anything could be possible. Most just wrote it off as people trying to explain a world they didn't understand.

"I never would have made that connection," Julia said. What Dana had just said had given her goosebumps. "You really think that's possible?"

"Why isn't it?" Dana asked, still staring at the night sky. "We don't know where we go when we die. Maybe we become sky people."

"Maybe we don't go anywhere," Julia said, rolling her eyes a bit. She couldn't believe her friend had just mentioned *sky people*.

"I believe we live on somehow past this life. I believe this is just our beginning. I believe our best life is after this one."

"I've heard that idea before too, but I don't believe it. How and why would we have more than one life? If that's the good life, why even have this one? Do animals go to the sky too when they die?"

"I doubt it. I believe we don't need to eat in the next life. We raise animals mostly for food here, so we wouldn't need them in the next life. I think we have many lives. I don't think this life was our first life. I think we slowly evolve in each lifetime until we are good enough to be sky people," Dana said, looking over at her surprised friend. "It sounds plausible to me."

"I have to disagree. I've heard all of those ideas from others too. That's the kind of shit John Henderson used to spew. He was the first person I can remember talking about a creator in the sky and that we get to be with our creator when we die. I remember us both thinking it was crazy talk. Now you're telling me you believe it?" Julia was shocked by what Dana was saying.

"I do, yes, at least I have been thinking about it a lot more over the past week. I *want* to believe there's more to life than just this. I *want* to believe Amanda is in a better place, not just a hole in the ground. I don't think it should have anything to do with who first said it. John was a despicable man but that doesn't mean his theories were wrong. A lot of good people believe that too, and I'm beginning to really think it could be true. Especially after seeing those shooting stars tonight. I know in my heart that was Amanda, Mallory, Greg, and the Pete guy telling us they are okay. We were just talking about how much we missed them all and they gave us a sign that they're ok. I felt that as soon as I saw those stars," Dana said. She knew Julia thought she was nuts at that moment, but she didn't care. Dana *needed* something to believe in, something that helped her feel better about losing a friend.

"John used that shit to control people. It was a way for him to make himself seem stronger and more powerful. He used it to mind-fuck people," Julia said. "He was an evil man—don't believe a word that came out of that man's mouth. Everything he ever said was calculated and meant to bend reality to get people to follow him blindly. And it worked for the most part. We all got the hell out of there, but most people stayed behind because for some unknown reason, they thought he was a great leader. He said awful things about women, especially, that most thought shouldn't ever be said out loud. But since the town leader said it, it was then okay for others to start talking and acting the same way. Every word out of that man's mouth was a lie, and you know it. Including the sky people nonsense."

"Julia, this isn't about John. He didn't invent the afterlife—he just talked about it. He had a platform where people had to listen to him. He did no good the entire time he ran that damn town, except maybe spread the word about a possible life after this one. If he did do one good thing, he gave people hope that there is something better out there for us after we die. I hate the man as much as you do, and like I said, this isn't about him or what he did to people. My growing belief in a life after this has nothing to do with him or who he was. Besides, I don't think the next life is how he made it out to be. I don't believe we have to be 'good' people or 'follow the rule of the land' to move onto the next life. He painted that picture to control people—you are right about that." Dana looked over at Julia again and saw a look of utter shock and disbelief on her dear friend's face. She knew she sounded crazy. They had talked at length about how crazy they thought John had been for talking like that.

"I just don't believe any of it. It is all too out there for me. It's a theory. It's fiction, Dana. A fictional tale made up by a delusional, psychopathic madman. For the sole purpose of controlling people. A way to make people blindly follow him."

"I don't believe he made it up. I do agree he used it to control people. I also fully agree he was a madman, but again this isn't about him. People have a right to make up their own minds about things. If people were naïve enough to blindly follow him, that's on them. We all got out. We didn't buy into his lies and rhetoric. He did have an end game, and the people that followed him deserve whatever happens to them. He could have and should have been overthrown, but there wasn't enough of us to do it, so we left. Something awful and terrible must have happened to him at some point in his life; people just aren't born that evil." Dana paused and sighed. "Let's move on from him. Cecilia said he died. He is no longer a concern. The truth is, Julia, I just want *something* to believe in. I want to believe this isn't it for us. I want to believe that we don't just make it through our time here and then end up in a hole in the ground forever. There *has* to be something else."

"Why? Why does there have to be something else? Why can't we just enjoy this life to its fullest and rest peacefully when it's over? That's my question: why does there have to be more? No offense, but it sounds greedy to me. We were blessed with this beautiful world, plenty of food, good friends and family—why isn't that good enough? Why *can't* that be good enough?"

Dana didn't reply right away. She stood there and contemplated what her friend had just said. Julia had made a good point: why wasn't this life good enough?

"I think we'd be robbing ourselves of our best life if we believed there was something better waiting for us after we die," Julia said after a moment. "What would be the point to enjoying this life to its fullest if we are focused on the possibility of something better? I don't think it gets any better than this. That's why I brought John into this. He didn't want people to be happy. Happy people don't tend to blindly follow a madman. He wanted people to be scared and angry so that he could play the savior. So that he could give just enough to satisfy the people and then tout himself as the best ruler in the history of mankind. He was a narcissist, and to a lot of us, it was blindingly clear, but to most, he somehow seemed like a good leader. They trusted him. He may not have made up the sky people theory, but he manipulated it to his benefit. I think we should remember that when we think about the possibility of a life after this one. If a madman can use something like that to take even more control, then there may be something fundamentally wrong about the theory."

Dana just stood there, looking at Julia. Julia had always had a way of bringing Dana back down to reality when she got worked up about something. Dana knew she was grasping at straws, just trying so hard to believe something so she would feel better about losing people close to her. Julia was right; if someone like John could use such an idea to control people, it probably wasn't true. As she stood there thinking about what Julia had just said, she slowly began to realize that there wasn't actually much possibility of a life after this one. But she also knew those shooting stars were Amanda, Mallory, Greg, and the Pete fella. She didn't know how, but she just knew it was them.

With tears in her eyes again, Dana said, "Thank you, Julia. Thank you for always bringing me back to reality. I don't know why I started to believe that stuff. Everything you have said makes perfect sense." Dana wanted to totally agree with Julia—it was how she had always thought—but the events of the past week and seeing those shooting stars had made her question everything. Most people would just say the stars were coincidence, but in her heart, she believed it was not just a coincidence. Dana loved and respected Julia and valued her opinions. Julia had made some good points, and her opinions did make sense, but Dana wasn't ready do give up the idea of a life after this one. She just wanted her friend to think she had.

"I know why you did. Believing there is something else after this life helps us feel better when we lose someone so close to us. We can't comprehend death. It seems so final—it *is* so final. We don't want to let ourselves believe that when it's over, that's it, it's over. We make up ideas and theories to make death easier to accept—and not just the death of others but our own death. The thought of dying is scary as fuck. I don't want to die, but I will. We all will, and knowing that to be a fact is what's so scary about it. I'm sure there have been all kinds of life-after-death theories floating about throughout the history of mankind. That's the thing—all we will ever have are theories. The only way we will ever know for sure what happens to us after this life is to die. And you can't come back and tell others what death is like." Julia paused and looked out over Leah's front yard toward town. "What I've learned from this week is that I need to enjoy the little things more often, like a good cup of spiked tea. I need to let the people I care about know how much I care about them more often through my actions and with my words. Amanda was younger than us, Dana. If she could suddenly die like that, any one of us could. I don't want to take this life for granted anymore, and if there is a life after this one, then great, but I'm not wasting what little time I have here thinking about it."

Dana nodded. She was crying again. Julia had made some great points and a lot of it resonated with her. She had been using the possibility of life after death to cope with their losses that week. She had cared deeply for Amanda and just wanted to believe she had moved on to a better place. Julia was right—what was important going forward was to live their best lives. Always to remember and honor the deceased but to live a great life while you had it. Because someday, she would be in that hole in the ground too.

"We should get inside and get some sleep," Julia said, snapping Dana out of deep thought.

"You're right," Dana said quietly, almost in a whisper. "You're right about all of it." She wanted Julia to know that she had heard her. Dana did agree with most of what Julia had said. But she knew you could live the best life here and still believe in a life after. She didn't know why she wanted to believe it so badly—she hadn't before—but it was at least comforting for the time being. She would reflect on it all more and make up her own mind about it all. She wasn't going to let Julia bully her into agreeing with her.

"You're just grieving and heartbroken," Julia said, putting her hand on Dana's shoulder. "I think things seem worse because Amanda was so close to us in age. If it had just been Mallory or Greg, it would be a little easier to take. First of all, we weren't as close to Mallory, but mostly because she was so much older. Sure, she passed away too soon, but she had lived a long, happy life. We will miss Greg coming into the store every day and telling us those silly jokes he always had. He was a regular part of our lives, but again, we weren't that close to him either. We were very close to Amanda, and I think that's what's hurting the most, and I think this was your way of grieving her. And it's perfectly normal to want some answers. It's perfectly normal to want to believe there is something else for us after this world."

"Thank you so much for talking to me tonight. I know you are hurting just as much as I am, so I really appreciate you talking all this out with me. I appreciate you being so grounded and down to earth about it all, even though you are grieving too. This is one of a million reasons why I love you so much!" Dana said and hugged Julia again.

"As always, my pleasure! I am and I always will be here for you no matter what. You are my best friend, and your friendship keeps me going every day. I love you too. With every part of my being."

"You are the best!" Dana said, releasing Julia.

"You are too!" Julia said. "Now let's go get some sleep so we're not falling asleep at work tomorrow." Julia chuckled.

"Good idea. Sleep sounds wonderful right now," Dana said, turning toward the cabin.

"Shit yeah, it does," Julia said, following Dana inside.

Leah had two couches in her living room. Dana and Julia each took a couch. They said good night and quickly fell asleep. The events of the day and the late-night conversation had exhausted them.

Cecilia and Marcus had made it to Henderson late that evening. Marcus and his wife, Alexis, had made up a spare room for Cecilia to stay with them. Alexis had made dinner for all of them, and they all settled in around the dining room table to eat. Cecilia was starving and plowed through Alexis's delicious dinner. The three of them sat at the table and chatted while they ate. The conversation was light and informal. They didn't talk about the upcoming merger or any other town-related topics. After they finished their meal, Cecilia excused herself for bed. It had gotten pretty late; she wanted to try to get some good rest before the big meeting the next morning. Marcus had arranged for everyone to meet at the sheriff's office in their briefing room.

It had been a long, draining day. A hot meal and sleep was what Cecilia needed. After she had changed into her night clothes, Cecilia read through her speech one last time. It wasn't a rah-rah type of speech, but she did feel like it would excite the other town leaders. Her main focus was to drive home the fact that things shouldn't change much. Day-to-day operations for each town should go on as they always had. The only difference would be they would be creating a supply chain between all of them. Everything would be fairly and equally priced. As it was before, a chicken from one town may have been priced double of that from another town; that was what she wanted to do away with. Cecilia also wanted to expand their land and create larger farms. More supply would drive down the cost of goods for everyone.

Cecilia felt good about the meeting the following morning. She was very excited to finally get things going. Marcus had told her that everyone was on board and excited about it except for the town of Everett. Everett's mayor had her doubts about uniting all the towns. She felt Everett had more to offer than any other town and felt like they would get robbed of their independence. Marcus had explained it wasn't mandatory for everyone to join in, but any town that didn't would be cut off from the united towns. Marcus talked her into at least coming to the meeting and hearing everyone out. Maybe she had some ideas that would make her feel better about joining the other towns. He assured Everett's mayor that Cecilia was a strong and brilliant leader; she would govern a successful society. Marcus had warned Cecilia that Everett's mayor was pretty odd. He had said that not only did she have a unique personality but she also had some kind of birth defect that made her look ghostly. All skin and bones.

Cecilia wasn't too nervous about having one town on the fence about the merger. It had made her feel good, in fact. She wanted the other town leaders to question her and the merger. That's how they would all collectively create a thriving community. Cecilia didn't want to be the supreme leader; she wanted to be a part of the system. She didn't want to be the system. It would take everyone to build a thriving society. Cecilia hoped they would have an open and honest discussion the next morning. She hoped everyone would be willing to be involved and have ideas to bring to the table. She didn't want to just go in there and give a speech and have everyone blindly agree. She knew a lot of those towns were struggling and they were biting at the bit to merge with the other towns. She hoped Everett's mayor would open up a debate and they could all hammer out a good plan.

Cecilia tucked herself into bed. The day had been exhausting, and she fell asleep quickly. Usually, it was hard to fall asleep in a new place and a different bed, but not that night. Cecilia slept hard that night. She woke up the next morning feeling rested and ready for the day.

Alexis and Marcus had prepared a large breakfast. Cecilia joined them at the table, and they all ate. One of Marcus's deputies stopped by to let them know the other town leaders were already gathered at the sheriff's office. Marcus and Cecilia quickly finished eating and headed for town.

Henderson was a beautiful town. Cecilia could tell it had been around for a long time. It had to be at least five times the size of her little town. Cecilia was beginning to think they should consider turning Henderson—or Jamison, as she wanted to rename it—into the capitol of their united towns. Henderson just had the size and the resources to base a government out of. As far as she knew, it was the only town with any kind of law enforcement, and they would need law enforcement moving forward. Cecilia knew once you started growing communities, the need for law and order increased with the growth of a society. No matter how fair and balanced policies seemed when they were rolled out, there would always be people who didn't agree with them. That disagreement and divide usually led to people causing trouble. She would need Marcus to address law enforcement immediately.

Marcus led Cecilia into the briefing room. The other town leaders stood up and greeted them as they came in. Cecilia knew right away which one was Everett's mayor; Marcus's description of her had been spot on. She did look like a skeleton with skin loosely draped over it. She had a long, misshapen head. Her eyes were dark and honestly creepy.

"Good morning everyone," Cecilia said after everyone had sat back down. She stood at a podium in the front of the briefing room. "I am Cecilia Rodgers. I am happy and excited to be here today! What a great honor it is to address you all about the wonderful prospect of merging our towns. We are at the beginning stages of building a beautiful, thriving society. I am excited to tell you my ideas, and I want to hear ideas and any trepidations you all may have. I am confident that this will work out well for us all."

Cecilia paused and looked around the room. She had everyone's attention.

"First, I want to suggest we rename Henderson to Jamison. Jamison was the last name of a young woman from our town who had grown up in Henderson. She recently passed away, and I thought it would be fitting to honor her memory by naming the new Henderson after her. Sheriff, will you float that idea through town for me?"

Marcus nodded. He thought it was a good idea, and he was certain the rest of the town would agree.

"The name change doesn't affect the rest of you any," Cecilia continued. "I just wanted to open with that. I think the first thing that needs to be addressed in a transition like this is the production and distribution of goods. Right now, each town is somewhat self-sufficient but still struggling in some areas. By coming together as one nation, we can all thrive equally. What one town has an abundance of can be distributed to the other towns. I would like to expand our territory and build new, bigger farms to raise crops and livestock. We will all work together on that expansion. Right now, we all pretty much fend for ourselves, and that just isn't sustainable any longer. Our individual communities are growing rapidly and are in a continuous need of more goods and supplies."

Cecilia looked around at the other town leaders again; she felt like she may be losing some of them. A couple had concerned looks on their faces. "I should stop here and say that I don't intend on being a ruler. I want to be part of a leadership group. A leadership group that includes everyone in this room. You all would stay in your roles as mayors of your towns, but we would all work together as a united nation. Each one of you would still govern your town how you see fit, but under the guidelines of the nation. By pooling all of our resources together, we will never have needs of our people go unmet again. Before I go on, are there any questions?"

The mayors of Everett and Williamstown raised their hands.

"Before you ask your questions, would you please introduce yourself to the room?"

The mayor from Everett stood up. "I am Eve Adams, the mayor of Everett," she said to the room. That name was extremely familiar to Cecilia. She assumed she had known the woman from her time in

Henderson. But still, there was something about that name and the woman that made Cecilia cringe. "As most of you are aware, I am not on board with this merger. What we have in Everett is perfect for us, and I don't feel we need much help from any of you all. I don't mean to sound selfish or indignant, but I don't see any reason to unite the towns. I think what we have now is working just fine." She sat back down.

"Thank you for your comments," Cecilia said, "but did you have any questions regarding the merger? Did I not do a sufficient job of explaining why uniting the towns benefits us all?"

Eve Adams stood up again. "I think you did a fine job of explaining how it benefits all of you. I guess my question then would be, besides my town being cut off from the rest of you if we don't join you, what benefit is there for us? We have the one thing you all want, and we have most of the crops we need, and we're working on building up our livestock. We are almost completely self-sufficient." Eve Adams sat back down.

"A society only works as a whole. We want every town united and working together. We don't want to end up having altercations down the road," Cecilia said. "Are there any other concerns?" she asked the room.

The mayor of Williamstown stood up. "I'm Dean Richards, mayor of Williamstown. Your doctor is my brother," Dean started. "I don't really have a concern—it's more of a suggestion."

"Oh yes, please, we want suggestions," Cecilia said to him.

"Well, I want to start with this—my town and myself are fully on board for uniting the towns. We are actually extremely excited about it," Dean said. "My suggestion is this: As a united nation, we will need laws, law enforcement, and punishment. I have the utmost respect for Sheriff Riley here, and I would like to nominate him to head up a nationwide law enforcement outfit. My town has a sheriff and one deputy—I can't lose either of them. Just as we all will work together as leaders, I would like to see Sheriff Riley work with other sheriff departments so we can implement a unilateral set of laws and regulations."

"I think that is a fantastic suggestion, and I have already mentioned that to him. He said he would be honored to do just that if he was asked to. We will need laws, and we will need punishment for those who decide to break those laws. I don't foresee our law enforcement officers being too busy—we all have great people in our towns. But regardless of how upstanding our citizens are, any society does need laws. Sheriff," Cecilia said, turning to Marcus, "is this something you are still willing to take on?"

"Yes, ma'am," Marcus replied. "It would be an honor and my privilege."

"Great!" Cecilia exclaimed. "That matter is settled. Sheriff, I will leave all of the law to you and a team you assemble to handle."

"Yes, ma'am," Marcus replied.

Eve Adams stood up again. "May I interject here?" she asked. "Why do you, Miss Rodgers, get to decide what is best for all of us?"

"I was asked and appointed to the job by everyone in this room. Or so I thought I had been," Cecilia responded. "As I said earlier, I don't want to be a ruler, just one of the leaders. But a healthy society only works with someone at the top to delegate and make final decisions. What I had in mind was a counsel of those of us in this room. We would vote on anything and everything that needed to be decided for the betterment of our nation. The people of our towns would also have a say. I want them to vote on issues that will directly affect them. In a case where we all cannot agree, then I would have final say. It is called a democracy. I have had experience running a democracy before."

"Again," Eve Adams began, "I'll ask, why you?"

"I was asked to do it," Cecilia said, getting annoyed with Eve. "I was going to say no, but everyone talked me into it. I will tell you this—in a few years, when we have everything settled and running like a well-oiled machine, we can hold elections to see who the people of our nation want as their next leader. At that time, you, assuming you join us, could run for the position. It will take time to build this great nation, so in the meantime, we go ahead as planned. I will be the governor and you all will be my deputy governors, retaining the roles you already have, just under a new title."

"Maybe we should have a vote right now to see who gets to be governor," Eve said. "I would like the opportunity to run against you. I think I could lead a great nation just as well, if not better, than you. And I mean no offense by that."

"No offense taken," Cecilia said. "At this point in the venture, it is too late to hold an election."

"What about a vote by the men in this room? The decision of who runs everything will greatly impact everyone in here. Probably more so than our townspeople. There's five of them in here—majority vote gets to be governor. No hard feelings. If you win, my town will join the new nation, and I will work with you to create a thriving society. If I win, I expect the same from you."

Cecilia stared at Eve for a moment. How had they gotten to this point? She had thought she was coming in to give a speech and get the ball rolling on uniting the towns. She hadn't been prepared to run for her position. Cecilia was pretty confident everyone in that room would vote for her. They had all tapped her in the first place. If they had wanted Eve Adams, they would've asked her first.

"Okay, fine. Let's do just that. The vote must be anonymous. We don't need to have the possibility of any animosity coming from this. Regardless of the outcome, we will all have to work closely together to pull this transition off," Cecilia said. She was frustrated with all of it, but she felt as though she had to go along with it at that point.

"I agree with you on that," Eve said. "How shall we proceed?"

"You tell me, this was all your idea," Cecilia said. That last question had pissed her off. This woman brought up the idea to hold a vote and then she wanted Cecilia to hammer out the details? No way. Cecilia wasn't going to play that game.

"Well, I think we should both get time to talk to our fellow mayors and campaign for the position. How about twenty minutes each, in private with the rest of them?" Eve said, smiling. It was a creepy smile.

"Fine. Would you like to go first?" Cecilia asked.

"Sure," Eve said.

Cecilia grabbed her notebook and left the room. She went out to the waiting room in the front of the office and sat down. She was furious. Her heart was pounding, and she felt rage in her chest. That damn woman had thrown a big old wrench into Cecilia's plans. Now they were wasting time holding a useless vote.

Twenty minutes later, Eve Adams strolled out like she owned the place.

"Good luck," Eve said to Cecilia with that creepy smile.

"Thanks," Cecilia said with disdain in her voice. No matter the outcome of that vote, Eve was going to be difficult to work with.

Cecilia entered the briefing room and went to the podium. Marcus had sat down with the mayors from the other towns. She looked out at them and smiled.

"What do I need to say, gentlemen? You all asked me to run this new society. You all came to me. I would assume if you had wanted Eve Adams, you would have asked her. I feel as though she is just trying to undermine all of us. She clearly didn't want to be a part of our new society, and now she is trying to sabotage us. When Marcus first approached me about this, my gut reaction was to say no. My town is doing very well despite the events of the past week. I was happy being the mayor of that town. I still am. But the more I thought about what Marcus had proposed, the more I began to love the idea. The more I loved the idea, the more I wanted to be an integral part of it. You all know what I want to do moving forward to get this society going. You all are great leaders, and I have faith that together we will create the greatest nation mankind has ever seen. The people of our towns will thrive. My number one priority is the townsfolk. I don't need to be governor—like I said, I was perfectly content running my little town—but I would like to be governor. I would love to represent our people and move our communities into a new phase of life. Together we can do just that. I'm not going to tell you that you should vote for me because I will be better than Eve Adams. I am going to ask you to vote for me because I believe I can do a better job. I will work endlessly to be the best governor possible. This is a dream we all had. Let's continue with what we had already set into motion. Thank you, gentlemen, and I will respect your decision." Cecilia walked out of the room again.

Cecilia returned to the waiting room. Eve Adams was sitting with her unnaturally long legs crossed. She looked at Cecilia and smiled.

"You know I'm not trying to undermine you, right?" Eve asked Cecilia. "I have not been on board with this merger idea from go, but if it's going to go forward and my town will basically be forced into it, then I want to run it. I have always thought of you as a great leader, I truly have, but I believe I could do a better job. I feel like I have more experience leading a large number of beings—I mean human beings of course. You all have forced my hand here." Eve paused and looked out the front window. "I like you, Cecilia, I really do. I will work with you if the men pick you, but I will not follow you blindly. I will challenge you when I see it fit to do so. No one should have absolute control—it never works out well for anyone. It never has, and it never will."

"I'm not asking anyone to blindly follow me. I have never wanted absolute control. I want a democracy. I hope we can all work toward that as well," Cecilia said, sitting down across from Eve. Eve seemed to be calm and collected. Cecilia was nervous and anxious, but Eve seemed like nothing bothered her.

"Democracies don't work either, at least for long. They seem great at first, but corruption always brings them down. Always," Eve said.

"I don't agree with that. We can control corruption. What form of government do you propose?" Cecilia asked, honestly curious. This woman had been nothing but an annoyance from the moment Cecilia had met her, and she wanted to know why.

"Personally, I don't think we need a government at all. I think things should stay as they were. Aside from having trouble growing wheat and not having enough livestock, my town is thriving as is. Every once in a while, we need to acquire some wheat and cattle from Jonestown, and that's fine. It works. I feel like you all are bullying me into joining you. Threatening me with being cut off and potential violence down the road."

"We never threatened violence," Cecilia interjected. "I don't ever want to see violence again."

"You did threaten violence. It was a veiled threat, but it was there," Eve said, still so calm and collected. She looked like she was thoroughly enjoying all of this.

"No one threatened you in any way," Cecilia said. "And I don't like being accused of anything of that nature."

"You said you didn't want any altercations down the road. That was your way of telling me that if I don't go along, there would be trouble down the road. Do you all think if I don't join you that you can eventually just overthrow me and take my town? Is it that important to you that I join up?" Eve asked.

"You should know that was not at all what I was implying. I just met you, but I can tell you're smarter than that," Cecilia said. Eve smiled at her. It was a creepy, indignant, and smug smile. "I would have hoped you would have known I meant if we don't merge the towns now, there could be altercations down the road over land and goods."

"There have never been any altercations, what makes you so certain there will be?" Eve asked.

"Towns don't get smaller as time goes on. People don't get less hungry. As the population of each town grows, so does the need for more goods. The size of our crops now will not be big enough to sustain growing communities, and eventually, each town will need to branch out. If we are a united community, we will all share equally in goods and services, so expansion wouldn't be an issue."

"Sounds like you have it all figured out, Miss Rodgers," Eve said.

"I thought we did," Cecilia responded. "Is it something I said? Is there something about me you don't like? Is that why you're so against all of this?"

"No not at all. As I said before, I like you a lot, Cecilia, I always have. I have a lot of respect for you and I think you are a rare and one-of-a-kind leader," Eve said. "Look, let me level with you. I wasn't supposed to be here. Something happened beyond my control, a direct threat to my very existence, and I barely escaped that. I ended up here with the rest of you. That was never part of the plan. If I may be blunt, I fucking hate it here. But since I am stuck here, I want to do things my way, and that's what I've been doing from go. Most people don't like me, and I honestly don't give two shits about it. I am well aware that I weird people out. It's mostly my appearance, but it's also because I don't give a shit about any of them. I built a town that has been very successful. You see, Cecilia, I too have leadership experience. You're not the only one around here who has run a large society before. I know you remember being more than just a mayor—I can see it in your eyes. That's another reason I like you so much—you are a tough lady. You have a lot of passion and fire inside you. I respect that."

"Excuse me, ladies," Marcus interrupted. "We have all voted. The anonymous votes are sealed in an envelope and locked in my desk drawer. I am going to go to city hall and get the town clerk, Melanie, to come count the votes. I don't think any of us should do that."

"That sounds like a good plan, Sheriff," Cecilia said. Eve nodded in agreement.

"I will return shortly with Melanie," Marcus said as he exited the office.

Cecilia returned her focus to Eve. Eve was staring at her.

"So let me see if I understand what you just laid out," Cecilia began. "You weren't supposed to be here and you hate it here, but since you're stuck, you want complete control of your environment. Is that accurate?"

"Yeah, pretty spot on," Eve said.

"Why not leave? Go back to where ever it is you came from?" Cecilia asked.

"I can't. It's too late for that now," Eve answered.

"Do you even care about your townspeople? Or do you just care about the power?"

"I have grown attached to a lot of them. The power isn't what I seek, Cecilia. I want the control. I don't like doing what someone else tells me to do. I don't like feeling helpless."

"You're not making me feel very good about the future," Cecilia said. "Sounds like no matter how those men voted, you and I will have issues moving forward."

"No, Cecilia, we won't. If I win, I want you as my second in command. You have a way of speaking to people that is both calming and respectful. People trust you. Your words have meaning and impact. You are a brilliant speaker," Eve said.

"Well, thank you," Cecilia said, a bit confused. She had really gotten the vibe that this woman didn't like her, despite continually saying that she did. "And if I win?"

"Same, I expect to be your second in command. I have the most experience, and I think we'd work well together. I can tell by your expression that you're confused. I'm sure by my gruffness and argumentative nature you got the vibe that I didn't like you, even though I told you otherwise. Look, sometimes, people need to be challenged to come back down to earth. Sometimes people can develop an ego and need to be reminded that they are indeed human and capable of making mistakes. Now I'm not saying that is the case with you or this situation per se. I guess what I'm trying to say is that I wanted to remind you that you're not the only one capable of this position. The truth is, the only reason I even considered all of this was because of you. Once I learned they had tapped you, I had to at least hear what the plan would be for this venture. And then once I saw you standing at that podium, I realized that could and should be me. So there was a bit of jealousy, but I assure you I respect you and I will respect the vote of those men."

As if on cue, Marcus walked through the front doors with Melanie.

"You two ready for the count?" he asked them. Cecilia and Eve nodded and stood up.

Everyone followed Marcus back into the briefing room. Marcus went to his desk and unlocked the drawer. He pulled out the sealed envelope and handed it to Melanie. Marcus, Cecilia, and Eve sat down with the other men. Melanie stood behind the podium and opened the envelope. She pulled out five folded pieces of paper and began to count each vote out loud. Four votes for Cecilia and one for Eve. The room awkwardly applauded. Cecilia thanked everyone. Eve looked angry but kept quiet. Cecilia knew she was going to have problems with Eve. It didn't matter what Eve had said; Cecilia didn't trust her. There was something about her that just screamed "liar." Eve knew how to manipulate people. She knew how to tell people what they wanted to hear. Cecilia had dealt with difficult people before and would deal with Eve appropriately. For the time being, she just wanted to move on with the planning stage of the merger. She just wanted to get everything settled and be done for the day. There were going to be many speed bumps on the road to a new community, not just Eve. Cecilia wanted everyone on the same page and hoped she could get everyone's cooperation. She knew at least four of the men in that room would be cooperative. As long as she had the support of the majority of the other leaders, she would be able to move forward with her plans fairly easily.

Melanie left and returned to City Hall. The rest of them spent the afternoon hammering out details and splitting up responsibilities. To Cecilia's surprise, Eve was very engaged and helpful in the planning stage. She assumed it was a ploy to stay in good graces with the other leaders and Marcus. Eve was smart enough to know she had to play the game if she wanted a chance to win the next election. Cecilia hoped that Eve's desire to eventually win the top seat would lead to her playing ball and being cooperative. Cecilia wasn't going to hold her breath, though; she knew she would get the real Eve in private, while everyone else saw the fake team player Eve.

One of the mayors, Jeramiah Cummings, looked angry and uncomfortable the whole time. He worked well with everyone, but every time Eve spoke, he got a look of hatred on his face. Cecilia could tell that man did not want to be around Eve at all. Cecilia tried not to worry about any of that; she honestly didn't care about whatever petty differences Eve and Jeramiah seemed to have. She really just wanted to get to work on uniting the towns.

After several hours of planning and discussion, everyone parted ways for the evening. Cecilia went back to Marcus's place with him. Alexis had prepared another delicious dinner for the three of them. Despite trying for years, Marcus and Alexis had never had any children, so it was nice to have company. Especially for Alexis. Marcus was gone a lot for work, and Alexis felt lonely a lot of the time. She busied herself with chores and tending to the garden, but she craved human interaction. She loved her husband and enjoyed his company, but it was nice to have someone else around for a little while.

Marcus and Cecilia filled Alexis in on the happenings of their day. Alexis wasn't surprised that Eve had caused problems. Everyone in Henderson knew of Eve and her overbearing personality. Eve had tried to talk John into some kind of partnership; the details of it had never gone public. John's hatred and distrust of women had put a stop to any of it before it could even get going. That had infuriated Eve, and she had cut Henderson off from any goods or services they had gotten from Everett. The most damaging being they had been cut off from Everett's metal. Eve and her townspeople had figured out how to manufacture metal. Being cut off from Everett also meant Henderson had to find a new town to trade with for corn. Henderson didn't have enough land to grow enough corn to support the town's needs, so they had to supplement it from surrounding towns. Once they had been cut off from Everett, they could only rely on Mayfield. That drove up the cost of corn, meaning most in town had to go without. That was why the entire town was not only on board with the merger but ecstatic about it.

"So do you think she'll go along with all of this?" Alexis asked after they had told her what Eve had done that day.

"I'm hopeful she will," Cecilia answered. "I think her desire to be governor someday will make her play nice for now, at least publicly. I fear she will be a nightmare for us, though."

"That's too bad. It's too bad we can't just leave her out of all of this," Alexis said.

"I kind of wish we could too, but that would be a logistical nightmare. I wasn't aware of this until today, but Everett is basically in the middle of three other towns. Trying to work around it would be next to impossible, especially with a pissed-off Eve. I think our best course of action is to just include them and do our best to work with her instead of against her. She's the type of person who needs to have control, so if we just make her feel like she has some control, we should be okay. I also believe once we have everything settled and our new society is booming, she'll come around even more," Cecilia said. She did really believe that.

"And we all need their metal, for now, let's not forget about that. She thinks she has everyone by the balls with that. But we are close to being able to manufacture it as well," Marcus added.

"Yes, of course that goes without saying. Hopefully we can all work together on that front as well," Cecilia said.

"I hope she'll go along. I hope she will play nice. We all saw firsthand what John's 'my way or no way' approach did to people. She strikes me as a similar type of person. Probably why they hated each other so much," Alexis said, getting up and clearing the table.

"That kind of stuff won't be happening anymore. We won't allow it. We are creating a fair and balanced society. We want to lead the people of this new nation, not control them. We want the people to have a say in everything," Cecilia told Alexis. "There will never be a supreme leader again. We will have elected officials from each town who will bring their town's needs and concerns to the table to be addressed and taken care of. This will work and it will work wonderfully, despite people like Eve."

Alexis returned to the table with tea for the three of them. "Marcus, I'm curious, who do you think voted for her?" Cecilia asked him.

"I am positive it was Lowell Pattison, the mayor of Jonestown. He was the only one who would work with her. They have had an alliance for years. He's a good man, but she has him wrapped around her little finger," Marcus replied.

"Will he be a problem for us too?" Cecilia asked.

"No, like I said, he's a good man. I'm sure he knew the rest of us would vote for you, so he just voted for her to stay in her good graces. I've had long chats with everyone, except for Eve, and Lowell is one hundred percent behind this merger. His town is struggling, especially with winter looming. He needs this as much as the rest of us, if not more. He'll play ball, I guarantee it."

"Okay, good. As long as we have everyone else's support, Eve shouldn't be much of an issue," Cecilia said.

"There will be issues with her, I have no doubt about it. She will be a pain in our side," Marcus said as he sipped his tea. "She played nice after the vote—it's a tactic I hear she is good at, doing and saying what she thinks people want to hear so she can manipulate you later. We'll have to keep an eye on her."

"I get all that. I don't know her well, and I'm still hopeful we can get her on board once she sees that what we're doing will make life so much better for everyone, including her," Cecilia responded.

"No one knows her well, that's part of the problem. One thing I've heard that is consistent about her, though, is that she's very manipulative. She seems like an angry person in general too. The couple of times I have spoken with her didn't turn out too well. She is extremely condescending," Marcus said.

"That she is," Cecilia agreed. "We pretty much know where we stand with her and that she will potentially cause us problems. We just have to deal with her as we go. Now tell me about the others. I got a good vibe about Dean Richards. You've told me a little about Lowell Pattison. Who are the other two mayors? What are they all about?"

Marcus was confused at first by Cecilia's questions; she should have known a little bit about each of them. They had all been around for a long time. But then he remembered she had mentioned she was struggling with some memory issues.

"Well," Marcus began, "Carl Mayfield, the mayor of Mayfield— creative town name, huh?" He chuckled. "Is a fine man. Mayfield is the closest town to Henderson, and so I've had a lot of dealings with Carl, and all of them have been more than pleasant. I even consider him to be a friend. He and John didn't get along at all, so all town business went through me. I have no worries about Carl. He is also one hundred percent on board. He speaks very highly of you too and is very excited to work with you on this. So that leaves us with Jeramiah Cummings, the mayor of Freeland. He too is a good man, but he has a temper. A wicked temper that gets worse with every drink he takes, and the man loves his liquor. He's totally on board as well. He and I had many conversations leading up to today. He's glad you are going to be leading all of this. My only concern with Jeramiah, besides his temper, is his feelings toward Eve. He absolutely hates that woman. Despises her. Everett and Freeland used to have a decent working relationship back when Eve's husband, Daryl, was still alive. Jeramiah and Daryl had worked out an agreement on trading goods. I don't know the details of the agreement, but it sounded like it was fair and worked out well for both sides. Well, when Daryl passed away a few years ago, Eve changed the agreement in her favor. Jeramiah obviously didn't like that so she just did away with it and him. She black-balled him and his town, completely cut them off. That's when she went to Lowell and basically forced him into an agreement. She bullied them both to get what she wanted. So I can see big problems arising between the two of them. Jeramiah will work well with the rest of us, but he won't deal with her. I have heard him say he wished her dead many times."

"Well, we can work around that. Eve told me that she respects me and will be willing to work with me, so maybe I can just play liaison between the two of them. It's good to hear the others are all on board and excited, it should make this process go smoothly. I don't know about you, but I came into this knowing there would be a lot of bumps in the road. I knew this wasn't going to be a picnic. We're upending everyone's way of life. We're fixing to change how our whole world works right now. It's not going to be easy or fun. But it is necessary," Cecilia said.

"I agree, Cecilia," Marcus said. "I came into this with the same mindset. But I think it will be fun even though it will be a lot of hard work and stress. The end product will make the journey worthwhile."

"For sure," Cecilia agreed. "I have never backed down from any challenge in my life, and I don't ever plan to."

"Neither have we," Marcus said, looking at his wife sitting next to him. "We've been through a lot together and we've always come out stronger people. This will be no different." He leaned over and kissed Alexis on the cheek.

"We have been through a lot," Alexis said. "But we've done it together, and that's what matters most. Now we can all pull together and create something no one has seen before. Marcus has told me everything about the plans to unite the towns, and I think it's a wonderful idea."

"Thank you both," Cecilia said smiling.

"You bet," Marcus said. "Is there anything else you're curious about?"

"Well, there was one thing that struck me odd. You mentioned Eve was married and that her husband did deals with other towns. Was he really involved with running Everett? I only ask because Eve doesn't strike me as the kind of person willing to share power," Cecilia asked.

"You're right, she certainly is not. But she is also very smart. She knows she intimidates people. She knows people are weirded out by her. Daryl was the opposite—people loved him. He was bright, funny, and charismatic. Eve used his likability to her advantage. She manipulated Daryl into thinking he had something to do with running that town, so he would do her bidding. She used him every step of the way to get her way. Hell, she even used their kids to get what she wanted. They had seven kids, all boys." Marcus paused for a second. "I don't mean to be rude, but you really don't remember much, do you?" he asked Cecilia.

"No, I don't," Cecilia responded, a little embarrassed. "I don't know why either. We had a bizarre lightning storm not too long ago. I went to bed that night, assumably with my memory intact and woke up the next day with totally different memories. Really out-there and strange memories. But the more people tell me, the more I am beginning to regain my memory. Things you have said to me start to click with me. So if you don't mind, please tell me more."

"That is bizarre, but I have heard of people losing their memory before. I feel for you, that's for sure, it's got to be frustrating," Marcus said. Alexis got up from the table to get more tea for them.

"To say the least," Cecilia said. "But I have come to terms with it, and I just want to move on from it. I remember everything that has happened since then, so I'm not really worried about it anymore."

"Hopefully you continue to regain some of it," Marcus said. "As I was saying, Daryl and Eve had seven sons. She used being the mother of seven boys as a way of making people respect her more. She used being a mother to make people see her as more human. You've met her—she is not the most humane person in the world. She is off and frankly kind of scary. The boys all seemed to be fine, well-behaved boys growing up. They are all now married and have a lot of kids themselves. Pumping out seven or more kids must run in that family. All of their sons have at least seven kids or are working on that many. Everett allows some strange things—most notable is having more than one wife. The men of that town are allowed to marry as many women as they would like—well, except for Daryl. He was not allowed to have more than one wife. Now that I think about it, I don't think anyone was until their sons came of age. Yeah, that seems right. I feel like that practice was put in place after Daryl died. But anyway, all of Eve's sons have multiple wives and many children with each one. It's way too strange for me to even try to understand. I couldn't imagine a life like that."

"That is strange, but I have heard of that practice before. I would never live that way either," Cecilia said.

"No way," Alexis added as she returned to the table with fresh tea.

"Most people wouldn't," Marcus said. "Her sons seem to be the ones manufacturing the metal. They all live on a big chunk of land, presumably owned by Eve, and are rarely ever seen by anyone. Their land is surrounded by huge walls and fences. No one knows what they are up to in there. That whole family is very strange and not forthcoming about anything. I tried to see if they would share their technology for manufacturing metal, and they would not. A man that had worked for them for a bit while Daryl was still alive moved away from Everett as soon as Daryl had died. He came to Henderson. He knew some very basic things about making metal, primarily how to mine the ore. Before he could teach us much of anything, he disappeared. His body was found in the woods a couple weeks later by some hunters. He had been decapitated. Everyone knew it had to be Everett that had done that, but there was no way to prove it. I opened an investigation, but no one in Everett would talk to me. Eve told me it had to be someone from Henderson—no one from her town was capable of such violence. I know she had him killed. I am positive of that. I just can't prove it. I'm not sure if any of that will be of any relevance to what we are doing here, but her unstableness worries me in general."

"As it does me too. Any odd behavior is concerning, especially murder, while we try to unite the towns. Everett has to be one of them. We need their land and goods. I wish we could exclude them, but that would lead to bigger problems with them down the road. We need to get this done as soon as possible to avoid any further resistance from Eve and her town. I don't feel like we need to worry about her sons until they give us a reason to," Cecilia said. Everything Marcus had just told her did sound strange and extremely worrisome, but none of it really surprised her. Eve was an odd duck through and through, so nothing would surprise Cecilia at that point.

"I agree with that," Marcus said. "I have some good friends in Everett that will keep an eye on Eve and her sons. They will remain anonymous—I cannot risk their safety. They are the town hunters, and we've had a weekly meeting set up in the woods for some time now. If Eve ever found out about that, my friends would be killed. One of their daughters is married to one of Eve's sons. My friend tried to forbid that marriage, but his daughter went along with it anyway. She was brainwashed by Eve, her sons, and the other wives. My friend is furious about it but doesn't let his daughter know that. His daughter visits him regularly. She won't say much about what goes on there, but she does say enough for him to have some good information for me every week." Marcus paused and stood up to stretch. It was getting very late, and they had another busy day ahead of them. "I am more than willing to tell you more at a later date, ma'am, but I think we should all get some sleep. It's terribly late, and we have another busy day tomorrow."

"That sounds good to me," Alexis said, stretching and yawning.

"I appreciate everything you have told me this evening, Sheriff. You have given me some great information that will help me navigate this process ahead of us. I look forward to more information as we go along," Cecilia said, standing up from the table. "I also want to thank you both for your kindness, hospitality, and company. I have really enjoyed my time with you two."

"You are so very welcome," Alexis said. "You are welcome here anytime."

"Yes, ma'am, you are always welcome here with us. We have thoroughly enjoyed your company as well," Marcus said. "Well, good night then. We'll see you tomorrow morning."

"Good night to both of you and thanks again." Cecilia smiled and headed for her room. She could hear Marcus and Alexis chatting as they got ready for bed. She couldn't understand what they were saying; she could only hear their muffled voices through the walls.

*****

The next morning, Marcus and Cecilia arrived at the sheriff's office about an hour early so Marcus could handle some town business. Lowell Pattison was already there. Cecilia and Lowell took a seat at a table in the briefing room and began to chat while Marcus took care of what he needed to do.

"Good morning, Lowell," Cecilia said, settling into her chair.

"Good morning," Lowell replied. "How was your evening?"

"Oh, I had a great evening. I am staying with Marcus and his wife. They are wonderful hosts. How was your evening?" Cecilia asked.

"It was okay. I am staying at the inn downtown. The other men wanted to have drinks after we left here, but I declined. I'm not much of a drinker, and I wanted some sleep. Dean didn't stay out long. I was outside smoking a cigar when he came back, and he joined me out front to smoke for a bit. Those other two guys must have really tied one on, though. I heard them come back to the inn quite late last night," Lowell said. Cecilia wasn't surprised Lowell hadn't joined the other men; he seemed to be somewhat of a loner.

"Sounds like they had a good time," Cecilia chuckled. "But I'm with you—I would opt for sleep over drinking any night too." She looked across the room at Marcus. He was at his desk, scribbling away in a notebook. "So, Lowell, tell me how you feel about what we are doing here?"

"Honestly, ma'am, I love it!" Lowell responded with excitement in his voice. "I couldn't be more excited about it! As you probably know, I have been forced into an agreement with Eve and her town for years. Excuse my language, but she's had me by the balls for a long time." Lowell paused and looked around the room. Cecilia assumed he was making sure Eve hadn't come in already. "Not too many people know this, but I became mayor after our original mayor suddenly died. There was a lot of speculation that he did not die of natural causes. He had had a falling out with Eve after her husband passed away…" Lowell lowered his head. "Daryl was a good man," he added, shaking his head. "I'm not sure what he ever saw in that woman, but he always said he loved her. You see, I was the town's sheriff, originally and I loved that job. When Tom, our first mayor, died, I assumed his son would take over, but he didn't want anything to do with the job. After Tom's funeral, his son moved away and has never been heard from again. It's assumed he's dead too. I was told by the town's council that I would be mayor. I politely declined, and I was told that wasn't an option. I was told that it had to be me or else. I was never told what the 'or else' meant exactly, but I knew it meant 'Do this or you will also suddenly die.' So I did. It has been a nightmare, honestly. I didn't know how to be a mayor. I didn't trust anyone on my council. But I toughed it out, and now we're here. That's why I couldn't be happier. With you running everything and Marcus in charge of law enforcement, I am confident my town will thrive once again. Thank you so much for a being a part of this!"

"It's my pleasure. I've been hearing a lot of really negative things about Everett lately. I am glad we can all come together and build a new community. There is strength in numbers, you know," Cecilia said.

"I do know. That's another reason I am so excited," Lowell responded.

"You know we will get Eve to go along, right?" Cecilia asked.

"Yeah, until she gets pissed off about something. She kind of has an upper hand."

"The metal?" Cecilia asked.

"Yeah, the metal. She pretty much has us all by the balls with that," Lowell said.

"I'm not worried about it. We can learn to manufacture metal as well. She won't hold the monopoly on it for long. Besides, we have her by the balls too. If we cut her off, her people go hungry, and she knows it. She can have all the metal in the world, but they can't eat it—they need crops and they just don't have the infrastructure for growing them. She won't be pleasant to deal with—that I am sure of—but she will have to play ball," Cecilia said. "She's only one person. We can't let her intimidate us. I certainly won't be intimidated by her."

"I just hope more people don't end up dead. Death seems to follow that woman," Lowell said quietly.

"I won't let that happen!" Cecilia said. "People won't be killed on my watch!"

"I hope not. I've seen too much of it already," Lowell sighed.

"Trust me, I won't let it happen. *We* won't let it happen," Cecilia said.

Dean Richards walked into the briefing room. He looked around the room and headed for Cecilia and Lowell. Dean joined them at the table and said good morning to them.

"Good morning, Dean," Cecilia said. "It's nice to see you again."

"It's nice to see you again, too, ma'am," Dean replied. "And you too, Lowell." The men shook hands.

"Always a pleasure, Dean," Lowell said as they shook hands.

"How's my brother doing, ma'am?" Dean asked Cecilia.

"He's great," Cecilia responded. "He is a terrific doctor and an even finer man."

"That's great to hear," Dean said. "We were all so sad to see him move away, but our town already had a doctor, and that's all my brother has ever wanted to do with his life, to be a town doctor."

"Well, we sure are glad to have him as our doctor," Cecilia said. Cecilia hated small talk, but she knew it was part of life and especially a part of conducting business. These people weren't her friends; they were colleagues, and colleagues exchanged a lot of small talk. "He's helped us all through some tough times lately. He is a wise and very kind man. You should be proud of your brother."

"I am. I am extremely proud of him for following his dreams. He could have worked with me on the town council, but he had always wanted to be a doctor," Dean said.

Two of Marcus's deputies rushed into the briefing room. The commotion of their frantic entrance distracted Cecilia and the two men at the table. The deputies rushed to Marcus and whispered something in his ear. Marcus jumped out of his chair with a look of panic and disbelief on his face. He shouted, "Take me there!" and ran out of the room with his deputies. Cecilia looked at Dean and Lowell; they looked as confused as she felt.

"What could that be about?" Dean asked the table.

"Who knows, but it looked like an emergency," Lowell responded.

"I'm sure if it pertains to us, Marcus will fill us in later. He does still have a town to police and run. He needs to handle town business first," Cecilia said. "We will wait for Eve, Jeramiah, and Carl to arrive and then move forward with the day's work with or without Marcus."

Dean and Lowell nodded in agreement. Cecilia opened her notebook and started looking over the talking points for the day. Lowell and Dean opened their notebooks as well. The three of them sat in silence for a while, studying their notebooks. Cecilia felt for Marcus, Henderson was the biggest town out of all of them. As the sheriff and now the acting mayor, Marcus had a lot on his plate. Cecilia was beyond impressed with Marcus; he handled everything so well and did it all with a smile. She had a ton of respect for the man. She hoped whatever was happening wasn't too serious, although it sure had seemed to be very serious. Marcus's reaction to whatever his deputies had told him had been severe. She knew it was something really bad, but at the same time, she hoped she was wrong. But his face when he heard the news told her she wasn't wrong.

Shit! Hopefully it didn't have anything to do with Alexis. A pit began to grow in Cecilia's stomach. *Oh, please don't let it have anything to do with Alexis,* she thought.

Carl and Jeramiah entered the briefing room. They both looked tired and haggard. It was clear they had had a long night of drinking. Jeramiah looked worse off than Carl. Carl and Jeramiah joined the rest of them at the table. Jeramiah looked like he hadn't slept all night and he smelled like a tavern.

"What's going on?" Carl asked. "We saw Marcus and a couple of his deputies running toward town on our way in here."

"We don't know," Lowell responded. "Looked extremely serious though."

"Yeah, they sure did have a look of panic on their faces," Carl said. "I hope everything turns out okay."

"Did you say they were headed into town?" Cecilia asked.

"Yes, ma'am. Headed for downtown in a full sprint," Carl replied.

Cecilia let out a sigh of relief. That was the opposite direction from Marcus and Alexis's place. That made Cecilia feel better; it obviously didn't have anything to do with Alexis.

"Well, gentlemen, should we begin or wait for Eve?" Cecilia asked.

"Let's just begin without her," Lowell said. "She probably went back to Everett."

"Yeah, that would be my guess too," Dean added. "I didn't see her at the inn this morning."

"I didn't either." Lowell said. "I know that woman all too well, and I know when she doesn't get her way, she just checks out. It's her way or no way. I bet she went home furious last night."

"I have no doubt she did," Dean added. "Let's just get to work, and if she does end up showing up, we'll fill her in then."

"Okay, sounds good to me," Cecilia said. She flipped back a few pages in her notebook and began to lay out some ideas. Everyone else scribbled down notes as she spoke, adding their input when needed.

*****

The deputies led Marcus to a room at the inn. There was another one of his deputies standing outside of the room. Marcus walked into the room and his jaw hit the floor. The pungent smell of blood filled his nostrils immediately and turned his stomach. He slowly walked to the bed. Lying on the bed was Eve. Her throat had been slit almost all the way through. Blood saturated the straw mattress. Her dark eyes stared up at the ceiling. Her eyes were creepier than ever. Marcus hesitantly reached out and closed her eyes. He just stood there in shock, staring at her. Whoever did that to her had a lot of hate in their heart. Marcus could see the hatred in how deep that cut was. He sighed and turned around. Marcus left the room.

"Who reported this?" he asked Travis Pounders, the deputy who had been standing guard at the door.

"Mr. Jenkins. He said he was doing his rounds, waking people for breakfast, and she didn't respond. He said he tried knocking and yelling for quite a while and no response. So he finally entered the room and found her like that. You shoulda seen him, boss, he was white as a sheet." Travis explained.

"I think I have a fairly good idea who could have done this," Marcus said. "But I'd like to talk to Mr. Jenkins."

"He said he'd be in his office if we need anything else," Travis said.

Marcus told the deputies to stay put and headed for Mr. Jenkins's office. Paul Jenkins owned and operated the inn.

"Please, come on in, Sheriff," Paul said after Marcus knocked on his open door. "Wish we were seeing each other on better circumstances."

"Me too, Mr. Jenkins," Marcus replied, sitting down in a chair across from Paul. "Tell me everything."

"Well, Sheriff, as I told Deputy Pounders, I was doing my rounds this morning—you know the breakfast wakeup calls—and that woman from Everett didn't respond when I knocked on her door. Usually, people will at least acknowledge me when I knock. I didn't think much of it at first—she is an odd duck, you know. Honestly, I didn't even want to rent her a room yesterday, but I kind of had too. She creeps me out, Sheriff." Paul looked at Marcus and noticed he had a 'Get to the point' look on his face. "Anyways, I tried knocking again, and still nothing. So I hollered and knocked, still no response. I was gettin' a little irritated. I thought she was just being rude and ignoring me. Either that or she had already left, but I hadn't seen her leave. I can see people come and go from my desk here. After a few more attempts at a response, I hollered I was coming in. I figured if she had just been ignoring me, she'd at least respond to me saying I'm coming in. But no response to that either and now I know why. I opened that fuckin' door and slammed it right back shut. I almost lost my breakfast, Sheriff. It was gruesome. Never seen anything like it before, and I never want to again. I will never get that image out of my head."

"Did you see her come in last night?" Marcus asked.

"Yea, she and those other fellas from out of town all came in at the same time yesterday. Probably 'round seven. They just missed dinner," Paul replied.

"Did she leave again at any time last night?" Marcus asked.

"No, sir, not to my knowledge. I close up at eight every night. My son, Paul Jr., watches the doors overnight. I asked him about that, and he said he never saw her leave," Paul explained. "Junior did say that them fellas left shortly after they had returned—well, three of 'em at least. One of them returned 'bout an hour later. The other two were out quite late, didn't come back 'til middle of the night. Musta closed down old Lucky's last night, be my guess."

"Did Junior say anything else about the goings on around here last night? I'd like to talk to him too, if I could."

"Sure thing, Sheriff. He didn't mention anything else to me. I'll go fetch him for ya." Paul stood up and left his office. He returned shortly with a very tired Paul Jr.

"Hello, Sheriff," Paul Jr. said as he took a seat next to Marcus. Paul Sr. sat back down behind his desk.

"Hello, Junior," Marcus said. Everyone in town called him Junior. "Tell me what happened here last night, if you would."

"I saw them fellas from out of town leave right after I took over for my dad, three of em at least. The other fella kept going out front to smoke, even though I said he could smoke in his room. One of the fellas returned 'bout an hour after they had all left. He stood out front and smoked with the fella that stayed back. Them other two fellas stayed out very late. They must've closed down Lucky's last night. They were quite drunk when they came back," Paul Jr. explained.

"What about the woman?" Marcus asked. "Did you see her at all last night?"

"No, sir, I didn't see her at all. In fact, I haven't seen her the whole time she's been here. Dad says she's a weird one though," Paul Jr. replied.

"None of that matters, Junior. I just need to know what went on here last night, because something clearly happened here last night. She didn't do that to herself. Did you hear anyone arguing or fighting last night?"

"No, sir, it was all quiet 'round here last night. Seemed like a normal night to me." Paul Jr. said. "Them drunk fellas was kinda noisy when they came back, I told em to keep it down. They did. They seemed like good guys to me."

"After you asked them to keep it down, did you hear anything else after that?" Marcus asked.

"No, sir. Like I said, they kept quiet after that. Probably went to bed and passed right out. They was drunk!" Paul Jr. replied.

"Okay, thank you guys," Marcus said, standing up.

"You have any idea who would do such a thing, Sheriff?" Paul Sr. asked. "Are we safe 'round here?"

"You all are safe—this was definitely focused solely on her. Whoever did this obviously wanted her dead and wanted it badly. I don't see this as the beginning of some kind of killing spree if that's what you're worried about," Marcus said.

"Thank you, Sheriff. If you need anything else, we'll both be here," Paul Sr. said.

"Thank you, guys. I'll be in touch," Marcus said and left the room.

Marcus returned to his deputies. Marcus sent the other two back to the station and told them to bring Cecilia to him. They ran off to go get her.

"What did you see after you got here, Deputy?" Marcus asked Travis.

"Same thing you just saw, boss. Fuckin' ghastly, isn't it?" Travis responded.

"It is," Marcus agreed. "What else did you see? Who else did you see?"

"Not much else, boss. A few people milling about. This is the busiest I ever seen this place, with all them mayors in town," Travis said. "One thing caught my attention, though. Everyone that walked past me looked at me with a curious look on their faces, except for one man. Don't know who he is, but I know he's one of the mayors in town meeting with you all."

"Short guy, kinda chubby? Black hair and a beard?" Marcus asked.

"Yup, that's the guy. I thought it was weird, boss, he wouldn't even look at me. Everyone else kinda stared at me and then at the door to the room here." Travis motioned at Eve's room's door behind him with his thumb. "But not that guy—he just stared at the floor and hurried past me."

"Well, that is very strange indeed," Marcus said, scratching his chin. He knew exactly whom Travis was referring to. "Sounds like I'll need to interview everyone who stayed here last night."

"Yes, sir. You'll be busy, boss," Travis said. "It's a damn shame. Shit like this ain't supposed to happen in our town."

"No, it is not. I am furious, Deputy."

The other deputies returned with Cecilia.

"Give us a minute, guys," Marcus said to his deputies. "I have the scene secure. Go get some tea or something."

The deputies left, quietly chatting among themselves. Cecilia was confused. What scene? She looked at Marcus and saw the stress and anger etched into his face.

"What is it, Sheriff?" she asked.

"Eve was found murdered this morning," Marcus said.

"*What?*" Cecilia shouted. "*Are you fucking serious?* How? What happened? Who would do that? You can't be serious!"

"Unfortunately, I am serious." Marcus sighed. "Someone cut her throat. And cut it deep."

"Holy shit, Marcus! You *are* serious! How did this happen?" Cecilia exclaimed.

"I don't know how it happened—should've never happened on my watch, but it did," Marcus replied.

"Don't beat yourself up, Sheriff. This isn't your fault by any means. Where is she now?" Cecilia asked.

"In this room here," Marcus responded, pointing to the door behind them.

"Can I see her?" Cecilia asked.

"If you want to, ma'am, but I must warn you it's gruesome. It ain't pretty."

"I've seen some gruesome shit in my life, Sheriff. I'll be just fine," Cecilia reassured him.

"Okay, let's go," Marcus said and slowly opened the door.

They stepped into the room, and the stench of decay made them both gag. Eve's grayish skin was melting off her like an ice cream cone in the July heat. The smell was overpowering. They quickly left the room, gagging.

"I've smelled that before," Cecilia coughed. "At Doctor Richard's office after we found that young man."

"She wasn't like that thirty minutes ago!" Marcus exclaimed. "She was intact last time I saw her."

"We've seen this before. It happened to the young man and Mallory," Cecilia said. "Doctor Richards said he found microscopic bugs feasting on their remains. We should get him here to look at Eve's remains."

"I'll send for him immediately," Marcus said. "Would you mind standing guard for a minute while I fetch my deputy?"

"No, I wouldn't mind at all," Cecilia said.

Marcus jogged off and returned within minutes with Deputy Pounders. He told Travis to stay put and not let anyone near that room no matter what.

"No one is allowed close to this room unless I am with them," Marcus told Travis.

"Yes, sir," Travis said.

"Come on, Cecilia, let's get someone on their way to fetch Doctor Richards," Marcus said.

Marcus and Cecilia headed out of the inn and back to his office. Marcus sent two of his deputies to go get Doctor Richards. The other mayors were still sitting around the table. All of them, except for

Jeramiah, looked very confused. Marcus asked Cecilia to step out of the room with him. He led her to his personal office and closed the door behind them.

"I think I know who did this," he told her as they sat down across his desk from each other. "I want to announce what happened to the other mayors and see how they respond to the news."

"You think it was one of them? Jeramiah?" Cecilia asked.

"I do, yes. I think he did it. That's why I want to gauge everyone's reaction. He should confirm my suspicions just by how he reacts," Marcus said.

"And then what?" Cecilia asked. "We arrest him?"

"No, I don't want to spook him, and I need to do an investigation. Besides, technically, I can't arrest him, even if he did do it. I would need to involve his sheriff, but he won't be any help. Jeramiah's sheriff is his brother, Julius. He hated Eve just as much as Jeramiah did. Julius will protect his brother," Marcus said.

"So what can we do then?" Cecilia asked. "If we do determine it was Jeramiah, we need to bring him to justice. Just because no one liked Eve doesn't mean she should have been murdered. We cannot have people killing each other. We have to set an example here, Sheriff."

"I know we do, and we need to figure out how to do just that. Jeramiah was smart about it, if he did do it. He did it before we were all united. Before we had one unified legal system. I'm sure he believes he'll get away with it because he knows his brother won't arrest him and he knows I can't," Marcus said, a little dejected.

"If he did it, we will bring him to justice. I will not stand for murder in this community. I've seen far too much of it already. It ends here with us!" Cecilia exclaimed. She could see that Marcus was dejected and felt helpless. She would do whatever it took to bring whoever did that to justice. "Let's go tell those men and test your theory, Sheriff."

"Let's," he responded, standing up and opening the office door for Cecilia. They went back into the briefing room.

The other mayors were sitting at the table, chatting among themselves. They all knew something bad had gone down and were floating theories around the table. Eve being murdered was not one of their theories. Not a single one of those men would lose a minute of sleep over her death.

"Gentlemen," Marcus began, "we have some terrible news to share." The room hushed, and everyone except for Jeramiah looked at Marcus. Jeramiah stared at the table. Marcus sighed and continued, "This morning, Eve Adams was found murdered in her room at the inn. It is a gruesome scene and one that should have never happened in my town."

Cecilia watched the other mayors to gauge how they reacted to the news. Everyone looked shocked, except for Jeramiah. He looked like he already knew what Marcus was telling them. Jeramiah just stared at the table. His face and body language convinced Cecilia that he had indeed done it. Now they just had to prove it.

"There is no place in our new society for violence and murder!" Marcus continued. His anger and frustration was visible to all. "We will find out who did this and bring them to justice. Mark my words, whoever murdered her will pay for their crime! We will not tolerate this shit around here!"

"Excuse me, Sheriff," Jeramiah said, standing up.

"What is it?" Marcus asked coldly. He had noticed Jeramiah's reaction, and it had convinced him that Jeramiah had done it.

"Correct me if I'm wrong, but you don't have the jurisdiction to hold whoever did this responsible. I mean if whoever did this wasn't a resident of Henderson," Jeramiah said with a shaky voice.

"The crime happened in my town, therefore, I do indeed have jurisdiction," Marcus replied.

"I don't believe you do," Jeramiah said. "I doubt whoever did this will ever come forward, and you will have some trouble figuring it out—again, especially if it wasn't one of your own that did this."

"Do you know something the rest of us don't?" Marcus asked. "Why does any of that matter to you so much?"

"Look, no one in this room liked that woman. At all. None of us will miss her. Are we going to go on down to Lucky's tavern and celebrate this? No, but we ain't sad about it either. In my opinion, we should bring her remains to her family and call it a day. Our goals of uniting the towns and building a new society just got a hell of a lot easier without that woman. Let's just move on," Jeramiah said and sat down.

"We cannot do that," Cecilia said. "We cannot let people think they can get away with murder, no matter who the victim is. Whether she was liked or not is irrelevant. We can't have people getting killed, period. We've all seen far too much of it in our lives, and no matter the circumstances, it is always horrific. It stops here and now. We will make an example out of whoever did this."

"Alright fuck this!" Jeramiah shouted, standing up again. "You know what? I was on board with this whole uniting towns thing, but I'm starting to second guess it now. If we all weren't here right now working on this merger, none of us would even give two shits that woman is dead. Fuck, we would probably celebrate it if it didn't happen at this moment in time. She was a horrible, nasty, controlling bitch and I for one am glad she's gone! I will not stand here and listen to this shit anymore! Drop it now or my town is out!"

"Jeramiah!" Marcus yelled. "Sit down and shut the fuck up!" The room fell dead silent. Marcus never spoke to people like that. "Your temper is getting the best of you again," Marcus said, a bit calmer. "I'm tired of this shit too. I should arrest you right now!"

"*For what?*" Jeramiah exclaimed. "For speaking my mind? For having harsh words for that woman? Go ahead, Marcus, arrest me!" Jeramiah stared down Marcus. "That's right, you can't!" Jeramiah stormed out of the room.

Marcus turned to follow him, and Cecilia grabbed his arm. "Let him go, Sheriff," she said softly. "He's too wound up to deal with right now."

"He did it," Marcus whispered to Cecilia.

"I know," she whispered back. "We'll get him somehow."

"One way or the other, he is mine," Marcus snarled.

"Well, gentlemen, in light of what is going on around here today, I think we will have to postpone our meetings for the day," Cecilia said to the remaining mayors. "I appreciate all of you and your commitment to what we are doing here. I hope you all can have a good day, and please, keep what went on in here today to your-selves. Thank you, gentlemen."

The other mayors slowly got up, gathered their things, and left the room. They didn't say anything to anyone; they just qui-etly exited the sheriff's office. Cecilia knew the men would all end up together somewhere and talk about what had happened. That was of little concern to her, as long as they kept it to themselves. Jeramiah had been correct about one thing: no one had liked Eve. No one was going to miss her. But her murder could not go unpun-ished. She wanted the other mayors to keep quiet about it so word didn't get out too soon. She didn't want people figuring out the loop-hole Jeramiah had and get their revenge on people before they had a new law enforcement in place. This merger had to happen soon. Immediately, if at all possible. Jeramiah was now going to be the problem with moving forward. She wished they could just arrest him and get past it all. They didn't have any evidence, though. As badly as she had wanted to get the merger done as quickly as possible, Cecilia knew they had to investigate the murder first. And fast—Eve's body was decaying rapidly. They were fighting the clock too.

Doctor Richards was in his office, writing an essay on what had happened to those bodies when someone pounded on the front door. He got up and went out front. He saw two Henderson sheriff's depu-ties standing out front. Doctor Richards unlocked the front door and invited the deputies inside.

"Good afternoon, Doctor. I am Deputy Mathew Burke, and this is Deputy Elijah Campbell. Sheriff Riley sent us to bring you back to Henderson. We have a body that is decomposing rapidly. Your mayor said you would know something about that," Deputy Burke said.

"Oh, shit, another one?" Doctor Richards said. "Yes, let me gather a few things and we can be on our way." Doctor Richards rushed to his autopsy room and gathered his instruments. "Okay, deputies, let's go," he said as he returned to them. "Time is not on our side."

"Yes, sir," Deputy Burke said.

As they filed out of his office, Doctor Richards saw Scarlett approaching them. She looked at them and came over to Doctor Richards.

"Everything okay, Doctor?" Scarlett asked. It was very concerning to her to see two deputies from Henderson with Doctor Richards, who was clearly in a hurry.

"They just told me they have a body that is rapidly decaying. Cecilia wants me to look at it," he replied.

A feeling of relief came over Scarlett; if Cecilia had sent for the doctor, then she was okay.

"Well, don't let me hold you all up any longer," Scarlett said. "Safe travels, gentlemen."

"Thank you, Scarlett. I'll return as soon as possible," Doctor Richards said and rushed off with the deputies.

Doctor Richards and the deputies made record time getting to Henderson. The deputies took him to Marcus and Cecilia, who were waiting at the inn.

"Thank you for coming, Doctor," Cecilia said. "We have a body that looks like it's melting. There isn't much tissue left. She's almost all bone already."

"Sounds like what happened to the Pete fellow," Doctor Richards said. "One minute I was examining his body, and the next thing I know, he's decaying before my eyes. I will take a look," Doctor Richards replied.

"Thank you," Cecilia said. "The smell is horrendous. And, Doctor, she was murdered. We need to collect evidence to hopefully find her killer."

"Okay, I will do my best, Cecilia, but if it's as bad as you say, I don't think we will get much of anything. How was she killed?" Doctor Richards asked.

"Someone cut her throat. Almost decapitated her," Cecilia responded.

"Oh shit, that is brutal. I may be able to tell you what kind of blade was used, if I have any viable flesh left on her neck. Let me get in there and get to work."

"Yes, please, Doctor. And thank you again," Cecilia said.

"You're welcome," Doctor Richards said, tying a handkerchief around his mouth and nose.

Marcus opened the door to Eve's room for Doctor Richards and immediately gagged at the smell. They could smell it from the hallway, but upon opening that door, the odor smacked them all in the face. The first thing Doctor Richards did was go across the room and open the little window. Hopefully that would help with the smell somewhat.

Doctor Richards began his examination of the remains. There wasn't much tissue left, and what was left was unrecognizable at that point. The yellowy-orange goo under the skeleton of the woman could have been anything. There was no way of telling what parts of her he was looking at. Doctor Richards started with the woman's neck. There was no more flesh or tissue on her head or neck. The front of her spinal cord had a large cut almost all the way through it. He examined it closely but could not tell what kind of blade had been used. Every person in that town—hell, in every town—carried a blade; it would be impossible to determine whose blade had been used to slit that woman's throat. Everything he saw was just so violent. Whoever had done this to that poor woman was very angry and had done it with much force. It sickened Doctor Richards to think someone was capable of such an act. The fact that someone had so much hate and violence in their heart that they could do this to a poor, helpless woman infuriated the doctor. He wished he could find some evidence that would help the sheriff find the person responsible for that gruesome crime. But the body was far too gone, and the murderer didn't seem to have left any physical evidence behind.

Doctor Richards cut out a section of her arm bone and studied it under his little microscope. Just as he had expected, those tiny, almost robotic insects were feasting on her bones. He walked around to the other side of the bed to get a sample of the rotting flesh. As he stepped around the end of the bed, he noticed a six-inch length of a leather strap. It was about the thickness of a shoe lace. Doctor Richards picked it up and looked at it more closely. One end of was frayed, as if it had been torn off of a longer piece. It could have belonged to the killer and could have been ripped off him in a struggle with the victim. Doctor Richards took the piece of leather strap out to Sheriff Riley.

"I found this on the other side of the bed. I think it could have belonged to the killer. Maybe a tie for his shirt or something," Doctor Richards said, handing Marcus the leather strap.

"Oh, this is great! If we can find the rest of this, we may be able to find the killer," Marcus said. He looked at Cecilia. "I think we know where we need to look first."

"Yes, we do, Sheriff," Cecilia responded.

"Deputy Pounders, stay here with the doctor. Get him whatever he needs," Marcus said to Travis.

"Yes, sir," Travis responded.

"We're going to go interview someone we suspect may have done this," Marcus said to Doctor Richards. "Anything you need, Deputy Pounders is here to help."

"Thank you, Sheriff," Doctor Richards said. "I just want to examine the remains for a bit longer."

"Let us know what you find," Marcus said.

"Will do," Doctor Richards replied.

Marcus and Cecilia took off to Mr. Jenkins office.

"We need to know what room Jeramiah Cummings rented," Marcus said to Paul.

"I'm afraid you just missed him, Sheriff," Paul said. "He checked out an hour ago. He was in quite a hurry too."

"Shit!" Marcus exclaimed. "He'll be back to Freeland before we could ever hope to catch him. Fuck!"

Cecilia and Paul stared at Marcus. They could see the anger and frustration written all over his face. Marcus knew without a doubt Jeramiah had killed Eve. Him running away only cemented it. Marcus was furious. He mumbled a few more curse words under his breath.

"Come on, Sheriff, let's go for a walk," Cecilia said, gently grabbing his arm. "Let's take a few moments to calm down, and then we can come up with a plan of action. I never like to operate when emotions are high."

"Okay, ma'am, that's probably the best thing to do for now," Marcus sighed. "Thank you, Paul, and please excuse my outburst."

"No worries, Sheriff. Stresses are high 'round here, totally understand your frustrations. Please, let me know if I can be of any more help."

"There is one thing," Marcus said, pulling the small piece of leather strap out of his pocket. "Do you recognize this at all?"

Paul looked at it closely. "No, sir, can't say I do," Paul said after a minute.

"Thanks again," Marcus said.

Marcus and Cecilia left. They went outside and walked toward Marcus's place. They walked in silence so they could collect their thoughts and calm down a bit. Marcus thought going home for a bit and having lunch with Alexis would help him calm down. He was still furious, and that anger wasn't going to go away anytime soon. But he did need to collect his thoughts so they could devise a plan to deal with Jeramiah.

Alexis was surprised and excited to see her husband in the middle of the day. She was happy to see Cecilia as well, but she could tell something was wrong right away.

"Tell me what's on your mind while I whip up some lunch," Alexis said.

They all gathered in the kitchen while Alexis and Cecilia put a quick lunch together. Marcus explained what had happened to Eve and how he was convinced it had to have been Jeramiah Cummings that had done it. The fact that Jeramiah had left in such a hurry only confirmed it to him. He explained to his wife how furious it all made him. "How dare someone come to my town and commit murder!" Alexis could see him get angrier as he told her the whole story. Cecilia stayed out of it; she knew it would be good for Marcus to vent to Alexis.

"Come, sit," Alexis said, grabbing the food and heading to the dining room table. Cecilia and Marcus joined her. "That is terrible news, honey," Alexis began. "I know it's not my place, but do you actually have to do anything about it?"

"Yes!" Marcus exclaimed. "He killed someone in my town!"

"Settle down a bit, honey," Alexis said. Marcus settled right down. "Now hear me out, please. You two sat here at this very table last night going on and on about what a horrible lady she was. Of course that is no excuse for killing someone. But honestly, aren't we all better off? I don't mean to sound unsympathetic, but it's kinda true. A lost life is always a sad thing, and to have someone do that in our town should be unforgivable. I agree that under different circumstances, he should be punished to the fullest extent."

"And he will be!" Marcus interrupted.

"Babe, please, let me say my piece. You're the sheriff and you will do what you want, but give me a chance to talk all this out with you. I strongly believe there is an alternative way to handle this. A way that will satisfy all."

Marcus looked at Cecilia, and she nodded. She wanted to hear what Alexis had to say.

"Sorry, baby, please go on," Marcus said.

"Look, my point is this, a terrible thing happened here today. We are pretty sure who did it but can't prove it. I say we quietly return her remains to Everett, tell her family she passed away in her sleep, and try to get whoever takes over that town on board with us. As far as Jeramiah goes, freeze him and his town out. After a while, they will have to play by our rules or their town will crumble." Alexis paused and sipped her tea. She could tell she had shocked Cecilia and her husband. The wife of the sheriff suggesting they just let a murderer go free? It should have been unthinkable, but it didn't sound half bad. "Eve was pretty old and sickly. People would buy that she just passed away," Alexis added.

"I don't know, honey. I can't just let him get away with it, no matter how much we all disliked Eve. No one deserves to be brutalized like that," Marcus said.

"Sheriff, if I may interject here," Cecilia began, "I think your wife here is on to something. We don't have any evidence except for that little piece of leather, which for all we know could have been part of whatever she had been wearing. The more time that goes by, the less evidence we will be able to come across. We're fighting a losing battle. We have already spooked Jeramiah—he won't be of any help to us if we keep going after him. I say we go with Alexis's plan for now and get right back to work merging these towns. Once we have our new government set up, then we go after Jeramiah. I feel like he will mess up again. We just have to stay diligent here. Is my heart broken that we lost Eve? No, it's not. Am I angry as to how we lost her? You better believe I am! But we are losing time here, Sheriff."

"I need to think on it," Marcus said. "Let's do this for now, Cecilia. You and the remaining mayors get back to work on creating a new government. I trust you all to make the right decisions. I will work with Doctor Richards while he is still in town on what to do about Eve and her remains. I am still going to investigate this murder. I will not sweep it under the rug. I will do so quietly and with only my most trusted deputies."

"That sounds fair," Cecilia said.

"I'm proud of you, baby," Alexis said, taking his hand. "You are a good sheriff and an even better man. I love you."

"Thank you, babe. I love you too."

Cecilia smiled at their interaction. It was so obvious that they truly and deeply loved each other. There was a huge amount of respect for one another as well; it made Cecilia's heart happy. Knowing there were more people in the world like Marcus and Alexis than people like Eve and Jeramiah made her feel even more confident about what they were doing. They could and would build a thriving society. A society of love and respect for your fellow man. A society of hard work, determination, and eventually great success. With all of that, they would not only succeed with their plans but they would also thrive. Cecilia strongly believed that people were inherently good and an extremely small percent went bad somehow. She guessed that when some folks met adversity, some would change for the worse. Seeing how Marcus reacted to Eve's murder made Cecilia feel good about the man that would become the chief law enforcement official. Marcus had grit and determination, but he was also very level-headed. Sure, his gut reaction had been to go after Jeramiah, but he listened to reason and adjusted his plan of action.

Cecilia felt great about what Alexis had said, and she felt confident that they had all made the right decision on how to move forward. Cecilia agreed with Marcus; murder should not be swept under the rug. But in this case, she agreed with Alexis more. Eve was not a good person and would not be missed by most. Jeramiah was a loose end, but Cecilia didn't believe he posed any threat to anyone else. He had, as far as they could tell, killed Eve out of anger and resentment. They couldn't even be a hundred percent sure it was Jeramiah. Lowell had had a very tumultuous relationship with Eve as well. He wanted to be part of the merger so badly just to get out of her grasp. Maybe she had told him she would never let him go; she would always still control him? Maybe that set him off? Any number of things could have gone down the night before. Any one of those men could have done that to her. They all had motive and opportunity. At that point in time, they were all in a gray area between independent towns and a united nation. Perfect opportunity to commit a crime of that nature. Cecilia didn't want to just brush past a murder, but she did want to get the new society going. She and the other mayors would hammer that out in the next couple of days. That would be done no matter what.

Cecilia got up and excused herself, saying she was headed back into town to round up the other mayors. She told Marcus and Alexis she didn't want to wait until the next day after all. She told Marcus she had faith in him and Doctor Richards and she wasn't going to spend another moment worrying about that end of things. Marcus and Alexis wished her luck, and Cecilia left.

Marcus kissed Alexis goodbye and said he was headed back to the inn to investigate the murder a bit more. He said he'd be home in time for dinner. Marcus gave Alexis one more kiss; there was always one more kiss, never enough for the two of them, and he left for the inn.

When Marcus got back to Eve's room, Doctor Richards was still in the room. Marcus wondered how the doctor could stay in there so long with that smell. Marcus pulled a handkerchief out of his pocket and tied it around his face. He took a deep breath and entered the room. Even with the handkerchief, the smell was overpowering. He didn't think he'd ever get that smell out of his nostrils.

"What'd you find, Doctor?" Marcus asked as he closed the door.

"Well, I found the same microscopic bugs I found on two people who had died in the woods back home. As you know, we lost four people within a day not too long ago. Two of them had these insects feasting on them, even their bones. The other two did not. I examined all four of them extensively, well, everything I could examine at least. I thought the bugs had something to do with finding the bodies in the woods, but we found a young woman's body in the same spot we had found a young man. The young man had these insects. The young woman did not. So long story short, I have no idea what they are or where they come from," Doctor Richards explained.

"We should have Doctor Willis look over the body too," Marcus said. Doctor Willis was Henderson's town doctor. "He's becoming an expert on bugs and decay. He is fascinated by insect life."

"Has he ever said anything about bugs like these? Have you all ever had a body decompose like this?" Doctor Richards asked.

"Just once. John's body did this too. His men wouldn't let anyone examine the body. They buried him quickly. They all ended up sick and then died too, but none of their bodies did this," Marcus replied.

"Strange," Doctor Richards said, shaking his head. "I'd like to go talk to Doctor Willis."

"I'll take you there," Marcus said, heading for the door. He couldn't get out of that room fast enough.

"Thank you, Sheriff," Doctor Richards said, grabbing the samples he had taken from the body and then followed Marcus out of the room. "Where was that woman from?" he asked Marcus as they walked out of the room.

"Everett. That's Eve Adams, the mayor of Everett. Why?"

"Her skeletal structure is like nothing I've ever seen before," Doctor Richards said, removing his handkerchief and putting it in his pocket. The stench of death lingered in his nose.

"How so, Doctor?" Marcus asked.

"She had an elongated skull. Her jaw and mouth were the smallest I have ever seen on an adult female. Her arms were longer than I have ever seen, and her fingers were unnaturally long and thin. And all of her bones were unnaturally thin. Honestly, I'm surprised she could even get around," Doctor Richards said as they walked across town.

"I don't mean to speak ill of the dead, but she was a very strange-looking woman. Creepy looking in fact," Marcus said. "Everyone has always just assumed it was a birth defect. She never spoke about it, and no one ever asked her about it. She wasn't the most approachable person either. Most people kept their distance from her."

"I suppose it could have been a birth defect," Doctor Richards said, mulling over what Marcus had just told him.

They arrived at Doctor Willis's office. Doctor Willis invited them in. Doctor Richards asked if they could go to his lab and look at the samples under a microscope. The doctors headed to the lab, and Marcus went back to the inn. He was going to brave that awful smell and try to find some evidence that would back up his theory that Jeramiah had committed that murder.

"Wow! This is incredible," Doctor Willis exclaimed as he studied the samples. "Have you ever seen anything like this before?" He looked up from the microscope.

"Yes, I've seen them three times now. Everybody I've found them on had decomposed at a rate that shouldn't be possible, I mean within a day," Doctor Richards replied.

"Holy shit, that can't be possible," Doctor Willis said.

"I know, but I've now seen it happen three times. Happened to a few pigs back home too."

"These things look robotic," Doctor Willis said, looking into the microscope again.

"I know, almost like they're synchronized. Usually, insects are running over themselves to feed, but these things look like they are in an organized march as they feed," Doctor Richards said.

"Strangest damn thing. Ants behave like this to a degree. I have seen something similar to these bugs, though," Doctor Willis said. "I was fishing a while back and I was digging in the dirt for worms when I came across what I though was an ant nest. It wasn't any ant I had ever seen before. They looked very similar to these things here but bigger. You could see them with the naked eye. Little gray beetle-looking insects. They noticed me too. As soon as I uncovered their little nest, they swarmed me. I had to jump into the lake to get them off of me. Nasty little things, that's for sure. May I try something with these bugs?" he asked Doctor Richards.

"Of course, do whatever you want. I would love to find out what they are," Doctor Richards replied.

"Okay, great." Doctor Willis said. He grabbed his tweezers and plucked one of the tiny insects from the dish it had been in. He put it on a slide and put a drop of water on it. He slid it under the microscope. The tiny insect squirmed in the water. It looked exactly like what he had found at the lake, only microscopic. "Those bugs I found down by the lake didn't like the water when I jumped in, and this little guy doesn't seem to care for it much either. This thing looks exactly like what I found down by the lake, only a lot smaller obviously. Whatever this is must be related to whatever I found."

"That's odd," Doctor Richards said. "How would they find the body so quickly?"

"I don't know. Maybe they're already inside. Maybe the people you found that have had them stumbled across the bigger ones and they somehow laid eggs inside of them. The eggs hatch once the person dies and feast on the remains. Maybe that's why this only happens to some of the bodies and not all of them," Doctor Willis theorized.

"That could very well be. I didn't know these things existed outside of a body," Doctor Richards said.

"We can't be sure of anything. I'm just theorizing here," Doctor Willis said.

"We should go see if we can find any of the bugs you discovered down by the lake. Compare the two," Doctor Richards said.

"That's a good idea. I'll take you to where I found them," Doctor Willis said.

The doctors put on their coats and headed for the lake. It was a beautiful sunny day but chilly. They took some specimen jars with them. Doctor Willis found the spot where he had found the bugs and began digging in the hard dirt. Within seconds, little gray bugs started filing out of the ground. The doctors captured a few of them and got out of there.

Back at the lab, they studied the new insects, and they did seem to be the same as the ones found in the bodies of the recently deceased. The insects collected from the lake did appear to have a hard outer shell that was missing on the tiny insects, but they figured the tiny ones eventually grew that shell once they had fed on the remains.

"How many bodies have you examined in your time as a doctor?" Doctor Richards asked.

"Too many to count. Why?" Doctor Willis responded.

"Same here, a lot of bodies. It's strange we have never seen this before. Why all of a sudden are these bugs showing up?" Doctor Richards wondered.

"Evolution, maybe?" Doctor Willis replied. "Insect life is fascinating, but we don't know much about it. Could be something the wildlife has carried forever and these things have finally evolved to the point where they can jump to us now. I have no doubts these big guys are relatives to the tiny ones. I'm going to keep studying them. I'll send any findings to you."

"Thank you, Doctor. I agree with your theory. I don't see any way of preventing this down the road. We can't keep people out of the woods. They need to hunt and fish. It's just sad to watch a body decompose like that," Doctor Richards said.

"I agree, it is sad, but it's the same end result. These insects speeding up the process doesn't change the fact that we all become a pile of ash in the end. Sounds morbid, but it's a fact," Doctor Willis said.

"That is so very true," Doctor Richards agreed. "Thank you for your time, Doctor Willis. Please stay in touch."

"I will. And thank you for bringing this to my attention."

"No problem. We'll talk soon," Doctor Richards said, putting his coat back on.

"We will. Take care," Doctor Willis said and escorted Doctor Richards out.

Doctor Richards made his way back to the inn. Sheriff Riley had left already. His deputy told Doctor Richards that Marcus had gone back to the station. Deputy Pounders told Doctor Richards how to get there and sent him on his way. Doctor Richards found the sheriff's office easily. A deputy at the front desk went and got Marcus for him.

"Hey, Doctor," Marcus said as he came up front, "were you and Doctor Willis able to find anything out about those bugs?"

"We did, yes. We have a theory. I would like to tell Cecilia about it all as well. Do you think you two would have a few moments to chat with me?" Doctor Richards asked.

"I'm sure we can make that happen," Marcus said. "Follow me."

Marcus led Doctor Richards to the briefing room. Cecilia and the other mayors were busy working out plans and ideas for the uniting of the towns.

"Excuse me, Cecilia?" Marcus said to the room. "The doctor here has some information he'd like to share with the both of us."

"Actually, I'd like to tell everyone in this room what we discovered. It will most likely be valuable information for everyone here," Doctor Richards said.

"Go ahead, Doctor," Marcus said, sitting down at the table with Cecilia and the other mayors.

"As Cecilia knows, I found microscopic insects in the remains of some people who recently died in our town. These insects decompose a body within a day instead of months or even years. Has anybody experienced rapid decomp in their towns recently?" Doctor Richards asked the room. Every one of the other mayors raised their hands. "Okay, so it is universal now. Well, Doctor Willis and I have determined these insects are most likely already inside of people when they die. We are assuming they are dormant until the person dies and then they awaken and literally feast on the remains. We found almost identical insects in the woods by the lake. We believe those insects somehow lay eggs inside of people that happen upon them and those eggs eventually become the little ones that feast on the recently deceased, and then we assume they grow into the bigger ones and the cycle is repeated. We don't believe these things cause any harm to us while we're alive—it's just what they do to us once we have died. But as Doctor Willis pointed out, we all decompose no matter what, so having that process sped up isn't too much to worry about, in our opinions at least. Any questions?"

"Why is this happening now? How come we have never seen this before now?" Cecilia asked.

"We think it's just the evolution of the insects. They've probably been around forever and just recently evolved to a point where they can infect us now too," Doctor Richards explained. "Doctor Willis is going to continue to study the insects and keep me posted on his findings. It doesn't appear there is much we can do about these bugs."

"Well, Doctor, it is nice to have some idea of what is going on with those things," Cecilia said. "We thank you for the information, and will you two please keep the rest of us updated as well?"

"Yes, ma'am, we certainly will," Doctor Richards said. He turned to Marcus. "Doctor Willis has a solid handle on things, so I think I will make my way home."

"Sounds good, Doctor. Thank you for your time and coming all this way to help me with my investigation. Normally I would have just gotten Doctor Willis to help, but Cecilia said you had experience with bodies decomposing like that."

"You're welcome, and unfortunately, I have far too much experience in that field now. Thank you all for your time, and have a good day. And good luck with the momentous task you have ahead of you."

Everyone thanked Doctor Richards and said their goodbyes. Doctor Richards stopped by the inn and gathered his gear before heading home. He made really good time; he made it home just before dark. Doctor Richards unloaded his supplies at the office and went home for the night. He needed a night off from everything. He poured himself a stiff drink and settled into his reading chair with a cigar. Doctor Richards felt good about the day's work. It felt great to finally have some answers. Those insects had really confused him. It had been good to get a second set of qualified eyes on them. Doctor Richards was more than satisfied with what they had come up with. One less thing to stress about moving forward.

CHAPTER 16

United They Stand

Scarlett stood in the front of Bob's tavern in front of a packed house. The entire town had shown up for the town hall meeting. Everyone was excitedly awaiting Scarlett's announcement. People were quietly chatting among themselves. They all knew what the announcement would be but still couldn't wait to finally hear it. Cecilia, Hope, and Gwen stood behind Scarlett. Scarlett was a bit nervous, but it was an excited nervousness. Cecilia and the other town mayors had succeeded in uniting all the towns, even Everett. The addition of Everett had been on the fence after Eve's death, but her eldest son had taken over mayoral duties and was more than excited to join the union. Scarlett raised her hand, and the crowd went silent.

"Good evening, all," Scarlett began. "I am so happy and excited to be standing in front of all of you as your new mayor!" The crowd applauded her. Whoops and hollers filled the smoky tavern. "What a great pleasure and honor it will be to serve you all. We have a great town full of tremendous people. I am proud to call you all my fellow townspeople. I will approach my job as mayor with the mindset of being a fellow townsperson, not just a leader. I want to work with each and every one of you to keep this town thriving. The past couple of months have been something else to say the least, but we all came together and kept things running smoothly. You all should be very proud of yourselves! Give yourselves a round of applause!"

The crowd erupted into applause again. People were shaking hands and slapping each other on the back. The room was alive with excitement and merriment. True, unbridled bliss. "We did this together. Cecilia worked her butt off with the other mayors to unite the towns, but we all played a major role in it as well. Without the love and support from all of you, we could have never done this!" Again, the crowd applauded. "Now down to business, folks." The crowd settled down and people took their seats at tables around the room. "Not much will change on a day-to-day basis in any of the towns—we will all still operate as we always have. The most notable changes will be the new supply chain. Everything produced and distributed will be strictly controlled by the new government. This is so that there will be no more price gauging or special deals. For example, corn will be the same price per pound here as it will be everywhere else. Metal will be available for every town now, not just the ones Everett had deals with. That kind of back-door dealing won't be allowed anymore. That is an arrestable offense now. Keeping costs down on goods and services is our number one priority now. No one person or entity should have a monopoly on anything. That too has been deemed illegal. This is a union now—it's not every town for themselves anymore."

Scarlett paused and looked around the room at her townspeople. "We did it!" she shouted, and the room erupted into applause yet again. "Let me hand it over to Cecilia." Scarlett stepped aside.

"Good evening, ladies and gentlemen!" Cecilia said excitedly. "I am beyond thrilled with what we have all accomplished in the recent months. We have successfully established what will be a thriving democracy, and I couldn't be happier. This has been a dream of mine for a long time. As you all know, I was on the fence with this at first, but as I pondered it, I quickly grew very excited about it. I am glad I was a part of this. As many of you have heard, we did face some steep challenges in the beginning stages of this. We were met with division and some animosity. Some of the other town leaders didn't want to join up with us. I feel they were afraid of losing some of their control. I am relieved that everyone quickly saw the benefit to this and came aboard, not only willingly but excited as well. We dealt with everything from nerves to outright violence, but we stayed the course and wound up here. This united nation of ours will benefit all of you more than any of us. That's why we worked so hard to get here. We wanted a better life for all, not just some. A true democracy and united society shouldn't make the leaders rich and all powerful—it should make its citizens' lives easier and more fruitful. That is the goal we will continue to strive for. We don't want to see anyone left behind."

Cecilia paused and looked around the crowded room. "It has been long enough that I can talk about this now. Very early on in this process, day one in fact, one of the other town's mayors was murdered." The people in the room all gasped. "We had a damn good idea who had done it, but we had no evidence at that time. The person we believe committed this horrendous act hung themselves two days later. Sheriff Riley was able to gather some evidence that did implicate the person we believed had done it. We put the case to bed and moved on with our many other duties. I bring all of this up to say this: crime will not be tolerated in any fashion going forward. Murder especially. Sheriff Riley is our top law enforcement official now, and he is fantastic at what he does. There will be no more deals to get out of trouble. No more friendly looks the other way. A great nation needs law and order to thrive. Crime will never pay, and it will get you locked up for a long time. Murder will be met with death for the murderer as well. I know this is all heavy stuff after Scarlett's wonderful speech, but it has to be said. I have no worries about any of you in this room now—you are all fine, upstanding folks. I am going around to each town and giving the same speech, except for Everett—we have already dealt with them. Please, folks, just know that you are all appreciated and we all see you as tremendous people. I am so proud and honored to have had the opportunity to be your mayor. You are in better hands now." She chuckled and looked at Scarlett. The townspeople broke out into cheers again. "As you all probably know by now, starting this week, I will take up permanent residence in Jamison, formerly known as Henderson. Jamison is now the capitol of this great new nation, so I will live there full time to do my job properly. I will miss you all very much. I will miss your smiling faces every morning as I walked to work. I love you all so much. I won't be a stranger, though. I will make many trips back here to see you all and conduct business with Scarlett. Thank you all for everything you have done for me and this great town!" Cecilia waved to the crowd, and they all jumped to their feet to applaud her.

"Thank you all for your time this evening," Scarlett said to the raucous crowd. "Now let's all celebrate the momentous occasion!"

The townspeople cheered, clapped, and hollered. The tavern was loud and rowdy with joy and excitement. The party lasted well into the night.

Malcolm and Bethany approached Scarlett and congratulated her. Scarlett had promoted Bethany to be her deputy mayor. Malcom took the position as the town's new sheriff. He hadn't wanted the job at first but was beginning to enjoy it quite a bit. It did afford him the opportunity to work closely with Bethany and Scarlett.

"Great speech, Scarlett," Malcolm said. "You got me all pumped up!" He chuckled.

"Thank you. You know I was a lot more nervous than I thought I would be. I knew I had nothing but good news to tell everyone, but still I got so nervous. I probably worked myself up from the excitement of the moment," Scarlett responded.

"Well, you didn't seem nervous at all," Bethany said. "I'm excited to work with you, and I'm honored you chose me."

"No one else I would have even asked," Scarlett said. "Are you guys sticking around for a while?"

"No, we're going to head home. Bethany gets so tired lately, and I'm pretty beat too," Malcolm said.

"Carrying around another human inside you does tire you out quite a bit," Scarlett laughed. "You guys take care. We'll see you tomorrow."

"Thank you, see you later," Bethany said.

"Have a good evening," Malcolm said as they turned to leave.

Malcolm and Bethany stepped out of the tavern into the freezing cold night. The sky was clear and full of stars. The full moon lit up the entire town. It was a frigid night but a gorgeous one. Malcolm took Bethany's hand, and they headed for home. As they walked through town, they looked up at the beautiful starry sky. As they watched the sky, three bright, bluish-colored lights streaked through the sky. They were gone as quickly as they had appeared.

"Wow, those were some bright shooting stars!" Bethany exclaimed.

"Yea, they were. So beautiful too," Malcolm said and squeezed his wife's hand.

"There's so much to this world that we know nothing about," Bethany said. "Do you ever feel small and insignificant?" she asked her husband.

"It is a vast and undiscovered world out there, but we learn new things about our world every day. We will keep learning things too. I wouldn't say I feel insignificant but maybe small. I think we are all a vital piece of this world," Malcolm said. "We are definitely small though." He chuckled.

"Do you think we're alone?" Bethany asked.

Malcolm stopped and looked around. "Yeah, I don't see anyone else. Why?"

"No, not us right here and right now. I mean do you think we're alone in this world?"

"Yea, well us and the animals," Malcolm said, a bit confused by her question.

"Do you think anything lives up there?" she asked, pointing to the night sky.

Malcolm chuckled. "No, babe, that would be impossible. Does this have anything to do with those weird dreams you were having a while back?" he asked.

"Maybe," Bethany replied. "I just think it's a little arrogant for us to believe there couldn't be life anywhere else. It's like, we're here—why is it so hard to believe there isn't life other places too?"

"I'm not saying there can't be. I'm just saying I doubt there is," Malcolm said. They had reached their cabin, and Malcolm opened the door for Bethany. She grunted her way up the few steps and into the door.

"I'm ready to have this baby already." She laughed. "It's like carrying around a boulder all day every day."

"I know, baby. I'm ready too. You are going to make such a wonderful mom," he said and kissed her.

"Thanks, love. You're going to be such a great dad too." Bethany hugged and kissed Malcolm. "I'm going to go lay down. My everything hurts."

"Sounds good, baby. Do you need anything?" Malcolm asked.

"Some hot tea would be wonderful. Thanks, babe," Bethany said and headed for their bedroom.

Just minutes after she had gone into their room, Malcolm heard her cry out in pain. He dropped what he was doing and ran to her. She was clutching her very pregnant belly and crying.

"*Is it time?*" Malcolm exclaimed.

"I don't know. Something's not right," Bethany panted.

"I'm going to go get Doctor Richards!" Malcolm said and ran out of the house.

He ran all the way back to town. He hadn't grabbed his coat or hat but didn't even notice the cold. Malcolm quickly found Doctor Richards among the crowd at Bob's tavern. He and the doctor ran back to Bethany. The tea kettle was screaming on the stove, but no one paid any attention to it. Malcolm and Doctor Richards rushed into the bedroom. Bethany was lying on the bed in considerable pain. Her face was scrunched up; tears and sweat glistened her cheeks.

"Get me some blankets and towels!" Doctor Richards told Malcolm. "Looks like she's having a baby tonight!"

Malcolm didn't stick around long enough to respond. He ran out of the room and gathered the supplies the doctor had asked for. Malcolm was scared and nervous but very excited as well. Bethany looked like she was miserable, and that hurt him to see. He hoped it would be quick and she could eventually get some rest. Malcolm didn't know anything about childbirth, but he did know she was in good hands with Doctor Richards; the man had delivered a lot of babies in his life.

"Something's wrong, Doctor," Bethany cried.

"I'm sure everything is just fine," Doctor Richards responded. "Let me examine you. I'm pretty sure you're in labor."

"But it's too soon," she cried.

"Not necessarily," he replied. "You could be a lot further along than we had thought. It is almost impossible to determine how far along a woman is early on. You have good weight on you and you seem to be very healthy. Bethany, I think everything will be just fine," he said.

Doctor Richards began to examine Bethany. "Oh yeah, you are definitely in labor!" he exclaimed. "You're having a baby tonight!"

"Doc, it hurts so bad. Something has to be wrong. Muscles I didn't even know I had are like freezing in place. The cramping is like nothing I ever knew was even possible!" Bethany panted through the tears.

"That's all normal. That's actually really good. That means your baby is ready to join us!" he tried to reassure her. "I'm not going to lie to you and say it'll be easy on you. This will hurt like nothing else."

"It already does!" she cried.

Malcolm rushed back into the room with every blanket and towel they owned. Doctor Richards chuckled a bit. He thought it was adorable how frantic Malcolm was.

"Malcolm, please go warm up some water and put it in a large bowl," Doctor Richards said. "Make sure the water is just barely warm—we don't want hot water."

"Okay, Doctor," Malcolm said and rushed out to the kitchen.

The tea kettle was still screeching on the stove. He removed it and set it aside; that water would be way too hot. Malcolm put a pot of water on the hot stove. The water warmed up quickly, and he transferred it to the largest bowl he could find. The water sloshed around the bowl and splashed over the sides as Malcolm hurried back to the room.

"Soak a small towel in the water and wipe your wife's face with it. Be by her side now. Comfort her through this," Doctor Richards calmly said to Malcolm. Doctor Richards knew he needed to bring the stress level down. Bethany's stress level seemed to increase every time she saw Malcolm franticly rushing around.

Malcolm pulled a chair up next to the bed. He gently wiped Bethany's face and forehead with the warm, damp towel. She seemed to relax a tiny bit. Malcolm took her hand in his other hand. She squeezed his hand tight. He set the towel aside and brushed her hair away from her ear. He leaned over and kissed her cheek. He whispered, "I love you, baby. You got this!" into her ear.

Bethany suddenly sat straight up and screamed. That startled Malcolm to his feet.

"She's okay, Malcolm. This is a contraction. The baby is coming. Now that you know what that feels like, Bethany, I need you to push when it happens again, okay?"

"Okay, Doctor, that really hurt!" Bethany said, trying to catch her breath.

"It's all normal. Part of giving birth. It does hurt, but this baby is ready to come out. It shouldn't be long now," Doctor Richards said. "Malcolm, hand me a blanket please." Malcolm handed him a blanket, and he spread it out on the bed under Bethany's legs. "Now hand me a towel please," he said to Malcolm. Malcolm handed him a towel. Doctor Richards spread it out over the blanket.

Malcolm sat back down next to Bethany and took her hand again. Another contraction hit, and she squeezed his hand. He thought she was going to break his fingers. This all went on for a while until a healthy baby girl was delivered. Bethany lay back on the bed, panting and crying. Malcolm was bawling as well. His baby girl was so beautiful. His wife was a warrior. He was so proud and impressed with her. He couldn't have done what she just did. No way. Malcolm was overwhelmed with joy and love. He could see in Bethany's eyes that she felt the same way. They had done it. They had brought a baby girl into the world. Malcolm hadn't realized you could fall in love with something so quickly. He didn't know he was even capable of that level of love. He had always loved Bethany with all of his heart, body, and soul, but this was a different love. Their baby girl was now the center of their universe.

Doctor Richards had the baby all cleaned up and wrapped in the blanket. He set the baby girl on Bethany's chest, and she clutched her daughter close. The baby girl looked up at her mother with dark, beautiful, and sparkling eyes. Bethany melted at the sight of her gorgeous girl. Tears of joy and love streamed down her red cheeks.

"Congratulations, Mom and Dad!" Doctor Richards exclaimed. He pulled a cigar out of his pocket and handed it to Malcolm. "You two have a very healthy baby girl there. I am so happy for the both of you. I will return in the morning to check on you and the baby."

"Thank you, Doctor Richards," Malcolm said.

"You are so very welcome. Delivering babies is by far the best part of being a doctor." Doctor Richards said. "Have you thought of a name yet?" he asked before he left.

"Yes," Bethany said, looking at Malcolm. "We're going to name her Amanda."

"Oh, that is a wonderful name!" the doctor exclaimed. "I love that name for her." He turned to the bedroom door. He gave Bethany some instructions on how to take care of herself after giving birth and some basics for Baby Amanda as well. "Again, congratulations Mom and Dad!" Doctor Richards said as he walked out of the room.

Bethany asked Malcolm for some water. He went and grabbed some water for them both. He returned to the room and climbed into bed next to his wife and daughter. Baby Amanda had fallen asleep on her mother's chest. The new parents watched as their precious baby slept soundly. Baby Amanda slept peacefully without a care in the world. She had two amazing parents that would take care of her every need and raise her to be a wonderful woman someday.

Malcolm and Bethany drifted off to sleep, holding their perfect baby girl. She had no worries, no stresses. She hadn't been jaded by life yet. She hadn't experienced the highs and lows of life yet. She hadn't made any memories yet. Everything was brand new to her. A truly fresh start. A new beginning.

ABOUT THE AUTHOR

Joseph Cubbage is from Spokane, Washington and is married with three children. He enjoys the outdoors, hiking, camping, and lazy days next to the pool. Joseph and his wife like to travel and see new cities as often as possible. These adventures inspire a lot of his writing. He is a full-time author and spends his free time with family and friends. He has two previously published books, *The Last Job* and *Zombie Clean*. Both are available on Amazon with a quick search of Joseph Cubbage, or they can be found on his Facebook page, https://www.facebook.com/jacwriting. To contact Joseph, please visit his web page at https://josephsbookstore.godaddysites.com.

CPSIA information can be obtained
at www.ICGtesting.com
Printed in the USA
LVHW022022151121
703363LV00001B/7